PRAISE FOR *ARCHANGEL'S LIGHT*

"Longtime fans will be delighted by the torturous pining in this slow burn." —*Kirkus Reviews*

"Singh . . . masterfully balances the love story with the complex paranormal plot. Fans will be delighted." —*Publishers Weekly*

"Exquisite. There is no other way to describe *Archangel's Light*, a book for which fans have been clamoring for years. . . . Master storyteller Nalini Singh is at the top of her craft with Illium and Aodhan's story—a book rife with loyalty, friendship, loss, unbreakable bonds, and LOVE." —*Harlequin Junkie*

"Nalini Singh remains at the very top of my auto-buy list, she just dazzles me with every new release. *Archangel's Light* is so well done, all at once moving the series plot arc forward, while taking readers on a journey through the past, and building a believable romance between two beloved characters in the present." —*Smexy Books*

"A tense, emotional, and fantastic story, revolving around the disaster from the deceased archangel, and the impaired relationship of two people we have always loved. . . . As in just about every book I read from Nalini Singh, I could not put this book down." —The Reading Café

"A fascinating read. . . . Fans will love it!" —Fresh Fiction

"A love story that will touch the heart of every reader [who] delves ⋯⋯⋯⋯⋯⋯⋯⋯⋯⋯⋯⋯" —Addicted to Romance

Archangel's Resurrection

A Guild Hunter Novel

Nalini Singh

BERKLEY ROMANCE
New York

BERKLEY ROMANCE
Published by Berkley
An imprint of Penguin Random House LLC
penguinrandomhouse.com

Copyright © 2022 by Nalini Singh
Penguin Random House supports copyright. Copyright fuels creativity, encourages
diverse voices, promotes free speech, and creates a vibrant culture. Thank you for buying
an authorized edition of this book and for complying with copyright laws by not
reproducing, scanning, or distributing any part of it in any form without permission.
You are supporting writers and allowing Penguin Random House to continue to
publish books for every reader.

BERKLEY is a registered trademark and Berkley Romance with B colophon
is a trademark of Penguin Random House LLC.

ISBN: 9780593198162

First Edition: October 2022

Printed in the United States of America
1 3 5 7 9 10 8 6 4 2

Archangel's Resurrection

Immortality is a gift incandescent.

Immortality is a curse obscene.

—Unknown scholar

The First Ending

1

Lijuan, Archangel of Death and Goddess Over All, gloried in the howl of her power as battle raged around her, Raphael's once-glittering city now broken and scorched. Impudent *child*. He should've listened to Lijuan, listened to his *goddess*! She'd told him what to do, had attempted to guide him. But no, he would make the wrong choice. He would choose to tie himself forever to a mewling mortal.

It mattered naught that his consort now bore wings and other trappings of immortality. She was nothing, a worm to be crushed under the boot, as Lijuan had once crushed her own worm. Because worms dug inside you, creating runnels and holes. Weaknesses. Fractures. Vulnerabilities.

Raphael had all of those. And today he would pay the price. They would all pay.

She laughed at the temerity of the archangels who'd gathered into an alliance against her. Together, they thought they could defeat her. When all they'd done was made things easier for her by congregating in one place. They might've been the apex predators on the planet once, but Lijuan alone held that throne now.

They were nothing but her servants.

Ignoring the chaos all around her, she scanned the area until she pinpointed the archangel she most wanted to remove from the equation. There she was. Small in stature, with skin "like the night, eyes that held the stars, and hair of violet moonlight"—or so she'd been described by the idiotic poet who'd written a scroll devoted to Zanaya, Queen of the Nile.

Lijuan had researched Zanaya as part of her investigation into all possible Sleepers who might prove a problem in the future . . . but she'd paid a little extra attention to the so-called Queen of the Nile. Not because she was more of a power than the others, but because Zanaya had managed to obtain the one thing that Lijuan had never been able to capture: the love of Alexander, Archangel of Persia.

Oh, he'd been kind to Lijuan, had told her that she was too young and that perhaps after another seven thousand years, they could come together. Only later had she realized that he'd simply been letting her down with kindness—by then, she'd seen true passion in a man's eyes, had understood with bitter clarity that what she'd seen in Alexander's had been . . . gentle, yes. Twined even with affection. But passion? No. Not even the merest inkling.

Why her and not me?

A gnawing question inside her ever since she'd learned of Zanaya and Alexander's history. Because that's how most ancient scrolls were written—with their two names linked. As if they were so much a unit that it was understood that should Zanaya walk the earth, Alexander would belong to her and no one else.

Rage burned through Lijuan.

How dare he choose this mere archangel in place of Lijuan, who was a goddess? How dare he *still* look at Zanaya in a way he'd never once looked at her! She shouldn't have noticed how their glances met, shouldn't have noticed anything beyond what was necessary to win this war, but she had—and the reminder of her pathetic past self enraged her.

Fueled by the lifeforce of those who'd sacrificed themselves to their goddess, she turned noncorporeal . . . and then she flew straight to the archangel who mocked Lijuan with her very existence. Lijuan had no weaknesses. After she killed Zanaya, she'd take care of Alexander. She'd *consume* them both, and once they were inside her, she would control them.

Zanaya never stood a chance.

Appearing behind her, Lijuan sank her fangs into the archangel's neck, and drank of her life. Those fangs usually only emerged in angels during the Making of a vampire, but Lijuan could call them up at will. Yet another sign of her difference from these creatures who sought to humble her.

Sudden savage winds whipped at Lijuan's hair as Zanaya called up her power, the archangel's body twisting to respond to the attack, but it was a futile effort. Lijuan had swallowed up too much of the potent power that made up a member of the Cadre, and Zanaya was fading, fading.

Lijuan's rage, however, oh, it continued to scald.

Because it did, she made a critical error. She eased her iron control on the vicious power which made her a goddess—and created a leak. A whisper of her own power flowed into Zanaya, a gift of which she was utterly unworthy. But no matter. Zanaya was dead anyway. At least now, Lijuan knew not to get so entranced by the refueling process that she lost her grip on the screaming endlessness that was her glory.

Sated for the moment, she dropped Zanaya's shriveled corpse and turned noncorporeal once more. There would never again be a scroll written that paired Zanaya with Alexander.

What a terrible shame that their love story had come to such an inglorious end.

Her lip curled when she saw golden-haired and silver-winged Alexander race to catch his lover's desiccated body before it could shatter against the earth. What a fool he was;

so unworthy of the goddess she'd become. How odd that she'd once wanted him. Now, all she wanted was his death. His end. Nothing could exist in this world that reminded her of personal failure.

She was a goddess. She. Did. Not. Fail.

2

Alexander saw Lijuan attack Zanaya.

Fighting to get to her, he witnessed Zanaya's wings droop, her body go limp.

But her mind, it was yet functional, yet held enough power for her to reach out to him along a pathway so old that it was part of his most elemental being: *Xander . . . kill me. She must be sto—*

Even had he the heart to follow her whispered plea, it was too late. Lijuan went noncorporeal again, dropping Zanaya from the sky. And his Zani's wings were crumpled, her body dropping, akin to a broken bird's. *Zani! Zani!*

Silence, nothing but silence from his quicksilver lover with her wicked tongue.

He caught her before she could hit the hard earth, his Zani, her spirit so bright and beautiful. Making a hard turn in midair, he arrowed his way toward the Tower infirmary.

"Hold on, Zani. Hold on!" It was an order, but she was beyond hearing him.

Her body was a whisper, so light that it was as if she were made of air. Her skin had turned to paper, the flesh of her curves just gone and her skin cold, so cold. Cradling her as close as he could while not hurting her, he kept on talking to her, kept on trying to make her respond. But all he heard was a silence without end.

Then, and through all the hours that followed.

"You promised you'd speak to me after the battle," he whispered to her after they'd vanquished the monster Lijuan had become, and he carried Zanaya's broken body to Cassandra's fire.

The seer of legend had promised to hold her safe.

Again, his Zani, who'd never hesitated to speak around him, said nothing. Her silence was a wound bigger than any other she could've inflicted on him.

He pressed a trembling kiss to her lips, and it tasted of the salt of his tears. "I can't exist in a world where you do not." He'd only lived this long because, no matter his anger at her, he knew that she Slept whole and unharmed. "Come back to me, my Zani."

Silence.

Until the very moment when he forced himself to give her into Cassandra's embrace. The seer's lilac hair was licked by the gold and orange of the enormous, impossible fissure deep into the earth above which they hovered, and the seafoam auroras of her haunting—haunted—eyes were tender, her arms careful as she cradled Zanaya against the floating softness of her gown.

"You will care for her." It came out an order.

Cassandra didn't tell him he had no right to give her orders. Gaze lost in the terrible gift that drove her to a madness that had her clawing out her eyes when she could no longer stand it, she said, "Alexander, Archangel of Persia, Child of Gzrel and Cendrion, before you lie two paths."

Her tone was eerie, echoing as if spoken in a great chamber.

Gut tight, Alexander clenched his fists. It took everything he had to keep his tone civil. "I don't wish for blurry prophecies that could mean anything and need to be interpreted. I want to know if Zanaya will rise and when."

Cassandra looked down at the body in her arms, a body she'd already wreathed in her flame. "This I do not know." Her face was soft now, her voice softer. "But I know this, Alexander, this is an ending . . . but it isn't the last ending. That, too, will come. Choose with care, for it will be the forever last."

Then she was gone, taking with her his Zani with her brilliant spirit and warrior's heart.

His own heart broke.

Always, no matter what, he'd known she would return. He'd been nursing a grudge against her for millennia, getting ready to have the fight that he was owed. He'd known she'd laugh at him for refusing to let it go, but then she'd have fought with him. After which, they'd have ended up in each other's arms. That was how it was meant to have been; that was the future for which he had waited for *so* long.

This . . .

Pain a raw knot inside him, he didn't know how he made it through the time that followed. He felt glued together by nothing but his own will when he finally returned to his territory. Once in his lands, he went not to his fort, but to an isolated ridge of mountains where no one could hear his heart splinter.

Wings flared out, he screamed out his grief and his rage till it brought him to his knees, but still the wound inside him continued to bleed. He'd survived the loss of Zanaya before, but then, it hadn't been a true loss. He'd known that she would rise again, that her timeline would cross with his again.

He no longer had that surety.

His Zani might Sleep forevermore.

Alexander screamed again, and his pain turned the mountain molten, a river of gold and silver and rarer precious metals that crept down every crack and seam, where they'd freeze at some point, a sculpture of astonishing beauty carved out of Alexander's grief.

3

Cassandra twisted and turned, unable to settle into rest.

The flames in which she slept were comfort, barriers against the slipstreams of time that showed her too much. But she could only fully escape those slipstreams when she was in a deep and true Sleep. And that she couldn't fall into when she had within her care angels who were a sprawling weight of power and history.

Astaad, Michaela, Favashi, and Zanaya, they were all . . . caught in between.

But it wasn't only these archangels that Cassandra watched. Another, too, Slept an unnatural Sleep far from her. Yet that being was connected to her by a thread tied to another, their blood bonded deep beneath the surface. Perhaps their pulses would beat in time . . . but not today.

Today, none of the Sleepers had a pulse, showed any signs of life.

She didn't know if they dreamt, but she did know that they had no awareness of the world. That was a mercy given their injuries. Yet she could feel their minds, huge and powerful, and those minds were . . . not at rest.

Had one of her brethren asked her how she knew these facts, she couldn't have answered them. All she had were guesses. Perhaps it was because the wounded archangels Slept in the embrace of her fire, their minds linked to her by threads tenuous that allowed her to monitor their lives. For, despite all outward appearances, they lived, the spark within flickering but not extinguished.

Yet.

She couldn't see any of their future timelines, not even the merest glimmer. Each led to a tangled knot so tight that it was pure darkness.

Yet she caught other things in the slipstreams that impinged on her shallow rest. Her owls fluttered around her, their feathers soft and white as she jerked and twitched in her Sleep. Sensing what awaited, she tried not to look at the slipstream. She was so very tired, her mind a stained-glass window so fractured with cracks that it could never be whole again.

The colors of her were the colors of him.

Qin, her Qin.

Tears rolled down her cheeks as she fought the compulsion to *look*, but she'd never won that fight in the eons since her "gift" was first bestowed on her. At times, when she was sane, she wondered if part of her anger was because of how she always lost the battle. Was she so very vain and arrogant that she was enraged by her constant inability to win?

Laughter, a touch mad.

Oh, that was her.

No, she wasn't angry. She'd long ago moved past anger, through terror and rage, into a sorrow so heavy that it was her very breath. Sometimes, she thought she must be born of tears, nothing to her but saltwater.

Her mind kaleidoscoped, shattered again, more fractures on the stained glass.

And the slipstream opened out in front of her, showing

her countless threads, millions of lives, millions of possibilities. One choice could lead to this, another to that. But some choices . . . some choices led always to a single thing. Roads funneled into a single choke point. Those were the futures set in stone.

As was the future that pulsed red in front of her in the shape of scarlet wings that glowed.

Red as blood.

But beautiful.

Even as the thought passed through her mind, the wings began to darken. To a rich ruby that was lovely. Then edged with blue. Still lovely. On a sigh that made her flinch, the blue and the red started to mingle but rather than the violet hue that should have resulted, the wings turned a sickly green.

Droplets of blood crawled down the feathers, each droplet a viscous black that splattered on the slipstream and coated the highways of it in a quickly spreading plague that decimated all future timelines. Feathers fell off the wings, further spreading the plague.

She jolted, her heart echoing the twisted tapestry of the rotting pair of wings.

"No." A whisper. "No. They have paid the price. They have survived." This should be a time of rebuilding and hope.

But the wings continued to contaminate the slipstreams with their poison.

One.

By.

One.

Over.

And.

Over.

Until the wings were nothing but bone rotted through with infection and the entirety of the future a noxious stranglehold with no way out. Screaming, she lifted her hands to claw out her eyes . . . but her owls stepped on her fingers, reminding her that she could Sleep, could fall deep, *deep* below the surface and allow herself to drown in nothingness.

But she couldn't hear her beloved owls today. Couldn't see them. All she could see were the rotting bones of the wings, breaking, falling, spreading more poison. Digging her nails into her eyes, she clawed them out. Blood coated her fingers, slick and iron bright. But it didn't matter how much damage she did to herself. She still saw. She still knew.

Her owls, distressed, fluttered their wings in an effort to calm her, but still she screamed.

Until . . .

A single thread of the slipstream that glittered with black diamonds. It split off from a thicker line. The main line was coated in the poison and went into the knot that was the end of eternity, the end of everything. The diamond-dark one flowed into a future beyond which lay more endless possibilities, stars blinking to life one after the other.

Cassandra wanted to cup her bloody hands around that single thread of hope, but that wasn't how her gift worked, how it had ever worked, was why she was always a little mad. "A single crossroads." Her murmur reached no one, caught in the fires she'd set up to stop her thoughts leaking into the minds of others.

Elena, that mortal child turned angel, she deserved a little peace from the whispers of a mad Ancient.

So it was only her owls that heard her screams, her words.

For the archangels she held in her arms couldn't hear, couldn't listen, were in a place far beyond pain, beyond this world, perhaps beyond healing.

Closing eyes that were already regenerating, Cassandra fell back into a fitful Sleep. She would continue to listen for her charges and for the other. Perhaps one would wake. Perhaps she would glimpse a joyous surprise in the slipstream. It had happened before. Some forces were greater than fate itself.

For she had seen Elena alive in only a single fragile timeline.

The mortal had fallen in the arms of her archangel, broken and dying, in every timeline. But in every other one, she'd died. Vanished, and with her, all the timelines that rippled off her, the world a wholly different place.

A place fetid and of death.

A place so terrible that Cassandra had interfered. She'd laid breadcrumbs of foresight that led to actions that led to other actions. Lijuan had woken Alexander because she thought he *would* wake, but it was the Archangel of Death who'd set that chain of motion into action.

So many painstakingly laid breadcrumbs, so many butterfly wings in the ether.

Because while Cassandra couldn't change the future, she'd learned that she could influence it dependent on which of her visions she shared. Share that Lijuan would rule all the world and it would be a weight on the shoulders of all those who battled, stealing their will and their strength. Share that she'd seen a scorched and devastated landscape and it became a horror whispering on the back of the neck.

So she'd shared other things. Dark truths . . . but not the darkest.

And today, in her madness, she understood that she *had* altered the future. But only to an extent. Because in the end, it had come down to a mortal's will to live and the force of an archangel's love. That she couldn't change, couldn't manipulate. That was where her power ended.

But . . . perhaps it was enough. Perhaps she could live with seeing the future if she could alter it even a fraction.

A fading thought as she slipped deeper into rest.

Yet as she did so, she saw one final image that turned into a silent prophecy: *Lovers fall and lovers rise. The river stops flowing. This time will be the end.*

The Beginning

4

The boy was born with a cry loud enough to startle the neighbors. They were unused to such disturbance from the home of two scholars known for their calm ways and steady bearing. The scene inside that scholarly home of stone and wood and a reverence of knowledge was one of even more astonishment—and of love.

Neither Gzrel nor Cendrion had thought to have another child after many thousands of years without such a blessing. Why, their son Osiris was already a man of some two thousand years! But now here he was, this boy so fierce and with such strong lungs, his wings nothing but a whisper of translucence on his back.

Gzrel cradled him close to her tender breasts, her tears overflowing as she pressed a kiss to the roundness of his cheek, while Cendrion took their son's tiny, fisted hand. "Alexander," he murmured, for they had already decided that their child would be named after Gzrel's mother, Alexandre, who was the reason that she and Cendrion had come together.

So shy Gzrel and Cendrion had been; they would've never made a move that might threaten the quiet friendship that sustained them both. But Alexandre had seen their love for each other, arranged it so that they would be stuck together during a fierce winter storm—enough time for each to see the longing and devotion of the other. Now here they were, thousands of years of love later, with a second living symbol of that love in their arms.

Osiris they'd named for Cendrion's father, he who had passed through the veil beyond which immortals so rarely traveled. He'd fallen in battle, obliterated in the fire of an archangel's wrath. So it was that Gzrel and Cendrion's children, Osiris and Alexander, would carry pieces of their family's history on both sides.

"He is fierce," Cendrion said, his voice deep and the gray of his eyes soft and warm against the pale gold of his skin and the burnished brown of his hair. "I'm quite sure I didn't yell so when I was born." A stunned joy in his tone. "Did Osiris do the same, or were we just younger then?"

That joy, that shock at becoming parents again was still with them when Ojewo, who was said to be distant blood kin to Cassandra herself, came to visit Alexander some few days later. Gzrel wanted to hug her precious babe close, protect him from the seer's strange sight and yet at the same time, she wanted to thrust him into the seer's arms so that Ojewo could tell them what dangers the future held for their boy.

Gzrel was no warrior and neither was Cendrion. They'd eschewed the path of violence eons past, but violence wasn't the only choice when it came to the troubles of life. They both had minds clever of thought. Surely if they knew of danger, they could find a way to protect Alexander from it?

Ojewo, with his air of youth despite his years, smiled as he entered their home, and that smile was so full of light that Gzrel handed over her child with a smile of her own, certain that Alexander would be safe in the arms of this handsome angel. So many sighed after him, whispering of the smoky green of his eyes and the deep brown of his skin, the slenderness of his build and the mystery of his smile.

Gzrel, in contrast, always wanted to mother him, though she knew that Ojewo had been an adult before she'd ever been a spark in her mother's eye. Perhaps because he reminded her of a young Osiris, slender and slow to smile, but with eyes that lit up when he did.

"You carry a youthful heart," she'd said to him once, bemused enough at how that was possible that she'd forgotten her natural reticence. "I'd always heard that seers are haunted by what they see, that it causes them to age before their time. I'm so happy this isn't the case for you."

She'd blushed in the immediate aftermath of her words, her hands flying to her face. "Oh, what has come over me? Forgive me for stepping where I have no right to go."

Ojewo would've been right to be insulted by the personal comment, but he'd laughed a laugh warm and bold that embraced her until she could do nothing but smile. "Ah, Gzrel, you need not fear to say such to me—you have earned the right after your many kindnesses to others."

He'd leaned in close, as if sharing a secret. "The truth," he'd said, his skin warm with the scent of the wild berries that grew all over the Refuge, "is that my sight is but a whisper in comparison to that of my most legendary ancestor. There are no records, no birth histories, but it is said in my family that she and her beloved Qin had a child. However, that child was born before her natural sight turned into . . . a fury and an agony."

No laughter now, nothing but sorrow for a woman he'd never met. "So, even if I am blood of her blood, a direct descendant, the sight I have inherited is a faded painting in comparison to the startling truth of hers. And I celebrate that gift every day of my life."

Gzrel had recoiled inwardly, her anguish for Cassandra as sharp as her horror. For Ojewo already saw too much, carried too much. To know even *more* . . . It made her wish peace and comfort to Cassandra where she lay, locked in a never-ending Sleep.

Immortals, to Gzrel's way of thinking, should see the future even less so than mortals. What was the point of seeing a grim future when that grim future might be thousands of years distant? All it would do was shadow the present. She'd always been grateful that Ojewo had given them no fortune for Osiris. All he'd said was that, like most newborns, he'd have many opportunities, many forks in the road to his destiny.

"If I speak for him a future, I will color his entire existence," Ojewo had murmured as he held their firstborn, and for a moment, Gzrel had thought she'd glimpsed the darkest of shadows cross the seer's face, but then Ojewo had lifted his head and smiled and the foolishness of the thought had passed.

Osiris was a babe, innocent as the fresh-fallen snow.

Relieved by the reminder of the seer's refusal to give fortunes to the very young, she settled into the visit and into the pride of being a new mother. Ojewo was so gentle with Alexander, so careful in how he touched the boy's little fists.

Opening them out, Alexander gripped at the seer's finger.

Ojewo's teeth flashed bright, his eyes sparkling. "Oh, you will be a strong one." The slightest shift in his voice toward the end, a certain tone that made the hair on the back of Gzrel's neck prickle.

She'd heard that tone before, knew what it heralded. *"Ojewo."* She went to pluck her child from the seer's arms . . . but it was too late.

"Wings of silver," Ojewo murmured. *"Such* wings. Such strength. Silver fire." A sudden blinking, then the feeling of a *wrench*, as if the seer was pulling himself out of the vision with force.

Gzrel swallowed, waited. Her gut was ice, her spine cold iron.

But Ojewo's smile only deepened. "Oh, I'm sorry to startle you so, Gzrel. This one is adamant in his path—and it will be a glorious one." Lifting the child he yet held, Ojewo pressed his lips to the babe's forehead. "He will shine like the stars."

Gzrel gasped out a breath, her hand on her chest. "Goodness. I thought you were going to tell me something awful!"

"And all I've said is that your babe will be glorious." Ojewo laughed again. "Do not all parents believe so of their children? It is a law, yes?"

Gzrel was still smiling hours later as she related the story to Cendrion, who'd had to miss the visit due to already having plans with a fellow scholar who was about to leave the Refuge for many years.

Cendrion laughed that quiet laugh that was her touchstone. "Ojewo is right," he said afterward. "It is a law." Taking Alexander from his crib, he said, "Oh, my love, an angelic courier handed me a letter from Osiris as I was coming home. It's in my bag."

"Oh! It's been too long since we've heard from him." Unable to wait till after dinner, she found the letter and read it aloud while Cendrion played with Alexander.

Their firstborn was a man of study and innovation, though his work was more hands-on and experimental than theirs. She and Cendrion both agreed that Osiris was a brilliant scholar, one who'd long eclipsed them—and they couldn't be more proud to be so eclipsed.

In this letter, he'd sent them copious notes on his latest projects.

Gzrel's chest burst with warmth. "I wonder what discoveries Osiris will make in his lifetime. He's so far along already."

"I can't wait to hear more on his project," Cendrion said, and they spoke on that for a while as Alexander watched them with eyes that had begun to change from an infant's fuzziness to a gray so striking it was heading toward silver.

He already had hair as gold as Gzrel's and per Ojewo, his wings would be silver, too. She could already see the shape of the boy he'd become, so beautiful and intelligent and the apple of their eye.

"What discoveries do you think our vocal younger son will make?" Cendrion said at one point during their conversation. "I'm certain he'll do the wildest experiments of us all!"

That Alexander, too, would be a scholar seemed a self-evident truth. Every angel in his maternal *and* paternal line as far back as memory could reach had chosen that life. No deviations except in specialization.

Of course Alexander would be a studious child.

As the years passed and their boy grew, Gzrel and Cendrion forgot about Ojewo's words except as a happy confirmation that their child would be all they believed children could be.

The sole person who didn't forget what he'd seen that day was Ojewo himself.

As he walked the ice-crusted pathways of the jagged mountains beyond the Refuge, he thought of the visions that had erupted into his mind with such brutal force that they couldn't be contained: the glory of an archangel of molten power, the choice he would one day have to make against the blood of his blood, the murmur of a fog of black hovering on a horizon so far in the future that even Ojewo's mind couldn't reach it . . . and the awareness that Alexander would experience both great happiness and great sorrow in his time.

His life would be one writ large and it would leave a permanent mark on the world.

"I wish you well, little one," he whispered to the ice and the snow, his breath puffs of white in the air. "And I hope that I am awake to witness your ascension."

Ojewo had long ago understood that to give a child a fortune was to weigh them down until they drowned, so he never spoke of what he saw.

That didn't mean he saw nothing. Far from it.

There remained, of course, faint forks in the road, including futures where the child *didn't* ascend, but Ojewo didn't believe these to be real possibilities.

The visions had been too visceral, too full of color.

Ojewo's heart ached for the pain and loss to come in Alexander's life, and he hoped that beyond the horror and agony lay joy. But Ojewo couldn't glimpse it, unable to see beyond the noxious black fog. Perhaps that was the limit of his sight . . . or perhaps it augured a thing so terrible that it engulfed the entire world.

5

Alexander loved to visit his big brother. Unlike many of his friends who had siblings older than them—though no one in school had a brother who was *so much* older—Osiris didn't ignore Alexander except for a present on his birthing day.

Mama said that Osiris had come to visit Alexander when Alexander was a fledgling with wings that didn't even open, and he'd been there for Alexander ever since. Mama and Papa had taught Alexander a lot, but it was Osiris who'd actually *shown* him things. His brother had allowed him to mix powders and liquids in the laboratory to see how they reacted, taken him to watch animals so Alexander could learn their behavior, and even taught him to swim!

Alexander was sure that his brother was the smartest person in the whole world.

Today, Osiris gave him a thinking look as Alexander ran back across the black sands of the faraway island of sunshine and water where Osiris lived. The sand burned so he ran as fast as he could, yelping and laughing at the same time.

"Such a wild thing you are," Osiris murmured, a tilt to his

lips and the silver of his eyes bright in the sun. They shared those eyes and even the gold of their hair, but Alexander's was straight like their father's and Osiris had curls like their mother's.

Alexander loved that they were so clearly brothers. The only obvious difference was that Osiris's skin was more sun-browned than Alexander's. The sun burned so hot here that Alexander's brother mostly wore a tunic that came to the middle of his thighs, sandals, and nothing else.

Alexander didn't bother with clothes at all. He knew he'd have to one day, but right now everyone still treated him like a baby, so it was allowed. Grinning at what his brother had said, he pretended to growl and be a tiger like the one they'd watched in Refuge territory once.

Osiris chuckled and rubbed his hand over Alexander's head—just as a vampire with big brown eyes and long dark hair, a frangipani bloom tucked behind one ear, came out from the trees. Her tunic was woven from strips of brown and black and had tassels that hung at her thighs.

"My lord," she murmured, her gaze lowered. "It's almost time to eat."

Alexander knew Livaliana was Osiris's favorite concubine. Osiris had explained concubines to him, so Alexander knew they were special friends his brother loved, and Livaliana was the *most* favorite. Alexander liked her too—she was kind and gentle like his mother, and she sang him beautiful songs at bedtime.

"Come, wild child." Osiris held out a hand. "Our lady beckons us."

As Alexander walked between them, one hand gripping his brother's and the other holding on to Livaliana's, Osiris said, "What do you think of sampling warrior training, little brother?"

Alexander stopped, stared up at Osiris, his heart thumping so loudly that he couldn't even hear the ocean waves anymore. "Really?"

"Yes." A look so serious that Alexander could feel it inside him. "I do believe our shy and noncombative parents may have created a warrior child—my own senior guards have come to me to say that they see such an energy in you, the same energy that lives in them. So I had the thought that we should offer you both the scholar's path and the warrior's, and allow you to make up your own mind."

Alexander couldn't speak, didn't have the words; he just flung himself at Osiris's legs and held on tight. Chuckling, his brother ruffled his hair again. "I should've known. You flew high and straight before most of your brethren could even get in the air. I have a feeling, young sib, that you're not meant for the family's favored way of life."

Alexander's happiness was so big he felt like his skin would burst and it stayed that way until his return to the Refuge, to wearing clothes again, and to the start of his training.

He met Callie on the second day of his training. She had eyes so blue they almost hurt to look at, and was a little older, but since there weren't that many children in the Refuge for this "season of life"—as his mother put it—they all had to practice together.

When the trainer asked Callie to show him an exercise she'd already learned, Alexander told himself to be careful—because even though she was older, she was smaller, more slender. Then she kicked his legs out from under him, landing him hard on his behind, and he realized she was tougher than she looked.

He stopped holding back.

Given that he was the newest member of the class, he never had a chance against her, but she didn't laugh at him for his mistakes, just told him why he'd lost and what he could do to fix it. A week into the lessons, he went to sit with her for their break. She allowed it, but later, on their walk home, he decided to climb a tree and somehow fell out of it. The movement dislodged a heavy bunch of ripe fruits.

They splattered and burst on her neat and tidy tunic.

"Alex!" Face red, she ignored his apologies to stomp off home.

It soon became clear that Callie *did not* consider him a friend. Not that he was sad. He liked her but he couldn't imagine anything worse than being invited to a lunch or party where he had to be on his best manners—because that was what Callie liked to do. He didn't understand. She was an incredible fighter . . . then she went and had honey cakes and tea with her friends, all of them in their best clothes.

In training though, it was different. He understood her there—she continued to push him with each lesson, each time she put him on the ground . . . until one day, he put her on the ground.

They both stared, eyes wide.

Then he threw his hands up into the air and did a lap around the training ring. "One to me, one hundred to Callie!"

Lying there in the dirt, the black of her hair sticking to her face, she laughed so hard that she cried, and he knew that she didn't mind that he'd beaten her.

Their bouts got better and better from then on, Alexander's body stronger and more flexible, his thoughts less childish— and his future path ever clearer. But he didn't tell Osiris or his parents that. Not yet. Gzrel and Cendrion had taught him to consider things before he decided, whether it was his opinion on a new kind of food, or his thoughts on a piece of information.

Alexander hated waiting. It was a waste of time. He always knew his mind straightaway and never changed it, but he also knew that his family liked to spend time thinking. Yesterday, he'd walked in on his mother just staring at the wall where she'd chalked drawings to do with her work even though she should have been packing.

A hard knot formed in his stomach when he remembered why they had to pack: because a senior member of their archangel's court wanted their home on the edge of a cliff. He'd argued with his parents that they should fight the preemptory relocation order, but they'd looked at him with faint smiles on their faces that weren't about smiling at all.

His father had said, "We're no one to the archangel, Alexander, simply two low-level scholars who are only attached to her court because it means others can't steal our research without picking a fight with her. It's not as if our dry specializations give any particular cachet to her court. She'd consider our request a petty matter, be annoyed by it."

"It's not petty!" Alexander hated that people could just push his parents around this way.

"Oh, baby." His mother had patted his chest, leaving chalk dust in her wake. "We lose nothing by not wasting our energy on this. Our new residence has room for all our scrolls and tablets and the like, and we shall be together. Politics don't interest us, so we don't play them."

Alexander could've said a hard thing then, a cruel thing about weakness and lack of spine, but he hadn't. Because he *loved* his mama and papa and they'd never ever done anything to hurt him.

That was also why he pretended to think even though his mind was made up.

And this decision . . . "I don't want to hurt their hearts," he told Callie one day when he was a youngling halfway to adulthood, long legged and lanky, and she'd decided she could stand him for small periods.

They still weren't friends, but he knew he could trust her and he hoped she knew she could trust him. "My brother has already guessed, I'm sure," he added, "but my parents have a vision of a continuing line of scholars."

Caliane bumped his shoulder with her own. "They won't mind, Alex. They won't understand, but they're so sweet, they'll love you regardless."

Alexander clung to that reassurance when he spoke to his parents about his choice at last. "I wish to follow the path of the warrior," he said, swallowing hard. "It fits me like it's always been meant to be my skin."

No anger or disappointment on their faces, just the love that had always been a part of his life.

"Whatever makes you happy, Alexander." His father squeezed his arm before turning to look at Alexander's mother with a tenderness that made Alexander blush. "Gzrel and I've always known that you'd walk your own path. Haven't we, my heart?"

His mother's laughter filled the room with sunshine. "I remember telling you that you couldn't stay on with Osiris when you were little, and the arguments you gave me about it!" Dancing eyes. "Another child might've thrown a tantrum, but you used every one of the words in your vocabulary to try to convince me that I was wrong, wrong, *wrong*. If memory serves me, I believe you used exactly those words in that tone."

Alexander couldn't help but grin, and when his mother put her slender arms around him to hug him tight, he hugged her in turn. And it struck him how small and fragile she was; he was already taller and stronger than her. People could so easily hurt her.

Hit by a wave of raw emotion that clogged up his throat, he hugged her even tighter.

Afterward, his parents asked him if he intended to discard scholarship altogether, and Alexander shook his head. "My brother has often advised me that the warriors who rise the highest are the ones who are smart as well as skilled on the field of battle."

"Those who stand in the courts of the archangels," Osiris had said, "are more than brawn. They're highly intelligent thinkers and informed strategists. Look, learn."

Alexander had done exactly that, using the skills he'd learned at his parents' knee to research the angels and vampires who stood as the seconds and senior courtiers of archangels. Not a single one could be labeled as brawn alone, though a number of them were lethal on the battlefield. Then had come the surprises. One second was an administrator with no battle experience whatsoever; still another wore the robes of a healer.

Alexander intended to get to the heart of those choices—as his parents had taught him, he wanted to *understand*. He didn't want to just *know*. One was the surface of the lake, the other the deep waters beneath.

"I must admit I'm happy to hear that," his mother said in response to his answer about his continuing scholarship, her fingers worrying the amber pendant she never took off. "Though it'll be a path that will demand much from you. You'll be careful of your health, won't you, my son?"

When he complained to Callie about his mother's over-protective worrying, she said, "That's her job as a mother. At least that's what my father tells me." No twist of emotion on her face, an absence of memory.

Callie didn't have a mama. Her mother had died giving birth to her. As a child, Alexander hadn't understood how that could be so—immortals lived forever aside from in some very specific circumstances, most of which involved severe insult to the body, including beheading.

Older now and realizing he still didn't truly comprehend any of it, he went home and asked his mother to explain it to him.

Gzrel was busy, but she put down her work, tucked her arm through his, and they walked all the way to the crack in the earth of the Refuge that had been there as long as Alexander could remember.

6

"It appeared some hundred years ago," his mother said, having followed his gaze, "and it's looking to develop into a gorge. I wonder what it will be in a thousand years, where it will stop its expansion."

Alexander was used to such non sequiturs from his mother, especially when it came to the study of rocks and the earth, Gzrel's specialty. "What do you think?"

"It's too early to be certain," she said with a frown, "but I disagree with those who are convinced the crack will swallow the Refuge. I believe it'll stop expanding once it's reached an equilibrium—though exactly when that will be remains a mystery."

Alexander tried to think about what it must be like to be as old as his mother or father—*thousands* of years old!—but it felt like a rock on his chest, the idea of it. He wondered sometimes who he'd be if he ever reached such an age, but it was too far for him to imagine. Today was his reality, and today, he was listening to his mother talk about Callie's mother. "Ma?"

"Yes?" She'd looked up at him, blinked. "Oh yes. Sorry, my son." Patting at his arm with the hand she didn't have tucked through it, she said, "Death in childbirth is unfortunately common among the mortals. Many things can go wrong while birthing a child, but as immortals, our advanced healing abilities ameliorate any such wounds to the extent that we never feel them."

"Callie's mother's body didn't heal?"

To his surprise, she shook her head. "As far as we know, it did. She didn't die *in* childbirth—she died the day after. Even in his grief, Caliane's father was adamant that the healers cut open his beloved, find out the reason why, for his daughter must have an answer. It must've been the hardest decision of his life—but it was the right one. No child should believe themselves the reason for their mother's death."

Alexander swallowed hard, his throat thick. He couldn't speak, so he just stared ahead and let his mother think he was simply concentrating on her words.

"What they discovered was that Caliane's mother was destined to die—an element of her heart had never formed correctly. While such irregularities in growth are unusual among our kind, they can and do occur."

Though his mother stopped there, Alexander was old enough to understand that Callie's mother's heart had collapsed badly enough to kill an immortal because of the power it took to birth a child.

Callie was smart. She'd know that, too.

Which was why Alexander would never ever bring up the topic with her. They might not be friends, but she'd always looked out for him and now it was his turn to look out for her. That was what it meant to be loyal, to be a good battlemate.

"Gzrel!"

His mother stiffened at the sound of her name shouted in an unfamiliar male voice, though her expression remained neutral. Skin prickling, Alexander stayed silent as a good-looking and tall warrior with curls of dark brown walked over to them. The stranger's leathers were well-worn but a cuff of gold and precious gems encircled his wrist—a symbol of favor from Rumaia, the archangel to whom all three of them owed fealty.

"Oh, who's this?" the man said with a wide smile that made Alexander's muscles tense. "Don't tell me this is your babe?"

"Indeed. This is my son Alexander." His mother's voice wasn't quite right, her cheer too bright, too hard. "Alexander, this is Phiron, who stands fourth to Archangel Rumaia."

The man laughed, hearty and long. "Oh Gzrel, will you not tell your son that we were almost more once upon a time?" Pale blue eyes twinkling, the man looked at Alexander. "I pursued your mother as a youth, was mad for her. But she had eyes only for Cendrion."

"It was an age ago," his mother said. "We were barely grown."

"Quite right!" Phiron agreed with a clap. "But you must let me say that you still speak as sweetly. The sound is delicate music to my ears."

"It is an honor to meet you," Alexander said before his mother felt forced to respond, because, quite unlike his parents, he already knew how to play political games, to say one thing and mean another.

He studied political maneuvering as assiduously as his mother studied rocks and the earth.

Phiron slapped him on the shoulder. "I hear you're in warrior training," he said, giving away the fact he knew more about their family than he'd initially let on. "Perhaps I'll have time to give you a private lesson while I'm in the Refuge." A grin. "And now I must go. But we'll meet again, Gzrel."

His mother held her tongue until they were home, then she turned and gripped at Alexander's upper arms. "My son, do not accept any invitation to be alone with Phiron. If you can't get out of it politely, take Callie with you—her father is Rumaia's weapons-master and of equal standing to Phiron. She isn't a child who Phiron will dare mistreat or bully into silence and so he'll be forced to treat you well."

Having never seen his mother so distraught, Alexander fought his churning stomach to say, "Ma, what is it? Did that man hurt you?" Fury was a sharp and jagged sun inside him.

A shake of her head, her eyes skating away. "No, but . . . He holds grudges, Phiron, and he doesn't forgive rejection." She gripped the pendant that hung in the hollow of her throat. "I'm being foolish—it's been so long and we weren't much more than children. Yet . . . He has broken with his lover of many years, and I—"

She gnawed at her lower lip. "He carries anger behind that false smile, Alexander. His beauty is but a mask for inner ugliness. And we exist in front of him, a family that loves. It might not seem much, but, when in a mood, Phiron never needed much to bathe in rage. I fear he's fixated on us this time around. Promise me you'll be careful."

"I promise," he said without hesitation, already hating Phiron for the panic he'd seeded in Gzrel. He was also no infant—he knew his mother had lied. Phiron *had* hurt her; she just didn't want to tell Alexander.

His hand fisting, he fought the impulse to go to the warrior angel, pick a fight. That would be stupid. He'd lose. He was a boy and Phiron the fourth to an archangel. He'd flick Alexander off like an annoying fly.

Far better for Alexander to find another way to deal with the threat.

But Phiron struck far faster than any of them could've expected. Four days later, Alexander came home to find his father bloody and beaten on the floor of their home, his face not much more than pulp. Cendrion's wing bones had been crushed, the bloody imprint of a boot yet on them, and he'd lost an eye, but he was crawling to the door.

A long streak of blood on the polished wood of the floor Alexander had swept that very morning bore silent witness to his horrible journey.

"Papa!" Alexander crashed to his knees beside his father. "Papa! I'll get the healer!"

Cendrion grabbed at him with hands that were mangled,

his draftsman's fingers shattered and twisted and his wrist missing the bracelet of metal and amber that was a constant on his body. "No," he gasped out past the blood. "Gzrel . . . Phiron . . . has . . . Gzrel."

The panic in Alexander turned ice-cold. But he didn't freeze. No, he used the ice to think, to strategize, to bridge the gap between the boy he was today and the man he intended to become. "I understand, Papa," he said with chilly calm. "I know what to do."

Fear burned in his father's single remaining eye as he tried to speak again. "Rum—"

"I know," Alexander interrupted, for his father needed to conserve his strength. "I won't go to Archangel Rumaia." Phiron might've crossed a line that should be unforgiveable, but he was Rumaia's fourth and as Alexander had learned when they were forced to give up their home to another of her favorites, she was indulgent with her inner court; she was as likely to tell Gzrel it was an honor to be so wanted than to punish Phiron.

Moving quickly now that he had a plan, he found a blanket and put it over his father's broken body with tender care. Broken but not fatally. An angel could survive even this nasty a beating. And he knew the choice his father would want him to make. So instead of going to the healer, he flew hard and fast to General Akhia-Solay, second to Archangel Esphares.

Esphares and Rumaia were mortal enemies. And General Akhia-Solay was Esphares's most trusted confidant—the general was also one of the seconds that Alexander most admired. From all Alexander had observed and heard, Akhia-Solay was *smart*, was a large part of the reason why Esphares held so much territory.

But more than that, Akhia-Solay had honor. Even young as he was, Alexander understood honor, understood what it was to be a good person. He'd been raised by people who were honorable to the core—so honorable that they didn't understand the depth of malevolence that existed in others.

He'd seen how his mother had questioned herself about Phiron despite having experienced his malice first hand.

As he understood that, he understood that Archangel Rumaia's honor was tainted and without value; that realization had been coming to him in fits and starts, but after today, he no longer had any doubts. Phiron wouldn't have dared his actions had he believed he might suffer any real punishment.

Archangel Rumaia cared only for herself and those close to her; she didn't protect those outside her inner circle. And to Alexander, to protect those who were weaker lay at the heart of what it meant to have honor. General Akhia-Solay, in contrast to Rumaia, had been known to personally fly children and other enemy non-combatants out of the field of battle.

Archangel Esphares also had the most disciplined army in the Cadre of Ten because of Akhia-Solay. The general didn't permit raping and pillaging in war, much less in peacetime. And he kept on winning, his troops confident in the knowledge that their archangel—informed by their general—would reward them for their fidelity and hard work.

Driven by desperation, Alexander didn't bother to look for sentries as he crossed three Refuge borders to get to the section that belonged to Esphares. He knew he must've been spotted, but he was a child.

Most sentries had orders to allow children to fly as they wished.

He'd planned to go to the stronghold of Archangel Esphares and ask for the general, but fate had mercy on him and he spotted the general standing directly outside the stronghold, in conversation with a robed courtier.

Heart pounding and breath painful, Alexander dropped to land bruisingly hard mere handsbreadths from the two. His knees vibrated from the impact, his teeth clenching shut. Instead of reacting with anger, the adults looked at him with startled amusement. Again, because Alexander was a child yet, no threat to anyone.

"Sir." Alexander went down on one knee in front of the general. Not two. Because Akhia-Solay also appreciated strength. Alexander would not beg. He'd treat this as if he were a full-grown warrior rather than a stripling, approach the general in that avatar. "I would speak with you. It is most urgent."

He could feel the general's piercing gaze on the top of his head. Akhia-Solay's deadly black eyes were legend, but now Alexander lifted his head and met those mysterious orbs. They sat in a face that was all sharp lines and angles beneath skin of a rich brown, the only softness provided by the general's shoulder-length hair.

A liquid black, he wore it open today, only a single feather woven into it to speak of his allegiance to Esphares. Because that feather was brown speckled with blue—the shade on the underside of Esphares's wings.

"Rise, child," he said, his voice a touch impatient, then turned to bid farewell to the courtier.

Alexander waited only until the courtier was out of ear-shot before saying, "Sir, I need help." The general wasn't known for his patience with people who didn't get to the point, so Alexander got to it. "Phiron, Fourth to Archangel Rumaia, has kidnapped my mother, and grievously wounded my father."

Akhia-Solay turned and spat onto the grass that encircled a tree planted in the courtyard. "Rumaia runs her court like a brothel." As an insult, it was a grave one, but then the general said, "But my archangel will not war with her over this."

Alexander had his answer ready. "I know. I'm not asking for the help of Archangel Esphares. I'm asking for yours." He continued to hold those strange, dangerous eyes. "A dispute between a second and a fourth will be exactly that—a dispute between warriors. A personal matter." One Phiron wouldn't want escalated should he lose, because to do so would be to draw attention to the fact that he'd proved weaker than another senior angel. The bastard would be trapped by his own arrogance and pride.

Akhia-Solay stared at Alexander for a long time. "You realize this will end your parents' protection under Rumaia?"

Alexander couldn't help the rage that seeded tremors in his voice. "She gives no protection. Rather, she makes us prey." A stark difference. "And my parents are highly intelligent scholars. My mother leads the field in the study of rocks and the earth—and I know Archangel Esphares has many earth shakes in his lands. She'd be a valuable resource for him."

The general waved that aside. "I'll do this, pup, but not because of your mother's scholarship. Because I want you under my wing and under my command. You have a heart like a lion's—and a mind that is too bright. You need discipline and the right kind of guidance so that you don't make the wrong decisions as you grow."

He gripped the side of Alexander's neck. "Now, you must stay here. Phiron is a peacock I can crush with ease. If only I could wring his neck and pull it off his body, but that might actually start a war. I'll leave him alive and extract your mother. I don't need to be watching out for a fledgling at the same time."

"I'll go to the healers, sir," Alexander said, his pulse a stampeding beast. "Get help for my father."

"Good. So long as you stay out of my way. I'll bring your mother to the infirmary. Let us hope she doesn't need it for herself." Stepping back on that, the general took off in a blast of wind.

Waiting only until he wouldn't have to fight the backdraft of the general's flight, Alexander rose into the air—and went exactly where he'd said he would, no matter the nausea that burned his throat and scalded his gut. The general knew how to strategize an attack far better than Alexander; Alexander wouldn't ruin the operation by being a child who couldn't listen to necessary orders.

His chest squeezed.

Later, much later, while his father rested in the infirmary, his mother—unharmed on the outside but broken inside—

took Alexander's hand in her trembling one. "I'm sorry you were put in that position, my darling boy." Tears rolled down her face. "I never thought Phiron would stoop to such horror."

Alexander felt as if he'd aged a hundred years in the hours past. So he didn't berate his mother for not facing up to the cold, hard truth. He just put his arm around her and said, "It's all right, Mama. It's not your fault." That was as true as the fact that his parents preferred to be blind to the darkness in the world.

"It's all right," he said again as his mother cried as if her heart was broken. "I was born for this. To protect. To fight for what's right."

And to understand that power *mattered*.

Else people could crush and belittle and humiliate you.

No. Never again.

To keep that vow, he needed to gain so much power that no one would dare treat him and his as prey. A goal toward which he'd already begun to walk—General Akhia-Solay had made it clear that, fledgling or not, Alexander was now under his command.

Good.

7

Alexander was already a seasoned member of a junior squadron under Akhia-Solay when he graduated to adulthood at a hundred years of age. Callie, having hit the century milestone before him, was also well established—as an angelic courier for another court. Not Rumaia's, for Callie was too clever not to see the fetid corrosion of that court.

No, she flew under the banner of Archangel Sha-yi, she who was old enough to be termed an Ancient, and who had eyes so deep and wise that even Alexander found himself unsettled around her.

"You're not in a squadron?" he'd asked when Callie first told him of her position.

"Every fledgling warrior that joins my sire's court must first serve a decade as a courier alongside our usual physical training," she'd explained. "It's to ensure that we know all flight paths inside out, and have scouted our own emergency landing sites when it comes to the longer flights over water."

Struck by the importance of both pieces of knowledge, Alexander made sure to volunteer as a courier for his court when the call went out. And he didn't only take from Callie—he shared his knowledge with her too, so that their information was pooled, and they both became better, stronger.

"You have so much ambition that, when we were younger, I expected you to hoard all you learned," Callie said to him many years down the road. "Why do you share?"

Alexander had to think about that. "Perhaps because I have a brother and parents who've always shared what they know with me?" He rubbed his jaw. "And . . . I think it's also because when I look around at the most powerful among our kind, I see teams. Very few archangels and senior angels are true loners. Having bonds of trust on which you can rely is an important aspect of long-term power."

Caliane looked at him with those eyes so blue they outshone the rare gems coveted by mortals and immortals both. "Sometimes, Alex, you scare me."

He raised an eyebrow. "You're just gentler in how you wear your ambition, Callie. Neither one of us will be content to remain mere foot soldiers. We'll be generals."

He was proven both right and wrong.

He was the one who became a general, while Caliane became second to Sha-yi. They argued over it over a mug of mead now and then, whether he'd been right or not. He pointed out that being second was an even higher position than being a general, and she pointed out that she still wasn't a general.

Along the way, he made other friends, built other bonds of trust. But in all of this, he remained unbound by the heart, a powerful man who took lovers when the urge struck, and who treated them with kindness, but felt no desire to tie himself down.

Then fate laughed at him.

8

Zanaya had never been face-to-face with an archangel. Hardly unusual. Many young angels never came in contact with an archangel unless they had one in the family, or they ran into them by accident while the archangel was visiting the Refuge. Most of the time, the members of the Cadre lived in their territories, while angelic young grew up safe in the protective arms of the Refuge.

Zanaya, however, hadn't even had that opportunity. She was one of the rare children who'd been raised away from the angelic homeland. That was also the reason why she knew no other angels her age as she walked into service as a trainee in the forces of Archangel Inj'ra. At least, thanks to her mentor, Mivoniel, she wasn't coming in as a complete novice.

She'd thought she was prepared for this, but as she entered the barracks, where she was to live with ten other young angels, she had no idea what to do. They'd all grown up together in the Refuge, were sharing jokes or conversation while she pretended to be busy putting away her clothes and boots in the old trunk at the foot of her bedroll—which she'd already laid out. More busy work, more things to keep her from looking like she was lonely.

Zanaya ignored the feeling. She was used to ignoring it.

"Zanaya, right?"

Jerking at the soft voice at her shoulder, she spun on her heel to find herself facing the person she'd have judged the least likely to speak to her. Where Zanaya was dressed in a rough tunic with a rope around the middle, Aureline wore soft leathers of a pale brown that had clearly been made with intense care, then worn so often they molded to their wearer's body.

Zanaya had one pair of leathers—she'd been gifted them by Mivoniel, and she treasured the set, would never wear it while just in the barracks. As for her tunic, it wasn't as if she couldn't afford better—her father had done his duty by her there—but that she had no idea what women her age wore or what was acceptable.

The hamlet in which she'd grown up was populated by retired warriors for the most part, not a girl or youth among them. Old leathers, simple pants, or rough tunics, that was the usual dress code. Zanaya had worked out for herself that her mother's preferred gowns weren't apt to be the right choice for her new life either. So she'd gone for the simplest item, the one least likely to subject her to ridicule.

As it was, one of the other young soldiers had snickered and called her a "feral" when she walked in. She'd wanted to kick him in the face, but Mivoniel had warned her that her temper was her greatest weakness. "Control it or you'll be the one who comes out the worse off. No archangel wants a hothead in their ranks."

So she'd stifled her rage and kept to herself.

Now Aureline, with her beautiful leathers, her skin like dark gold and her mane of hair of a thick and shiny sable, a shade that was echoed in her wings, was talking to her. Zanaya didn't know what the other girl wanted, was ready for a knife to the ribs, but once again, she fell back on what her mentor had advised.

"Watch for betrayal, but don't expect it of everyone. A fighter alone will always fall. And I'm not talking only of battle. Walking a solitary path through life . . . you've witnessed your mother do it. It's a hard existence. I wouldn't have this for you. And, for a warrior, battlemates can become kin over time."

Zanaya couldn't imagine Aureline being any kind of kin to her—she'd seen the other girl laughing with the others, could already tell she was one of the most popular people in the group. Far more likely, she'd come to spare a crumb to the outsider, feel good about herself. But Zanaya kept her tone civil as she said, "Yes, I'm Zanaya."

Aureline's smile deepened, revealing dents in her cheeks that made her even more lovely. "I'm Aureline, but all my friends call me Auri. Did you truly grow up in the outside world?"

When Zanaya nodded, Aureline's eyes—a striking translucent brown—widened. "I've never met anyone who did that! You must have such amazing stories." She rolled her eyes. "My parents barely let me go past the edge of the Refuge, even after I wasn't a baby any longer."

Zanaya didn't know why she said it, but she did. "I've ridden a horse." It was a strange thing to say, but Zanaya wasn't going to pretend to be like the others. Because she wasn't. Her whole life had been different.

Aureline all but jumped, her wings opening out a fraction to reveal hints of brighter autumnal hues among the sable. "No!" Her cry attracted the attention of the others, but she ignored them to say, "Was it terrifying?"

And that was the beginning of Zanaya learning that Aureline was nice. Just . . . *nice*. She discovered that the girl who was going to become her best friend in the entire world had been born to nice parents who'd raised her with love and affection, and that she'd grown surrounded by others who were also nice.

As a result, Aureline was that rare being who was plain

good. She had no hidden agenda, no sly side, no awareness that people could be two-faced. It drove Zanaya to distraction at times, how Aureline just believed the best of others—but she also came to see that most people tried to be their best with her . . . because it was very hard to hurt a person who saw only the best in you.

"I was raised to see such openness as a weakness," she said to her friend some ten years later, after they'd long settled into a friendship tight and true. "My mother taught me that to open yourself up to people is to invite them to cut out a piece of you, then discard you."

Aureline passed over a wedge of the fruit she'd just sliced as they sat on the low wall of the training salle, watching older warriors do a bout. "She must've been awfully hurt by someone she trusted."

"Yes." The man who'd sired Zanaya had forever altered Rzia's path. But—"I think at a certain point, a person must take responsibility for being their own person. To look forever backward . . ." She thought of the pile of returned letters her mother hoarded in a trunk, letters Camio hadn't even bothered to open. "It's stagnation and obsession."

Because no matter how often Rzia cursed Camio for destroying her life, she also cried for him night after night. Zanaya was certain that should her father walk back into Rzia's life, Rzia would accept him into her bed with open arms. Camio was the sun to her, and she'd shriveled and grown sour without the light of his attention.

"Aren't you afraid?" she said to Aureline before her friend could ask what she knew of obsession. "Of trusting and having it end in betrayal?"

Aureline chewed as she thought. Because that was the thing with Auri—she was kind and generous, but she wasn't simple in the least.

Right then, the spotted kitten who'd deigned to permit Zanaya to look after her, jumped up on the wall between her and her friend. Anisha yawned to show off her sharp teeth, accepted Auri's exclamations on her beauty, then curled up to nap. The only sign of her affection for Zanaya was the tail sleek and dark that rested against Zanaya's thigh.

Zanaya adored the haughty beast.

"I suppose I haven't been kicked by life yet," Auri said at last. "And I'm not going to live in fear of things that haven't yet occurred." She passed across another piece of the sweet star-shaped fruit. "I'll keep on trusting until I get kicked so hard that I begin to flinch."

It was Zanaya's turn to think as she took a bite of the crunchy treat. "I suppose I've never been kicked, either." She hadn't ever thought of it in those terms. "But unlike you, it's because I don't trust many people."

"I'm shocked." Auri's voice was bland. "It's not like you're still holding it against poor Meher for calling you a feral."

Zanaya elbowed her best friend. "I plan to hold that grudge forever."

"Even though he has bowed down on the floor to beg your mercy and admitted he was being a stupid dick-waving kid trying to look big in front of his friends?"

Zanaya snorted.

Pointing her small knife at Zanaya, Aureline said, "I believe him. It was a horrible thing to say, no doubt about it, but he's not bad when he's not waving his dick around."

"Perhaps I'll run mad and try to be more like you," Zanaya said with a scowl. "Give people a chance. Even Meher."

That turned out easier said than done, but . . . Meher didn't break her trust after she gave him a grudging chance.

The redheaded and wide-shouldered asshole actually became her friend, loyal and true.

It was *this* Zanaya, a woman capable of a fledgling trust, but with scars far deeper and stubborn, who first saw General Alexander. She'd heard about him, of course. It seemed like half the women she knew—*and* half the men, to be fair—couldn't stop sighing over him. Golden hair, eyes of captured lightning, a honed body straight out of a fever dream, that was what they said.

The half that weren't sighing over him were in awe of his battle tactics. Meher waxed lyrical on the topic at any given opportunity. "They say he's Akhia-Solay's battlefield heir, ruthless, calculated, and built with honor."

Zanaya hero-worshipped no one and had no intention of starting now. She was also immune to pretty men. Her father was one of the prettiest men in the angelic world, and while Rzia's obsession was a flaw her own, Camio wasn't blameless. He'd fed on Rzia's adulation when it suited him, hadn't he? He'd fueled her dreams of forever.

Then he'd decided he was bored and moved on, leaving carnage in his wake.

No, beauty didn't sway Zanaya. Neither did the kind of arrogance Alexander no doubt possessed.

She had zero doubts about her ability to resist his allure . . . until the moment she locked her gaze with one of inhuman silver.

Her world stopped. Just stopped.

All those words people used about General Alexander? They weren't anything near enough. He was *power* and he was beauty—and he was danger. And it all sang to her in a way nothing else in her life had ever done.

9

Alexander wasn't ready for Zanaya. A blooded general of three thousand years of age, a man both feared and revered, and she took him down like he was the stripling when *she* was the one barely past her majority.

Her hair was astonishing—curls that reached the middle of her back and were a shade unlike any other: silver kissed by purple, soft and luscious. Twilight in living form. But its beauty was eclipsed by that of her skin, for it was the color of night when the moon didn't rise, flawless and smooth. She was small but shapely in form, her eyes an intense dark brown that gave nothing away, her wings midnight with a dusting of silvery white.

He could've handled her arresting beauty; there were many lovely angels and vampires in the world, and he'd bedded a great number of them. But he had no chance against her spirit. She held his gaze with a fierceness unexpected in one so young.

Drawn as he was to her, he was no predator. She might believe herself ready to tangle with him, but in immortal

terms, she was but a babe. It wasn't the same with mortals—
he could lie with a mortal woman of a bare twenty or so years
without guilt, for mortal lives moved much, *much* faster.

That woman in her twenties was apt to be seasoned by
life, and know herself. Most mortals of such an age were already long married, with babes of their own. They saw him
as another adult, albeit a pretty angelic one. And even there,
he was careful about the women he bedded. Never any who
were married or entangled with another, for one. After that,
it was a thing of heart and spirit. He could count his mortal
lovers on one hand—and he remembered and mourned each
and every one.

Hanisha so sweet and graceful but with a backbone of
steel.

Sukhon, a fellow wild child who'd have lived life naked if
she could.

Adah, a maker of music driven by her art.

Eir, swift of foot and lithe of body.

Isane, a calm wind, her blind eyes seeing things he never
would.

Alexander had been but a fleeting indulgence to all of them.
Not a one had showed any signs of obsession—a significant
threat when it came to relationships between mortals and
angels and one that some immortals enjoyed.

But Alexander had chosen women who'd all been ob-
sessed with other things: art, the desire to have children, expansion of the mind, and so much more. Against them, *he'd*
felt the callow youth. Such wouldn't be the case with Zanaya,
no matter how much she might believe it to be.

"At a hundred and fifteen," he said to Akhia-Solay, who'd
seen his interest in Zanaya *and* seen him walk away, "I thought
I knew it all when in truth, I was an untried boy. I won't be
the one to clip her wings or reshape them as I see fit."

The general, who'd turned from mentor to friend, raised
an eyebrow. "I think no one will shape that girl, Alex. She
has a will that is a dazzling fire—but yes, even fires can be

snuffed out by rough handling." A curt nod. "This is the integrity I saw in the boy grown into the heart of the man. I'm proud to call you my friend and battlemate."

On the journey home from their courier run, Zanaya told Aureline and their third squadron mate to go on without her. The three of them had been sent to different parts of Esphares's territory, their job to deliver documents or small goods, and it had made sense to meet up to fly home. "I need some time alone. I'll catch up."

Auri's expression said she saw far more than Zanaya wanted her to see, but she didn't interrogate Zanaya. "We'll fly at a steady pace, and watch for you at nightfall."

After the two vanished over a distant ridge of mountains, Zanaya landed on a remote island in the middle of nowhere just so she could *think*, could find her balance again.

That single moment of unexpected eye contact with General Alexander had left her shaken, the foundations she'd thought as solid as rock suddenly nothing but crumbled stone. She'd caught his response, too. An awareness of the madness that could be. He wasn't proof against her—but from the way he'd broken the eye contact, she knew he wasn't going to do anything about it.

Breath harsh and fast, she kicked at the barnacle-covered rocks at her feet, releasing the scent of dead fish into the air. The stink seemed apt, seemed a fitting judgment on the insanity that threatened to take hold of her.

She knew what he'd tell himself, that she was too young, that she didn't know her own mind—but Zanaya had never been one to flinch from a decision. She *knew* what she felt, and she knew it hovered on the brink of obsession.

"*No.*" A rigid promise to herself.

She had no desire for an obsessive romantic love. She'd witnessed far too much of it in her mother's bitter, empty life and in her simultaneously pathetic and angry devotion to

Camio—who truly couldn't give a fuck. Just like Alexander didn't give a fuck about Zanaya; she might've caught his eye in the moment, but the man was no abstemious monk.

As with her father, Alexander had plenty of lovers and none of them permanent.

Zanaya would *not* be another notch on the general's bed-post.

Muscles tense enough to snap, she lifted off after her squadron mates, determined to follow the path she'd laid out for her life. But as seasons passed, she couldn't stop her ears from listening for word of Alexander, even as she gritted her teeth and threw herself into becoming the best of the best.

"You're beyond the rest of us," Auri told her one day, her face damp with sweat and her chest heaving. "You've always been better but now you're outpacing and out-strategizing everyone but me, and even I'm barely keeping up."

"You can't not keep up," Zanaya declared. "I intend for you to be my lieutenant when I'm a general."

Her friend shoved tendrils of hair off her face. "There's that Zan confidence." Words said with love, Aureline well aware of Zanaya's ambitions. "What if I want to be the general?"

"You don't." Zanaya knew her friend as well as Auri knew her. "You're too nice and hate the idea of disciplining anyone."

Aureline winced. "Perhaps you have a point. But that would make me a terrible lieutenant too."

"No, because then you'd just be following the rules laid down by your general—and you never have any issue with that." Aureline's tendencies didn't make her weak, just different from Zanaya. That was a subtlety Zanaya had learned from her best friend. "Now, lift your sword so we can fix the error in your technique that allowed me to beat you."

Their swords clashed, the vibration going straight to Zanaya's teeth.

In truth, Zanaya didn't have to do much to ensure Auri progressed through the ranks with her—her friend had the ability, just not Zanaya's driving ambition. She was, however, loyal to the bone, and willing to tie her flag to her best friend's.

"So you'll never be alone," Auri said to her one day, while Zanaya's faithful hound, Balan—his smooth coat jet-black and his ears sharply pointed—walked alongside Zanaya. "So you'll always have a lieutenant at your back who you can trust without hesitation."

Zanaya's chest ached. "I'm counting on that."

"And don't forget Meher," Auri pointed out with a wicked grin. "He's still keeping up."

"As he should." Zanaya had long forgiven Meher his initial rudeness, but he'd never be to her what Auri was—the friend who'd embraced her before she knew anything of Zanaya's skill or ambition. "The weapons-master has summoned me to a meeting."

Auri's eyes widened at her confession. "He's going to promote you."

Auri was proven right. At three hundred, Zanaya was brutally young to be a senior squadron leader, but that was the position she held after the meeting.

She was on the road to the kind of power that would put her in control of her existence. No being beholden to her mother's resentful care or her father's absent largesse. No having to bow and scrape to angels who considered her an uneducated blot on polite society. No pressure to mold and lessen herself to fit the world.

Zanaya intended to make the world fit *her*.

As for Alexander . . . Her cheeks burned, her chest tight. She'd glimpsed him from a distance last summer, and the madness, the obsession, it had hit as hard and as low as before.

Whatever this was, it wasn't dying.

Alexander kept quiet track of Zanaya in the years that followed their first meeting, raised a glass to her when he heard she'd been promoted to senior squadron leader in the army of an archangel on the other side of the world from the archangel whom Alexander had once served. These days, Alexander served no one, his power such that he was considered a threat by most.

All of them waiting, watching, to see when he would ascend.

When it happened, however, it happened to Callie first, the sky a cauldron of jewel blue alive with white lightning, and all the waters in all the oceans and lakes in the world ice-white fire that sparked and glittered.

She'd always been strong, but now, she glowed with the power of an archangel, and for a single moment in time, they considered whether he could act as her second—but there was a repulsion between them that shouldn't have existed, and that foretold the future to come. Two archangels couldn't be in close proximity for long periods of time.

"You will ascend," she said to him one day a year after her ascension, as they stood side by side in front of a frozen lake high in the mountains of the Refuge, while the mountain winds howled around them. "Will you be my enemy, Alex, or my friend?"

"Friend," he said at once.

But Caliane shook her head. "I'd like to think so, but the power of an archangel . . . It's this enormous force within, one that could devour the weaker, and that pushes even the strong. I sometimes wonder if archangels are built for war, if we are the control on the world that ensures none of us ever becomes too settled, too haughty, too much for this land."

Callie had always been the more introspective of the two of them. Alexander was far more pragmatic. Crouching down, he picked up a piece of shattered ice and slid it across the glossy ice of the lake. "I'll be your friend because it'll be advantageous in the long run. Have you not seen that the archangels who've ruled the longest are the ones with strong ties to at least one other in the Cadre?"

The Cadre of Ten was full at present, but at least five members were Ancients with one foot already out of this world. Alexander was confident that when they went into

Sleep, they wouldn't come back out for eons upon eons—if ever.

"Sometimes," his mother had said to him of late, "we live too long. Far beyond our time. We must Sleep and allow the young their time."

Alexander's heart clenched. "My mother is thinking of Sleep," he said to Callie, without waiting for her to respond to his statement about power in the Cadre. "Father will go with her, of course." Cendrion's love for Gzrel was as enduring as hers for him.

"You know what I've always liked about your parents?" Callie said. "That they're kind to each other. Did you ever notice? Your mother always makes your father his evening tea, and he always puts out her slippers in the morning so that when she steps out into the garden, her feet won't be cold."

Her voice turned contemplative again. "When I was a girl, I thought love meant high romance and great drama, but now I understand that love that lasts is a constellation of small kindnesses." She put a hand on his shoulder where he remained crouched beside her, his wings on the ice and snow behind them. "You'll miss them."

He shrugged, but not hard enough to dislodge her hand—she was one of the few people from whom he'd accept comfort, for they had no imbalance between them, not even now that she was a member of the Cadre. Had he not been so powerful himself, he *would* have stood as her second. They might butt heads, but they also trusted each other without question.

"It's foolishness," he muttered. "I'm no infant or youth. I'm a full-grown man strong in my power."

"Love has no use-by date, Alex," Callie murmured. "You'll love them all the eons of your existence, and you'll miss them, too. But I think if they Sleep, it won't be forever, not when they have two sons they so adore. They'll wake now and then to watch over you. This is their way."

Alexander couldn't speak, his heart expanding hugely under the power of her words. He clutched at them a decade later, when his parents told him and Osiris that they would Sleep now. One last hug from his mother's arms, one last touch on the shoulder from his father, memories he carved into his mind in stone.

"We tried so hard to stay awake for the next step on your journey," Cendrion murmured to him. "But the tiredness weighs heavy on our bones now, son. We'll wake in future times to see you in your glory." A glance over at where Osiris was distracted with talking to Gzrel. "You'll watch over Osiris? I know he's your elder, but he becomes lost in his alchemical experiments these days, and we worry—"

"There's no need, Father," Alexander reassured the man who'd brought him up with a gentle hand—far too gentle for a child of Alexander's rebellious bent had Osiris not also taken a hand in his raising. "I'll make sure my brother is safe and protected, even as he wanders the pathways of the mind." It was as if their positions in life had been reversed, with him the elder now, watching over his increasingly more cerebral brother.

The last of the tension washed out of his father, his face becoming startlingly youthful.

When he went into Sleep with his beloved Gzrel, it was under the watchful eye of two sons who made sure their parents' place of Sleep was protected and inaccessible to anyone but the two of them. Afterward, Osiris returned to the island he'd turned into a giant laboratory.

There were no concubines now, only a small number of assistants and other staff.

"I am no longer of the body, little brother," Osiris had said the last time Alexander and he had spoken on the topic. "I see so much." A fist thumping into the open palm of his hand. "If only I could make it real."

"I'd help you if I could, Osiris, but you've always been the smarter of the two of us."

Deep laughter, his brother's warmth embracing Alexander as it had done when he was a child—and yet there was a near-manic quality to Osiris now, one that unsettled Alexander. "In some ways, brother," Osiris had said, "and in others you are the master—the strategist no one will ever beat in battle."

As Alexander flew away from Osiris this momentous day, his thoughts went back to that instant, that conversation, and he had the sudden blinding thought that Zanaya would one day out-strategize him. It should've been an infuriating thing to imagine . . . but it wasn't. Because should she get to that point, she'd be old enough and strong enough that he'd no longer have to fight his compulsion toward her.

Alexander's entire body burned at the idea of it.

10

It was darkfall by the time Alexander flew into the territory that he "managed" for Esphares—the truth was that he did as he pleased with no oversight now that Akhia-Solay, too, had gone into Sleep. Alexander had been given the land because none of the Cadre wanted him out of their sight. He wondered if they thought he would foment rebellion.

Alexander snorted as he worked out in the beaten dirt of his home practice ring the next dawn, his feet bare and his body clothed in nothing but streaks of paint made from the local pigments. Alexander was no idiot. He knew that no angel, no matter how powerful, challenged an archangel and came out the winner.

Archangels were as far beyond angels as angelkind was beyond humankind.

Spiking his fighting staff on the ground, he spun up, then around to land on both feet, sending up puffs of dirt. There was no applause, no cries of encouragement. He did these morning sessions on his own, pushing himself to the edge and beyond. To his mind, a true general should be in the same or better form than his soldiers.

That was what it meant to lead.

Alexander planned to be that way even after his ascension.

But as the years passed, ascension seemed nothing but a foolishness laid on his shoulders by others. The lack of growth did have one positive outcome—Esphares began to use him as a general in truth once again. So it was that Alexander flew into ruthless battle against the army of another archangel.

But where that archangel's general stayed safe behind the front line, Alexander was right at the forefront. That was why he brought home victory, winning another massive stretch of land for his archangel.

When Esphares stirred in Callie's direction, however, Alexander talked him down. "She's a young archangel, barely born," he said, talking to the ego because archangels this old were all ego and nothing else. "You'll gain more from becoming her mentor. The biggest threat to those in the Cadre is age and distance—she'll anchor you to the world, and her power will become yours."

The latter was a lie; Callie would always know her own mind, and she'd be no one's puppet. But the rest . . . yes, that was true enough. Now that he was working so closely with the Ancient who was his archangel, he'd begun to see that this being was in no way similar to angelkind. Half the time when Esphares looked at Alexander, it felt as if an alien intelligence, cold and distant, was weighing him up as food.

"Is that who I'll become one day?" Callie said to him when Esphares invited her to dinner and she accepted so she could visit with Alexander. "A *creature* devoid of empathy and humanity?"

"I don't know." Alexander couldn't imagine his friend so— of all their childhood peer group, Callie was the most empathic, the one most apt to speak on behalf of the underdog. "I guess we'll find out."

Laughter, Callie's hair a black river under the sunshine. "Oh, Alex, you do keep me from diving too deep into the weeds."

He shrugged. "What's the point of worrying about a future we can't see, can't know? Live the now, and deal with the rest later. Cassandra wouldn't have gone insane if she could do that."

"You're right," Caliane said, but her eyes were soft, hazy. "Yet I sometimes have the strange sensation of fate bearing down on me, the knowledge that there exists a future I could avoid if only I knew of it. It's too bad Ojewo has vanished—we have no living seers any longer."

Sighing, she shook her head. "Or perhaps all archangels are a touch mad." A slight smile as she glanced up at him. "Could be you'll be the one making such pronouncements soon."

Scowling, Alexander shook his head. "I'm not going to ascend. I'm strong but clearly not the right person to be an archangel or I would've become Cadre by now. I plan to be the best general the world has ever seen."

Callie continued to watch him. "You'll never be satisfied with that."

"It is what it is." All the talk of ascension had spoken to his pride. And a prideful fighter was a dead fighter if he didn't have the skills to back himself up. "Perhaps I can be your second after all. You still haven't found a permanent second?"

"No. Though there are possibilities. But you and I?" She shook her head. "You have too much arrogance in you, Alex. We'd be in constant battle over who was right and who was wrong."

He couldn't argue with her on the point. "Then I hope that I don't ever have to lead an army against your troops in battle, Callie." Quiet words, quieter than Alexander ever spoke. "It would scar my heart."

A touch of her fingers to his arm, a quick wince from them both as a result of the repulsion effect that didn't seem to be fading even as it became clear he wasn't destined to ascend. "I think you're safe enough for now," she said, rubbing her fingers on the fabric of her gown. "Whatever you said to Esphares, he seems to be trying to set himself up as my guide on the Cadre."

"Sorry about that." Alexander shrugged. "My fault."

"No. He is the archangel who well knows the unspoken rules of the Cadre." A steely-eyed look. "He has forgotten that all the members are equals. But no matter. I can learn from the old while never forgetting who I am."

She tightened her lips. "You know he should be Sleeping? I won't ask for your opinion on the point, for it would be akin to treason for you to agree with me, but we both know I speak the truth. Our kind may be immortal, but we're not meant to take up limitless time and space."

"We're young," Alexander said, simply to rile up his friend. "I wonder if we'll feel the same when we're doddery old Ancients."

Callie shot him a sharp look . . . and then they were both laughing at the idea of being as old as Esphares and refusing to Sleep. Alexander knew it was highly unlikely he'd ever make it to such a grand old age. As a general for an archangel prone to war, he went into battle far more than most of his compatriots.

There would come a time when he'd find himself fighting against someone who was faster, stronger, better trained, and that would be the end of Alexander, first general of Archangel Esphares. He wouldn't rail against a death in battle— he'd been born for battle and it made sense to him that he would one day die on a battlefield.

So it was that he continued to fly into battle after battle in the years that followed, while Esphares became increasingly more maddened—to the point that Alexander began to see that the rest of the Cadre was starting to come together against him, Esphares considered such a threat that they were willing to set aside their petty grievances against each other.

And on this subject, Callie couldn't talk to him, because that *would* be to lure him into treason, and whatever you might say about Alexander, no one had ever called him disloyal. However, neither was he one to follow blindly. So it was that as the dark clouds of a war to end all wars swirled on the horizon, he went to speak to Esphares deep in the cave-like court he kept in the mountains covered in the constant snow and ice that were part of his territory.

Esphares no longer had a second now that Akhia-Solay had gone into Sleep, had come to treat Alexander as if he held that position. Today, he ranted and raved as he paced around a stone table on which he'd placed markers to show how he wanted the troops positioned for the latest fight.

Alexander waited until his sire had worn himself out of his first anger, then he took his life into his hands. "If we put troops here," he murmured, pointing out one section, "your enemies can collapse the cliff onto them, killing or badly injuring thousands in a single strike."

When Esphares remained silent, his eyes glittering, Alexander continued to slowly and methodically decimate his archangel's "plan."

Esphares's wings began to glow, never a welcome sight. "Are you calling me stupid, young pup?" Fury turned his features into a caricature of the handsome angel he'd once been.

"No, sire. I've looked up to you for thousands of years. General Akhia-Solay was brilliant, but he couldn't have won all he did without working side by side with an archangel as brilliant." He held Esphares's eyes, though it was a painful thing to hold a gaze brimming with archangelic power. "You would've *never* made a single one of these mistakes then."

The deadly glow didn't dim, but something of Alexander's passion seemed to get through to Esphares and he stared at the stone table. "Why did I not see?" It was a question almost to himself.

But Alexander answered. "Because you are tired, sire, and

a tired fighter always falls on the battlefield. It's a law you taught me yourself, when I was a fledgling in your army."

"Archangels don't get tired, child," Esphares said, and the way he addressed Alexander was a deliberate insult.

Alexander ignored it. "How many memories do you carry, sire? How much of the weight of history do you bear? How powerful is the crushing force of it all?"

Esphares spun around, his wings opening and snapping closed in a violent motion that created a powerful gust of wind and knocked over all the pieces on the battle table. "I am an archangel! I have the capacity to be endless!"

"Yes," Alexander said. "But there's a reason the Cadre is only ten or less. Never more. Else our world would burn ever more, as archangels lived atop archangels. There's a reason we Sleep. We can be infinite, it's true, but my mother used to say that being infinite is also our hidden curse. We see no end, and so we live without urgency. We begin to dim in ways small and terrible without ever seeing it."

Esphares stared at him, death in his eyes. "Do you say I dim, Alexander?"

Alexander went down on one knee, his wings flared behind him. "I will never again serve anyone of your strategic skill, sire. I will never again know a man with such a wealth of battle knowledge in his mind." He looked up, held that gaze that might yet be the final thing he saw. And he stuck true to his convictions. "But I would rather die today than live to see your light fade mistake by small mistake."

A blink, a sudden absence of motion.

Then Esphares exhaled. "Is it so bad then, Alexander?"

Aware the danger had passed, Alexander yet stayed on bent knee, for Esphares would always have his respect. "It's getting there, sire. Another year and you won't listen to me. You'll strike me dead and end up surrounded by those who fear you and will say whatever it is you wish them to say."

Esphares, the scar on one side of his face an element of his history that he'd never explained and that no one else knew the answer to—for it defied the healing abilities of angel-kind, came to Alexander and held out a hand. Taking it, Alexander allowed his archangel to haul him to his feet.

"You were never my second in the official records," Esphares said, "but you have acted with the fidelity and courage of a second, and I won't forget it. Go now, Alexander. I must think."

"Sire." Alexander bowed out of the room, near certain that this would be the last time he'd see the archangel with the wings of a gray falcon for eons to come.

He was right.

Esphares vanished into a place of Sleep secret and unknown and the storm clouds of war whispered away, the Cadre now nine. Alexander had the task of storing Esphares's most precious belongings and he handled the task with all respect. Only after it was done to his satisfaction would he turn his mind to seeking his next position.

He'd long left behind all thoughts of ascension. So it was that it came without warning, a spike of impossible power that sent him soaring to the sky, alongside a raven caught in the inferno of his updraft. Then they both went down, the raven burning up as Alexander was struck by a lightning bolt that spread metal through his bones and fused him to the stone of the isolated mountaintop on which he'd landed.

The raven's feathers were caught in the fusion, black filaments against the metal.

Alexander screamed and from his mouth spilled silver lightning that turned into liquid gold that burned. Across the world, metal melted, spiraled its way across landscapes, became frozen in strange and beautiful shapes. The sky flashed silver then violent gold with a flickering sheen to it.

There was no night.

Only a dazzling metallic day.

When it ended, he'd broken out of the stone and sat crouched on the mountaintop, his blood feeling like liquid metal and his power so vast it reached into forever. And he understood why Esphares hadn't wanted to go into Sleep. He understood what it was to be greedy with and for power. He understood that he was now one of the ten most powerful beings on the planet.

11

When the sky turned to gleaming metal above Zanaya, deadly as a blade, it was a spear through her heart. She knew what had happened even before news spread across angelkind that First General Alexander had ascended. If he'd been beyond her reach before, he was now impossibly past it.

Zanaya wanted to scream at the sky, then at herself.

"I will not be my mother, obsessing over a man until that obsession is all I am!" she yelled to Auri as they sparred, her best friend the only person who knew of Zanaya's reluctant fascination with the unattainable Alexander. "I will not!"

Blocking her move with one arm, Auri swept Zanaya's feet out from under her, but Zanaya rolled back up with quicksilver swiftness.

"You're hardly your mother," her friend said, her breathing rough as the two of them circled each other. "It's not like you've put yourself into near-seclusion and refuse to even look at another man. If I recall, you tumbled a rather delicious bite at the last border meeting."

Zanaya spun out with a dangerous kick, but her friend was

fast, grabbed her foot and flipped her, evading Zanaya's wings as they snapped out to knock her over. Zanaya gloried in sparring with a warrior who so evenly matched her. There were very few moves she could pull that Aureline hadn't seen a thousand times over. Which constantly pushed her to be better, faster, more innovative.

"I'm hardly going to allow my sex to dry up and blow away while he's working his way through a harem," she muttered during the next span of quiet as they restarted the bout after a tussle that had ended in a draw. It wasn't that she was jealous of Alexander's lovers. That would be madness indeed when the two of them had literally *never touched*, but she hated this hold he had on her that meant she was even aware of who he bedded.

As for Zanaya . . . she was just as bad, wasn't she? She never promised her lovers anything, gave them only her body and her affection, and always cut matters off before passion could fuse with emotion. "My obsession is in the form of the mind," she admitted to Auri, infuriated by herself for it. "As if now that I know Alexander exists, I can't fully give myself to any other. Makes me *exactly* like Rzia."

"You've said your mother has pined for your father until she's made herself and her world a small and toxic place," her best friend argued. "Zanaya, you might have a fascination with Alexander, but it has done nothing to stifle your growth."

Zanaya grunted and blocked a blow from Aureline. "I'd rather not feel the fascination at all," she gritted out. "It's like a bee buzzing inside my skull. I want rid of it!"

Aureline straightened from her fighting stance, held up a hand to signal a pause. "You know, if it was anyone else, Zan, I'd tell them to seek a healer, get past the obsession."

Zanaya flushed. "Yes?"

"Yes. Because the idea of reaching for an archangel? It would be a hopeless goal. But it's not anyone else. It's you." Aureline's lovely and intelligent eyes held her in place far more effectively than any sparring hold.

"Your drive is the first reason I don't believe you to be

delusional," her friend said. "The second is that I was waiting for you in his court when you crossed paths with Alexander. I witnessed how he looked at you in turn. It's not in your head—the reaction between you was . . . potent. Unsettling in its intensity, if I'm being truthful."

Aureline bit down on her plush lower lip. "But it's going to be a long journey, my friend. The man he is? When it comes to being with a fellow warrior, he won't ever lie with anyone below a general. It'd be different if you weren't a warrior. He's attracted to you because of that, because of who you are. But he also won't lie with you—to do so would be to change the course of your existence."

"Donkey shit," Zanaya muttered, thumping a fisted hand against the stone wall of the training ring. "I have full control over my life."

Aureline gave her one of those curiously wise looks. "You may believe so, Zan, but the years that separate you, the power differential . . . can you not feel it around even our sire? It's a pressure on the skin, a thing of such vastness that it's elemental.

"And you're no mortal," Aureline continued, "to grow in the body and the mind at chaotic speed. You're an angel, your growth constricted by the demands and gifts of immortality. You aren't tough enough or old enough to take on an archangel and remain yourself. Your mind is too malleable yet." Walking over to the table that held an array of weapons, she grabbed a fighting staff. "But we'll get you there."

"My ambitions are my own." Zanaya caught the staff Aureline threw across. "I won't alter them for any man."

"Didn't say you would." They clashed in the middle of the ring, both of them holding the pressure on their staffs. "I'm saying Archangel Alexander sees that power in you and is waiting for you to grow into it and that perhaps we can accelerate the process."

Zanaya hesitated, ended up with Auri's staff at her throat. Ignoring it, she said, "Do you truly believe so?" It remained painfully hard for her to allow herself to be vulnerable, but if there was anyone of whom she could ask this question that cut through her external armor to reveal her soft insides, it was her closest friend.

Pulling back her staff, Aureline wiped the back of one forearm over her brow. "Yes. The two of you . . . that moment . . . Such a demanding bond, it's not for me, Zan. It's too much, too violent. But for you? Yes."

Aureline searched her face. "But are you sure? I don't think such an attraction will ever be comfortable. It'll always demand everything, threaten to crush you in the passion of its grip."

Zanaya thought of Auri's parents and their sweet kindness to one another. After witnessing it, she'd decided she wanted that kind of love. A love warm and of the heart, and nothing akin to the dark obsession of Rzia's desire for Camio. And yet she was her mother's daughter—and the only man with whom she could imagine spending eternity was an archangel who probably wasn't good for her.

Just like Rzia and Camio . . . but for one crucial factor.

"If I am ever with Alexander," she said at last, "it'll be as solid a thing as the stone of the mountains. He won't play games of trust. The general who lives within him has too much honor for that. And fidelity, Auri, is more precious to me than any gemstone."

Aureline's nod was slow, her gaze pensive. "I wish you luck, Zan. You know I hope for only the best things for you."

Zanaya cherished that knowledge more than Aureline could ever understand. "All the way, Auri," she said. "Together. General and lieutenant."

Auri grinned and raised her staff. "All the way."

Two days later, they had to deal with a skirmish on the border after the neighboring archangel got into a state over some ridiculous slight or transgression. A contretemps that was so common that all of them rolled their eyes. Zanaya put out extra food for her most assuredly spoiled twin cats, then they got on with it.

It was a normal day in the sky above the border, with no one out for blood . . . until Aureline took a heavy battle spear directly through the throat.

The weapon was so brutal that it all but decapitated her.

Screaming, Zanaya sliced off the head of the angel who'd dared come for her best friend with such a deadly hit when they all knew this was a fight for show, for nothing but ego. The rest of them—on both sides—had been careful not to do anything that could lead to a final death. Such restraint was an unspoken rule when it came to border skirmishes that would blow over by the next day.

Her squadron locked in a vicious line above Zanaya, blood in their eyes.

Stunned by the speed of both the blow and the retaliation, the other side fell back as Zanaya landed beside Aureline's crumpled body. Terror such as she'd never before felt shot through her veins, cold as ice. She didn't want to see her best friend's head separated from her body, wings twisted and torn. But she made herself look, for she wouldn't give up on Auri unless all hope was lost.

Her best friend was a broken sculpture painted in red.

That horrific spear pinned her to the earth, her legs and spine shattered from the violent impact of her fall from the sky, and her pretty wings crumpled so badly that it looked as if she lay on a bed of blood-soaked feathers. But her eyes . . . "Auri!" Zanaya's heart started to beat once again. "Auri, hold on."

Eyes of translucent brown, the pupils huge pools of black, clung desperately to her own, but Zanaya could already feel the life of her drifting away. Aureline was young, without the healing capability of an older angel. But if Zanaya could keep her throat from ripping apart, her head from separating fully from her body, she might be able to keep Auri alive long enough for a healer to work on her.

Hands trembling from the force of her need to *do* something, Zanaya halted her instinctive desire to pull the ugly weapon from her throat. That would tear Aureline to pieces. Instead, she yelled up to the squadron. "Meher!"

Their friend landed beside them an instant later, his face a mask of rage and pain. "What do you need us to do?"

Zanaya realized he believed Aureline dead, was ready for vengeance. "She's alive, but I need to cut off the end of the spear so I can fly her to a healer."

Expression crumpling for a heartbeat, Meher then recovered and put away his battle-ax to pull out the short sword with the teeth of a sawblade that he'd brought from the homeland his parents had chosen after he was old enough to leave the Refuge. It was a traditional blade in a mortal tribe there, one given to youths after their majority.

Where many angels would've just taken the blade without regard to the traditions of the mortals, Meher had actually completed the landbound tasks required to earn it. It had been a difficult odyssey for him because of his wings, and he often boasted about his prowess. But there was no sign of that laughing, bigheaded Meher today.

His skin taut over the bones of his face, he crouched down beside Auri.

While Zanaya held Aureline's neck and head steady, Meher began to saw gently at the end of the spear that stuck out of their friend's throat. "Don't go, Auri," he whispered as he sawed. "I haven't built up the courage to ask you to walk with me yet." Tears rolled down his strong, stoic face, but he never hesitated in the sawing. "I've been making a courting gift for you. Please don't go."

Zanaya's heart was breaking, but she made it stone as she held her hands around Aureline's head. And when she saw her friend's eyes begin to flutter shut, she said, "*No*," in her harshest tone. "You don't get to die, Auri. I forbid it."

Aureline's lashes lifted, the barest hint of laughter in them. But she couldn't speak, blood bubbling out of her mouth. Zanaya heard her all the same. "Yes," she said. "I have no problem with confidence. Now you *stay*. Otherwise I'll have to console Meher, and you know how I feel about redheads."

Meher continued to saw, flecks of wood falling onto Aureline's face and chest.

It took a long time. Zanaya knew there was no way to rush it without killing Aureline, but every one of the muscles in her body was bunched up with the urge to yell at Meher to go faster. And in the end, Aureline couldn't stay conscious anymore. It wasn't a matter of will; her body no longer had the strength.

"She's still alive," Zanaya told Meher when he began to breathe in short hard puffs, his hands shaking. "Complete the cut."

He did so with gritted teeth.

In the interim, one of the other members of their squadron had flown down and ripped off her tunic of a fine handwoven fabric—to reveal a skirted loincloth and breasts strapped in place by the wide bandages used by most fighters whose breasts weren't small enough to not become painful from the intense motion of combat. Since their wings didn't permit a simple around-the-body strapping, their squadron mate's bared body was a complex matrix of lines in cloth.

Right now, her focus was on the tunic she was tearing into long panels.

As Meher completed his task and threw aside the piece of the spear he'd cut, Zanaya slid her hand under Aureline's neck with extreme care and placed her fingers around the other end of the spear. Perspiration chilled her skin. "Tip's buried too deep in the ground. We can't pull it out without hurting her." She thought fast. "We extricate Auri by sliding her neck up over the top end of the spear." It was short now, the exercise doable.

Meher helped her stabilize Aureline's head as they gently, gently, *gently* got her free. Then they worked at rapid speed to wrap her wound with the bandages formed of their squadron mate's tunic. It didn't matter if they made it tight; angels could survive without air for long periods. It wouldn't be comfortable, but it was better than Aureline's head detaching from her body.

Because there was no coming back from that for anyone but an archangel.

"Is she still alive?" Meher asked as they finished wrapping the final bandage.

"Yes," Zanaya said, though she wasn't sure. "Hold the line." With that, she gathered Aureline up in her arms. Her friend was taller than her, but Zanaya had built up considerable strength over the years—in all honesty, she was far stronger than she should be, given her size and outward appearance. A little gift from her father no doubt, because it certainly hadn't come from Rzia's willowy and ethereal line.

Just grateful for the strength that meant she had no trouble doing a vertical takeoff with Auri's body cradled in her arms, she tucked her friend close and, hoping against hope that Aureline could fight just a little longer, she flew her friend home.

12

Alexander saw Zanaya again a bare season after his ascension, while he was in the process of trying to put together his court. She came into his world as a squadron leader in charge of escorting a renowned scholar whom Archangel Inj'ra had kindly permitted to guest in Alexander's court for a period, the scholar's task to assist Alexander in certain matters.

If Zanaya had been a punch to the solar plexus before, she was now a grip around his throat. But if she'd been forbidden then, she was now verboten.

An archangel and such a young angel?

It would be an abomination.

Yet she stood under the banner that bore his sigil—a raven in flight—and held his eyes with impudent arrogance, challenging him to see her, know her, have her. But there was something different about her this time, a tension that hinted at pain. And that Alexander couldn't stand, so he closed the distance between them.

"What's happened?" he asked, as if they'd been having

this conversation throughout the years between their first meeting and this. "Why do you hurt?"

She would've been well within her rights to tell him it was none of his business, but he'd startled her out of her martial calm by striding over to stand so close to her. So she told him the truth. "My best friend is gravely injured. She might die."

Alexander wanted to hold her. To face the specter of death so *young* . . . "She isn't dead yet," he said. "And Inj'ra has a corps of healers that outshine any other."

"Yes." Hope in her tone now, her face younger and more innocent than it had been a bare moment ago. "Thank you, Alexander." She should've called him Archangel Alexander but of course she wouldn't, not this warrior woman who refused to treat him with diffidence. "Will you walk with me today?"

Gut clenched against the desire to hold her, comfort her further, he said, "I do not consort with babes." It was a cruel thing to say, but he had to be cruel. Or he'd doom them both.

Her expression grew hard as granite, all softness erased. "You'll regret your words one day, *Archangel Alexander.*"

He should've been furious with her for speaking to him in that tone, but Zanaya made her own rules when it came to Alexander. The only rule he wouldn't permit her to break was the one that would lead to her touching him. At least not until she was a thousand years of age or more.

He could not—would not—take her to his bed while she remained dewy with youth. He'd seen such things happen between angels and it never ended well. Either the youth outgrew their elder, or the elder crushed the youth's growth. All of it due to the fact that angels grew *slowly*, including in their maturity.

Needing to speak of Zanaya even if he wouldn't permit himself to have her, he found himself telling his second—and friend—all of it. "It may be condescending to say that, squadron leader or not," he said at last, "Zanaya doesn't know herself yet—"

"—but that makes it no less true," Avelina completed for him.

Tall and taut with the muscle of a honed warrior beneath her well-worn leathers, she had eyes of a brown so pale it was amber, and skin the shade of purest onyx. Though it made Alexander's chief of "soft" operations, Zakariah, groan at the "cruel waste of beauty," Avelina usually wore her mass of tight black curls in fine braids threaded through with strings of shimmering bronze.

"I'm a warrior, Zak," he'd heard her say dryly. "I'll leave the fashion to you. I'm more interested in hair that leaves my field of view clear and is easy to maintain. There are, sadly, no hair maids on the battlefield."

Avelina had been his lieutenant when he'd ridden into battle as a general, had agreed to stand as his second for the moment. It wasn't that she didn't wish to be in his court. Quite the opposite. "I'm a good lieutenant," she'd said to him, "and I will of course walk by your side as you grow into your power. But seconds have to be so much more than lieutenants and I won't hobble you due to your loyalty."

When Alexander had scowled, she'd laughed, her trademark husky tone warm with affection. "Oh, Alex, you know how you are. There's arrogance there, but it's well earned—your most enduring trait, however, is that you are loyal to those you choose as your own. You might now be an archangel, but that doesn't mean you're no longer the same warrior I followed into battle and who I knew would have my back in any situation."

Only very few people still spoke to Alexander with such openness. That was a reality he hadn't understood until he ascended. Now it made so much sense to him that Callie had never put distance between them; she'd needed the frank honesty of a friend. Such was a gift, one that became near impossible to find when you were one of the most powerful beings in the entire world.

Today, Avelina nodded over at where Zanaya was departing the court, her squadron fed and rested and ready to take off from the desert sands so prevalent in his territory. Much of his land was colored in the hues of sunset, and Alexander would have it no other way. As Osiris had his lush tropical island, Alexander had his land of whispering sands, date palms tall and proud, and hidden aquamarine oases.

He and Avelina stood on a high parapet of the old fort of rich red stone that had already been in place when Alexander took over these lands. He'd build his own fort, to his own specifications, but until then, there was nothing wrong with this one—built by another warrior archangel, it was designed for defense and offense both.

"She is lovely and strong," Avelina said, "and I see how she looks at you." A slight narrowing of her eyes as the desert breeze blew across the scents of the bustling marketplace just outside the walls of the fort. "There's arrogance there too—but it isn't earned. Not yet. She's young, a little foolish. But we were so as youths, too. Do you remember?"

"Far too well," Alexander muttered as he watched Zanaya take off in a sweep of wings that reminded him of the stars at midnight, diamond pinpricks in the black. "It's all I can do not to pull her back, not to have her by my side, but I know that in so doing, I'll change her." It was inevitable.

"Yes." Avelina pushed back from the parapet. "One day, she'll understand that."

Until then, he thought, she'd think him a coward unwilling to take a risk. Alexander would've raged against anyone else who dared have such thoughts—but Zanaya *was* young and a little foolish. That was the way of things.

"Come," he said to his friend and acting second, "we need to finish our sweep of the eastern border. The fortifications there are crumbling."

"Yes, it's lucky that you have Sha-yi on that border," Avelina said as she put space between them so they could take off without tangling wings. "She's old and pondering Sleep and not in the mood to pick a fight with a young archangel."

Alexander paused. "Do you think it's odd? So many of the old ones starting to slip away?"

Avelina made a face. "These are not things I think about, sire. I'm a battle hand."

On that blunt statement, they flew out to the border that had none of the forbidding and ice-laden mountains that could be found in other parts of his territory, but the question was yet on Alexander's mind when he met up with Caliane the next winter. She'd flown to him for the visit, for her land was now far more stable—she'd had longer as an archangel, was already becoming known in the Cadre for her calm way and unyielding spine.

When he brought up the subject with her as they sat side by side on rocks perched on a snowy mountaintop that was part of a much bigger range, the two of them feasting on the dried meats, nuts, and plump dates they'd brought along for lunch, she said, "I've noticed it too. I even spoke to the Librarian, asked if we had records of past Cadres."

"You mean he hasn't keeled over dead yet?" The Librarian was so old that Alexander was certain he must have cobwebs growing in his full white beard.

Caliane blurted out a laugh. "Alex!" A punch to his shoulder.

Alexander grinned and tore off a piece of dried meat. "I mean he has to be *old*," he said after he'd chewed and swallowed. "He actually looks old!" Immortals didn't show age after they reached a certain point of adulthood, their physical progression from that time on so imperceptible as to be nonexistent.

"He's always had white hair, you idiot. All his family does. As you well know." Lips still curved, she dug into the bag for her favorite dried berries. "But yes, he does look a touch older than is usual among our kind—which makes him a great Librarian and Historian. He knows so many pieces of our history that I sometimes wonder if he even knew the Ancestors."

A cold wind swept through Alexander's bones at the mention of the angels said to Sleep below the Refuge. Angels who were so old that they might well be another species altogether. "Have you ever asked him?"

"Once, when I was a child. He gave me an inscrutable smile and said I was too young for some knowledge. Perhaps in another few eons, he'd share all with me." A shake of her head. "He has no fear of anyone, you know. Not even archangels."

"That's because he's outlived all of them," Alexander pointed out, throwing a tidbit to a curious bird of prey that had landed nearby. "What did he say about the Cadre?"

"That things appear to happen in cycles. Some long, some short. An entire group comes in or goes out—the transition might be scattered over a few decades or a century, but it's a pattern that holds. He says the current cycle has been one of the longest—many of the present Cadre weren't even close to being Ancients at the beginning of their reign."

Alexander whistled. "A long time to rule." Considering this new information, he said, "Makes sense, doesn't it? The cycling. It means that each Cadre has enough time to become a battle unit in case it's ever needed. You can't do that as effectively with constant change."

"Can you imagine a storm that unites us all?" Caliane murmured, the date she'd taken forgotten in her hand. "It'd have to be a terrible threat indeed."

"Let's hope it never comes to that." It might well augur the end of the world. "How goes it in your lands?"

"Rumaia's stirring on my border for no reason but that she's bored. It's like a game to the old ones, their loyal warriors just bodies to be fed into the fire to fuel a brief respite from ennui."

Alexander's muscles tensed, his skin frigid—and it had little to do with his hatred of Rumaia. "Is that our future, Callie? An aimless existence devoid of challenge or growth?"

"I hope not, Alex," Caliane said, but he knew the fear would haunt her, as it did him.

"Let's vow to stay young in our hearts. Always." He held out a forearm as snow began to dust their shoulders. One of his ravens landed on his shoulder at the same instant, stark black against the falling white.

Though Caliane returned the hold in the way of warriors, her expression was solemn through the snow. "I'm not certain that's a vow we'll be able to keep. Immortality is a slow and relentless march that crushes everything in its path. We are but its foot soldiers."

13

Nine hundred years.

That was how long it took for Zanaya to rise to the post of first general to Archangel Inj'ra. No one could've predicted that she'd make it to the position so startlingly young, but she'd proven herself many times over—and she'd brought Aureline and Meher with her.

For her best friend had survived the blow that haunted Zanaya to this day.

Two years they'd spent without her, while she lay in a healing sleep. Not *anshara*, for she'd been too young to take herself into that rest designed to allow a badly wounded angelic body to heal. This had been a rest induced and enforced by the healers.

Two long years that Zanaya's world had been too quiet, too solemn. It would've been easy to say then that loving people wasn't worth it, that it led only to devastation and anguish. But Aureline had made Zanaya better than that, had taught her to understand subtleties of emotion that Zanaya's own mother had long forsaken. Yet Rzia had taught her something too: that to hold on to rage forever was to poison your own existence.

With each step she took, Zanaya moved further away from Rzia and the coldhearted and isolated child she'd attempted to raise. Those very steps had also brought her to this moment where she wore the intricately carved golden arm sheaths that were the right of Inj'ra's first general.

Aureline and Meher, as her first and second lieutenants respectively, had been presented with a single metal cuff each. The two had forced themselves to keep up with her as she blazed her way through the ranks. Neither wanted Zanaya in a leading role without her most trusted people at her back.

"You have enough ambition for all three of us," Meher said on that memorable day after Inj'ra promoted Zanaya to first general.

He was lying flat on his back on the grass as they spoke, staring up at the cloudless blue sky. "I'm exhausted from just being in your shadow." Except he was smiling as he said that. "My entire clan is agog—I was meant to be the black sheep, the jokester they loved but who never achieved anything important, and here I am, in an archangel's most elite squadron."

Shooting Zanaya a salute from his supine position, he said, "Thank you for forcing me to be ambitious, though I'm sure I'd have made a perfectly charming layabout."

"I don't think it was me," Zanaya replied, amused at his antics. "You were following Auri." Theirs had been an *interesting* love story to say the least, but when it had finally begun in earnest at long last, it had been like watching two interlocking pieces come together with a satisfying snap.

Zanaya had never been anything but happy for them. Well, except for the times they'd aggravated her during their courtship. Heavens but they'd been young and dramatic. As she'd been so painfully *young* without ever being aware of it.

To think she'd believed she could handle an archangel!

She snorted inwardly. Confidence was one thing, foolish arrogance quite another.

Today, she watched from her seated position against a tree

as Aureline flopped over onto her stomach beside Meher, then leaned across to kiss him. "You sell yourself short, sweetheart. You're steady and relentless and indefatigable. You just need a cause or a leader you trust—and we have that."

There went Auri, being so gently wonderful again, Zanaya thought as she picked up her goblet of cider, her hound, Maslan, lying quiescent under her hand. Of her cherished Balan's line, his coat was a glossy black in the sunlight, his body lean and long. To look at him thus, you'd never know him for a master of the hunt.

"We are both off duty today, are we not, Maslan?" she murmured with a smile as she scratched him between his pointed ears before taking a sip of the cider.

It had been a gift from Aureline and Meher, the bottle left to chill in a cold stream well before the ceremony that had elevated Zanaya to her present rank. Aureline had also sweet-talked the kitchen staff into packing them a near-banquet, and Meher had scouted this sun-dappled location in which to gather.

Mivoniel had joined them for the first half of the celebratory meal, having been invited to the ceremony by Archangel Inj'ra herself. It was a thing of great honor to Zanaya that her archangel valued her enough to make such an effort, but she'd been even more honored and overjoyed that her mentor had traveled so far to witness her triumph.

"If I ever decide my old bones wish to once more join an archangel's troops," he'd said, "I'll be applying to you." A grin. "Have to use those connections."

It had been a laughing joke, but Zanaya had responded seriously. "I'd have you at my back anytime, Mivoniel. You're one of the best fighters I've ever known—but more than that, I trust you to the core."

A thoughtful look from the most influential figure in her life. "You know, I decided I wanted out of all this"—a wave at the archangelic stronghold in the distance—"about the time I met you. Too many years of fighting, too many battles for nothing but pride. A quiet life suited me . . . but now . . . Perhaps I'll apply to you one day after all, my young Zanaya."

Now, with Mivoniel homeward bound, she sat in the sun with her friends and she thought about the archangel who'd been her obsession at one point in time. It had been nine centuries since they'd last crossed paths—an immense span of time by mortal standards, but little enough when it came to an archangel newly ascended and a woman determined to control her own destiny.

Especially when Inj'ra and Alexander were friendly. Zanaya had no reason to come up against him or his troops, and the same for him.

Be honest, Zanaya. You avoided him purposefully at the start.

True enough, she admitted. But that had been an age ago. Theirs were just lives that had never again intersected. Angelkind sprawled across the world, their numbers on the rise this past millennium as a result of the peace that had held since Rumaia and other warlike Ancients vanished from the living world.

Would it still be there between them? That brutal bolt of attraction?

It should've been an amusing memory, nothing but a reminder of the folly of youth, but she'd never quite been able to reduce it to that. Part of her remained hung up on the echo of her long-ago obsession. Well, she'd get the chance to confront memory with reality soon; generals of her new stature moved in circles that included frequent contact with members of the Cadre.

What she didn't expect was to come face-to-face with Alexander mere days hence, during a visit to Inj'ra's Refuge territory. Muscles tight from her long flight, she'd decided to go for a walk, shake things loose. But the ice and snow on the outskirts of the angelic homeland chilled her to the point that she was muttering at herself for having become soft, when she felt a prickle along her spine.

She turned . . . and there he was, in this same remote corner of the Refuge, far from the bustle of the inhabited core. It felt akin to taking a blow from the spiked ball at the end of the hard shaft of a morning star—a bright explosion of need potent enough to claw through her armor, break her. But she didn't go to him, this golden angel in the snow.

Hell no.

Zanaya would beg after no man. Ever.

Putting her hands on her hips, she held his gaze and raised an eyebrow.

His irises that astonishing silver she'd convinced herself she must've misremembered, he walked to her while holding his wings with perfect warrior precision. The air between them was suddenly no longer the ice of their surroundings. It burned as hot as the heart of the turbulent volcano she'd overflown on her journey.

"First General Zanaya," he said, coming to a halt less than half a foot from her. "It suits you. As did Squadron Leader and Wing Commander."

Though her heart was thunder, she maintained an outwardly cool expression. "Keeping track of me, are you?"

"Always. From the first moment I saw you."

It shook her, how he admitted that without hesitation. "Some would call that obsession."

A shoulder lifted in a lithe shrug. "You could as equally call it devotion." Lifting his hand, he cupped her cheek.

Zanaya could've easily avoided or rebuffed the touch. But she wasn't here to play those games. Not when the slight contact had reignited a firestorm of raw need that she'd only ever experienced with *him*. That need was far from being only of the body—obsession, devotion, whatever name you put on it, this *thing* between them allowed neither heart nor mind to stand separate.

It asked for everything.

"Put your cards on the table, Archangel Alexander." It was deliberate, her use of his full title. "I'm not here to guess at your motives."

Lightning in his eyes, he dipped his head to complete the kiss that had begun with their first moment of eye contact. It was . . . There'd been no kiss like this in her existence. It cut her even as it claimed her, and then she was the one who was doing the cutting, doing the claiming, each as hungry as the other.

The cuts formed into scars, into invisible marks that would never fade.

A single kiss and she knew young Zanaya hadn't been foolish after all. "It was always meant to be this," she said against his kiss-bruised lips when they came up for air. "It was always meant to be *us*."

"Yes," he agreed, but then hardened his jaw. "But to have taken you then would've been to take an infant. Tell me that you're the same woman today as you were then."

Zanaya liked to win arguments, but she didn't like to lie. So she scowled . . . but kissed him again, because she was the moth and Alexander the beckoning flame—or perhaps it was the other way around. He might be one of the Cadre but he didn't hold the power in this relationship. Neither did she.

When he took her into his arms and flew into the sky, she was a full and enthusiastic participant in a dance frenetic and wild. She forgot everything she knew of this act. He lost all technique.

And they came together in a pleasure so deep it was pain.

Afterward, their naked bodies sheened with sweat and protected by the archangelic cloak of glamour—which made them invisible to all but other archangels with the same gift, he flew her to his home in the Refuge and to his bed. Where they lay side by side to give their hearts and breaths time to calm, and Zanaya said, "I don't share, Alexander. Pension off your concubines."

Zanaya wasn't about to throw any woman onto the streets, but neither was she content to have Alexander's concubines flitting about. A generous pension wasn't only the decent thing to do, it removed any guilt from the situation—because as far as she knew, Alexander had remained as emotionally unattached as ever. The concubines could have had no illusions of love or forever.

"If you don't," she said, "I'll cut off a part of your body anytime I see you."

He didn't point out that he was an archangel and could crush her in a heartbeat. He just said, "I've not had a harem for many years, my Zani. Since the moment it became clear that you were heading toward becoming a senior general."

A literal skip of her heart.

Turning her head, she looked straight at him to see if he was playing her. But no, it was the warrior—blunt and up-front— who looked at her, not the archangel well versed in the politics of the Cadre. She was tough, but she wasn't hard of heart, not when it came to him. It mattered, that he'd done this, begun to treat them as a possibility the moment it appeared it might become one.

Shifting to fully face him, she kissed him with a sweetness that came from within. The instant it was over, she felt unmoored, vulnerable. How foolish, to show her heart with such openness . . . but Alexander nuzzled her right then, holding her with as much tenderness.

Don't use my vulnerability to hurt me.

The words stuck in her throat. Because to speak them would be to teach him that he could hurt her. Far better to wait and see what came next in this strange relationship that had built over more than a millennium.

This was just their beginning . . . and as she'd seen from Rzia and Camio, a beautiful beginning was a sign of nothing. It could still end in tears and recrimination and rage.

14

But what came next was a thing most unexpected that twisted up her heart and threatened to stop her breath. A mere three turns of the moon into their relationship, while she was on a fleeting visit to his territory, Alexander said, "I have a gift for you, Zani." Shifting on his heel, he walked to the large trunk at the foot of his bed, all honed muscle and sleek grace in the sunlight that poured in through the open balcony doors.

He was bare to the skin but for a simple leather skirt that shielded his manhood. Alexander was anything but shy, had only pulled on the short garment because they intended to walk to the stables prior to Zanaya's onward journey. Alexander had promised to show her his newest stallion, a "big and bold creature with a storm in its heart."

Zanaya loved horses even though she rarely rode these days. It felt unfair to her steed to make it put up with such large wings—the infrequent times she did ride, she stood in the stirrups with her wings sleeked back, she and the horse a single organism that flew across the landscape. Today, she intended to cadge a treat for the animals from the kitchen, spend some time petting and admiring them before she left.

The reminder of how soon she'd have to take flight was a stab to the gut.

The pain chilled her skin and iced her heart, her mind roiling with images of how Rzia had watched for Camio even as bitterness swallowed her whole. So it was that she finished pulling on her flying leathers in a gnawing panic. "I'm not one of your concubines," she bit out, the words far harder than they should've been. "You have no need to coddle me."

Rzia had kept every single memento from her time with Camio, each bauble and trinket hidden in a wooden box that Zanaya was forbidden to touch. Even in her sour resentment of Camio, Rzia had been more protective of him and that box of memories cruel and cold than of her living child.

At least once a month, Zanaya's mother would sit down and open the box just as the sun was about to set—then, in the flickering glow of candlelight, Rzia would touch and fondle the pretty and meaningless objects while sobbing. At least that had been the case when Zanaya was younger. Later, Rzia had spewed hate . . . while continuing to hoard the trinkets that were all she'd ever had of Camio.

"I can buy my own baubles," Zanaya added, for good measure.

Alexander glanced over his shoulder, no insult in his eye and a smile wicked and beautiful on his lips. "Do you think I don't know you at all, Zani?"

He looked young and wild and he made her pulse race. Which only added fuel to the fire of her need to take a step back, retreat from the visceral depth of what he did to her.

Then he opened the trunk and bent down to retrieve the item.

She sucked in a breath when he rose, because lying flat across his hands was a sword that she knew from a glance had been crafted by the most gifted weapons-maker in the world: Master Llisak. Given the sheer length of his waiting list, this sword had to have been ordered a long, long time ago.

For her.

She knew that the instant she took the hilt in her hand, lifted it up. It felt like air and it felt like danger, a weapon designed specifically for her body and muscle mass and the way she fought. The blade was lethal grace, the hilt embedded with opals that sparkled in the light while being set deep enough that they'd be no impediment.

When she swung the blade in a rapid dance of movement, it sang.

Perhaps, in the grip of her dread about the intensity of what she felt for Alexander, she might've rejected any other gift—but she was too much the warrior to reject *this*. "Lover, this isn't a gift," she said after she came to a standstill. "This is a treasure." Her voice was husky, her skin hot from embarrassment at her earlier disagreeable behavior.

When she met his gaze, she expected satisfaction, perhaps a little smug arrogance. But what she saw was a glitter in the silver, a flame that wasn't about the flesh. "You are magnificent in motion."

Flushing, feeling like a youngling gawky and awkward, she glanced at the hilt, rubbed her hand over a blue opal with a red heart that flickered in the sunlight. "Firelight," she murmured, raising the blade to watch the sun kiss the gleaming metal of it. "A sword like this needs a name. And this one is created of fire and light."

"As are you." Gilded by the sun, Alexander crossed to kiss her where she stood beside his tumbled bed.

Firelight held at her side, she was sinking into the heat of the lushly intimate connection, her breasts pressed to the warm muscle of a man who'd been born to be a warrior, when she felt an indentation in the hilt that she'd assumed was a part of the design . . . but now she frowned. The indentation was too deep, made the hilt a fraction imperfect. And none of Master Llisak's work was imperfect.

"Wait." Breaking the kiss, the scent of Alexander in her breath and his hand on her hip, she moved back enough that she could lift the sword, look at the indentation.

Only, it wasn't an indentation. It was the setting for another gemstone—but that gemstone was missing. "Master Llisak doesn't make mistakes," she murmured, confused by the error.

"No." Alexander's tone . . . it held time and power and a fury of emotion that gripped her by the throat.

Alexander felt his heart thunder. He'd thought this a small matter, a mere symbol of what was already true, but there was a potent resonance in this moment that stunned him. Swallowing to wet a throat gone dry, he moved back to the trunk to retrieve a small drawstring bag he'd kept there alongside Firelight.

Zanaya watched him in motionless silence, her pupils dilated and her breathing unsteady.

As was his.

Foolishness.

Yet his hand trembled when he returned to stand in front of her, then undid the drawstring and dropped the gemstone within onto his other palm. A piece of amber of a hue so deep it might be mistaken for a ruby, it wasn't smooth and round but cut in facets that would fit perfectly into the empty space in Firelight's hilt.

He wasn't sure either one of them was breathing when he met her gaze and said, "Will you wear my amber, Zani?" A roar of sound in his ears.

Alexander had never before asked anyone to wear his amber. Amber wasn't a gift cheaply or oft given in their kind. It might not be the rarest of the gemstones, but amber held *history*, held time. Amber was endless. And amber was shared only between lovers who were so deeply entangled that they had no wish to be unentangled.

His mother had worn hers as a pendant, his father his as a bracelet of metal with an amber centerpiece, the jewelry such a familiar part of Alexander's childhood that he hadn't truly ever *noticed* it—except when it was missing. That had happened exactly once, the bloody and brutal moment carved into his memories. Otherwise, his parents' amber had just been, a constant representation of their intent to be together.

Zanaya, his windstorm of a lover, just stared at the gem on his palm.

Alexander had never had a problem with standing his ground, but today, he almost closed his fingers over the offering, his mind working out how to pretend it had never happened . . . but then she lifted a hand and touched a single finger to the amber.

That finger trembled.

Exhaling in a rush, he gave a half laugh. "We are acting like halflings."

Her eyes were huge when she looked up, but a smile broke out over her lips at his words. Then she laughed, too, the sound a little rough around the edges, but her eyes bright. "It's not every day an archangel asks me to wear his amber."

"I should hope not." He tried for a grim tone, but he was too happy to be here with her to manage it. "If you need time, Zani—"

"No." A quick, firm word. "I was just startled." She blinked. "I never expected amber in my life."

When she looked away the instant after those words left her lips, he realized she hadn't intended to say them. And though he knew little of her family, he knew that, unlike his, her parents had never been a unit. To him, amber with her had always been a given. To her, it was a surprise.

Tenderness swamping him in a crashing wave, he cupped the back of her neck, the soft silk of her braid a caress against his knuckles. "I thought if I tempted you with a sword, you'd be more likely to wear it."

His words teased a smile out of her. "I think you're right, General." Then, at last, she picked up the gem, held it to the light. "Such a deep hue. Wherever did you find it?"

"In a secret place in my lands. I'll show you when you can

next visit for longer." As he watched, she lifted Firelight in a way that meant she could settle the amber inside the spot created for it in the hilt.

"A perfect fit," she murmured. "It'll break my heart to leave Firelight here so that Master Llisak can affix the amber, but"—she looked up with a dazzling smile—"that'll give me time to find your amber."

Alexander's chest expanded, sunshine in every drop of blood in his body.

15

Four centuries of loving Zanaya later, Alexander blocked a blow of dazzling ocher light as he returned the volley with his own power. He wasn't quite fast enough and Sha-yi's angelfire clipped him on the shoulder. Hissing out a breath as the angelfire tried to burn through to bone, he nonetheless kept up his aggressive attack. It was a glancing wound, nothing his immortal blood couldn't heal.

Not that that stopped it from hurting like acid.

He didn't bother to ask Sha-yi to surrender. His previously sane, stable, and wise neighbor had gone mad over the bitter winter just past—long after she should've put herself to Sleep so that her mind could repair itself. The Ancient had turned instead into a constant antagonist with no control and delusions that her power was greater than Alexander's. It wasn't, the two of them equally matched.

What would turn the tide here were their armies.

Alexander's was a ruthlessly oiled machine, his soldiers in lockstep. Then there was the Wing Brotherhood, who were a lethal strike all their own. A small and tightly knit unit that chose to mark their skin with his raven, they were both advance sentinels and expert stealth fighters. And they simply did not surrender.

Sha-yi's army, in contrast, was a shambles. It hadn't been so while Caliane acted as her second, but it had been many centuries since Caliane left that position. Perhaps the first sign of Sha-yi's decline was that she'd never replaced Callie. Neither had she replaced the generals who'd chosen to work out their contracts, then follow Callie to her new court.

The latter wasn't an unusual move. Neither was it a dishonorable one. A new archangel's people often came from various other courts—many older angels and vampires enjoyed the challenge of setting up a territory under a newborn archangel. It was an expected thing that an ascension would shake up long-settled courts.

The problem was that instead of putting out the call for qualified warriors who wished to join a highly stable territory, Sha-yi had simply promoted more junior people into the open senior positions. Those junior people had been nowhere near suitable—and this was the outcome.

"Surrender, you upstart!" the other archangel yelled, her once-content eyes red with blood fury and the burnished sunlight of her skin streaked by golden paint; it was all she wore but for a short loincloth, her taut breasts also painted gold.

Alexander's paint was silver, his own loincloth covered by a short skirt studded with metal. He still fought naked at times, but there was something to be said for not having his private parts exposed to the wind and the rain and the snow.

"Your time is done, old one!" Alexander yelled back, burying Sha-yi in silver lightning. "Look below! My people have swarmed your stronghold!"

Sha-yi looked down for but half of a moment—and that was all the time Alexander needed to land a fatal heart blow. He was no bloodthirsty monster, didn't usually go for a death blow when fighting another archangel. Most of the time, the battles came out of pent-up aggression, with neither party willing to battle to the death.

Sha-yi, however, was far beyond any reason or sanity. To leave her alive would be to prolong the war, lose more innocent lives. Because both their people were dying for her madness.

Now, she screamed, a burning star of angelfire in her chest.

Alexander flinched, hit by a wave of pity woven with a breathtaking sense of loss.

Sha-yi had been an unquestionably good archangel once, a woman Alexander admired deeply and wished to emulate. She'd helped him countless times over the years, and they'd broken bread anytime the other felt the need to converse with a fellow archangel without flying to a more distant territory. Of all the older archangels on the Cadre, she'd always been his favorite.

Now, she was dying in front of him.

Battle had stopped the moment the armies realized what was happening, and the world was silent when Sha-yi fell from the sky. They hadn't been so high that she'd break apart . . . not that such a thing was an issue any longer.

Alexander fell with her, and the fighters below all pulled back to give both archangels space and privacy. She looked so fragile as she lay on the churned-up ground, her white wings now muddy and her limbs without power. And though Alexander had struck the heart blow that even now ate away at her, stealing the life of this Ancient who'd done so much good in her time, Sha-yi gripped the hand Alexander held out.

"Thank you, my young friend," she whispered and though blood dripped out of her mouth, the rich brown of her eyes was clear for the first time since they'd begun to fight. "I waited too lo—" Releasing his hand, she arched her back, her mouth open in a silent scream.

The explosion of angelfire blinded him.

When he could finally see again, Archangel Sha-yi was gone, millennia of life, of memories, of wisdom obliterated.

Nothing was left in the aftermath but a scar on the landscape that would take decades to fade.

Shaken and wounded in a way he couldn't have predicted, Alexander went through the necessary motions . . . but he broke when Zanaya walked through the doors of his private suite halfway through the night.

Her hair was drenched in sweat, her face hot, bearing witness to the grueling pace she'd set herself. "Alexander, I heard." She opened up her arms.

He went into them, into the only pair of arms in the world he'd allow to hold him as he mourned the loss of a magnificent life that shouldn't have ended in pain and madness. It didn't matter that Zanaya was so much smaller; she wrapped him up in her wings and in her fierceness, and he could just *be*.

Zanaya watched over her lover as he dozed restlessly. She'd known Sha-yi through Alexander's words about her, could understand the depth of his grief. The other archangel had been a great help to Alexander when he first ascended, and in the end, he'd been forced to end her immortal existence. It would be akin to Zanaya having to kill Mivoniel.

That Sha-yi had thanked him for it might one day ameliorate his pain, but not today.

"Shh." She brushed her fingers through his hair, soothing him as he frowned and turned. "Sleep, lover. Rest."

While he did eventually fall into a deeper rest, she found herself wide awake and afraid in a way she'd never before been. Because Alexander was an archangel, too. As full to the brim with power as Sha-yi had been. Could it happen to him? A madness insidious and total?

Narrowing her eyes, she made a promise to herself that she wouldn't permit him to ignore the need to Sleep. He'd told her that Sha-yi herself had been trying to say that she'd stayed awake too long. Zanaya would do everything in her power to ensure that Alexander never ended up losing himself to the insanity that had turned Sha-yi from archangel to maddened monster.

"Alexander-mine," she murmured, brushing her lips over his. "You are the heart of my entire world." Words she'd not say to him while he was conscious—perhaps she'd get to that point one day, but she couldn't yet see that future.

Especially not when she was still stinging from the news that Rzia and Camio had reconciled. She'd never seen her mother so giddy and happy, a child who'd found her favorite toy after losing it for centuries upon centuries. Her father, meanwhile, was all grace and warmth, the smug candle flame around which her mother hovered.

No matter her feelings on her parents' relationship, she hadn't said a word. There were some mistakes you couldn't stop people from making. But to Sleep or not? Yes, that was one mistake she'd ensure Alexander didn't make. Her lover wouldn't die because he'd been too arrogant to rest when it was his time.

16

"We are nine now," Alexander said to Caliane when they met in the Refuge not long after Sha-yi's death.

"I fear it may be eight," she murmured. "Dragan has vanished as of the past half moon, and I'm certain he has gone into Sleep. Else he'd never be this quiet."

She was proven right on the next full moon, when Archangel Dragan's second informed the Cadre that his sire had chosen to Sleep.

So it was that the Cadre was eight for one thousand years until an ascension no one saw coming.

Zanaya was her archangel's right hand by then, her most senior general in name, and her second in truth. Inj'ra's long-serving second and cherished friend had perished in a personal fight that had gone too far.

And while Alexander's Zani might be ruthless, she was also loyal; she'd liked and respected the lost second, so the fact she effectively held his position was a thing of circumstance rather than a conscious effort on her part. That she didn't bear the title of second *was* a conscious action, a way to honor the lost friend who Inj'ra would mourn for eternity. For as Avelina had been by Alexander's side since before his ascension, so had Inj'ra's second.

Today, he stroked his hand over the sleek curve of Zanaya's flank, the beauty of her skin unlike any other in angelkind. Even the most stunning vampire couldn't compare to her; she was unique, a dark flame so hot it incinerated. She might be small in stature, but she made up for it in the violence of her will and the fury of her temper.

He'd watched her fight in battle and roared with pride because she was his.

He dreamed of her when she was in her archangel's territory, and he'd made friends with Inj'ra for the mercenary reason that it meant he could visit Zanaya almost at will.

Sliding her hand down to his cock, she gripped it, squeezed hard. "Do you think I don't know that you talked my sire into positioning me in your court for the turn of the moon? Your generals need my guidance about as much as mine need yours." That black fire in her astonishing eyes. "I'm not a doll for you to move as you wish, Archangel Alexander."

He could've met anger with anger, but he cupped her cheek, the melded onyx and amber of the strong and powerfully unique ring she'd given him a warm familiarity on his finger. Unlike most such rings, his didn't feature a piece of amber— rather, the amber and the onyx had been worked together, so that the sunlight of the amber wove through the obsidian of the onyx.

She laughingly refused to tell him how she'd done it. But that she'd taken as much care with his amber as he had with hers meant everything. "I can't sleep when you're far from me," he said. "I did it once, waited more than a millennium. Never again. I'll cheat, lie, and bargain to have you close."

A startled blink, her fingers releasing him at last, her hand coming to lie flat against his chest. "You shouldn't say these things, lover," she murmured. "I will take advantage. To control an archangel would be a power indeed."

He knew that she told the truth, that part of her was exactly that merciless—and he loved her all the same. Because she'd forgotten one critical factor. "Are you in control then, Zani?" A single kiss was all it took, her answer in the primal pumping of her hips as she rode him, and in the bites she left all over his body.

"I will own you," she said, her skin aglow with heat in the aftermath and her eyes glittering. "Until you're in me and I'm no longer this mad creature around you."

"Try," Alexander said in challenge as he began to kiss his way down her body, to the shadowed juncture between her thighs.

She screamed her pleasure, her hands wrenching at his hair and her thighs clamping around his head. He rode her bliss, licking her into oblivion even as he spilled his own seed onto the bed like a callow youth with his first woman.

He should've been embarrassed, full of shame—but there was no such thing with Zanaya. They were both as greedy, both as ruled by obsession, and when the time came that he had to let her go so she could return to her archangel, he had to fight his basest instincts. They wanted to cage her, keep her.

"I would rather cut my own throat than live in a cage," she said to him when he spoke his desire aloud. "Poke out my own eyes so that the needles go straight into the brain. Drop my body onto a spike that obliterates my heart. Anything it takes, I would do. I will not be a caged bird, Alexander."

Then she kissed him, her nails leaving clawed trails down his chest.

"It's insanity," he said to Callie the next time they met. "How we are with each other. It's not normal in any sense of the word." At times, he felt as if Zanaya was the most dangerous creature to him in all the world. "And yet I can't let her go."

"It worries me, too," Callie murmured. "This obsession I see in you. Will you start a war for her, Alex?"

He clenched his jaw. "No. Because to do so would be to lose her. She will fight for her archangel."

"I'd hate her for doing this to you," Caliane said, "but there is the loyal heart you both share. She's ruthless and arrogant and all too aware of her own power, but she also has a heart full of devotion. I watched her, you know. For you. I checked to see what she does when she's away from you. She fights. She trains. She cares for her hounds and spoils her cats. She supports her friends and comrades. And she never lies with anyone else."

Alexander hadn't needed Caliane to tell him that; he knew. How could Zani lie with anyone else when what burned between them was an inferno that scarred until neither could be with any other? Alexander lay with no other, too, his devotion as dark and as brutal as her own.

That devotion continued to build and build until it was too dark, too demanding. Jealousy took root inside him in slow whispers fanned into rage by distance and loneliness, a green-eyed snake that craved to possess her, to *keep* her. The rational part of him knew that was the worst possible thing he could demand of her, but he wasn't rational anymore.

"I love you!" He slammed a fist into his heart, the two of them alone on a desolate mountaintop cloaked in night. "More than is sane for me to love! Yet you'd rather spend far more time with other men!"

"I'm a general, you ass! Those men are part of my squadrons! I'm the one with room to complain!" The mountain winds howled as they moved through the peaks, blowing Zanaya's unbound hair back from her face in a tangle of purple-hued silver. "Do you think I don't see all those angels and vampires fluttering their eyelashes at you and all but falling out of their clothes whenever you walk by?"

He waved off the ridiculousness of the idea. "Are you questioning my word?"

"Are you questioning mine?" she yelled back.

"Zani." He gritted his teeth. "It's you I love."

"Your love comes with conditions," she snapped back. "You would make me one of your minions, simpering at your feet."

Anger made his wings glow, his hands fist. "No one simpers in my court!" Alexander had no desire to be surrounded by those who'd say yes regardless of their true opinions. That way lay a weak and spineless court. "How dare you accuse me of such!"

"I dare because *you are not my archangel!*" She kicked at the remains of a calcified tree with her booted foot. "You will never be my archangel! I will never move into your territory! I do that and our relationship is over!"

"That is shite!" Shoving both hands through his hair, he strode halfway across the mountaintop in a futile attempt to release the angry energy inside him—only to turn around and come right back to stand toe-to-toe with her. "Archangels have lovers that live in their own territories! Relationships continue!"

"I am not those lovers, and you are not those archangels," was the harsh rejoinder, her wings snapping open in a martial movement before snapping shut as hard. "You don't know how to be anything but the ruler of all that you survey. I will not be ruled by my lover. Not now. Not ever!"

"I don't wish to rule you!"

"Wishes matter naught when you're an archangel used to getting your way!" Her face was incandescent with heat, her feet set apart, the two of them so close that her chest brushed his with every breath. "You say all these pretty words, but when it comes down to it, Archangel Alexander, *you like to get your own way.*"

"I've bent and bent for you! I even turned away from war against Inj'ra because you call her your liege!"

"Can you hear yourself?" A snarl. "You make every decision based on cold-eyed politics—and now, you try to use one of those decisions against me. Your love is a thing that strangles!"

When his wings blazed so bright that the glow lit up the

night, he decided he had to get out, leave this madness. So he just stepped back and took off, up into the high cloud, where the air was so cold it hurt, and so thin that even an archangel's lungs protested.

But while he might've managed to hold back the implosion, the need to keep her in his grasp grew and grew. As did her opposing refusal to accept *anything* from him. As if the smallest gift might lead to servitude and bondage.

Each rejection infuriated him—and each attempt on his part to possess her enraged her . . . until there came a time when they were literally fighting each other, two warriors who'd devolved to the worst parts of their natures. She couldn't win, not against an archangel, but she bloodied him and he was furious because she made him hurt her when she wouldn't stop.

"Enough!" It was a roar as they stood face-to-face, chests heaving and bodies bruised.

Zanaya wiped the back of her hand over her mouth. "I can't do this anymore. It's driving me to frothing madness."

"You'll get no argument from me."

That was the first time they walked away from each other, and it was like the universe was being torn in two, ripped apart by bare and vicious hands. Alexander felt fragile within, a part of him irreparably damaged.

The split lasted a decade, and then one day, he saw her on a narrow street in a town built of red stone, a warrior dressed in faded black leathers with a sword in a spine sheath and the glory of her hair in a single pragmatic braid.

The flecks of white in the midnight of her wings caught the light, shimmered.

As he stood frozen, she moved as if she'd sensed his piercing regard. Their eyes locked . . . and time unraveled. There was no decision, no need for a decision. The next step was as inevitable as the summer monsoons and the winter snows—and soon they lay in each other's arms in a bed with a gauzy white canopy on the second floor of an ancient home, the sounds of the market outside and the world within a haze.

He touched her with hands that ached with need.

She kissed him with a wet shine in her eyes.

There were no words at first, only a longing so deep it was agony. They communicated by touch, by breath, by the slide of skin against skin, wing against wing. He shuddered at the feel of her fingers stroking over the arches of his wings; she shivered when he returned the intimacy.

It hurt, his need to touch her and be touched by her.

He mapped her body with his mouth, kiss by kiss.

She traced the lines of him with her hand, a tactile portrait.

At last, when it felt as if they'd break apart into innumerable shards, they came together in a primal tenderness that made his throat burn and his arms clench tight around her, his small and fierce Zani.

It was much later, the two of them having spent that time entwined skin to skin in an effort to assuage the continued ache of need within, that words finally entered this room in a town on the edge of a desert.

"It'll be different this time," Zanaya said, her fingers caressing his cheek. "We'll be different. We're older. Wiser."

"Yes." Alexander rubbed his cheek against her hand. "I have missed you, my Zani. I swear I won't make the same mistake, won't attempt to grip you tight, keep you in my grasp." It would be akin to trying to hold the wind.

"I've . . . I've looked back," Zanaya said, her face stark. "And I did reject things too hard and fast at times. I vow not to react reflexively, vow to truly listen."

"So will I. You began to reject my offers when I started to corner you." He'd spent many a night railing at himself for his stupidity—he must've been actually insane to attempt to cage a woman who had *told him* she would rather die than live in even the most gilded cage. "We ended up in a cycle of destruction."

A softness in her expression at the raw honesty of his confession. "You stalk me in my dreams, lover."

They were tentative with each other this time, more careful about the words they said and the wounds they inflicted. The hesitation felt awkward but the kind of awkward that can be borne for the promise of better things—and there was so much good between them. So much laughter, so much adventure, so much trust.

They went flying through the ravines of the jagged and glorious mountain range that acted as a natural barrier between the Refuge and the mortal world. They camped atop a towering natural plinth deep in the lands of her archangel. They visited Osiris in the tropics and ate sour fruits that made their faces shrivel and their tongues go numb.

He never felt as young as he did when Zanaya was by his side.

She made the world come alive for him in the wildest, most beautiful way. His favorite times with her though, were the rare moments when she allowed her guard to fall, revealing the sweetness at her core. A sweetness that meant she always bought treats for the urchins in any market through which they passed, and that led her to rescuing lost or abandoned animals to the point that she'd hired a vampire to look after her menagerie.

That vampire, of course, had been badly broken by his past. Another wounded being for Zanaya to pick up and take home. Putting him in charge of the animals had been a stroke of genius on her part. He'd healed through healing them, and was utterly devoted to both the creatures and to Zanaya.

"My mother had no tenderness in her when I was a child," she told him once, as they lay in the dark looking up at the stars, the waving golden grasses of Alexander's territory creating a secluded cocoon around them. "She taught me that the world would crush me if I wasn't faster, harder, with an armored shell."

Alexander scowled. Rzia was far from his favorite person,

but he couldn't erase the fact she was Zanaya's mother. "You understand that she was speaking out of anger?" An anger she'd nurtured and taken out on her child—creating a toxic environment from which Zanaya's father had never bothered to remove her.

No, Alexander would never respect either one of Zanaya's parents.

Zanaya took so long to reply that the night insects began to buzz again around them, lit by the glow of the gravid moon, and he thought the conversation was over. Then she spoke, her words without tone. "Over the years, I've met people who knew her when she was a newborn adult. They say she was naïve, soft, tender as they come."

Sitting up, she put her arms around her knees, her hair a soft silvery waterfall down her back. "I can't imagine her that way, no matter how I try. All I remember is her coldness, and how she taught me that the weak get crushed, that the world uses them up and spits them out."

A smile without humor. "My father, when I met him as an adult, do you know what advice he gave me? To not allow life to become stagnant. It sounds like excellent advice for an immortal, doesn't it?"

"But for Camio, it applies to people, too. Get bored? Move on. Too broken? Move on. Too needy? Move on." A sharp huff of sound. "Babies are needy. A child is needy. It's as well he's not one of our more fertile brethren and I'm his only offspring."

Alexander sat up, frowned. "Was he Rzia's first experience of love?"

"I don't know. It may surprise you to learn that my mother and I aren't close enough to discuss such intimacies." Dry words. "But you see the stock from which I come. One who uses and discards without compunction. One who pickles herself in bitterness and obsession. Does it not scare you off?"

After the way they'd broken so savagely, Alexander took conscious care never to act in any way overbearing with Zanaya—her need to be free and independent was a storm.

He couldn't blame her. A number of years into their initial relationship, she'd shared that Rzia had wanted to raise her in total isolation, that she'd only settled in the hamlet and permitted Zanaya to interact with the warriors who lived there because of the fear she'd otherwise be ordered to return to the Refuge—which was a regular haunt of Camio's.

Rzia had tried to stifle Zanaya's spirit at every turn nonetheless, clip her wings. She might've told herself she was doing it for Zanaya's own good, a twisted way to protect her, but it had been nothing of the kind. It had been the action of an angry woman who'd had no one on whom to expend her rage but a small and defenseless girl.

So yes, Alexander understood his Zani's need for freedom above all things. He might've made a mess of it once, not comprehending the true depth of his lover's scars, but no one had ever called Alexander a stupid man. So today, he made no demands; rather, he laid his heart at her feet and said, "Let me hold you, Zani. I need to hold you."

For the first time in their life together, she didn't argue, just tucked herself against his chest and let him wrap his arms and his wings around her. And for a moment in time under the moonlight, they were the best they could be to each other.

Hope and trust and love. So much love.

17

It was two years later, while Zanaya was to be in her archangel's territory for a significant duration that Alexander flew to see his brother again. Osiris greeted him at the door to his sprawling laboratory with mussed-up hair and a dreamy look in his eyes. It faded to be replaced by crisp clarity when he recognized Alexander.

"Little brother!" He embraced Alexander with the joyous warmth of a man to whom Alexander would never be anything but his younger brother, no matter how old or powerful he became.

Grinning because that was exactly how it should be, Alexander hugged him back. Osiris's body was thinner than optimal, but from the strength of his embrace, he wasn't forgetting to eat to the point of it becoming dangerous.

"Isn't it a bit dark in there for experiments?" he said when they drew apart. "Why have you covered all the windows?"

Osiris grinned. "Come and see."

Alexander sucked in a breath after his brother shut the

door. The entire space glowed with specks of light. "Osiris, what is this?" It was glorious, whatever it was.

"An oceanic organism I discovered recently. Astonishing, isn't it?" He opened the door again. "But you're right. I've been in the dark too long. Let's go for a swim and get fresh air into our lungs and you can tell me what you've been up to these past years."

Alexander wasn't quite ready to leave the wonder of Osiris's lab, but he didn't like the paleness in his brother's face— Osiris really must've been locked in there for days. "I'll have to come see this wonder again before I leave."

"Anytime you like." Osiris beamed. "I must admit to a vainglorious pride in my success in replicating the organism— getting them to breed so to speak."

With evening about to fall, the air was warm rather than uncomfortably hot, and the black sands had cooled to a bearable temperature. Alexander had stripped off his sandals and tunic when he first landed, wore nothing but a short leather skirt that protected his modesty. Not that he had much of that; most warriors didn't. But it was the accepted way of things in this season of life.

Osiris wore one of his sleeveless thigh-length tunics, but he, too, kicked off his sandals so he could walk barefoot on the sand. It was enough of a pleasure that neither one of them mentioned taking to the air and flying to their favorite little oceanside cliff—from where they'd always loved to dive into the tropical blue.

Alexander drew in the warm air and said, "When did you start to become interested in living organisms? I believed your chief interest lay in chemical reactions?"

"I've always enjoyed animals," Osiris said, just as a brazen bird with feathers of red and green screeched overhead. "Even that bad-tempered scold." Laughing when the bird screeched again, he said, "I suppose it's just time. I've been alive a lot longer than you. Altering the focus of my studies keeps my mind interested and energized."

Alexander nodded, for he, too, thrived on challenge. "You continue to keep no lovers?" He wouldn't usually ask such a question but he was beginning to worry about Osiris's isolation; these days, his brother employed a bare skeleton staff and didn't interact much even with them.

Alexander knew that because he had a loving spy among the staff—Osiris's vampire housekeeper had been with him so long that Alexander considered her family. She felt the same about him and Osiris, and so had no compunction in reporting her worries about Osiris's lack of interaction with others to him.

"I think I'm beyond all that," Osiris said right then. "No interest whatsoever."

Alexander didn't make a knee-jerk reply, instead thinking on the topic; he was aware of immortals who did indeed have no interest in the carnal side of life. He'd grown up with a battlemate who'd never had any inclinations that way—and didn't to this day.

Unlike that angel, Osiris obviously hadn't always been thus, but he *was* older, had once lived a life full of concubines and carnality; it might well be that he'd glutted himself and was now done. Fair enough—but that didn't ease Alexander's mind when it came to his general reclusiveness. "You're not lonely spending so much time on your own?"

A slap to Alexander's shoulder. "Never! My mind loves the silence, and I come up with my best breakthroughs in that space with no other voices." His smile wicked and affectionate, he said, "I know Lemei complains to you, but she has no need to worry. I feel I'm becoming . . . a more centered being, one content in myself."

As Osiris appeared happy and balanced except for his pale skin and thin frame, Alexander left it at that, and the days they spent together passed in laughter and the easy conversation of brothers.

"You came at a good time," Osiris said as they swam in the cold waters of a river pool one day, the jungle a vibrant tropical green around them and the screeching bird rebuking them from the shore. "I was attempting to fix a problem by smashing my head against it over and over and that never works. Today, I find myself seeing a solution and I wasn't thinking about the problem at all."

"I would visit more often, brother, but the Cadre is in flux." They were short two archangels, the world not in a position where he could vanish for long periods.

"Don't worry about that, Alexander. Truth is that I'd be a terrible host if you were to fly to me more often—I need large swaths of time alone to work on my research." He shoved wet strands of hair out of eyes the same shade as Alexander's. "That's another thing I need to work out."

Alexander raised both eyebrows in a silent question.

"My work area," Osiris said, switching from the local language they'd been using to the tongue that had been their first. "While it was perfectly acceptable in terms of my previous area of specialization, working with living organisms requires a colder climate." He rubbed his jaw. "I don't, however, wish to leave my island."

"If you need assistance locating a colder place," Alexander said, "a number of areas in my territory never thaw out—mostly in the mountains."

"Thank you, little brother. I may well take you up on that offer." Osiris looked at the bountiful green all around them. "I hesitate only because there's so much life here, so much inspiration. I'm not sure I'm ready to leave it. At least I can put off the decision awhile longer—for now, my experiments are stable enough in the workspace I've built. Layers upon layers of dirt formed into walls keep it cool inside."

"Yes, I noticed."

"It's a technique some among our kind consider archaic, but it works far better than many newer innovations." Osiris waved his hand on the heels of his words. "But enough about that. I notice you haven't mentioned Zanaya. Have you two parted ways again?"

"No. We're together." He rubbed a fisted hand over his heart. "She is the brightest star in the sky for me."

Osiris was quiet for a moment. "She's your weakness, is she not, brother?"

Alexander had never quite thought of it that way. "Zanaya isn't weak in the least. But if you speak from the point of view of others in the Cadre, then I suppose you're right."

"Yes, that's what I meant." Osiris drew down his eyebrows. "She still refuses to join your court so you can protect her?"

"It would destroy us. She can't ever be my subordinate."

"I suppose I see that." Osiris sighed. "I know our parents thought me lost in my world of alchemy and experiments, but I worry about you, too. The last time you two parted ways, you were . . . unlike yourself. Angrier."

"We're different people now," Alexander assured his brother. "Our relationship has grown and matured."

"I hope so, for your sake," Osiris said before he dove down into the dark green depths of the pool.

Alexander thought nothing of their conversation until after the next winter, when he went to see Zanaya and found her laughing with a fellow general who had far more than admiration in his gaze.

Of course he did. How could he not when Zanaya was a star vivid and compelling?

His jealousy where she was concerned, his need for her devotion to mirror his own came to violent life inside him, a thing so vicious that it almost signaled the end for that general. While the general survived due to Zanaya literally standing in Alexander's way, Zanaya's fury was knives coming at Alexander.

"Either you trust me or you don't," she said in the aftermath. "Decide!"

"It's not you I don't trust."

"Can you even hear yourself? That's the platitude of a being who can't control his own emotions." Her eyes glittered.

Alexander fisted then opened his hands. "I understand and accept that you can't live under my rule." It was hard, so fucking hard, to keep his voice even, but he refused to allow this to devolve into harsh words without reason or sense. "But why won't you take a position in a territory that neighbors mine instead of one so far distant?"

"Because I'm my own person, with my own dreams and my own plans." She thrust a thumb into her chest. "You are not the sun around which I revolve!"

He felt as if she'd stabbed him. "You're my sun," he said quietly.

"Lover, you're an archangel who only visits me when politics allow you to leave your territory." She held up a hand, palm out, when he would've spoken. "I'm not blaming you for it. It is what it is. All I'm saying is that if I make you my sun, the balance between us breaks. For I will never be your sun, regardless of what you might believe."

That day, that argument, bruised and battered them both, and it was the start of a rot. Not birthed by anger this time, but by a kind of disappointment that had them pulling away from the relationship as each nursed their own emotional wounds, certain in the knowledge that their love could never be returned in the way they needed it to be returned.

Their very devotion became a poison in its voracious demand.

It asked them to fall into each other—and *only* each other, shutting out the rest of the world, all their responsibilities, all their friendships, anything else that might steal the air from the inferno that scalded them. It was a thing of madness that could never be satisfied, a devotion so pitiless it could lead to murder and to war.

It refused to allow either of them to breathe.

And in so doing, it succeeded in choking the life out of the love that bound them to one another, until one day . . . they just weren't together anymore. It hurt worse than the first break, because their love had been deeper this time around, their understanding of each other much more profound.

Alexander didn't rage, just threw himself into his work as an archangel. And, after a century of silence between them, he took the odd lover. No one who'd ever be to him what

Zanaya had been, but safe choices, women who asked nothing of him but what he was willing to give, women who would never make him question a single decision, much less threaten to push him into the abyss. He knew Zanaya must've moved on, too, but as he'd once listened for news of her, he now blocked all knowledge of First General Zanaya.

He also began to accept that they were too combustible together, hurt each other too much. Love that deep wounded and bruised and destroyed. The loss of her had brought him to his knees, turned him hollow for decades.

Far better to stick with the safe choices.

Then one night, the entire world turned dark in a roar of silken silence as opulent as a panther's fur and he *knew*. "Zanaya has ascended," he said to Avelina while staring up at that luminous sky, while a melody beyond the ability of any musician to mimic filled the air . . . along with scents as lush as Zanaya's night. "My love has ascended."

Because no matter what, that would never not be true: she was his love and would *always* be his love. That had never been the problem between them. And now, she was his equal in power.

Hope he'd believed long dead unfurled its wings inside him, the youth he'd once been alive in the scarred heart of the archangel.

On the other side of the world, Zanaya's back snapped out of the vicious arch into which it had been bent in the air, her wings back under her control. The power that had poured out of her mouth and eyes to drench the sky in midnight shut off, but the windstorm that held her aloft did not.

It cradled her, brutal power and speed that exhilarated.

Laughing at the primal beauty of it, she danced in the tempests before sucking them into herself. It was pain that sent her spiraling to land hard on the ground—and it was ecstasy that had her hair streaming back as scents sensual and wild wove over her skin, through her veins.

Her outward form may not have changed, but she was far bigger than she'd ever been, could touch every point in the universe.

And she knew what she was now, what she'd *become*.

An archangel. One of the Cadre of Ten.

A being unkillable by anyone but a fellow archangel.

18

Alexander planned to go to Zanaya, court her until she was his, this time forever, but she came to him mere days after her ascension, just flew into his arms. Their kiss was a joyous homecoming, tears streaking both their faces. So overwhelmed was he that it took him a moment to notice the flickers of silvery light in her irises that must've come with ascension.

Earthbound stars. As if she truly was a piece of the night sky.

"Zani, my Zani." He pressed his forehead to her own. "Archangel Zanaya."

No one had predicted this, for while Zanaya was a power, so were multiple other angels of her age. Yet it made perfect sense to him that it would be her. Zanaya had always burned as bright as a star, magnetic and impossible to ignore. Now, that star controlled a territory, and they were equals on every level—including raw power.

They were also archangels who couldn't be in the same space for long periods of time without stirring violence in one another, but they made it work. It got ragged at times, and they did fight, but they were a unit for a hundred of the best years of his life . . . until war broke out among the Cadre and they found themselves on opposite sides of the issue, neither willing to back down.

Alexander was convinced of his choice.

Zanaya was convinced of her choice.

He saw in her refusal to even consider his point of view the impulsive stubbornness of a young archangel. She saw in his rejection of her stance an infuriating condescension.

There was no middle ground.

But Alexander refused to strike against her and she wouldn't strike against him. Neither, however, did they support each other. The aftermath was as bitter as the fruit on Osiris's island that even the animals wouldn't eat, both of them angry at the other for their choice and unable to forgive.

"It's damaging to what the mortals call the soul," Caliane said to him after war's end. "What you and Zanaya do to each other. Perhaps my friend, this love story is not meant to have a happy ending."

Her words inflicted a wound, for Alexander had begun to realize the same awful truth. Zanaya was to him what no one else had ever been or ever would be—a literal piece of his heart—but they were akin to two opposing elements that, together, could create great beauty . . . or great carnage.

Despite his acceptance that he and Zanaya just weren't meant to be, two people whose love wasn't enough to bridge the differences between them, Alexander fell back into her orbit more than once in the eons that followed—as she fell into his. In time, they grew past covetousness and jealousy, in no doubt that their hearts belonged to each other alone. It was a truth evident and unassailable that no one could ever truly come between them.

Their trust in one another was profound, their loyalty to each other unquestioned by even their worst enemies. All knew that Alexander would never make war against Zanaya, as she'd never make war against him. There was no point attempting to even foment such a thing, for that line Alexander and his Zani would never cross, not even in the darkest maw of anger. But the rest . . . the struggles of power, of two immovable opposing forces with their own scars . . . that, they could not navigate.

"We have to stop doing this, lover," she said one day when she'd long been an archangel, her wings brushing against him as he lay on the tumbled sheets of their bed while she sat on the side with her feet on the floor. The tiny kitten he'd gifted her slept undisturbed in its plush basket against the far wall.

"I know."

Then they did it again and again and again, locked in a cycle of hurt and love until one brutal day, when Zanaya threw up her hands. "I came here to make love with you for I plan to go into Sleep. And you do this!"

Alexander's blood ran cold. "Sleep?" Gripping her shoulders, he said, "What are you talking about?"

"I'm tired, Alexander." Shoving him away, she stalked to the other end of the room to stare out the window at the rolling sands of his territory. "We've dealt with more wars in the past ten thousand years than in many of the eons before."

A shift on her heel, a glance back at him. "You're tired, too, though you're too stubborn to admit it."

"Archangels don't get tired."

She snorted. "You keep telling yourself that and you'll end up a mad archangel just like Sha-yi." An unerring blow. "I promised myself I'd never allow you to go that far, but I was a hopeful fool. I didn't know how the lure of power would hold you to the world—to the point of ignoring the very real threat that looms over all our heads!"

"I'm in full control of my faculties!"

"You're *old*! So am I!" Thrusting her hands through her hair, she said, "Your compatriots, including Caliane, have all Slept for long stretches. You're the only one who refuses!

Don't do this, Alexander! Don't be what Esphares almost became! Don't allow your hunger for power to destroy you! Remember the words you told me you said to him. Do you wish to dim flicker by small flicker?"

Alexander shoved aside that irrelevant worry. "When will you Sleep? Where?" He couldn't bear knowing that she planned to go so far from him, to a place even an archangel couldn't reach.

"No, lover, this I will do in privacy."

He froze. "Do you not trust me to watch over you?" It injured him to the core that she'd believe he'd use her vulnerability to hurt her.

"Oh, Alexander." A sigh, her throat moving. "It's not that I don't trust you. It's that I trust you too much." Walking across, she took his hand, lifted it to press a kiss to his palm.

Star-flecked eyes locked with his. "We are each other's obsession, lover-mine. Should you know where I Sleep, you won't ever Sleep for the need to watch over me." A shake of her head. "I won't do this to you. We may be the worst for each other, but this I won't do to you. For I have loved you more than I have loved anyone else in my entire existence."

"No!" He reached for her, intending to kiss her, love her until she couldn't leave him.

The sword she wore like it was her favorite piece of jewelry was suddenly between them, the tip pressed to his heart. "No, not this time." A hard tone brittle at the edges. "I'm breaking us before we break each other in ways that can't be undone. I'll Sleep and when I wake, I'll be sane when it comes to you—instead of this half-mad creature I've become."

Heat flushed his skin, his shoulders knots upon knots. "Our love isn't a madness! The things we've done together, Zani. The adventures we've had, the discoveries we've made!"

"The blows we've landed, the fractures we've created in each other, the rages we've incited." She pushed the tip of the blade in further warning when he would've moved forward. "We *hurt* each other, Alexander. We do it over and over again. Neither one of us is innocent."

She continued on when he would've spoken. "Look how angry and out of control you are now. This isn't the calm and stable Archangel Alexander your people know and revere. As your Zani isn't the good-natured and even-tempered Archangel Zanaya her people follow. I don't like who I become with you when we fall into one of our dark periods."

Her words staggered him—all the more so for being pure truth. "We'll find our path," he said. "Don't go to Sleep, Zani. I would miss you for all eternity."

Her eyes shimmered for a second before she gave a harsh shake of her head. "I'll miss you even in my dreams, lover, but we've proven many times over that I'm not the right woman for you. And I refuse to stay awake and watch you dim into the madness of an archangel who will not Sleep for fear of losing his grip on power. Forget me."

He didn't run after her when she left, furious and heartbroken in equal measures. And despite her resolve, she must have rethought her decision, because she didn't go into Sleep right then. Still angry with her for scaring him, for showing him just how much emotional power she could wield over him, he kept his distance . . . and a decade later, even though he was an immortal, there was no more time.

Zanaya went to Sleep in a place of her choosing of which he had no knowledge.

"You've broken my heart, Zani," he said to a night dotted with starlight, but nowhere near as beautiful as the darkness that had heralded her ascension. "I'll never forgive you for leaving me."

It was a lie, of course. Had she woken then, he would've fought with her—then kissed her. Because Zanaya was as much a part of him as his own beating heart. But she didn't wake. Not that century. Not that millennium. And not in the millennia that followed.

His Zani Slept through age after age after age.

Cascade

19

Zanaya knew there was something wrong with this waking. An archangel's waking should be self-mandated, but this felt outside herself. As if a huge hand had come down through the earth and wrenched her out of her well-earned rest.

She hadn't made her decision to Sleep in haste, had intended to stay in this suspended state for millennia upon millennia. But now here she was, being shaken awake by someone who clearly didn't know that she was a most terrible beast in the mornings.

Perhaps it was Alexander. Impatient with her as he was often wont to be.

Another violent tug, that invisible hand viciously powerful. More powerful than any archangel.

Not Alexander then.

Not wanting to waste energy when she didn't know anything of the enemy, she allowed the unknown power to wrench her from her rest. The sands of what had once been the territory of her beloved parted around her like golden water as she rose from the secret place she'd made beneath. A place only an archangel could make, and only an archangel could survive.

Her power stretched out as she woke, and she knew that the world was now a moonless night. That was how it'd been when she ascended, a lush ebony night filled with a thousand scents that mesmerized and haunted. It was said that mortals and immortals both had gone into eternity searching to once again scent the mysterious beauty of her ascension.

The finely woven and short length of cloth in which she'd gone to Sleep, the hues of it starlight and sparkle, hugged her with delicate grace as she rose. The fabric was as soft as a baby's skin, and as fine. It covered her breasts and her torso, and only fell to her upper thighs, but what use did a Sleeping archangel have for anything more? She'd preferred to rest in beauty and softness—but for Firelight, of course.

Her beloved sword had lain beside her in her rest, but she slung it down the sheath along her spine as she rose. Her dress might be nothing but moonlight and stars, but beneath it was a softness of leather, a sheath and harness.

Her first breath of the desert air was colder than expected, the landscape around her glittering white rather than the golden sands through which she'd risen.

Her brow furrowed.

A stir in the air, a whisper of a familiar wingbeat.

Her heart sighed . . . and felt no surprise when he landed in front of her, an archangel of such classical beauty that the mortals had wanted to worship him as a god. Hair of gold and skin kissed by the sun, his eyes a startling silver and his wings the same, Alexander was the most beautiful man she'd ever known.

He was also as hard as stone, a honed warrior who'd shot down any attempts to worship him. "I am no god, Zani," he'd said. "If such exalted beings exist, they are far more evolved than I."

Arrogant the general might've been, but he'd also been earthy and honest.

"Xander," she said, her voice lazy from Sleep and her language the one they'd spoken most often prior to her rest. "We meet again." It felt inevitable that he should be here on her waking; their lifelines had been entwined for an eternity, had they not?

"That is my grandson's name now."

Delight in her breath, her eyes widening at the idea of such a thing. "You jest? You are a grandfather?" It was impossible to do anything but smile at the thought. "I have Slept long."

"That is a matter of opinion." A grumble.

Laughter bubbled out of her, his bad temper a familiar thing. "Oh, Alexander, do not say you are not happy to see me." It was such temptation to play with him, to knock at that hard head. "I am crushed."

Feeling stiff and in need of movement, she reached her arms toward the sky as the sun began to emerge from behind Zanaya's endless night. Her bare toes dug into the snow, her wings stretching out to their maximum width before she closed them in and turned her eyes to the ground. "It did not snow in this desert when I went to Sleep." Crouching down, she gathered a handful of the cold white. "Does my Nile yet flow, or is it ice?"

"It's begun to ice over," was the most unexpected response. "We are in a Cascade. You are the only Ancient I know who has woken with such suddenness, but there are signs Aegaeon is also stirring. Caliane woke before I did."

Smile wiped away, all playfulness erased, Zanaya rose to her full height. Once, lifetimes ago, she'd been a girl who'd railed against her short stature, but she'd long left that child behind, was at home in her skin, in her curves. Curves this very man had stroked with a possessive hand so many times that his touch was embedded in her flesh.

But those were pleasures not for a Cascade, those unpredictable points in time where archangelic powers turned vicious in their strength—and madness was only a heartbeat away. The pressure of a Cascade was an intense vise that had fostered many a war. "I will Sleep," she said at once, for too many archangels awake would equal catastrophe. At least this explained what had wrenched her from her Sleep. A Cascade respected no one, least of all the Cadre.

Inj'ra had once told her that "archangels are playthings to the Cascade." It had been her then sire's opinion that the Cascade was a natural event that took place to "humble" the most arrogant creatures in the world: the archangels.

Zanaya wasn't sure she didn't believe Inj'ra.

But Alexander gave a slight shake of his head. "I do not think the Cascade will let you Sleep." Folding his arms in a silent repudiation of her, Alexander said, "I will call a Cadre meeting about you, but first, I have to rescue a village buried under ice and snow."

She couldn't help it; she never could when he got this stiff and formal. "Why so bad-tempered, lover?"

Silver fire in his gaze. "I am an Ancient. Treat me as such or . . ."

"Or what?" She winked at him because she knew very well that he couldn't stand being winked at, but even so, her heart sighed to see him hearty and whole. Never would she want to be awake in a world where Alexander didn't exist— even if it was only in Sleep. "So, tell me what you've been doing since I decided I'd caused enough mayhem for ten immortal lifetimes."

His glare warned her that he hadn't forgiven her for going into Sleep while they were yet angry with each other. Oh, that's how he'd think of it, she was certain. Forgetting all the many, *many* times when she'd spoken to him of her need for Sleep—and *his*. Not that he'd ever agreed with her. Not Alexander.

Now, he snapped, "I have work to do," and lifted off.

Laughing because she knew this man, no matter if they'd been apart for millennia, she rose with him, her wings glorying in flight.

She was about to ask more about this Cascade when the

world turned a black that was flat and hard and cold. So, so, cold. Akin to the inside of a human crypt. With it came a silence that felt like a pressure on the lungs, a crushing force that would snap the spine and crack the skull. Then . . . the screams. Shrill, ugly, the most horrific sounds she'd ever heard.

"What is this cacophony!" Firelight in hand, she searched for an enemy, found none. "No archangel I know wakes with such darkness!"

"You do not know her." Alexander's tone was grim as he came to hover beside her, his wing just brushing hers. "Her name is Lijuan."

That was how Zanaya first learned of the Archangel of China, this being who could make the dead walk—and who believed that the shuffling corpses she produced equaled "life." Alexander told her that Lijuan had named her creatures the "reborn" but it seemed to Zanaya that they were nothing but the fetid and despoiled dead, blank and mindless.

"This Cascade," she said to Alexander some time later, after she'd absorbed all she could of the current world, "isn't like the others."

They'd both lived through other Cascades, many small, several large. None had threatened to break the world, leave it a crumbling ruin.

"No," Alexander agreed, his face tired in a way she'd never before seen it. "Lijuan treats us all with contempt, believes herself a goddess above even her former brethren in the Cadre."

Standing side by side with Alexander on the balcony of his fortress, Zanaya stared out at the snow that still draped his lands. The two of them had helped clear multiple regions of the crush of ice, but she knew without asking that such actions were only a temporary solution. "How do we stop her?" That was the true test, the true question.

"The Cadre is to meet soon." Alexander rubbed a hand

over his face, then put his hands on his hips again, his eyes trained on the lands beyond. "Too many of us are awake, Zani."

She might've teased him for thawing enough to fall back into using his old pet name for her. But that Zanaya was a creature of peacetime. Now was the time for her warrior avatar. "We must be needed," she mused, setting aside the shock that still reverberated through her at his earlier comment that Caliane had woken before he did.

If he'd *woken*, that meant he'd *Slept* at some point in time.

Zanaya wanted to ask him what or who had convinced him to take that step. Because Zanaya hadn't been enough—and yes, that wound throbbed to this day.

The pain of the woman, however, could wait. Today, it was the archangel who needed to reign supreme. "Perhaps it's the only way to defeat this Lijuan." And though she'd long forgotten fear, that was a terrifying thought. How could one archangel be such a power that the Cascade would wake so many Sleepers to stand against her?

There were more surprises to come—including a Cadre meeting beyond her experience. She'd expected them to fly to a central meeting point, or for it to be assumed that they'd use a mental power that was only of the Cadre—though Zanaya would've refused the latter, the price it demanded too high. To use the archangelic ability was to lose their empathy for at least half a day, become cold and heartless monsters.

Zanaya had used it exactly once. Never again. She would not allow herself to go into the Quiet, become the very creature her mother had tried to raise her to be.

If that meant flying a significant distance, so be it.

Alexander knew all of that and had never pushed her to use her power. So she wasn't surprised when he didn't bring it up. She *was* surprised when he led her into a large internal room with flat black paintings on the walls.

"If this is a new style of art, lover," she muttered, curling her lip, "I have no faith in the current state of civilization."

A chuckle before he could remember that he was meant to

be angry with her. "It's a communications system," he explained. "I can't tell you how it works. I leave that knowledge to the young. All I know is that it's useful."

Intrigued, Zanaya went outside to what Alexander referred to as the "control room" and watched a vampire named Richmond push buttons and touch what he told her were called "screens." His voice was crisp and clean and held the precise rhythm of a language unknown to her—but the language he used when he spoke to her was the *old* angelic tongue, which— per angelic law—had to remain unchanged in certain key aspects.

New vocabulary could be introduced to include new things in the world, but the old had to stay and the underlying structure of the language itself had to remain the same as when it had first been spoken. An event that had taken place so long ago that no one in Zanaya's lifetime had had any knowledge of it. Any natural evolution was forcefully crushed or pushed in the direction of the offshoot of the angelic tongue used in everyday life.

This *one* language, clunky though it might sound to any new generation that had to study it in childhood, had to remain a constant across eons.

Nothing else would work in a world of immortals who Slept.

All members of an archangel's innermost circle were tutored in it, so she hadn't been surprised when Richmond proved fluent.

"All is ready, sire," he said eventually into a small black button at his collar, and he had the politeness to continue using the archaic language Zanaya understood. "I will leave now with your permission."

Zanaya jerked when Alexander's voice came from directly in front of her . . . though he was inside the windowless room with the flat black panels. "Go," he said. "Keemat will take care of any new emergencies for the duration of this meeting—contact her if anything arises."

Keemat, she'd come to know, was his most senior general

but for Valerius. The latter—a loyal, honorable, and intelligent, if occasionally stodgy, angel—had been with Alexander in Zanaya's time, too, and today stood as his third. Oddly enough, given their differing personalities and views on battle tactics, Valerius and Zanaya had ever enjoyed each other's company. She looked forward to breaking bread with him once again.

Alexander, it seemed, had no second at this time as Valerius was firm in his stance that he wasn't the right person for the task. In truth, if he was much as he'd been before her Sleep, then she agreed with him. Alexander's third was many things, but gifted in the subtlety required of a second? No, that was not Valerius.

"Sire." The vampire, Richmond, rose before turning to bow deeply to Zanaya. "Lady Zanaya. Please excuse me. I'm not permitted to witness a meeting of the Cadre."

Realizing she was in his way, she stepped out of his path. "It's better that you not listen in, young one." Zanaya smiled then made a face at the thought of the pompous bombast to come. "You may lose all your illusions about your illustrious rulers."

A blink, a blush of color under the dark gold of his skin. Followed by the faintest smile. "I'm glad to have the chance to live in a world where you are awake, my lady."

The scamp was gone a moment later, closing the heavy doors firmly behind himself.

"Zani!"

Rolling her eyes at that impatient call, she slipped back into the room with the black screens. They were, however, no longer blank. Each showed a turning hourglass with writing beneath that her mind processed as a countdown, though she couldn't understand the language.

It wouldn't be much longer till she did, however.

Angelic brains old enough to trigger the Sleep state also absorbed new languages at a speed that couldn't be explained in any rational way. Which was why the archaic nature of the old tongue didn't matter; it was only used to ease the transition from Sleep to a wakeful existence.

The first screen cleared, to reveal a face. Followed by another screen, and another until each was filled by the visage of a member of the Cadre.

20

Zanaya sucked in a breath when she saw not one but *two* sets of eyes of a blue so distinctive it was a signature. *Caliane has a son?* she asked Alexander.

Yes. His father was Nadiel—who ruled and died while you Slept. An echo of pain in his voice, an indication of a bad end for this Nadiel who had won Caliane. *Raphael is the son of two archangels.*

It was instinct to want to touch his wing, his arm, offer comfort for a hurt the parameters of which she didn't know, but this wasn't the time or place. Alexander wouldn't want to acknowledge any vulnerability in such company. Instead, she attempted to distract him. *I want to stare. That would be rude, but I can't help it.*

The merest hint of a twitch of his lips. *I think you're safe to indulge. Everyone is staring at one another.*

So they are. After all, it wasn't every day that so many Ancients woke up and shook off the cobwebs. Then the discussion began and she came to the sour realization that several of these old ones should've stayed in their cobwebby bunkers.

You're not helping matters, Alexander muttered into her mind when she made another sly comment designed to irritate.

That idiot one with the blue-green hair makes me desire to burst my own eardrums so I no longer have to listen to him. Zanaya had never been able to stand big blustering types, though she had to admit she *was* charmed by Titus, son of Alexander's respected First General Avelina. He might well be a glorious exception to her usual stance. *What is his name again? Chief Idiot?*

Aegaeon, you know full well his name is Aegaeon. You were both awake at the same time in the past.

You don't like him, either, so stop pretending. And he's a donkey's ass in any time.

Alexander was far too controlled to throw up his hands, but she knew her lover. Yet despite her willingness—and tendency—to stir the pot, she paid attention when Titus "played" something he called a "recording." Alexander was mentally translating for her when the others slipped into newer languages, and she filed the new words in her rapidly building hoard of what appeared to be a tongue in popular use.

She soon realized that a "recording" was a way to make memories concrete, so you could relive them at will.

A true wonder, but this memory was so gruesome that shocked silence befell them all.

An oily black fog that didn't look like anything that should exist in their world had swallowed up Lijuan's territory. Small creatures that wandered into it—birds, stray dogs, and the like—fell dead on the spot or emerged with such horrific injuries that mercy was the only option.

A slow creep of ice over her skin. "She is the Archangel of Death." Horror curdled her stomach. "I see this now." Turning to two Ancients who'd been blowing hot air, she said, "Do you not see?" She couldn't understand their egotistical imprudence. "We wake before our time to take care of this menace." The understanding of the general she'd once been. "We are not meant to live in this world. It is *not* our time."

She'd spoken those last words—or ones similar to them—to Alexander once upon a time, in a futile attempt to make him understand that Sleeping wasn't surrender. It was simply an artifact of age and time. He hadn't agreed then, but though she didn't look at him now, she knew he was with her on this: Lijuan needed to be stopped.

But too many stupid old ones were also awake. They *refused* to listen—and at last, Archangel Antonicus declared that he would fly *into* the murderous black fog that blanketed China. He was certain in his belief that he'd remain unaffected.

"He either has far more power than we know," Alexander muttered to her after the meeting, "or he's driven by conceit and pride."

Zanaya tilted her head a touch to the side. "Have you become wise, lover? Time was, you were the most arrogant one of all."

A pause, eyes of silver meeting her own. "I was considered a great statesman in my time, Zani. I grew while you Slept. Perhaps I've grown far beyond you."

There it was; that bite of anger. He still hadn't forgiven her for leaving him. And she still hadn't forgiven him for not coming with her. "Oh, how you wound me." She clutched theatrically at her heart, hiding the extent of her love for him as she'd always done.

He'd have too much power elsewise, would hold all the reins. For the Archangel of Persia was and would always be her greatest weakness. While power was *his* greatest weakness and greatest need. His love for Zanaya had never been able to compare—regardless of what he might've told himself.

Temper a pulsing nerve in his jaw, he said, "We have a little time before we need to fly to Neha's territory to witness Antonicus's attempt to breach the fog. We're much closer to her than many others. I'm flying out to assist a region hit by a flash flood."

Not wanting to be around Alexander when he could hurt her with such ease—and perhaps even without intent, which was somehow worse—she said, "I'll fly over the closest of your mountainous regions, help anyone who needs it." She made sure to keep a slight smile on her face. "I look forward to learning more from you in the future, oh wise one."

Hands on his hips, he glared at her. "Why do you always manage to make me sound ridiculous?"

It hurt a little less when she saw that he was yet vulnerable to her barbs. "Someone has to keep you humble, Archangel Alexander."

"Half my life, I've spent wanting to strangle you, I swear," he muttered. "I'll come with you. Valerius and his squadron don't need me to handle the flood, and the mountain areas are the most isolated."

"No. Don't." She gave him a flat glare. "I need a little distance from you."

This time, the pause was longer. Then he said, "Have you not had enough, Zani? Eons of Sleep and still you don't want to be close to me?"

Her anger crumbled, her fury turning into a wild passion and need that had only ever worn his name. "Damn you." Striding across, she took his face in her hands, pressed her lips to his.

And for a moment that hung in time, they were just Xander and Zani, two lovers who had always been meant to be.

Then she was tearing away from him and leaving the room. So she could think. So she could breathe. Because their love? It had always been too much. Too big. Too demanding. If he wanted to strangle her, she wanted to push him away until she could be whole without him.

Except it was too late. It had been too late the first time she'd seen him.

She took off in a hard burst. And she didn't look back even though she wanted to do so with every fiber of her being.

He blamed her for leaving him and going into Sleep, but he'd left her just as much when he'd chosen a ceaseless reign over her desire to heal their aging minds and leave the world to the young.

I will never again be that powerless boy, Zani. I will never allow anyone to crush me and mine under their boot.

Words he'd spoken to her untold mortal lifetimes ago, when he'd told her of what it had been like to grow up an unimportant part of Rumaia's poisonous court. She understood that the angry and wounded boy he'd once been was a permanent part of Alexander's psyche; he'd settle for nothing less than a position as an apex predator. But she also understood another immutable truth that he'd chosen to forget: archangels weren't meant to rule forever.

Look at Antonicus. He shouldn't be awake; he was so clearly not of this time and not suited to it in any fashion. It wasn't simply a matter of being outpaced by new knowledge, like that which had faciliated the meeting of the Cadre. She'd seen great and wondrous inventions during her reign that— from what she'd experienced of the present world thus far— appeared lost to time.

Such was the way, even in a world of immortals. People forgot and discoveries were made over and over. The world was in constant flux. It could be that millennia from now, they might live once again in a time of chaos and brute power. That might be the right time for an angel like Antonicus—he could do good in such a world.

Civilizations rose and fell, even angelic civilizations.

The great civilization Zanaya had built, perhaps it remained in the echoes of history, in the memories of some old ones, but it would've fallen into the desert in its time, as was the right way. As the Nile flowed in new routes every eon, life changed, turned, became.

I grew while you Slept.

She hissed out a breath, the wound pulsing anew. And she wondered at all she'd missed of Alexander's life while she wasn't in this world. She'd missed a child, for one.

Thinking on that, she considered if she was jealous.
No.

Children were a gift, to be treasured. And they both knew the truth. No other lover either one of them had taken over their long, long lifetimes could end the tempestuous vortex that swirled between them. Sometimes, it got too much, demanded too much, and they looked to quieter, less demanding arms. Never accepting that they'd inevitably find themselves back in the vortex.

"I'd die if Meher lay with another," Auri had said to Zanaya once, during a time when Zanaya and Alexander were no longer a couple. "How can you bear it?"

"Because when we break, we *break*, Auri." Her heart had ached at the memory of each awful break. "We shatter into splinters. There's no us, only a memory of us—and a memory of anguish and hurt."

A solemn look from her closest friend. "That doesn't sound like love, Zan. That sounds like pitched battle."

Zanaya had laughed then, her amusement an ironic thing. "You speak truth. It seems I'm not built for a gentle and kind love. I'm built for war. So is he." And that was why they were forever doomed.

That knowledge heavy on her mind, she swept over the mountains and stopped to offer assistance where needed. The vast majority of the squadron commanders and ground crews had no idea who she was, but accepted her presence because it was obvious that Alexander had to know she was in the heart of his territory—the general had never run anything but a tight ship.

She saw some of them talking into small rectangular devices and narrowed her eyes, thinking of the "screens" through which she'd spoken to the others in the Cadre. It seemed to her that these were miniature versions of those screens, so likely they could be used for communication. No doubt they were requesting confirmation from the fortress that she was no threat to their people.

Well, she'd have time to learn about these new inventions

after the war was done. For now, it felt good to use her abilities for acts simple but necessary: to clear floodwaters, lift people or animals out of danger, or explode the eerie spikes of stone that had erupted out of the earth without warning, this Cascade truly a thing beyond.

Waves of tiredness rippled over her more than once. She shrugged them off, knowing they weren't related to physical exhaustion, had nothing to do with a need for rest. No, this was another kind of tiredness.

Of this constant pitched battle between her and Alexander. *Why do we do it?*

She had no answer to her question by the time she had to turn back in readiness to fly to Archangel Neha's territory. They were to meet on her border with this Zhou Lijuan who thought herself above them all, in readiness to witness Antonicus's heroics—or idiocy, the interpretation dependent on the individual.

"Despite the fact I believe him to be putting his life at risk for no rational reason," Zanaya said to Alexander as they flew, "I want him to succeed. For in so doing, he'd show us a path out of the horrors she has spawned."

Alexander responded to her archangel-to-archangel conversational overture in kind. They'd both been polite since her return, well aware that what was coming allowed no room for extraneous emotion.

"I feel the same," Alexander said. "Antonicus isn't an archangel to whom I feel any affinity, but I wish him well in this. We need him to succeed."

They didn't speak further until Alexander said, "Lijuan's territory isn't on our direct route, but I suggest we detour over it in order to gather intelligence."

"I was considering the same." Wars were won on information—or a lack of it. "We'll fly high until we see the edge of the fog. I can't imagine she has the power to send it up into the higher atmosphere, but let us not die because we have turned into prideful idiots like certain buffoons who give old angels a bad name."

Laughter in her mind, warm and masculine and reaching both her sex and her heart. One she could bear; the other might yet succeed in breaking her. *Agreed.*

So it was that they were high in air thin and frigid when they first overflew a border section of Lijuan's lands.

21

Zanaya was built to withstand cold, but her skin shivered at first sight of the stygian blackness beneath. No light peeked through, no hint of any civilization. Nothing. "It's like she's thrown a blanket over existence itself."

Alexander, who'd come to a hover next to her, pressed his lips together. "We can only hope her people aren't suffocating below."

She glanced at him. He caught her look, nodded. And they flew down for a closer inspection—but not so close that they were in any danger of touching the fog. What they discovered was that the fog was far from uniform. "Some patches are almost viscous," she murmured, pointing out one.

"Yes, but even the thinnest areas are opaque. China has become a locked room without windows." Alexander's words were grim.

They flew on, not landing until they reached the roof of a border fort in the territory of Neha, Archangel of India. There was no chance of making a mistake as to where they were supposed to land. This close, the location was a beacon to her senses—it pulsed with the aggressive power of the archangels who'd already arrived.

She landed, folded back her wings, and took in the lay of the land. Alexander had come down beside her, but was pulled into conversation with Antonicus. *Better you than I,* she muttered into his mind and walked to the edge of the rooftop.

Flaming torches lined this side of the border, casting a red-gold glow against the black fog that swallowed all life. Neha's warriors stood in a line against the black—but far enough back that there was no risk of accidental contact with Lijuan's murderous creation.

Black was Zanaya's signature. She loved the night, had ascended in a velvet darkness so opulent that bards had written songs about it. Her skin was as close as a mortal or immortal could get to that midnight shade, and if she'd had a vanity in her life, it was that skin so smooth and rich in color.

But this . . . this fog wasn't black. It was nature twisted, with a disturbing unctuous feel to it. Like an eel . . . but no, it was too sickeningly aberrant to compare to that slippery denizen of waterways, its coat gleaming wet and lovely in sunshine-dappled water.

A presence by her side.

"Lady Zanaya." Titus bowed his head slightly in greeting, big and bold and rather beautiful. "Alexander told me about you once, long ago."

"Oh? What did he say?"

Eyebrows lowering, he said, "That you had the ability to drive ascetics devoted to peace into a flaming rage."

Zanaya laughed so hard it made her stomach hurt. Afterward, she said, "You are a good friend to him indeed." There were very few people with whom Alexander was so open.

"He's a good friend to me, too." Titus measured her with those dark eyes, a sudden solemnity to them that told her he had far more depths than were apparent on the surface. "I'm not sure, however, that you're good for him, Lady Zanaya."

"Oh, young Titus," she said on a renewed wave of aching tiredness, "we were never good for each other." Not quite the truth—there'd been incredible moments, decades, centuries of beauty and grace between them. It was only that the years had been tempered by as much pain and anger and frustration. "Perhaps the question will be moot after this waking."

"Why say you that?"

She nodded at the fog peculiar and chilling. "I've woken to a terrible world. I don't know if I'll survive it."

A cold wind across her neck, as if Cassandra herself had brushed her fingers over her nape.

Zanaya straightened her spine, stilled her heartbeat. Death held no fear for her. She'd lived a vast span of time.

Then a masculine voice carried over to her on the night currents, familiar and beloved.

Glancing over her shoulder, she thought, *But I have not loved him enough. It will never be enough.*

This time, however, wasn't theirs, even had they not already been squabbling. This time was for the Cadre to step up and eliminate a menace that had been born of one of them. And it was to that topic they soon turned, discussing what knowledge they had of Lijuan's fog. At one point, Neha showed them a line of birds who'd all fallen on this side of the strange border. As if they'd begun to fly in, only to die.

Neha confirmed that, as far as they were able to tell, the birds had died the instant they made contact with the fog. Caliane followed that up with the information that Neha's people had discovered other small animals, including snakes, with their heads in the fog and the rest of their bodies in Neha's territory.

Dead as soon as they attempted to enter that oily miasma.

"Enough." Antonicus exercising his voice again. "It is time I do what must be done—I am not a child to be scared by ghost stories." His voice dripped with contempt for what he clearly saw as their cowardice.

Fool. A good general reviewed all information before making a decision. They didn't send people blundering off into the unknown. But if Antonicus wished to volunteer to blunder, then Zanaya would use the resulting knowledge. And as she'd said to Alexander, she still wished him well.

Antonicus continued on. "I will see you all after I return from speaking to this Lijuan who believes herself a goddess even over immortals."

Zanaya was aware of Alexander coming to stand beside her as all the archangels lined up on the edge of the roof to watch Antonicus's progress over the sea of black. He'd agreed to drop down into the fog at a point that would be visible to them, before rising to head on deeper, toward Lijuan's main stronghold.

She held her breath as he reached the first point. He turned to indicate that he was about to dive by raising his arm . . . then dived into the black that wasn't black. Her chest tightened as the moments passed and he didn't emerge. She truly hadn't expected the death fog to affect an archangel— and an Ancient at that.

No, there he was!

A sudden burst of hope . . . shattered when it became clear that Antonicus was injured.

It was Caliane's son, Raphael—the only archangel who, she'd learned, had a proven immunity to at least some of Lijuan's powers—that flew out to assist Antonicus. And it was Raphael who carried back an archangel wasted and hollow, Antonicus's eyes sheened by oily blackness.

Laying him down on a mat on the roof, Raphael was able to use his power to chase the black from Antonicus's eyes, but it was a temporary reprieve.

Zanaya had seen archangels die, but never in such a way. Always in battle, always in a blaze. This . . . Her gut clenched. She crouched beside the body alongside the rest of the Cadre, an honor guard of archangels as Antonicus's wings began to curl and go black, as his skin became a rotted green, and as his chest sank inward, as if his body was turning into viscous soup.

Until . . . it all stopped.

Antonicus lay frozen in a moment of decay and death. Perhaps because archangels could come back from many things.

Which was why Zanaya didn't argue when it was mooted that they shouldn't destroy his body but bury it in a distant place of ice and frost where he couldn't spread the infection that riddled his frame—and where he could lie in peace for eons as his body fought to repair itself.

"I don't know if I want to hope that he's alive or not," she said to Alexander as they flew ahead of the group some hours later, having already taken a turn carrying the sling that held the body. "The horrors in his eyes, on his face before he was no longer present . . . imagine being trapped in that moment for all eternity." For there was a chance that Antonicus wouldn't die—but wouldn't wake either.

He'd remain forever a partially rotted corpse.

"He had no mind at the end," Alexander said. "I'm certain of that. If he Sleeps, it'll be a Sleep devoid of all knowledge. Which may be what keeps him sane should he be alive."

Zanaya hoped Alexander was right when it came time to hold the burial. She and Archangel Elijah formed the hole where Antonicus's body would lie cradled in impermeable stone. Then they all joined together to lower Antonicus into the hole.

"To Antonicus!"

Zanaya's eyes met Alexander's as they said the name of the gravely injured archangel, and she could read his thoughts in his eyes: the general was afraid that they'd made a mistake, that they'd just buried a problem rather than dealing with it. Antonicus was infected with a darkness beyond anything either of them had ever before seen.

If he returned . . .

We must give him a chance, she said to Alexander, mind-to-mind. *It's the only honorable choice.*

Yes, he agreed at once. *But we will watch. We will be ready.*

22

Afterward, their mood somber, the Cadre split in various directions to return home, all of them knowing this was but the first strike.

"How has she become so?" Zanaya asked Alexander when they finally landed on the balcony of his main fort. "Zhou Lijuan? Was she always a great power?"

"I knew her as a young woman," Alexander said. "She was powerful but no more so than you or I. Had she not given in to this madness, I could've seen her becoming a strong Ancient." He thrust a hand through his hair as he led her inside and down a corridor carved out of the local red stone, paintings etched into the stone itself.

"I'd blame it on the Cascade," he said, "but Titus informs me that there were more subtle signs of change in her before this evil." He began to tell her of those signs; he'd always been generous when it came to information that was Cadre business.

Halting in front of a set of heavy golden doors, he held her gaze. "These are my rooms, Zani. Will you come with me this dark day?"

Perhaps she might've refused at another time, still bruised from their earlier altercation. But after witnessing what had taken place with Antonicus, she said, "Yes. But you, my general, will provide for me a bath first and foremost." She would not lie with him rife with the stink of death.

A tug of his lips, a smile so open that it showed her a glimpse of the youth she'd been born too late to know. "Only you would order me to draw you a bath." Hauling open one of the doors with an easy grace, he waved her in. "My lady."

Laughing, she strode in.

She experienced no surprise at seeing the relatively meagre furnishings in the initial area of his suite. He'd always gone for spare in his living quarters—except for in one place. "Ah, there it is." A huge four-poster bed complete with curtains that could be tied back, and luxurious bedding.

"Will you make fun of me for my continued liking of comfort when I sleep?"

"Never," she said as she took off her sword and kicked off the boots that a member of Alexander's staff had managed to find for her. "Not when I enjoy it so much."

Water ran somewhere close by and she knew he'd started to fill the bath. Padding toward the sound of that water, she dropped her clothing until she was bare to the skin, the air kissing every inch of her.

Leaning one hand against the doorjamb of the bathing chamber, she took in the floor tiles of gentle desert gold riven with streaks of a deeper gold; the color was reflected in the dark gold of the water spouts, but the walls were a simple cream, as were the thick towels that sat piled up in a woven basket to one side of what she assumed was a built-in bowl to wash the face.

Water gushed from one of the golden spouts, and given the steam rising up from the bath, that water was hot. No need then, to build a fire below the bath, or to have water heated elsewhere in the home carried up in buckets. How extraordinary . . . and yet somehow not startling.

Because even when certain things changed over the eons, they remained the same. This world might have technologies far beyond what angelkind had discovered when she went to Sleep, but people still needed to bathe, to wash their faces.

But the most intriguing thing in this room was the angel who stood beside the bath, half bent over it as he tested the water with his hand. His wings were a glory of silver against the muted colors of the space, his hair shining in the light that poured from a fixture in the ceiling. For the people of this time had also managed to harness light.

"Someone already came in and filled it two-thirds of the way up," he told her as he flicked the water off his fingers. "You won't have to wait—" Speech bitten off on a harsh inhale as he turned, saw her.

She smiled, and yes, it was pride that heated her blood. So many years they'd been apart and still he looked at her with that wild storm in his eyes. There was no shield of an archangel powerful and remote, and no sign of the general so inscrutable that his enemies could never guess at his motives or planned moves.

This was the Alexander that Zanaya alone saw.

Needing to touch him, she closed the distance between them. "You're overdressed, lover." A husky purr against his chest as she ran her hands down the beaten dark brown of his leathers, but it was a bittersweet joy that ran through her veins. "I could almost imagine these being the same set I gifted you once."

He closed his hand over her wrist, his hold rough with warmth. "I wore those until they fell apart. I was so angry with you, but still I wore them." Dropping his head to her own on that rough confession, he crushed her lips with his own.

She didn't mind.

Their love had never been a gentle thing.

Thrusting her hand into the thick silk of his hair, she

gripped hard as she kissed him back with just as much fury, just as much need. Being on tiptoes was her usual state when they kissed, even though he always bent for her, but never had she felt at a disadvantage. Here, they'd always, *always*, been equals.

When he took hold of her hips and lifted, she moved with him, ended up with her legs locked around his waist. He was so strong and warm against her, the fluid muscle of him obvious even through his leathers. They'd been in this position so many times that it felt as easy as breathing.

Zanaya could remember laughing and running to him on a visit, wrapping her legs around his waist as he held her while they kissed, utterly delighted to see each other. So many times she'd run into his arms, this archangel who was the only man in all of eternity who'd ever had the power to cause her pain.

Today, however, when they drew apart with their chests heaving, there was no pain, only an ache that came from having missed him even in her Sleep. "Hello, lover," she murmured.

He kissed the tips of her fingers when she ran them over his lips, and she remembered that no, they weren't always so passionate and almost angry with each other in bed. There'd been tenderness too, long ago, before the fractures grew too great. Before they both bled too much. Before the wounds hardened into scars.

Unable to look back at the unbearable sweetness of what had once been, she ravaged his mouth in another untamed kiss while tearing at his leathers. He got the message, pulled back only long enough to rip the top off over his head and throw it to the tiles. It fell with no sound, the leather beyond soft after so many years against his skin.

Running her hands over that skin, over the warmth and muscle of him, she gloried in the now, in this moment when Zani was with her Alexander. The steam from the bath floated in the air, lingered against his skin and her own, and when she dropped her mouth to his throat, she tasted salt.

A shudder, one of his hands fisting in her hair.

He'd always been sensitive along his throat. She kissed the strong column, her memories of him an imprint on her soul. Always she'd remember how he liked to be touched, how he liked to touch in turn. Even when they hadn't been able to speak to each other, mute with anger, they'd been able to communicate through touch.

"Zani." A rough caress against her temple as he pulled her mouth from his throat and claimed it with his own once more.

You'd think that after all eternity, she would've had enough of his kiss, he enough of hers.

But no.

It would never be enough.

The wanting had never been the problem between them.

She sank into the kiss, into him. And when he broke it to kiss the tops of her breasts while he used one big hand to caress each in turn, her wings fluttered restlessly. She might've felt akin to a trapped bird were they not so well matched. Because they were, she could surrender to the pleasure that was a stretching awake of nerves long asleep.

Shuddering when he took her nipple into his mouth, she said, "It hurts."

He stopped at once, looked up. "Zani?"

"It has been an eternity since I've felt such sensation." She swallowed, pressed her fingers to his lips. "Yet the need eats me alive." She stole a kiss, another. "Be with me. The rest can wait." She hungered for the sense of completion that came with holding his body in her own, in feeling him move in that most intimate of ways.

Cupping the side of her face, he pressed his forehead to hers. "I have *missed* you."

Her eyes threatened to tear up. She refused to let them. Refused to be so vulnerable all over again. Instead, she kissed him until he did as she'd asked and put her down so he could rid himself of the rest of his clothing. Then he was picking her up again, and she was sliding down onto him, this dance of theirs long perfected.

Yet still it wrenched a gasp from her, that moment of connection.

There was a sense of inevitability to it, a sense of rightness.

Unable to look too hard at that when they'd never got the rest of their relationship right, no matter how many times they tried, she wrapped him up in her arms as he wrapped her up in his, their wings entangling. The pleasure that awaited at the end of the dance, this wasn't about that. This was about . . . being. Just being.

Tears threatened again.

Burying her face against him, she let the hot beads of pain fall, mingle with the sweat between their bodies, the steam on their skin. Until at last, she became water and her entire self came apart in gleaming droplets that fell to the floor and shattered.

23

Zanaya sat in the huge circular bath with her back to Alexander's chest, her wings spread out so they wouldn't be pressed awkwardly against him. Even this position should've been awkward, but somehow, it never was. He sat with his legs on either side of her own, his hands busy in her hair as he sleeked it with the glorious-smelling soap he'd poured from a small earthenware jar.

A sudden stab in her heart, an icy fear engendered by this moment of care, of affection.

"Do you think we're trapped, Alexander?" she murmured. "Bound to repeat patterns of mistakes?"

"No, of course not."

Such a blunt answer. Such an Alexander answer. "So you believe immortality makes us wiser?"

"Not all of us. Some are imbeciles no matter how long they live. Case in point: Aegaeon."

She laughed, the joy unexpected. "Do you remember Rinri? He was far too honest and stalwart a being to ever be called an imbecile, but can you imagine him as a wise elder?"

He groaned at her mention of the angel who'd been in her training group when she first joined a martial squadron. "I have nothing against Rinri. He wasn't the least bit evil. He was also excellent brawn and loyal to his cause. But if that man had any thoughts unrelated to weapons, fighting, or carnality, I will eat my own foot with that atrocity of a sauce you once created."

Shoulders shaking, she fell back against him, relaxing fully at last. "It wasn't that bad."

"Zani, it tasted of charcoal with a hint of basil."

She snorted laughter at the scarily accurate description. "Do you know what happened to Rinri?" He might not have been the most scintillating conversationalist, but he'd also never intentionally harmed anyone aside from in battle. Not many could make that claim.

When Alexander went quiet, she knew. "Rinri is dead." Sadness spread through her for the amiable battle-obsessed boy she'd once known. "How?"

"He had a good life," Alexander told her as he picked up a pitcher full of cool clean water. "He fathered seventeen children."

Zanaya's mouth dropped open. "What?!"

Alexander tapped her shoulder to let her know he was about to pour the water over her head and she closed both eyes and mouth until he was done washing the soap out of her hair.

Afterward, he pulled her back against him. "I'll tell you about Rinri's feats of fertility if you lie here and let me work this cream into your hair that Lemei keeps telling me will make mine soft and glowing. I've pointed it out to her on multiple occasions that I am a general and an archangel. I do not need for my hair to be that of a pampered courtier's."

Her smile spread again. "Of course Lemei is part of your court. She probably gave her notice to her previous employer the instant you woke." The vampire *adored* Alexander and Osiris in a warmly maternal way.

"She had retired in my absence," Alexander said, which

told Zanaya that Osiris, too, must've gone into Sleep at some point in the past—else Lemei would've stayed on with him.

"Alas," Alexander continued, "she now has a new lease of life and runs my household with an iron fist."

Dark words, but she caught the love that underlay each one. Zanaya's smile creased her cheeks now. Part of why she'd always loved Alexander was that while he might be arrogant with his peers, he was never anything less than kind with those who had far less power or standing. He allowed himself to be lovingly bullied by Lemei and other house-keepers, ate ridiculous dishes so his chefs wouldn't have their feelings hurt, and, in times of peace, always held large feasts for all his staff.

It was why his people so adored him. Not that a single one of them would brag of any of his acts of kindness to others. Oh no, they were utterly invested in maintaining the pitiless image of their archangel. "I'm also a general," she pointed out in faux outrage. "Do you say my hair needs to be soft and to glow?"

He groaned and pressed a kiss to her shoulder, one big hand cupping her upper arm. "You are a star, Zani. You glow clad in nothing but dirt and sweat."

"Such charm you have, lover." But she relented. "Come, put this magical cream in my hair and tell me of Rinri. Did he die in battle at least? That was his most ardent wish."

"Indeed," Alexander confirmed. "During a confrontation between archangels. But before that . . . well, it turned out Rinri did have one other talent: fathering children on one and many a lover."

Then, as she lay there against him, her eyes closed as he massaged her scalp with knowing hands, he told her of Rinri's life, and that astonishing count of children. "Is it a record, do you think?" she asked at the end, her voice a touch lan-guid. "With angelic fertility being so low in general, it surely must be."

"Yes," Alexander said. "As far as I know, he fathered more children than any other angel in our history."

"Well, I can say he would've gone into death with a smile on his face after leaving a legacy such as that." She lifted an imaginary glass. "To Rinri. May you rest in peace, my friend."

"To Rinri," Alexander echoed, his voice resonant and beautiful.

He told her more things she'd missed in the time of her Sleep, and she told him of things he'd missed because they hadn't spoken for some time before she went into that Sleep. "Regardless of being wrenched forcefully from my rest," she said, "I feel so much stronger than when I went into that rest, so much more present. I'll never be sorry for Sleeping."

His arms, which he'd placed around her under the water, tightened.

"No, lover," she murmured. "Not even for you would I chance madness. It takes far too many of our old ones." As if the mind was only built to run so long without stopping, it began to decay and fracture the longer it was in continuous use.

"I did go into Sleep some four centuries ago," he told her, answering the question she hadn't been able to bear to ask. "My rest was foreshortened by the Cascade." A pause, then, "Have I told you about Naasir?"

Frowning, she went to push him about his decision to Sleep, find out what had precipitated it, but something in his voice made her hesitate. Pain, *such* pain. "Who is Naasir?" she said instead.

"Osiris's greatest achievement." His voice caught, hitched. "I had to execute him, Zani. More than half a millennium ago, I had to kill my brother because if I did not, he would've become an ever-greater monster—one who had no awareness of his evil."

A single hot splash against her shoulder.

It stabbed her more deeply than any blade. Alexander, she knew without asking, hadn't trusted his grief to anyone else in all the centuries since his brother's death. Because Alexander simply wasn't this man when he wasn't with Zanaya.

It was only with her that he gave himself permission to be a little softer, a little gentler.

Wrapping her arms around the ones he had around her, she didn't stay silent. Another might have, thinking he would tell her the entirety of this bleak piece of his history in his own time. But she knew the general—the fact he'd brought it up meant he wanted to tell her . . . had kept it locked up inside him until this instant. Because only with Zanaya could he rip his heart open.

Her own heart cracked open.

She couldn't bear it when he was wounded, wanted to kill anyone who'd dared hurt him. That it had been Osiris who'd inflicted this mortal wound . . . Her eyes went hot, threatened to leak, but today she had to be the one who held him. So she swallowed her tears and turned to press her lips to his upper arm.

"Tell me, lover," she murmured. "Tell me why your brother left you with no other choice." Because if he had, Alexander would've taken that other choice. He'd *loved* Osiris, looked up to him as a younger sib, even though he'd long moved past Osiris in emotional maturity.

Alexander took a deep shuddering breath. "I was tired, Zani." Rough words. "Tired enough that your words about fading in dying flickers had come to haunt me." His arms tightened, as if holding on to her as a talisman against pain. "But by then, I *couldn't* go into Sleep. A terrible gnawing worry kept me awake and in the world."

And then he fell hundreds of years into the past, taking her with him . . . until he stood speaking to Titus on a mountaintop in his friend's territory.

"My brother is no longer who he once was," Alexander said to Titus. The young archangel and child of his comrade-in-arms and most trusted general, Avelina, had somehow become his friend though they were separated by eons of life.

Big and brash and honest, Titus had filled a little of the void left behind by Nadiel's death, Avelina's decision to Sleep, and Caliane's descent into madness and subsequent vanishing. Nothing would ever fill the gaping hole that was the absence of his Zani, but he'd learned to live with that, had even come to see the wisdom of her actions.

Had she remained in the world, they might well have killed each other by now, their spiral of love and anger a toxic stew. She'd set him free to be a better man, a better archangel—until today he was known as wise, an Ancient who'd even acted the peacemaker. That didn't mean he wasn't yet half-angry and half-in love with her. As he'd accepted the wisdom of her choice, he'd accepted that she'd be forever a part of the tapestry of his existence—even should they never meet again.

Today, he stood with Titus on a flourishing green mountaintop, the wild monkeys chattering in the trees and the humid breeze carrying across the myriad scents of this land full of flora and fauna unseen anywhere else on the planet. As a young angel, Alexander had often overflown this region, racing the cheetah below and keeping company with the winged creatures, but he felt too old for such games now, his bones heavy and his heart on the edge of exhaustion.

Titus was often accused of not having a subtle bone in his body, but today, he said, "This is why you won't Sleep, even though you know it's past time."

Alexander narrowed his eyes at the young pup who'd never held back his words—which was the very reason why he was Alexander's close friend. "Are you calling me old, you young pipsqueak?"

Throwing back his head, Titus laughed that booming laugh that made him such a favorite among all. It was big and warm and beguiled all bystanders to laugh with him. Even Alexander, worry a heavy stone crushing his ribcage, couldn't help the upward tug of his lips.

Titus bumped his shoulder. "I told you I saw a white hair in your golden locks."

"Careful, child," Alexander said in his most pompous tone, and Titus laughed again.

Afterward, as they walked the plateau, the other man said, "You've never really talked much about Osiris."

"No, I suppose I haven't. Not since you've known me." Titus, after all, hadn't yet completed even his third millennium of life. "I adored him as a boy, looked up to him in every way, was so proud of his discoveries, his inventions." Osiris was responsible for many innovations that would go down in angelic history.

"I hear you speak only of the past, my friend," Titus said, his breastplate gleaming in the morning sunlight. "What has changed that you no longer talk of your sibling with pride?"

Alexander stared out into the distance, at the sprawling forests teeming with life. He'd seen a leopard prowling with feline confidence as they overflew the green, the creature halting to look up at the angels with a gaze that said it would take them down given half the chance.

Its confidence had memory piercing through him—of an archangel whose laughter made him a younger man, and who had eyes that held the silvery light of the stars. Oh, how Zanaya had adored her haughty felines and loyal hounds, spoiled one and all. She'd even made friends with the raucous birds on Osiris's island.

What would she say about his brother now?

"Osiris," he explained to Titus, "began his life working with natural elements—and that work, I understood." Alexander's own power was connected to the earth, most specifically to metal. "After a time, he began to move into plants, then small organisms such as those that live in the oceans."

Alexander hadn't comprehended that work as well, but he'd appreciated it. It was Osiris who'd pioneered the bioluminescent moss that many vampires and even mortals used in underground structures to safely light their way.

While it might not be an innovation that was directly useful to angelkind—for most angels didn't enjoy being underground—you couldn't say that it hadn't been of great benefit to their kind. Their vampiric and mortal servants could now safely use cellars and the like without having to go in with fiery torches or flickering candles.

"I," he continued, "was a touch disturbed when Osiris began to experiment with larger oceanic organisms, but he made the point that his work wasn't much different from hunting for food, and from all I saw, he did nothing that could be considered abhorrent. He did indeed do much the same as the fisherman who stabs his prey with a spear—only instead of eating his kill, he'd dissect it to learn everything of it, piece by piece."

Alexander's stomach had churned at the idea of it, but Osiris was so logical and methodical about the entire operation that his own reaction had felt naïve, devoid of maturity. "He never took more than what he needed and often far less than what I'd have on my own table as food.

"It would've been hypocritical to argue against his actions simply because I didn't appreciate his scholarship. And, in the end, his anatomical drawings of sea creatures became—and still are—a staple resource for other scientists and scholars."

"So what is it that now causes you to worry so much that it's a rain shadow hovering constantly above your head?"

"That's the thing, Titus. I don't know." Alexander thrust one hand through his hair. "Osiris has turned secretive over the years. Distancing himself from his colleagues, his friends, and yes, his brother. A half-moon ago, I suddenly realized that I no longer know where he lives and works—and haven't known for some time."

That keeping track of his brother had slipped his mind was yet another indication that he should be Sleeping; the general he'd been would've *never* made a tactical error so significant. "I went first to the large laboratory he set up in a cold area of my lands—but it had been cleaned up and shuttered, long enough ago that cobwebs matted the doors and there was significant snow damage to the buildings."

"You had no word of his departure from your people?"

"The location was isolated deep in the mountains—and I'd given Osiris that land. He was my brother. I never treated him as someone to be watched by my forces."

"Yes, of course. I would be the same with my sisters."

"The only things I found in the laboratory were a few of his meldings." Echoes of the little game his brother had used to play for the amusement and wonder of all. "A beaker melded to a table so it looks to be on the brink of falling, a bookshelf melded to the ceiling and shaped so it seems to undulate, a book melded to a knife so that the pages flow like liquid down the metal." That last had been astonishing, a true piece of art.

"I've never known any other angel who could do such a thing," Titus said.

"Yes, it's a unique gift. Osiris believes he gained it during a past Cascade." Alexander had taken the book-and-knife meld to his home, lest it be damaged by the elements. "It struck me that perhaps he'd become tired of the cold after so many years and decamped to his tropical island, so I went to visit him there—only to find it empty, with no signs of recent habitation."

The tropical vegetation had taken over the laboratory, while an entire banana palm had grown through the broken roof of what had once been Osiris's residence. Vines hung and crept everywhere, and he'd heard the chirps of birds from inside the buildings of the compound. Huge flowers that were clearly strange and lovely hybrids had bloomed with abandon, their scent cloying.

His brother's work, Alexander had understood, disturbed on a level he couldn't articulate.

"You think he is doing something he doesn't want you to see?" Titus frowned, lines furrowing his forehead. "Not just being secretive as scholars at times are with their most precious projects?"

Alexander nodded. "I know so. For while he'd cleaned up the laboratory in my lands, I saw disturbing remains in his abandoned island laboratory." Tiny insects of revulsion crawled over him. "Large animal bones lying near chains—as if he'd confined the creatures inside his dark and windowless workspace. Other bones showed signs of malnutrition, and of burns unnatural—not akin to bones in a burn pile, but as if the animal's limb had been amputated then cauterized."

He'd seen other things, too. Pieces of leather that had felt disconcertingly like mortal or immortal skin, a forgotten stone tablet with the carved image of a dissected angelic body, even its wing bones exposed . . . and worst of all, a pile of bones that had looked at first glance like those of mortal children. Thankfully, they'd proved to be of small monkeys, but the sheer number of them . . .

What use did Osiris have for so many of the chattering, mischievous creatures?

"My territory has many predators," Titus murmured, looking out over the landscape below, "but very few of those predators play with their prey. Such cruelty is a thing of angels, vampires, and mortals." His jaw was tight. "What help do you need to find answers, my friend?"

"I can't speak of this to others of the Cadre. I wouldn't condemn Osiris for simply being secretive. Many with his intelligence and quirks are so. And he may have a reasonable explanation that we aren't scholarly enough to divine."

Titus nodded. "Less friendly archangels might also see your concern as a weakness to be exploited."

"Yes. I need to find him before anyone else realizes that my brother has vanished—and I need to ensure that he isn't doing anything which shouldn't be done."

Tension locking his shoulders, he added, "That upstart, Raphael, has been asking me about my brother, saying he's heard troubling rumors." Alexander had no knowledge of those rumors and hadn't wanted to show his hand by asking Raphael for clarification. Which left only one option. "I need to find Osiris before Raphael beats me to it."

Titus raised an eyebrow. "You don't trust young Rafe?"

"He might be blood of Caliane and Nadiel, but he's a

pup," Alexander muttered. "Not even a thousand years old. This is a matter of adults and of family."

Titus said nothing on that point, both of them aware that Titus and Alexander were family of the heart. "I'll put my ear to the ground," Titus said instead, "and instruct my spymaster to do the same. Ozias would cut out her heart before betraying me, so your brother's location will be kept secret by her should she discover it."

In the end, however, it was Callie's upstart pup who discovered Osiris's location.

24

Raphael gave Alexander the location of Osiris's new residence, but refused to reveal the source of his knowledge. That would've irritated Alexander had this not been a matter of urgency. Because the rumors picked up by Raphael's people said that Osiris was experimenting not on animals, but on mortal *children*.

"No." Alexander sliced out a hand, haunted by the memory of that pile of monkey bones. "He wouldn't. My brother isn't evil. He wouldn't harm a *child*." Not the man who'd been so warm and generous and kind to his much younger sibling.

To his surprise, Raphael nodded. "I can't believe it either." The pup's eyes were as searingly blue as his mother's, the color of a high mountain sky at noon.

A wave of longing swept over Alexander at the sight. Oh what he'd do for Caliane's calm advice right now. But Callie had gone quite mad, and now Slept in a place unknown to everyone, even her son.

A son whose body she'd shattered to pieces when he'd

tried to confront her. That same woman had once almost cried because her "baby boy" had a skinned knee. People changed in dark and terrible ways.

The knowledge was a leaden weight on Alexander's wings.

"No matter our belief in him, we must investigate these rumors," Raphael added. "*Something* has so badly scared mortals in a region adjacent to his residence that they've abandoned long-settled villages. Those who can be coaxed to speak whisper of a monster that comes in the night and steals their children. It may be that Osiris has inadvertently loosed a weapon on the populace."

Alexander almost shuddered in relief. An out-of-control weapon was still a better outcome than his brother murdering children. And though he didn't want anyone in his family business, he gave a curt nod. He couldn't cut Raphael out of this when he had done the honorable thing and come to him rather than flying straight to Osiris. "You're sure all trails lead back to the land of snow and ice?"

"Yes. The affected villages are on the tip of the continent closest to it. A long journey by ship, but not for an angel on the wing."

What Raphael didn't say but Alexander heard loud and clear was that it wouldn't be a difficult flight for an angel of Osiris's age and strength *even if that angel were carrying a mortal child.*

"We go right now." Alexander couldn't stand to be in limbo, not with an accusation so horrific hovering above their heads. "I need no preparation. You may follow if you need more time."

"No. Even if the lost children have nothing to do with Osiris, we must uncover what's happening. Though should we need to fly to the villages, we'll have to gain agreement from Elijah. It's his territory, and the only reason he doesn't already know about the losses is because the area is so isolated."

"Why do you know?" Alexander snapped.

"I have a friend who likes to walk trails hard and isolated—he sees and hears much," was the cool response, one that told Alexander absolutely nothing. Raphael's informant could've been anyone, vampire, angel, or mortal.

Not that it mattered. What mattered was finding Osiris.

So it was that Alexander flew out, not quite side by side with Caliane's son.

He'd left his own son in charge of his territory. While Rohan was officially his weapons-master, in actuality he'd become Alexander's temporary second over the past decade. It wasn't a case of nepotism—Alexander didn't believe in raising blood over those with more ability. Rohan had earned every one of his positions and promotions.

Alexander's son was very, very good at what he did.

So good that other members of the Cadre had tried to poach him as their weapons-master, and four centuries earlier, Rohan had taken one of those offers. Because he was Alexander's son, full of warrior pride, and he wouldn't have it said that his title was nothing but a father's gift.

When he'd returned to Alexander's court at last, angel-kind knew him not as Rohan, son of Alexander, but as Rohan, weapons-master to an archangel. Alexander's pride in his son was immeasurable. The boy was all he could've ever wanted him to be, the best surprise of Alexander's life.

He hadn't loved Rohan's mother, wasn't sure he even had the capacity for such love anymore, and their union had been brief. When she'd come to him with news of a child, it had been the shock of a lifetime.

A beautiful shock.

"I wish to come with you, Father," Rohan had said when Alexander gave him a short debrief prior to leaving with Raphael. "You need people you can trust around you."

"This is no ambush, son. Raphael isn't built that way."

Callie's boy reminded Alexander of himself—perhaps the very reason why he was so irritated by the pup. "And I need you here. I have no idea what I'll find at my brother's new home, or how long I'll be absent. We can't both be away from the court."

Rohan, his skin a burnished light brown, the same shade as his mother's, and his eyes darkest ebony, his wings pale silver that merged into charcoal gray, had acquiesced at last. "I hope the rumors prove to be greatly exaggerated. Scary stories told by frightened mortals. Does the area not have wild cats of various kinds? Perhaps it is those cats that are hunting their children. The creatures have been known to become daring against mortals."

Alexander hoped against hope that his son was right, but the closer they got to the icy heart of Osiris's new home, the more his blood began to chill. His brother had chosen a place so remote that even angelkind rarely passed this way. It wasn't on any of their usual flight paths, and even had it been, Osiris's home was positioned in the shadow of a huge over-hang. That overhang would protect it from the snow and any resulting avalanches, but it also provided a shield against fly-ers above.

For Raphael to find this . . . well, Caliane's son had done her proud.

"The residence is smaller than I expected," he said after the two of them landed silently in the falling snow.

Snowflakes catching on the midnight hue of his lashes, Raphael said, "To have room for a laboratory, it must con-tinue underground. Makes sense in this environment."

Alexander's mind stirred, disgorging a long-forgotten conversation about Osiris's need for a colder place to do his work. The stealth with which Osiris had abandoned just such a space in Alexander's own territory was now fuel to the cold fire in his gut. Why set up in this desolate place when he'd already had safe access to an environment of constant ice and cold?

Alexander also didn't like the idea of his brother hiding in the earth. That wasn't the natural inclination of their kind. They belonged to the air and to the sky. But Osiris had chosen this remote and cold nothingness for a reason.

Dead things could be kept from rotting by such bitter cold.

Alexander's stomach lurched, a chill nausea threatening to take hold. "Let's go." He strode ahead.

Raphael didn't gainsay his right to be the one to confront Osiris.

Callie's boy had manners at least.

When he went to push open the door, however, it proved locked. The nausea turned into scalding bile. Because what need did Osiris have to lock a door in this place so far from any other hint of civilization that it was a sprawl of white nothingness?

Unable to speak past the fear that had a stranglehold around his throat, he used a pulse of archangelic power to break the lock.

He expected heat when he walked through the open door, but the inside of the home proved as frigid as the outside. "This isn't right."

Angels were built to survive extreme cold, but that didn't mean it was comfortable. He and Raphael were both dressed in heavy leathers, the insides lined to insulate against a landscape so painfully inhospitable.

Osiris had also lived in the tropics for so long because he didn't enjoy colder climes. Alexander could still remember how his brother had groaned at the temperature when they'd been scouting a location for him to set up a laboratory in Alexander's lands. Osiris's dislike of snow and ice was also why he'd so rarely visited the Refuge after Alexander was no longer a child, far preferring that Alexander come to him and a place "where our nether regions won't freeze off, brother-mine."

His older brother's laughter a ghostly echo in his head, he took in the icicles that dripped off the shelving across the way, the layer of fine ice that glittered in patches on the floor.

Having entered after him, Raphael crouched down to touch

his finger to the ice. "It hasn't set solidly." Once back upright, he placed a booted foot on the ice and cracks spread outward, the thin shell fracturing to release a trickle of liquid. "This isn't like the icicles—which I'm guessing formed out of trapped condensation. Water spilled here, began to freeze."

Alexander pointed out a metal pitcher that lay overturned in the corner. "There."

"There's no other sign of trouble." Raphael turned slowly around, taking in the entire space. "The books are still on the shelves, and look there—a plate of undisturbed food on the table from which the pitcher fell."

"Knowing my brother, he was distracted by an experiment or a sudden thought." Alexander's nausea began to recede, to be replaced by a surge of amused affection. For this was just like Osiris. "He's allowed the fire to go out, ignored the fallen pitcher in his rush to get to his lab."

When he strode to the heavy iron oven and opened up the door, he saw a few embers, the heat the barest kiss on his skin. Nothing enough to hold back the atmosphere of this land of snow and ice so desolate that even angels gave it a wide berth.

"Osiris must have other means of heating his home." Alexander shut the oven door. "This oven would barely make a dent." That was when he spotted the explosion of pipes that emerged from the back of the oven and realized his error. "Water ducts," he said. "They must run throughout this residence. The oven might be enough once the system is in stable operation."

Raphael wasn't listening to him; he was staring at a part of the far wall that appeared to have been damaged to reveal stone building blocks on the other side. As Alexander watched, Raphael put his hand on the stone, frowned.

"What is it, Rafe?" he said, falling back on the name he'd once called the boy—back when Nadiel was alive and Caliane in no danger of madness.

Back then, Raphael had been the cherished child of a beloved friend.

"I don't know." Lifting his hand from the stone, Raphael stared at it, then curled his fingers inward. "It disturbs me for some reason."

Despite his increasing belief that Osiris was just being Osiris, Alexander didn't disregard the young angel's words; the boy might be arrogant but he was the son of two archangels, his blood formed of violent power.

At this moment, however, Alexander didn't have time to look at walls. "Osiris must be downstairs." He'd spotted stairs to the right, just beyond what appeared to be his brother's kitchen and dining area.

He went that way, Raphael next to him. They looked down into a windowless stairwell to see ice dripping from the banister, the scene lit by the greenish glow of bioluminescent moss that was dead in large patches. "The cold," Alexander said. "The moss isn't designed to survive it." But enough remained to light the stairs.

No water, no ice on those stairs, but neither was there any extra space to maneuver. Alexander glanced around, frowned. "The interior of this home isn't as large as it should be if we measure by the size of the external structure."

"As if there's space hidden all around." Raphael turned those familiar eyes toward the wall next to them. "But what I touched behind the wood paneling was stone. Would your brother build stone tunnels around his home?"

"It would mean an enormous expenditure of power for no discernible reason," Alexander muttered. "It's not as if he needs to hide things from intruders—aside from Osiris, we're likely the first angels who've ever set foot here."

"Do you believe he built this place with his own hands?"

"Yes. Osiris has many gifts, many strengths—and he's patient." To keep his home a true secret, he'd have ferried every single piece of building material here piece by careful piece. "I'll go first."

Again, Raphael didn't attempt to stop him. Because this was a matter of family.

He heard the susurration of the other angel's wings as he followed, but all else was silent . . . until just before he was about to turn the corner into the final part of the stairs—which widened out enough to permit them to stand side by side.

Do you hear it? he said mind-to-mind to Raphael, for unsurprisingly, the child of two archangels had exhibited the ability to communicate in this fashion far too young.

Alexander rarely initiated mental contact with those outside his inner court, but it was easy with Raphael—because Alexander had spoken to the boy before this way, in the years after Caliane's disappearance. Sharine, who had always been Callie's closest friend, had taken the lead in helping Raphael recover from the catastrophic injuries his mad mother had inflicted on the son Alexander knew was a piece of her heart, but Alexander had been there in the shadows.

He'd made sure no one dared ostracize or ill-treat Caliane's boy—because there were those in angelkind who'd begun to whisper that surely the boy would soon end up mad, what with both his parents having fallen to that affliction.

He wondered if Raphael remembered. The talkative child who'd once ridden on his shoulders as Alexander walked with Callie and Nadiel had been . . . damaged by his mother's actions, and Alexander wasn't sure he'd been truly *present* for much of the immediate aftermath.

Not that it mattered.

While Alexander liked Raphael—upstart pup or not—he'd done what he had for Callie, the friend who'd stood by him through eternity. The friend who'd allowed him to scream out his rage and his loss when his Zani went into Sleep.

Small sounds, Raphael said now. *Movement.*

Yes, but not of an adult angel. These movements were smaller, almost . . . secretive. *It's likely an animal.*

You're probably right.

No more words, the two of them moving silently down to the wider section of the stairs . . . and then they walked into a large laboratory lit by multiple flickering lanterns. The oil was about to run out, Alexander thought as Raphael scanned the right half of the room, Alexander the left.

They both saw Osiris at the same time.

25

Alexander's brother lay flat on his back on the floor, his arms and legs splayed . . . and his face a clawed-out mask of blood. Flickering shadows danced over the nightmare of him. His throat was gone, torn to pieces until it was near to a decapitation. But that wasn't the most horrifying thing.

A small, *small* mortal boy, naked but for the blood that coated the warm dark of his skin, crouched on Osiris's left wing, over the torn-open cavity of his chest. His shaggy hair was a shock of silver, striking in its purity of color. The boy held something dark and wet in his tiny hands, was taking quick ravenous bites of it.

The child is eating my brother's liver. The mental words came out cold with shock, with the impossibility of what he was seeing.

How could this tiny child have ended Osiris?

Then a gurgle sounded from the angel on the floor and Osiris began to rise, his fisted hand moving with brute intent, as if to punch the boy.

A bolt of power—Raphael's power—slammed into Osiris,

shoving him back down before he could make contact with the child. Alexander made no move to stop Raphael. All the other man had done was protect a child. Angels didn't hit the young.

Why had Osiris, this big brother who had always shielded the child Alexander had been, even tried such an act?

Brother. Osiris's mental voice, shaky and weak. *Help me.*

At the same time, the child whipped his head toward Raphael and Alexander. A growling sound emerged from deep in his chest. Even as Alexander stared, trying to make sense of this situation, a kind of . . . ripple shadowed the child's skin. Stripes. Like a tiger's. And for a moment, the boy was a tiger given human form, his eyes a silver as pure as Alexander's own but far more feral.

Hissing when Raphael moved toward him, the boy scuttled back, leaving tiny footprints in blood on Osiris's wing, and dropping his prize of Osiris's liver on his brother's blood-splattered feathers. Those silver eyes darted toward Raphael, then at the liver, back again. The child was trying to calculate if he could get to it before Raphael.

A starving creature ready to fight for his food even against a bigger predator.

Alexander's brain finally processed how the boy's bones pushed against his skin, how his cheeks were hollowed out. The child needed to eat. Before he could say anything about getting food from the kitchen, Raphael crouched down, picked up the piece of liver . . . and held it out to the child.

Alexander knew he should intervene, should kill Raphael for treating Osiris with such callous disregard, but he had the sick feeling that his brother owed this child his blood and his flesh. So he stood in silence as the child weighed up Raphael's offer before racing forward with inhuman speed to grab the offering; he then scuttled to hide in the shadows under a large table to gobble it down.

Raphael looked over at Alexander as Alexander came down at his brother's right side, his gut a wrench of agony. "I believe," Raphael murmured, "the child has already taken bites of Osiris's heart." It was a low murmur, the kind a person used if they didn't want to startle a wild animal. "He has near-archangelic speed."

Silver eyes glinted at Alexander from under the table, the child's face once more a striped ripple that wasn't quite human. "Brother," he said to Osiris, and took his hand, "what have you done?"

Osiris replied mind-to-mind. *I succeeded, Alexander! I have fulfilled the promise of my melding gift! I have made a chimera!* Such excitement in eyes that were surrounded by dried blood and crusted viscera. The orbs had been clawed out, Alexander realized, then regenerated. But there was nothing of pain in Osiris's tone, only joy, such joy. *My name will be known throughout angelkind! Will be written forever in our history.*

Alexander glanced once more at the tiny starved child who behaved more like an animal, and felt his heart tear in two. *How did you do it? What was the cost?*

It was worth it, brother-mine! I have made a new creature! A new being! A stable meld of a tiger and a mortal!

As Alexander fought the tears that burned his irises, he saw Raphael rise and turn to explore the rest of the laboratory. The child's eyes glinted and then he was scrabbling out of his chosen hiding spot to tag along behind Raphael. Jumping up on tables with the ease of a cat, the boy prowled along with curious eyes.

Leaving behind a pinkish-red trail of footprints and handprints.

The child was astonishing and wild and he *should not have existed*. "A mortal is not meant to be a tiger and a tiger is not meant to be a mortal," he said to his brother, his voice like gravel.

I see two dead wolves in a large cage to the left, Raphael told him at the same time. *From the stiffness of their bodies, they died some time ago. They appear to have been torn apart by claws. Old blood coats the inside of the cage.*

Alexander tried not to think of the boy shut inside the

cage with wolves, but his brain refused to stop making the connection. Why would Osiris do such an ugly thing?

The child has fangs. Raphael's grim voice in his mind again, the other angel standing close to the far wall with the feral child up on a shelf above him. That extraordinary silver hair hung around the boy's face as he leaned out to see what Raphael was doing.

Did you Make him, brother? That would be an even worse abomination. Children weren't meant to be turned into vampires. *Ever.* It was a crime so grave that the only and irrevocable punishment was death.

Mortals were firefly flickers in an immortal world, but children were still children, to be protected and loved. Never to be abused and broken.

No, Osiris said, but he wouldn't hold Alexander's gaze. *I simply used a droplet or two of the Making toxin as part of the experiment.* His hand spasmed on Alexander as he mentioned the dangerous toxin that built up in angelic bodies, and could only be purged into a mortal—thus leading to the creation of vampires.

Osiris continued to speak into Alexander's mind. *It has merged with his blood.* Feverish excitement, a stunned and bright joy. *He's not angel, mortal, animal, or vampire. He's a true chimera.* Bloody coughing as the sound of Raphael tearing the back wall apart filled the air. *Help me, Alexander . . . little sib.*

"I will," Alexander said gently. "I will, Osiris."

A growling sound.

He glanced up to find the child staring at Raphael with fangs bared as Raphael stood in front of a section of the back wall that he'd torn away to reveal what lay beyond. Stone bricks. The odd thing was that each brick was a unique shape—as if the stone had been worked by angelic power.

"What lies here?" Raphael asked the child, as if the feral boy could understand.

Osiris's eyes shifted again, and Alexander *knew.* His already broken heart suffered a death blow. Still, he had to be sure beyond any doubt. "Where did you bury the other children? The other wild creatures? The failed chimeras?"

Nothing from his brother.

But Alexander could read Osiris's bloody face. *They are coffins, Raphael. My brother has surrounded himself with the bodies of all those children and animals he tortured.* Tears rolled down his face, his wings slumped to the floor.

Alexander, it hurts. Osiris sucked in a harsh gasp of air. *Please take me from this cold place so I can heal.*

Don't worry, brother. Alexander turned his attention to Raphael. *Take the boy from here, Rafe.*

The younger angel didn't argue. Neither did he try to grab the wild chimera. Instead, he just held out his arms, his hands streaked with dust from tearing apart the wall—and dried blood from when he'd picked up the piece of Osiris's liver.

The boy watched him with suspicious silver eyes . . . before jumping straight into his arms and clinging to him with sharp claws. Not wincing even though Alexander could see that those claws had sliced right through his leathers, Raphael strode out without a backward look.

The chimera hissed and growled at Osiris as they passed, even swiping out a small—so *small*—clawed hand, as if he'd tear off even more pieces of his tormentor.

Where is he taking him? He's my creation! Osiris struggled to get up, was too weak.

Don't worry, my brother. All is well. Justice said Osiris should suffer pain and torture for what he'd done, that he should scream as his innocent victims must have, but Alexander couldn't do that to the brother who'd once held his hand and taught him to swim.

Yet he knew Osiris couldn't be permitted to live. It was clear that he believed he'd done a great thing, that angelkind would honor him. And the terrible truth was that some in angelkind would, should his atrocity of a deed become known. Because evil existed in every species, mortal and immortal.

To allow Osiris to live would be to spread a cancer that would lead to more innocent deaths, more devastated parents and small broken bodies.

So he executed his brother with mercy, using a small pulse of archangelic power to still his heart and cut the connection to his brain. Before he did so, however, he went in with delicate grace and took all of Osiris's memories to do with the chimera. That wild and angry boy, should he survive, should he be sane and capable of understanding, would deserve to know his history one day.

He made sure Osiris felt nothing, that he died believing he'd soon be feted as a pioneer of legend. He went in peace . . . but Alexander felt none. In taking his brother's memories, he'd learned a thing even more terrible than what had gone before: Osiris *did* yet keep concubines, but they were nothing akin to clever and witty Livaliana, who'd once been so cherished of Osiris.

Rather, Osiris had specifically targeted women with simple minds and no curiosity, women who'd be happy with fripperies and a life of luxury and not demand anything more from him. He housed all four in a large stronghold far from other angels. Though he visited his lovers but rarely, the four concubines were all angels.

Osiris had attempted to sire an immortal child on whom to experiment.

Alexander crouched there with his dead brother's hand in his, and he cried. For a loss that would haunt him forevermore. Each memory of Osiris tainted, their shared laughter a cruelty now. *Everything* hurt. "I'm sorry," he said, speaking not to his brother but to all the dead children who lay in this place.

He could've sworn a cold whisper passed over his neck.

Looking down at his brother, he knew that Osiris was unwanted here. He was the intruder now. So after one last touch of his brother's hand, Alexander turned Osiris to ash, then used his power to gather all that ash into one of the containers in the laboratory. "He won't hurt you anymore," he promised the small ghosts who stood staring up at him.

An icicle broke to crash onto the floor as he turned to leave and he knew he was unwanted, too. Blood of the man who had done this abomination.

Chest a spiderweb of cracks, he left his brother's victims to their icy peace.

Stepping outside, he looked for Raphael and found him in the distance, the child in his arms and what appeared to be a sack at his feet. The angel had taken off his warm and heavily lined outer jerkin and put the child into it. That it had no sleeves mattered naught—the child was small enough that it enveloped his otherwise naked body. Not that the wild chimera seemed impressed with the item of clothing. He kept biting at the leather, but at least he wasn't trying to escape Raphael's arms.

Raphael had also wrapped the boy's feet in something and was likely using his own angelic body heat to keep him warm. Still, from what Alexander had gleaned from his brother's mind, the child wouldn't last long in this cold. They had to get him out of here. But first—*Raphael, I wish to transfer Osiris's knowledge to you. I shouldn't be the only one who knows the boy's history.* Even archangels could die—or go into Sleep.

I agree to the transfer, Raphael replied. *I also took what appear to be your brother's diaries from the bookshelf upstairs. The child may prefer to read them alongside, or rather than, being told of his history by you or me.*

Alexander saw the awful sense in that . . . even as he felt a dark revulsion against so much as touching the diaries that he knew his brother had hunched over with fanatical passion. Those memories had been vivid imprints in Osiris's mind. Osiris's hand had flowed across the page, the ink threatening to smudge from the speed of his need to put down the thoughts of his breakthrough.

He had called the beginning of his descent into evil "a glorious moment of genius."

Alexander didn't challenge Raphael's right to hold the diaries in trust for the boy. All he said was, *I will complete the memory transfer now.* So it was done, the terrible knowledge now a burden borne by two. *I can't destroy this stronghold,* he said to Caliane's son. *It is a burial ground. But it can't stay here to be discovered. What happened here can't ever be known.* With that, he rose into the air.

In the distance, Raphael did the same, the boy as well as the diaries in his arms.

Then, with Osiris's ashes held in one hand, Alexander used his power to collapse the ground under the stronghold in such a way that it formed a uniform crater that cradled the house. And though no ravens could ever fly in this cold place, a raven's feather fluttered to land atop the roof.

He made sure the stronghold remained undamaged as he dug the crater deeper and deeper. Until at last, the stronghold sat so deep that no one would ever accidentally find it. To further make sure of that, Alexander turned the rock shelf below which it had sheltered into dust.

He erased all other rocky structures in the vicinity, too.

There were no longer any landmarks here for anyone to track, to find. *Go, get the boy warm,* he said to Raphael. *I'll cover the stronghold with the excavated dirt, then watch the snow fall until the landscape is pristine.* And his brother's crimes had been buried. Such was not Alexander's way—he believed in public condemnation, but this secret, if known, could spawn more evil.

So this was how it had to be. The child could be passed off as a disastrously failed Making by an unknown angel, his feral nature a byproduct of growing up in squalid conditions—and his distinctive eyes a result of Alexander using his archangelic power to try to ameliorate the damage done to him.

No one would disbelieve it. What reason would they have to? Chimeras, after all, were creatures of myth, nothing but a flight of the imagination. Alexander could safely predict that not a single person would so much as *think* of that as an option. And if an abused child might be saved, ninety-nine percent of angels would attempt it; in this situation, angel-kind wouldn't find it odd in the least that an archangel had expended his power on a mere mortal.

Still—*Do you agree with my decision, young Rafe?* He couldn't guarantee that his love for his brother wasn't clouding his judgment.

The blue fire in Raphael's eyes was apparent even from this distance. *Yes. This knowledge can't be permitted to spread. It'd find a foothold in the ugliest corners of our society and it would lead to more killing, more evil.*

Alexander wasn't one to ask for anyone's advice, but today he nodded. *The child is under my protection. Make it known.* He had a feeling that wouldn't be necessary for long—the chimera had bonded to Raphael and everyone knew the young pup would be ascending sooner rather than later.

The young angel's power might be termed catastrophic for someone of his age except that Raphael had a dark maturity to him. Watching his mother execute his father, then having that same mother crash him to the earth, smashing him to pieces . . . yes, it had all marked Callie's boy.

Raphael hesitated. *I'm sorry, Alexander. I never had a brother, but I know what it's like to lose family to madness.*

The boy was being kind in ascribing Osiris's decent into horror to madness. The truth, as Alexander had seen in his brother's mind, a truth of which he was certain Raphael was also cognizant, was that his brother had been very aware of the evil of what he was doing—he just hadn't cared. Osiris had thought his twisted version of "scientific progress" more important.

But Alexander just nodded to Raphael, waiting only until the other angel had flown away with the living symbol of Osiris's descent into the abyss before he began to use his power to bury the stronghold. His heart was a block of ice by the time he finished, but he landed and stood in the falling snow to watch the last part of it, the blanket of white that was to be the shroud of this burial ground.

And then, though he didn't understand why, he sent his power up into the sky in a shower of sparks. For all the children as bright and beautiful who'd never had a chance to bloom.

Rising into the air in the aftermath, he left the place where the dead could now rest, and he flew and flew and flew, until he was as far from the burial site as he could go. Then he dropped his brother's ashes into the heart of a volcano. The final ending. Because rather than being known throughout the world, Alexander would ensure that no one spoke his brother's name. As Osiris had erased the names and futures of all those lost children.

Eternity was a long time; Osiris would be forgotten soon enough.

A fitting punishment to a crime so malevolent and cold.

He flew home with another crack in his heart, another scar that took away a piece of the youth he'd once been. He'd become harder over the years—growth was inevitable, and his growth had included eons of being an archangel and holding vast power and with it, the responsibility for countless lives.

But this hardness . . . Would his Zani even know him when she woke from her Sleep? Or would she look at him and see a stranger grim and scarred to the point that he no longer had in him the man she'd loved?

Will you know her?

A whisper from the most pragmatic core of his nature, a question that almost stopped him mid-flight.

Zanaya had Slept for thousands of years while he was changing, growing. It wasn't only possible but likely that they'd be very different people when they met again in some distant future.

His heart cracked in half this time, and the scar that formed over it was rigid, his hardness a thing of unbreakable granite.

26

Zanaya could've never predicted the horror of the story Alexander was about to tell. "Oh, my love," she murmured when he fell silent, her throat thick. "You had no choice."

"How will I face my parents when they wake next?" The words of a son, not an archangel. "They tasked me with taking care of him."

"You did." She squeezed his arms. "You watched over him for an endless span of time. And even at the end, you didn't judge him at first glance, didn't condemn him without evidence."

But Osiris's crime had left Alexander no other option.

Angelkind might not value mortals except for the function they provided when it came time to purge the toxin in angelic blood, but children were sacred regardless of the future length of their lives. Angels had saved countless mortal children over the millennia. A number had even raised orphaned mortal children.

The one thing angels were never *ever* meant to do was harm a child.

"Osiris," she said when Alexander remained silent, "made a choice that left you with only a single one."

He didn't reply. He just held her, this warrior with a huge heart who'd had it torn to pieces by one of the few people he'd ever permitted himself to love. How could he believe that heart was as hard as stone when his grief was as potent today as that cold day in the snow?

But a mere breath later, there was no more time for them to sit still, for her to hold him and let him know it was all right to grieve. Alexander stiffened, his next words that of a general. "Valerius tells me we have reborn pouring out from the direction of the border with Neha."

Zanaya asked no more questions, just moved with warrior speed to ready herself.

They flew out soon afterward, and this time, she wore leathers that fit her surprisingly well for having been made by his staff in the short time since her rising. They were soft, the leather well worked, and she could move with ease.

Good.

Alexander had already given her enough information about reborn that she was prepared for what she might see once they flew past the line formed by the squadron that was keeping the creatures in check.

Strange, but the warriors seemed hesitant to kill, were just driving back the unliving beings with strikes close but not close enough to end them.

Then she saw. "Alexander, they are *children*." Her blood curdled with acidic horror, she couldn't stop looking at the atrocity below, the ugliness of what Lijuan had done so awful that it blew past the memory of even Osiris's terrible crimes.

"Yes." No surprise in Alexander's tone. "I received the information as we were flying here. I should've passed it on to you."

"It is no matter." She understood why he'd stayed silent. The news had been too much coming on top of the memories he'd just relived; he'd needed time to come to terms with it before he could speak of it.

"I was hoping perhaps," Alexander added, his tone harsh in the way it got when he was holding back strong emotion, "that they could be saved."

Zanaya understood his hope. But looking down at those twisted faces, those half-rotting bodies, she knew there could be no saving these blameless souls. "We must offer mercy." The words stuck in her throat; never in all her existence had she raised her hand to a child.

"She has done this on purpose." Alexander's voice was razored steel. "She knows it'll demoralize our troops to have to cut down children."

Such evil, Zanaya thought. "We must go first." Because they were both generals who led from the front.

"Yes." Alexander went to shift forward, paused with his head angled toward the west. "There are more." Harsh words. "Nests bursting open all across my territory. She has seeded the landscape with her malevolence." His jaw worked. "Neha must be facing the same, and possibly even Michaela. We're the three closest archangels to Lijuan. She wants us busy."

"I hope to get to kill her." Zanaya's eyes felt red with fury. "After this, there can be no more arguments about interfering in the territory of another archangel. She *must* die."

Alexander gave a grim nod, then flew ahead.

She allowed him to do so, for this was his territory and he had to strike the first blow. It would break his heart, this she knew. Because Alexander was not Osiris; her general had never hurt a child in his life.

And so began uncountable hours of horror.

They separated at some point, flying with archangelic speed to different areas of the territory. Before they did so, he told her that Michaela was flying to join them. Her territory had thankfully proved free of this spirit-crushing infestation.

Even with three archangels in the mix, however, the battle felt interminable, the dead children given false life accusing them with silent eyes as they fell under their power. Zanaya cried more than once and she wasn't ashamed of it.

There was no shame in crying for the murder of innocence.

Zani?

I'm holding, she told Alexander, knowing exactly why he'd reached out. *How are you?*

Dying piece by piece, was the answer spoken in a voice curt and martial. *But it must be done. They're no longer alive, no matter what Lijuan may have convinced herself.*

She tried to keep that thought uppermost in her mind in the hours that she spent on the fields bathed in the blood of beings who'd had nothing, *nothing* to do with this war. She was as merciful as possible, using her power wherever she could—so that they would die in a single strike, turned to ash before they ever felt even a touch of pain.

Such an act also spared the warriors who fought alongside her . . . at least a little. Because there were too many nests, and the reborn were pitifully small. They ran in different directions. They hid. And so the warriors, their faces streaked with tears and eyes raw, had to use their swords to strike them down.

Each blow broke another warrior's heart.

Zanaya knew from the blank looks on many of their faces that Alexander would be losing a chunk of his angelic army to Sleep as soon as this war was done. As for the vampires, they'd retreat into the isolation that was their version of Sleep.

Loyal and brave of heart they were, but this . . .

Even Alexander's unfaltering and ferocious Wing Brotherhood might not make it through this trial.

Zanaya didn't blame any of them.

Especially after she came within inches of a child who looked so lifelike that it would've been easy to believe that he was a lost mortal babe, caught up in this nightmare. Horrified that might be true, she looked into his mind . . . and heard only a scream of nothingness. No mind. No whisper of what the mortals called a soul.

No . . . there it was, a scant flicker.

Rage gripped her at the realization that some small fragment of personhood had survived. But that fragment was trapped within the horror, its body rotting as this creature fed on living beings. There was no way to save that fragment.

"I am sorry, little one," she said as she lifted her sword.

The child screamed and ran at her, its eyes turning red.

Then it was done, the head separated from the neck, and she had to move on to the next and the next. So many. A never-ending wave of death. *She killed the children of her territory!* Zanaya's fury was a black cloud that roiled with thunder. *That is the only way she could've created so many.*

Yes, was Alexander's grim answer. *I would've noticed if mortal children began to go missing with such regularity inside my own territory.* A terrible heaviness to his words, a reminder of why he was so sensitive to the topic. *These are her people. People she was bound to protect. That is our unspoken covenant with the mortals.*

She agreed with him, though many of their kind wouldn't. Too many believed angelkind above mortals and that was that. The truth was far more complex: angelkind would be a chasm of frothing madness without the mortals. She'd never known the whys of it, but the toxin that built up in angelic bodies could only be purged safely one way: through converting mortals into vampires.

Yet their angelic ancestors had done such a good job of convincing mortals that to become a vampire was a privilege that mortals *applied* for it. If only they knew . . . But would that change anything? Unlikely. Because any mortal uprising could have only one end: death for mortals.

But not this way. *Never* this way.

This act of Lijuan's broke the faith between immortal and mortal in the most fundamental aspect. Zanaya hoped that there was not another archangel in this world who agreed with Lijuan. If there was, she thought as she stood in a field of the dead given terrible life, then she would end them as brutally as they had forced her and Alexander to end these children.

Even archangels had to rest sometime.

None of them—Alexander, Zanaya, or Michaela—had done so for a twenty-four hour period, but aware they'd be useless should they allow themselves to burn out, they returned as one to Alexander's closest fortress when the waves of reborn children came to a lull.

"It's only a small reprieve," Alexander said after using a wet cloth to wipe the sweat, dirt . . . and other things, from his face.

Zanaya nodded her thanks to the small and thin member of his staff who'd run over the towels, and took one for herself.

Michaela did the same, before saying, "Yes. From what we're hearing from the other territories, Lijuan planned this very long-term. There will be multiple waves." She cleaned her face, but even with dirt on it, there was no ignoring her startling beauty. Skin of a smooth and sumptuous brown, eyes of striking green, masses of tumbling hair in rich hues of brown and gold, her wings a shimmering bronze and her body tall but with all the right curves.

Even her leathers were exquisite, a dark red that molded to her frame.

"There was an angel named Gavriel in my time," Zanaya murmured, thinking aloud. "Your skin is a tone or two paler than his, but you have a more feminine version of his face." The angel had been handsome beyond bearing, coveted by many. Zanaya had always thought him rather too pretty, with no edge to him, but from a purely aesthetic perspective, she'd appreciated that he was perfect.

Dropping her hand to the side, Michaela stared at Zanaya. "My father. He vanished after I was well into adulthood. I don't know if he Sleeps or if he is dead."

Zanaya wondered if she was imagining the question in Michaela's voice. "I can't help you there. But he was known to Sleep often."

Michaela glanced at Alexander. "You never told me you knew my father." A bite to her.

Ah, so the child has what the father lacked.

Not acknowledging Zanaya's mental aside, Alexander said, "I didn't know him. He was born in Zanaya's territory, was part of her court."

The slightest widening of Michaela's eyes, the first indication of the woman behind the mask of archangelic beauty and power. "I wasn't aware my father was in the court of an archangel."

"He was very good with the children and was always hopeful for a babe of his own," Zanaya told the other woman, not clarifying that Gavriel had been nowhere near her inner court. Rather, he'd been part of the pretty and frivolous crowd that softened up the harsh planes of a court helmed by a former general. "I liked him a great deal."

An important position after all, is it not, lover? The ones who aren't warriors but who make it worthwhile to go home? With their sweet songs and their colors and their ability to laugh.

Alexander's gaze flicked to hers. *I wouldn't know, Zani.* A tone as tart as a lemon. *I seem to be attracted to unsheathed blades.*

Hiding her laughter took effort . . . and even that urge to laugh lasted but a moment in time. "I'll tell you all I remember of your father," Zanaya promised Michaela, "but I think for now, we must focus on what is happening inside this territory and those of others."

Michaela inclined her head, regal as a queen. But as she'd gone out into the field with Zanaya and Alexander, and had fought with courage, Zanaya thought there was more to this woman than might be visible on the surface. "What news have you had, Alexander?"

"Lijuan's army has reached the heart of Raphael's territory and is a force beyond imagining." Leading them to the fortress's battle command, he went to a large sand table and laid out the facts in brutal clarity. "Keemat received the following information on their numbers while we were in the field."

By now, Zanaya had learned that Senior General Keemat was the most technologically proficient of Alexander's generals and, as such, was in charge of maintaining communication with the courts of archangels around the world.

"That makes no sense." Michaela frowned. "My spymaster was in her territory before the black fog, and saw no indication of a force that size. Forget about the mountains and other terrain where she might've hidden a troop—there's simply no place she could've hidden a group of warriors *this* big."

"Agreed." Zanaya gripped the edge of the sand table. "They'd have needed food, water, latrines, living quarters while they trained. No, it can't be done."

Alexander nodded. "I said the same. Keemat then asked me if I wanted the full nightmare brief while still in the field." His smile was tired. "I decided on a no. There's nothing we can do for New York just now and I wanted all our attention on the situation on the ground. It's terrible enough."

Zanaya wanted to bristle at his high-handedness in making that call, but in truth she'd have made the same one. Sometimes, even a general couldn't handle everything at once. Beside her, Michaela hissed out a breath.

Zanaya expected anger from the younger archangel, but Michaela surprised her again. "That bitch has done this to more of her people." She held Zanaya's and Alexander's gazes in turn. "If she can do this ugly thing to her *children*, she has no moral lines at all, certainly none to stop her from infecting adults."

Alexander stared at her. "You're talking of such astonishing numbers as to defy probability."

"The black fog," Zanaya said, thinking of the wreck of

Antonicus. "Her evil lives within it. She used it in some way to convert her people to these things she calls her reborn."

"We'll find out soon enough. Keemat tells me she has moving images captured in New York."

27

Michaela thrust a hand through her hair, which she'd pulled back in a loose braid at some point but had come mostly undone. "I need to be clean. My gorge roils at being covered in this horror—I'll be quick."

"She's right." Zanaya picked at her own clothing; it stuck to her skin with sweat and dirt and the veil knows what else. "A few minutes won't make a significant difference."

She could see Alexander fighting to gainsay them; he'd always had his little blind spots, had Alexander. They all did. But he gave a curt nod, and they left the command room. A waiting Lemei led Michaela to a guest suite, while Zanaya and Alexander flew up the central core of the fortress until they reached the level with their bathing chambers.

Alexander didn't invite her into his, and she didn't invite him into hers.

War didn't allow for such luxuriant sensation.

So it was that they scrubbed themselves clean as fast as possible and dressed in readiness to meet back in battle command.

Once more, Zanaya found herself pulling on leathers that fit her small and curvy frame to perfection. This time, the color was midnight black, the same shade she'd been known to prefer in her time—and it came with a built-in sheath for her sword. Someone had taken great care to make this for her.

Lover, she said mind-to-mind, *this is a minor thing in the scheme of what's happening right now, but can you ask Lemei for the identity of the people behind my clothing? I wish to thank them.*

A pause. *Organized by Lemei herself. Made by Shahira and her team. And Zani, it's not a minor thing that you care to thank them.*

She smiled as she left her room, felt even more joy when a sleek orange cat wearing a bejeweled collar walked over to her for affection. "Ah, a cat of the court, I see," she murmured, giving the creature its due. "You are most magnificent."

However, the burst of happiness was but fleeting; it faded as she walked into battle command and the reality of war. The command was a cavernous space, but unlike similar rooms in the past, it held not only the sand table and maps on the walls, but plenty of the screens that Zanaya had already witnessed. A number of other devices that flickered with lights and beeped now and then also sat in the room, along with their operators. Several of those operators were thin vampires who would've never passed warrior training.

Wars are not what they were in our time. Alexander's voice in her head, the general having beaten her back.

She wasn't surprised he'd divined the direction of her thoughts. *I wouldn't say so, lover. The smartest of the Cadre always enticed great minds to our courts.* People whose bodies weren't built for the physical act of war, but whose minds could turn the tide. *Don't tell me you've forgotten Ibanaya?*

A startled smile that creased his cheeks just as Michaela entered the room. *I never could beat him in a game of strategy.*

There was no more time for talk of the past then, because Senior General Keemat strode over to state that the "file" was "ready to play." Short and compact with muscle, her sharp eyes a dark brown and her skin a lighter hue of the same shade, her tightly bound hair a rich black, the commander had wings of darkest green threaded with gold.

Now, she led them to the largest screen in the room, then used a small device in her hand to initiate the display of captured memory.

Zanaya had prepared herself and still her breath caught at the unbroken wave of black-eyed evil over Raphael's city. "These fighters aren't like the reborn we've been battling."

"No," Keemat said, and her voice held a lilt that reminded Zanaya of the people of her Nile. "Dmitri—that's Raphael's second, Lady Zanaya—he tells me that these creatures have a certain level of intelligence in comparison to the reborn. Almost as if another mind is controlling their bodies."

"If Lijuan is able to do that with so many . . ." Michaela's voice trailed off, but they all understood the magnitude of the peril she'd left unspoken.

Alexander, his jaw a brutal line, said, "We must assist, but first we have to control the situation here. Elsewise, Lijuan will win by eating us all up in small bites."

Zanaya felt for Raphael's people. To face such an army . . . they would have to fight with courage beyond courage. But Alexander was also correct in his decision; should they leave his territory now, the children would likely spread throughout, creating *more* reborn.

It wouldn't matter then if they won the battle in New York—the war would've been lost to these creatures for they would've spawned and spawned by massacring anyone who came in their path. The entire system of angel-mortal-vampire would collapse without enough mortals left alive to process the toxin.

"Is there more?" Michaela asked.

Keemat briefed them on everything she had, and they talked over that knowledge as they ate with rapid speed. It was just fuel at this point, necessary to power their bodies. Afterward, they decided to put themselves on the field in rotation, so that the squadrons and infantry always had the support of one archangel.

"I'll take the first lone watch," Alexander said. "It's my territory and my responsibility. You two rest until you can take over. We'll fly to Raphael's territory after clearing up these reborn. We can't burn ourselves to the bone, need to be able to make the flight."

Zanaya walked out with him, while Michaela went into a private room set up with a communications system in order to make contact with her own people. The Archangel of Budapest wished to ensure her territory remained unmolested by the reborn threat.

Zanaya waited until she and Alexander were in the entranceway with no one else around before she took his hand; her discreetness wasn't about hiding who they were to each other. Anyone who knew even a piece of their history knew of Zanaya and Alexander.

No, it was about giving him a moment to lay down his head.

So she tugged him to her in silence, and he came in the same quiet to wrap his arms around her. And for a fragment of time, she held him, this general who she had loved all her lifetimes. She kissed him on the jaw when he pulled back and then she watched him put on his warrior skin once more.

"Thank you, my Zani."

He touched his fingers to her lips in a caress familiar and resonant.

Then he was striding out.

She stepped out in time to see him take to the skies, her general who'd have his heart broken over and over again this day. "If mortal hell exists, Lijuan," she whispered, "I condemn you to it."

In the days that followed, however, it was them and others around the world who lived in hell—a hell of Lijuan's creation.

As they had guessed, Alexander's wasn't the only territory Lijuan had infested with reborn children. Neha was dealing with the same—with Caliane's assistance.

Meanwhile Titus and Charisemnon battled a different wave of reborn, while Astaad and Aegaeon fought against a spreading wave of noxious insects that carried infection dangerous to vampires and angels both. The Archangel of the Pacific Isles and the newly risen Ancient had had to burn out multiple islands, razing the abundant green to stone, to contain the rapidly spreading plague.

But nothing was as bad as the situation in New York. That city had held the line thus far, its people refusing to surrender, but they couldn't go on forever.

So Zanaya wasn't surprised when Michaela said, "We *must* go to New York. The situation is dire!"

Alexander fisted a hand on the sand table around which the three of them stood, working on a strategy to funnel large numbers of reborn into a dead-end valley. "I won't abandon my people."

"The situation here is nearly under control," Michaela argued, her hands gripping the edge of the table. "A few more hours and your generals will be in a position to maintain the status quo if nothing else."

Alexander shook his head. "How can I leave this horror to my people to handle?"

"Because we'll lose the world if we don't win New York!"

Michaela and Alexander continued to argue for several more minutes before it became clear that they were at an impasse. "I can't agree," Michaela said at last. "I'm going to fly home, ensure all is well in my territory, then head to New York."

Alexander gave a brusque nod. "You have assisted greatly and for that, I thank you."

Perhaps, in another time, Zanaya wouldn't have liked this woman. From the little chatter she'd picked up about the Archangel of Budapest, she had a reputation for vanity and caprice. Zanaya didn't know if that was true, couldn't know. All she knew was that the Michaela she'd met this waking was a warrior and one with heart. She'd bled for each child she'd had to execute. "I'd fight with you in any battle, Michaela."

A slight narrowing of those striking green eyes, as if the other archangel was suspicious of Zanaya's words, but at last, she nodded. "As I would you, Zanaya." The faintest softening. "After the war is done, I invite you to Budapest. Perhaps you'll do me the honor of sharing stories of my father's youth."

"It'll delight me to do so. Gavriel was a favorite for the joy he brought to my court."

Michaela left then and there.

"Others say that she is vain and too consumed with herself," Zanaya murmured after she was gone. "Be that as it may, beneath all the gloss, she is an archangel true."

Alexander was quiet for a moment. "This is a different Michaela than I've ever before met. There's something . . ." He shook his head. "I can't quite put my finger on it. But whatever it is, I appreciate it. I wouldn't deal well with a capricious and demanding fellow archangel at this time."

When Zanaya's lips curved, he grimaced. "I was never that bad, Zani."

"No, lover. You were worse—in your own way."

"Let us deal with this situation."

So they did, were left sweaty and dirty and a little more emotionally broken in the aftermath, the valley below them filled with ash from the archangelic strikes that had ended the existence of over two hundred child reborn.

Only after it was done did she say, "I didn't interfere with your argument with Michaela because I'm newborn to this world, but lover, I think she's right."

She looked toward the rolling desert sands in the distance. "You don't abandon your people if you go now. They know this—and you have generals of strength and intelligence.

Valerius is an extraordinary battle commander, and Keemat is equally brilliant in her own right. Together, they can finish the cleanup."

Alexander's greatest flaw had always been his stubbornness. Today she saw it in his jaw and his rigid shoulders. "Will you go to New York then, Zani?"

She felt her heart crack. "It's not about us anymore, Alexander." When she raised her hand to touch his cheek, he flinched. "It's about the future of the world. *We* must go. You know this. You do not tarnish your honor by making this choice. It's the only right one."

A glitter in his eyes. "You could always talk me into things."

Dropping her hand, she stepped back. "I talk you into nothing." It came out a lash. "I simply ask you to stop being blinded by your territorial instincts."

Teeth clenched, he shoved a hand through his hair. "What will I return to if I leave them now?"

"What will the future hold if Lijuan kills the only archangel with any immunity to her?"

"A hard blow, Zani." He sighed. "And true. I will fly to Raphael's territory by your side. Let us end Lijuan once and for all."

28

The flight to New York was a grueling one, both of them pushing their bodies to the extreme. Michaela would've reached it while they were yet many hours distant, and Elijah had already been in the city for some time, his territory free of the reborn scourge.

Zanaya could only hope others in the Cadre were in a position to make the same choice. She knew, however, that Charisemnon was no longer an option—from the urgent report that had been blasted out to her and Alexander from Raphael's people, Charisemnon had been exposed as a traitor; he was no ally of the Cadre, was working with Lijuan. The report had been some time past, so she didn't know his current state.

She did know, however, that at least one archangel had died of late. There'd been no way to miss that news—it had come in the form of a thunderous boom of sound that reverberated around the world.

All she could hope was that good had won in this instance, that it was Charisemnon who was dead.

But she hoped the others would join them in New York. Because from the visual reports she'd seen coming out of Raphael's city, it was close to falling.

Is there any word on the others? Will they come to battle Lijuan? Though they flew side by side, she couldn't speak to Alexander aloud. They were moving too fast, utilizing maximum energy.

No word. Alexander's mental voice was grim. *Lijuan did well to seed so much chaos across so many different territories. She has broken us into pieces.*

Zanaya felt her own face tighten. *Were she not evil, she could've been a great leader.*

She did hold somewhat of that position in the Cadre prior to this descent into madness. That was before any Ancients were awake.

Zanaya shrugged. *As we discussed before the world turned to pain and death and sorrow, living a long time doesn't make us wise. It just makes us old and worn-out and—at worst—a threat to the world.*

A long pause from the man she'd loved for all eternity—but not enough to stay forever awake. As he hadn't loved her enough to go into Sleep for a millennium or two.

When he did speak, it was to say, *We'll talk about this after the battle. For now, she is the threat.*

Agreed. They weren't young angels on the cusp of their first love; they were Ancients and archangels, their priorities shaped by the needs of the people they ruled.

They flew on.

Until at last they hit the border of the city called Manhattan where the battle was taking place. Zanaya knew they must've been spotted by sentries long before so it was no surprise to find Raphael waiting for her and Alexander in the sky. But fascinated as she was by this child of Caliane's, she was even more compelled by the angel who hovered at his side.

Elena Deveraux. That was her name.

Zanaya had made it a point to find out that piece of information after she'd learned of this most unusual being. She'd thought to come face-to-face with a callow youth, or perhaps a scared mortal thrust into the world of archangels. But this woman with her hair the hue of white flame and her skin of dark gold, her wings formed of wild fire, was a warrior.

Forget about the fact that Raphael's consort bristled with weapons, like would always recognize like. But Elena Deveraux was something else, too. "A mortal turned angel," Zanaya said, giving voice to her wonderment. "How extraordinary. And such wings."

The newborn angel held Zanaya's gaze without flinching, and Zanaya found herself impressed again. Yes, she could see why this young one was consort to an archangel. She had within her a spark rare and precious.

Elena parted her lips as if to reply, but shifted her gaze toward the water in the distance a heartbeat later. "The sea aurora's back."

Zanaya looked at the ripple of multihued light on darkest blue turned translucent, haunting and lovely, and gave a small smile. "Qin's legend, that is what we called it in child tales. An old one." Older than Alexander or Caliane. "Will he rise, do you think?"

"He does or he doesn't." Alexander's tone came across as harsh but she knew that was because of his worry for the people he'd left behind, for the soldiers fighting a war that was knives into their hearts. "We must prepare for battle."

Giving a curt nod, Raphael and Elena led them to the silver spear of Raphael's sky-piercing Tower, and into what Raphael told them was the war room. The archangel had also done them the courtesy of informing them that the rest of the Cadre was already present. Barring, of course, the enemy, Lijuan, and that accursed traitor Charisemnon—Zanaya's hopes had come true on that point and the latter was no longer among the living. Titus had dispatched him before coming to New York.

Armed with foreknowledge of the Cadre's presence,

Zanaya walked into the war room prepared for the thrum of power in the air, the subtle—and not so subtle—posturing.

Rolling her eyes internally because some archangels would never learn, she kept her silence as she was wont to do when gathering intelligence. Alexander, in contrast, got right into the thick of it.

"I left my territory overrun by reborn to come here." His hand was a fist against the table around which they were gathered, the field of battle laid out on it in intricate detail. "We must end this here and quickly."

The discussion shifted to tactics and numbers and the best approaches. Zanaya was paying attention—she'd long been a general, would die as one—but she couldn't keep from glancing at Raphael and his consort. It intrigued her that Elena Deveraux made no attempt to push her way into the Cadre discussion, not seeking to treat Raphael's power as her own.

Some would see in that a diffidence that betrayed her mortal roots. They'd be fools. This was the confidence of a woman at home in her own skin and her own power. She had no need to rely on that of her lover. *I think I will like you, Elena Deveraux,* Zanaya thought to herself.

"Before we go any further," Raphael said at one point, while that idiot Aegaeon was blustering on like a peacock with its hideous screech, "you should all watch this."

The moving images that played against a screen that had dropped down from the ceiling told the story of the battles that had already taken place on this land . . . and the black evil that Raphael's people had witnessed. Zanaya's gut iced over—because what she was seeing was the impossible: an archangel *feeding* off her wounded, the very people who trusted and looked to her for protection. Instead, Lijuan had left them desiccated husks in her wake.

Feathers turned dusty and colorless, skin become parchment, faces frozen in twisted agony, only hollows where their eyes should've been. A few yet reached out even in death, as if pleading with their archangel to the final breath.

Silence overhung the war room.

Bile rising, she asked the question that needed to be asked. "Can this being she has become be killed?"

Caliane's eyes, so blue as to be gemstones, held infinite sorrow—and taut determination. "All we can do is try. The only other option is to swear allegiance to the goddess she believes herself to be and watch the world drown in death."

Her attention taken up with the resulting discussion of battle tactics, Zanaya was only peripherally aware of Elena slipping out of the war room. Strategy would be critical here. Which led her to say, "We must protect Raphael."

"Lady Zanaya," Raphael began, his features tight.

She sliced out a hand. "This is nothing about you being the youngest of us, Raphael. It's about you being our most powerful weapon. Our task must be to soften her up, yours to deal the death blow."

Zanaya held the young archangel's gaze again, and oddly enough, she could tell the difference between mother and child now. The same piercing hue . . . but Caliane's held a weight of age it was impossible to quantify, while Raphael's . . . carried a spark she couldn't quite put into words.

Perhaps she, too, she thought all at once, had eyes like Caliane. Old eyes.

Shrugging that aside, she kept it to the practicalities. "Bluntly speaking, Raphael, you'll have the most dangerous task of all. You'll likely need to come face-to-face with her to strike a mortal blow."

Alexander nodded from beside her. "Zanaya is right. We can't fight as solo units as we're all used to doing. We must be a team, with a single goal." A glance at her, a million memories in his eyes.

Across from them, Raphael gave a slow nod. "But we also can't have you wasting energy in active protection. Rather, we need to structure our strategy so you can focus wholly on wounding her—and in a way that leaves her flank open for my approach."

"Can you eliminate her with a single strike?" Neha asked.

Raphael's answer was a flat, "No. She's too engorged on the lifeforce she stole from her people."

"I truly wish to stab that bitch in the face," Zanaya muttered. "But as I'm unlikely to get my wish, let's work out how to wound and weaken her the most. I suggest we first annihilate her troops and overall support structure, forcing her to join the fight with no option to feed."

"I'm not sure why you're all worried," Aegaeon boomed. "She's *one* archangel! We can hit her hard and fast, and go back to our duties."

Neha stirred, her face a thing of regal control. "Remember what happened to Antonicus. Simply being an Ancient, with powerful energies, will not protect you." A strand of hair come loose from her braid touched the side of her face. "Don't be an arrogant fool."

Aegaeon puffed himself up. "Remember to whom you speak, girl. I was a ruler before you were ever a thought."

He might as well be a bull, pawing at the ground. Shall we fetch him a cow from the field to mount?

Alexander ducked his head a touch, and she thought she'd almost made him burst out laughing. *Behave, Zani. This is the most serious of business.*

Look me in the face and tell me you disagree.

A glance at her, the slightest hint of humor. *Now you have won and I must get my vengeance.*

Hiding her own smile, Zanaya turned her attention back to the discussion. By some luck or mercy, they'd come to an agreement on battle plans by the time dawn kissed the skies.

"The tiredness of our troops is no longer a handicap," Raphael said. "Not when we have all of you." Hands placed against the edge of the table and wings held back with warrior control, he met each set of archangelic eyes in turn "Even the sheer numbers at her disposal can't outweigh the power of ten archangels, four of them Ancients."

If his first words had been hopeful, his next were as dark as the grave. "If there is a risk that you will be taken by the enemy and rescue is unlikely, do what must be done. We cannot know how strong she'll become if she feeds on an arch-angel."

Aegaeon's big fists slamming down on the table. "You truly believe she would dare cross that line?"

Neha spoke the words in Zanaya's heart. "She turned children into infected vampires. There is no line she will not cross."

"Two hours until we strike." Caliane's son rose to his full height. "Prepare for battle."

29

The plan was set, their tasks determined. Before leaving to take up the position from where she'd decimate the enemy forces with her tempests while Titus broke the earth and Alexander melted its metals, Zanaya stood for a moment on one of the Tower's high balconies, her love by her side.

"I feel a sense of the portentous," she said, staring out across this strange and lovely city already badly scarred by war.

"Have you decided you are Cassandra's kin then, Zani?"

Laughing, she leaned slightly against him, overlapping his wing with her own. "Perhaps, lover, perhaps I am." No matter the lightness of her words, the weight of a future unseen and unknown lay heavy on her shoulders.

Shifting so they faced one another, Alexander lifted a hand to cup the side of her face. His expression was open in a way she'd rarely seen in the final millennia of their time together, more reminiscent of the first blush of their relationship. "Promise me that we'll talk after this war is over. That you won't just go into Sleep again."

She felt herself begin to bristle. "Lover, you can't ask without giving orders." But because arrogance or demands, she loved him all the same, she turned and pressed a kiss to his palm. "You're too used to having the world bend to you. I never will."

Holding those silver eyes that were now afire, she placed a hand over her heart. "But we will speak. It's past time, don't you think?" They had to work out what they were to each other now. Eons of love had left their mark, an imprint that could never be erased, but did that mean it was more than memory?

"Perhaps it's seeing young Raphael and his consort together," she said to him. "But I feel it, what we have missing between us. It's been gone a long time, has it not?"

Alexander slipped his hand to her nape, squeezed. "What are you saying, Zani?" His heart thundered, his breath coming short and fast.

Lovely dark eyes holding his without fear, as she'd always done. "I don't know," was the soft answer. "I just know that we can't continue this cycle endlessly." Rising up on tiptoe, she touched her lips to his. "I have loved you more than I have ever loved anyone or anything my entire existence, Xander, my Xander. But you still love power more."

"Zani." His heart felt as if it was being wrenched out of him. "You're wrong."

A faint smile, that sparkle in her eye. "Am I then? Well, we shall see after this war is done." Stepping back, she spread out her wings. "We'll talk later, lover. It's time for me to take position."

He watched her sweep off the balcony, catch a rising wind current, before spreading his own wings. "After the war," he promised the air, more than ready to have this out. Because if there was one thing he knew, it was that Zanaya was his yesterday and his today, and all the tomorrows to come.

His power stirred as he prepared himself for what was to come, his intent to melt all the metal around the enemy forces. Quite aside from the metal in the earth, many, *many* of the buildings in this city had rods of metal that acted as their spines. He'd felt it the instant he arrived, and he'd wondered if Raphael had forgotten what it was that the Archangel of Persia could do, the chaos he could cause . . . but then, Alexander had been gone from this world while this city—as it was now—was born.

As it stood, Raphael had no reason to be concerned. Alexander was no longer in the mood to pick fights with young archangels just going about their business. He hadn't told Zanaya of that irrational part of his history, was ashamed of it now that he looked back. Jessamy had been right to call him on his idiotic posturing, right to remind him of the wisdom he'd once owned.

"You are the only one who calls me wise," he'd told the slender angel with kindness woven into her very bones. "Everyone else believes I am a being of violence and war."

"You are both, Alexander. You always have been." A reminder that she was their Librarian now, the keeper of their histories, knew far more about him than he might imagine. "I think, if the test came again, you would stand on the side of right."

"You are so young, Jessamy. Foolish, many would say."

"Did they not call you the same when you stepped between two warring Ancients?"

He'd laughed then, delighted by her courage and her wit. Hers was the wisdom, he'd told himself, that had sent him into Sleep. What he'd refused to admit even to himself was that he was exhausted of living an existence devoid of his Zani. He'd been exhausted even before learning of Osiris's crimes—and he'd stayed awake from then on only to watch over the wild chimera.

That chimera had been full-grown by the time Jessamy spoke to him. And the hole in his heart where Zani was meant to live had pulsed with agony each and every day. He could no longer bear being awake without her. To see her rising from the sands . . . beneath his anger had burst a joy incandescent.

His Zani was awake, was back in his arms.

And now they went into war.

But it wasn't their first and wouldn't be their last. They'd survived eons upon eons. They'd survive this too, and then they'd talk.

The world roared, Titus lifting up the earth beneath the enemy's feet.

Landing hard on the asphalt of the abandoned road beyond which lay territory Lijuan's people had won, he crouched down on one knee and placed his hand on the dirt that Titus had lifted to the surface for him by purposefully cracking this section of the road.

The song of the metals within hummed through him, pure and resonant.

Smiling, he unleashed his power and every piece of metal that was touching the earth began to melt. A few weapons, other tools. Nothing but collateral damage . . . because Alexander's true target was the metal of the buildings that loomed over the enemy. "It's time for your mistress to learn that she cannot dance with the entire Cadre and win."

The air began to howl with violent winds the same instant that the buildings began to shiver and fall.

Smiling again and aware his eyes had gone a liquid and inhuman silver, he looked up.

To see his lover encased in a whirlwind as black as the heart of midnight as she trammeled the enemy, such a power as this world hadn't seen for eons. Oh how he loved her. He'd tell her after the war, and they would work it all out.

He was so certain of that outcome that when things went wrong, he refused to believe it was happening. He'd just decimated an entire wing of Lijuan's black-eyed army while Zanaya fought one of Lijuan's generals a short distance away, the man's eyes a hue that said he was fueled by his archangel, his power more than it should've been.

Zanaya was winning, of course she was winning . . . when Lijuan appeared right behind her, a nightmare out of mist.

Zani!

Even as he shouted out the mental warning and began to fly toward her, Lijuan gripped Zanaya's upper arms with fingers as thin as claws and struck with the speed of a cobra to sink her teeth into Zanaya's neck.

And Alexander's world ended.

Desolation

30

Lovers fall and lovers rise. The river stops flowing. This time will be the end.

Alexander jerked awake out of a terrible sleep, certain he'd heard an old, *old* voice in his head. Older than that of an Ancient. A voice he knew . . . but no, it was gone now, whatever nightmare it was that haunted him.

Twisting to sit on the edge of his bed, his feet on the floor and his head in his hands, he tried to reset his mind. For once, he was clean, his naked body devoid of streaks of dirt and other, more viscous substances. Hair that had been damp when he went into sleep was now dry, and his wings no longer carried the stench of the reborn.

He'd been fighting day after bitter day to cleanse his territory of the last traces of Lijuan's evil, and finally—months after that bitch's death—it was done. No more child reborn roamed the landscape, though he had sentries on constant surveillance and all the leaders of the towns and cities and villages knew to contact the fortress *at once* should there be any sign of reborn.

So it was that he'd finally lain down to rest for longer than an hour or two.

He was tired.

To the bone and beyond.

Even archangels could get tired when they didn't rest and barely ate. It was only Xander thrusting food into his hands that had made him remember to fuel his body. His grandson, who had already lost his parents and had been born long after his grandmother and grandfather went into Sleep, was the sole reason Alexander forced himself to continue on as more than an automaton tasked with cleaning up Lijuan's mess.

Some would say that he could now lie down into a final and eternal Sleep, slip into that silent unthinking deep where he didn't have to experience heartbreak every time he opened his eyes and remembered that his Zani was gone.

The only reason he didn't was Xander.

An angel of a bare two hundred with skin of dark gold and hair of a brown so dark it was moments away from black. Alexander knew that, though his wings appeared black when folded, the black faded into brown with hints of gold. The biggest surprise, however, was the underside of pure silver.

A silver identical to the shade of Alexander's wings.

Family. They were family. And his grandson was dealing with a grief not many angels his age ever had to experience, both his parents lost in a single act of violence. The youth was doing it with grace, but he remained fragile within. Oh, the child wouldn't put it that way—he was a warrior after all—but Alexander had mentored many a youth, and he'd raised a son.

He knew the boy was hurting yet. As he knew Xander would break forever if he lost his grandfather, too. The child had bowed in respect to Alexander when they first met, not knowing that Alexander wanted no such formality—he'd wanted only to hold this boy who was the last surviving piece of Rohan. The child of Alexander's child had been bewildered and grief-stricken then, and he didn't know Alexander.

But things had changed. Alexander no longer saw his

grandson as a memory of Rohan. Xander was far too much his own man for that—and what an astonishing young man he was; gifted in battle but also with a way about him that said he understood the pain and suffering of others.

Xander, too, knew him now not as a powerful Ancient but as the grandfather who'd race him across the plain, and who'd laugh with him when the boy made one of his rare—but always amusing—jokes.

No, Alexander couldn't go into Sleep. Not until Xander had healed and grown to the point he no longer needed the old man who was his only living family in the entire world. Because Alexander *felt* old for the first time in his existence.

Weighed down by grief and a missing that wouldn't end.

Always before, he'd known she'd wake. He'd been able to bear it because there existed a future in which she'd wake. Now . . .

"You miss her," his grandson had said a month after the war. "Lady Zanaya."

"Ah, Xander." He'd gripped the side of the boy's neck, tried to dig up a smile. "You're too young to be interested in the love stories of us Ancients."

But stubborn Xander, blood of Alexander's blood, had stood firm. "I wish I'd met her."

"I do, too. More than anything." However, his grandson's squadron had been on the farthest border from the fortress at the time of Zanaya's waking, and Alexander had thought he'd have plenty of time to introduce this bright young piece of his heart to the woman who *owned* that heart. "She would've liked you."

"I looked her up in the histories," Xander had added. "They're old, those histories, and most of the chapters are written from the accounts of the Ancients who were around at the time, but one thing remains a constant throughout: *many* of the fragments say Alexander and Zanaya or Zanaya and Alexander, as if to see one was to see the other."

He'd smiled then, a smile formed of pain and grief and

echoes of joy. "She'd be very angry at such an interpretation. Never say so to Zanaya."

A questioning smile from his grandson.

"She is fierce and proud and an archangel of power in her own right."

"But you're mentioned there, too. And you were older. Aren't you angry the histories have you so entwined?"

"No." Then he'd eaten the food Xander had brought in, and shaken his head at his grandson when he would've spoken further of Zanaya.

The wound had been too fresh, Alexander's pain bloodying him.

It was as fresh this day. Perhaps that was why he'd dreamed of swimming with her in a river of molten fire. She'd laughed and then dived, but when he'd tried to follow, he'd become lost, unable to find her even though he could hear the echo of her laughter rippling back to him.

Then a voice, old, so *old*.

And all at once, he remembered the words he'd heard just before he'd woken: *Lovers fall and lovers rise. The river stops flowing. This time will be the end.*

Alexander's heart pounded as he stared around the room. But no aurora-eyed seer stood over him, whispering words of doom. No woman with hair of violet shimmered into existence in a dark corner.

Lovers fall and lovers rise. The river stops flowing. This time will be the end.

Hope clutched at him. Rise. The word rise. Surely, *surely* that meant there was hope?

The river stops flowing. This time will be the end.

His heart clenched into a fist, his breathing ragged. He refused to listen to those words, refused to countenance their meaning. He would focus only on the first part. He would look to a future where his Zani rose again.

The Last Ending

31

Zanaya came awake with a jerk, her mind blurry and her limbs feeling *wrong*. Gulping the cool air inside the fiery cocoon that embraced her, she fought to stay calm. Perhaps another person would've panicked, but Zanaya was not another person. She was the Queen of the Nile and she knew that there was no power in this world stronger than a member of the Cadre.

The Archangel of Death.

A chill echo, a cascade of memories of her last awakening. She'd been in Alexander's territory then, safe in the soft black of her power far below the warm sands of his land. She'd kept to her decision and not told him that she intended to Sleep in his land. To do so would've been to tie a weight of love to his ankle, her Alexander stubborn and implacable, loyal and honorable.

She hadn't wanted that for him, not when she hadn't known how long she'd Sleep. And it was accepted fact that once an archangel entered the Sleep state, their power vanished from the world, no longer an impediment or provocation to any other member of the Cadre.

Else the world would be chaos, buffeted by competing winds of power.

Given their love, she'd known that Alexander *might* sense her had he dug down below the surface in the exact place in which she Slept, but otherwise, he'd never divine his Zani's presence.

So she'd allowed herself the comfort of going to Sleep close to him.

He'd been Archangel of Persia for so long when she went to Sleep that she hadn't been able to imagine any future world in which those lands didn't belong to him—and when she woke, she'd been proven right, for there he was. She'd been able to taste him in her every breath, her lover full of arrogance and power and a brutal love for her.

But there'd been no time for love then.

She frowned, the threads of the past unraveling in fits and starts.

And she remembered that she hadn't chosen to wake, though she'd been stirring, her body and mind rejuvenated from her long Sleep. She *would* have woken soon enough, but something had wrenched her prematurely out of her rest.

Her name is Lijuan.

Alexander had said that to her when she woke, while the sky turned a black akin to the grave, the air shredded by shrieks and screams.

There had been a war.

She'd risen because she'd needed to rise to help battle the Archangel of Death, she who would've spread her madness and her evil across the planet in a tide of death that was a facsimile of life.

Reborn.

That was what she'd called her shambling abominations.

Zanaya hissed out a breath hot with rage, still unable to comprehend how any archangel could permit themselves to fall so far into megalomaniacal madness that they'd believe they were doing a good thing in making the dead walk.

Blood in her fingertips now, her numb toes coming to life with stabbing pains.

Gritting her teeth, she rode the pain.

It hadn't been like this on her last waking. She might've been wrenched out of it prematurely, but she'd come awake as she should: in complete and total control of herself, her body at full fighting capacity.

Today, she was . . . incapacitated.

Face hot, she searched in her cocoon . . . and her hand closed over Firelight. It wasn't the same sword that Alexander had given her so long ago, but it was a worthy successor to the name. And it carried his amber. The two were always entwined—Firelight and Alexander's amber. She never wore one without the other.

As she never carried Firelight when she and Alexander were broken.

With the fingers of her right hand wrapped around its carved hilt studded with opals—the gemstones that Xander—no, he was Alexander now—Xander the name of his grandson— and how astonishing that he had a grandson!

Her thoughts skittered this way and that, gathering together the more frayed edges of her memories. This wasn't normal, she kept thinking, but at the same time there was no point in wallowing in the irregularities. She had to work out what was going on, what was—

A piercing stab that had her dropping Firelight to slap her hand over the side of her neck . . . where Lijuan had *bitten* her. Clinging to her like a mongrel dog and sucking her blood as if she were a vampire and not an archangel.

But no . . .

Zanaya squeezed her eyes shut, unraveled more tangled threads. Lijuan hadn't wanted blood. She'd been able to feed on the lifeforce of others—even archangels, it appeared. She'd *fed* on Zanaya.

Rage was a storm vortex inside her.

She'd fought back, she remembered, had called up the whirlwinds that were her trademark power, but Lijuan, this evil that had grown while Zanaya Slept, had been too powerful, a monster unleashed.

Zanaya had felt her body go cold as Lijuan sucked up all her energy, all her warmth, all her *life*! She'd seen her limbs begin to shrivel, felt her heart stutter. Her sight had faded at rapid speed, until the last thing she remembered was blurred gray. Then . . . nothingness.

She must've fallen from the sky, her wings crumpled and her body emaciated.

Half-terrified that she remained in that mummified state, that Lijuan had somehow turned her into one of her reborn, a shambling parody of life, she lifted one of her arms. Lit by the glow from the fiery cocoon, her skin proved as midnight dark as always, and as smooth, her flesh what it should be.

Her breath pulsed out of her in a ragged exhale, but she held back the wave of relief. Because she didn't feel like herself. Something was off. Perhaps it was her legs that remained shriveled.

Dropping her arm, she bent one leg at the knee, and the living fire of the cocoon rippled around her to make space. She looked, her skin cold, but her leg was whole, too, her flesh rejuvenated. Still uncertain, she ran her hands over her body—and realized she wore a simple linen shift that stopped midthigh. She made a face.

Zanaya didn't do linen or simple except when she was sparring or going into battle.

But she supposed it had been an emergency measure, the choice made by healers—who tended to be pragmatic by nature. She'd take care of it as soon as she rose and had access to her own resources. The thought made her wonder where she'd emerge this time around—she couldn't predict it, not when she wasn't the one who'd chosen the place of rest.

Alexander.

Her breath hurt in her lungs. She'd been trying not to

think of him but to not think of her beloved general was an impossibility. She'd glimpsed him fighting his way toward her as Lijuan sucked her dry, but she didn't know what had happened from that point on. Had he fallen victim to the monster, too? Was Alexander trapped in a mummified state?

Or even worse . . . had he borne damage akin to Antonicus?

Panic beat its wings inside her, her breath coming in short, sharp bursts. She could take anything but a world in which Alexander no longer existed.

Zanaya. You wake. The voice was beyond ancient, an echo of boundless time.

Zanaya went rigid, one hand on Firelight's hilt. *Who are you?* An archangel's imperious demand.

Laughter, the tone so very old that it made Zanaya's bones ache. Her stomach dipped. *Are you one of the Ancestors?* The old ones who were rumored to Sleep below the Refuge, the very first of angelkind.

Perhaps, child. Perhaps I am. I do not believe so, but I cannot remember my childhood any longer. A sigh. *I didn't expect any of you to wake so soon, yet I have Slept with one ear open, listening. Waiting. Your brethren continue to Sleep, caught in-between.*

Zanaya's muscles began to unclench. She hated that she was in this unknown place, with this unknown voice, and yet . . . She felt no sense of threat. It was warmth and protection that she heard, that she felt. *That witch bit me in battle.*

The voice shifted, became songlike: *Goddess of Nightmare. Wraith without a shadow. Rising into her Reign of Death.*

Every tiny hair on Zanaya's body shivered in a prickling wave. And some crumb of knowledge in the far recesses of her brain came to the fore, had her saying, *Archangel Cassandra?*

I was once her, came the answer. *Now, I do not know who I have become. Qin, my Qin, he knew me.* A world of sorrow. *I dreamed of you, child. Long ago. I had forgotten.*

Sky of silver.
Sky of night.
Wild tempests and a storm of gold.
Queen of the Nile.
Warrior beloved.
Battle born.
Death and resurrection.

Zanaya didn't realize she was holding her breath until Cassandra came to a halt. "That's it?" She threw up her hands, disrupting the liquid fire of her cocoon. "I know all that! I need to know what the future holds."

Laughter in her mind, unused, rusty, and yet oddly infectious for all its weight. *So many pathways I see for you, angel of tempests born. You could take any one of them. If I tell you the strongest thread I see, you will surely take the opposing one, so my sight is meaningless to you.*

Zanaya wished the Ancient were wrong about Zanaya's contrariness, but she wasn't.

"It's what makes me love you—and what infuriates me," Alexander had said to her once, laughter in that silver-kissed gaze. "If I say the sky is blue, you'll argue that it's green for no reason at all."

Sorry, she said to Cassandra. *I don't know why I'm like that.*

Do you not? Eons in her voice, such a heaviness of age that it threatened to crush Zanaya's ribs, compress her lungs. *Your mother was a woman who would hear only one voice. Her own.*

It had been a long, long time since Zanaya thought of Rzia, bitter and determinedly lonely, but now her stomach tensed. *I've moved far beyond that.* She was an archangel, a being of great power. *I'm no child.*

We are all our parents' children, was Cassandra's calm response. *But you . . . you carry a piece of another now.*

Ice in Zanaya's blood, shards in her bones. "Lijuan." She spat out the name like a curse. "She infected me with her viciousness?"

I have no answer to that, battle-born Zanaya. What I do know is that you're not the same archangel who woke prior to the war. Do you wish to rise now? I've protected you in my fire, but it is no cage.

Zanaya stared at the rippling golds and reds of the flames, thought of Sleep . . . and came to a screeching halt. *I can't initiate Sleep.* It was a gift that came centuries into adulthood and was a given; all angels past that age could choose to go into the state that suspended them between life and death.

Something is broken in me. Do you know what? Zanaya might be proud but she'd never been stupid; she was with Cassandra, Seer of Seers. To not ask the question would've been to waste a precious resource.

A long pause. *So many pathways,* Cassandra murmured again. *So many choices.*

Zanaya stayed silent, loath to disrupt the seer's thoughts.

Not broken . . . but damaged, Cassandra said at long last. *I truly cannot see your path beyond today, so I cannot tell you whether the wound is permanent or temporary. But one thing I now know, Queen of Tempests: you wake because it is your season to wake.*

Zanaya stared at the fire around her. Sleep or not, she could remain in this strange in-between place for a long time without going mad. She had the will. And if the world needed it, she would do it. Perhaps, however, such a sacrifice wasn't necessary. "How many archangels are awake in the world? Do you know?"

I listen as I watch over my Sleepers. I slip into a deeper rest now and again in an effort to avoid the slipstreams of time, but then I wake, and my owls tell me what I missed. Nine. There are nine.

Zanaya exhaled. "Then I will rise." The Cadre was meant to be ten, was the strongest and most stable at ten. And unless one among the Cadre wanted to hoard land, there was plenty enough territory to parcel out between ten. "Cassandra?"

Yes, Queen of Tempests?

Throat dry, she made herself say it: *Is Alexander awake or does he Sleep?* She couldn't even whisper the other option: that he was dead, had died in the battle against Lijuan.

The silver-winged warrior walks the world. A pause, followed by soft words almost drowned out by the roar in Zanaya's ears. *Silver wings and tempest winds. Storms unfettered. This time . . . will be the end.*

The liquid fire around Zanaya parted even as she struggled against the shock of those final words. *Wait! What does that mean?*

Her only answer was a whispered sigh, the brush of an old, *old* power over her skin . . . and then Cassandra was gone, returned to her watchful rest.

Zanaya rose.

32

Ten years after the war that had ended the reign of the Archangel of Death, and Alexander had managed to go on, managed to pretend that he was the same man as before the war. He'd fooled Xander, but hadn't even tried with Titus or Callie. It would've been pointless; unlike his grandson, his friends had known him far too long, seen him through too many seasons of life.

Now he stood atop Kilimanjaro, this demanding mountain in the lands of his friend. Clouds ringed the mountain, hiding the flat canopies of the umbrella trees he'd overflown on his way here, along with the forms of the many species of fauna that roamed this land. In contrast, the immediate area around him was an alpine barrenness.

Alone in the clouds, the Archangel of Persia found himself lost in a way he hadn't been for the entirety of his existence.

His mother, whose gentle heart would shatter when she next woke, had oft commented on his confidence. "Oh, my Alexander," she'd say with a laugh, "you've always known your mind. Such a strong will you had, even as a mere babe—why, you even managed to get Ojewo himself to give you a future when he never gave one to a child!"

That future had been unspecific in the extreme. When, as a halfling, he'd asked the seer to tell him his future, Ojewo had looked at him with a soft smile and said, "No angel should know the entirety of his future, Alexander, far less an angel of your resolve. You will shape your own future."

"One thing," a frustrated and barefoot Alexander had bargained. "Tell me one thing."

Ojewo had been dressed in a flowing robe of darkest blue at the time, his feet clad in formal sandals, and the dusky green of his eyes lined with kohl. He'd been on the way to a court function when Alexander had waylaid him.

But Ojewo hadn't been angry or impatient.

Tilting his head the slightest fraction, a mischievous glint to his eye, the seer had said, "She will be a luminous and fierce wind that lights up your existence."

Alexander, youthful and full of himself, had groaned. He'd hoped for stories of glory in war and of territories won. Instead Ojewo gave him what Alexander had privately labeled romantic fluff. Then had come Zanaya and at long last he'd realized that the seer had told him the *most* important piece of his future.

Because Zani was the fulcrum on which his existence turned.

So many years they'd spent apart, and yet when she'd woken, it was as if they'd kissed but a day ago. He knew her in his bones, loved her with every cell in his body.

. . . it isn't the last ending.

Words Cassandra had spoken when he handed Zanaya over to her care. Words he'd clung to for ten long, lonely years. Even more so than he'd clung to the echo of that ghostly prophecy he'd heard as he slept. That might well have been a dream, while the others were words Cassandra had spoken to his face.

Had he his way, he would've kept his Zani close, watched over her himself. But he'd known that his proud lover would hate that with every fiber of her being. Theirs had always been a relationship of equals. Midnight and silver, two streams that had crossed time and time again . . . but never blended.

Some might call that a broken love, but Alexander knew the truth: it had to be that way for their love to work. He and his Zani, neither one of them was built to bend. They *were* however, built to be loyal and to hold on to those they cherished.

"You are as arrogant as I," he'd said to her one memorable day, after she'd knocked him to the ground in combat training and was holding a sharp stiletto blade to his throat. She'd been dressed in one of those short shifts she liked to wear to fight, her arms lithely muscled, her hair pulled back in a braid, and her skin glorious in the sunlight.

His comment had been the continuation of a discussion they'd been having over breakfast, and that day, she'd thrown back her head and laughed before jumping up to her feet and reaching down to offer him her hand so he could haul himself upright. He hadn't needed the assist but he'd taken her hand nonetheless.

"Well, perhaps you're right, Xander." A wicked spark in her eye. "At least I'm not *old* and arrogant." Then she'd taken off into the sky with an unrepentant grin.

Growling, he'd taken off after her.

Zanaya was the only one who'd teased him long after they'd both settled into the Cadre, the only one who'd played with him. He and Caliane, their relationship had never been like that. Callie had always been calm, centered, a touch old before her time. Only with Nadiel had he seen her become a young woman, carefree and laughing.

As only with Zanaya had Alexander become a playful young man.

Alexander? Are you planning to moodily skulk on the mountain for much longer? Or will you join us for a meal?

Alexander scowled, reminded that he did now have one other person in his life who treated him with irreverence. *Your mother would be appalled by your manners, pup.*

Good thing she's still Sleeping. I have enough to deal with, given the refusal of my sisters to revere me as an archangel. Plague me they do.

Well aware that Titus adored his siblings, and often visited them to be so harangued and plagued, to be called "Tito" and treated as their beloved youngest sib, Alexander was hit by a wave of piercing melancholy. Oh how he missed his brother as Osiris had been before he became a monster. He missed laughing with him as Titus laughed with his sibs, missed their conversations and their swims.

It was as if his grief over Zanaya had breathed new life into that older pain.

His heart was as heavy as stone most days, but he tried never to reveal that side of himself to Xander. To his grandson, he was his grandfather, strong and well recovered and back to himself. Xander could believe it because he'd never met Zanaya; had he met her, had he seen her with Alexander, he'd have known that no man could ever get over a woman like Alexander's Zani.

To give himself strength to keep up the act, Alexander oft made it a point to think of the light in his life.

He had good friends in Titus—and now, Lady Sharine. She'd always been Caliane's closest friend and was apt to remain so for eternity, but Alexander had come to know her better over the years through her relationship with Titus. He'd come to understand why Caliane so cherished her bond with an angel Alexander had always thought of as an artist lost in her own world.

Then there was the youngest and most precious spark in his entire universe: Xander.

You jest? You are a grandfather?

Throat thick at the memory of Zanaya's joyous astonishment, he rose into the sunset sky. As was his wont every time he took to the sky, he looked toward the horizon in the direction of where Cassandra had vanished with Zanaya in her arms.

The seer's fire had been in Raphael's territory at the time, but Alexander wasn't credulous enough to think it remained there. An Ancient would never be so open about her place of rest—especially when she also watched over multiple other badly wounded archangels.

And Cassandra was beyond ancient; no one had any idea of the depth of her power or of what she was capable. Qin knew her best, and he certainly wasn't giving them any clues. The archangel who'd stepped in to watch over Astaad's territory rarely even spoke.

That was when it happened.

Sunset began to turn to midnight in a racing wave. Not the dark gray of encroaching night. The pure and soft obsidian of the Queen of the Nile. Heart thundering, he listened . . . and he heard her. The sweet and haunting music that was the wind in melody. Zanaya's song.

Alexander! This happened before the war. Titus's voice in his mind.

It's Zanaya. Alexander barely kept his mental voice from shaking when he caught a wave of scents lovely and unknowable. *She wakes.* And this time, she did so on her own terms, with her song and her scents.

A second longer, and he had it, her location. He couldn't do this with any other archangel and he didn't know if any other archangel could do it with anyone else. Usually, the members of the Cadre woke with a show—but in secret. No one not in close proximity would ever see them rise.

She's in your territory, he told Titus even as he set himself a hard pace in Zanaya's direction. He didn't want his friend surprised into aggressive action, wanted Zanaya to have a peaceful waking. *Somewhere in the north.*

Well, makes sense, Titus said with his customary pragmatism. *We need an archangel there.*

So they did. Titus was only Archangel of all Africa because there was no one else to take on the duty. The other archangel far preferred to handle only half the continent, truly give his people the care and attention he felt was an archangel's duty.

Zanaya wouldn't have to fight for territory.

She must be healed. Titus's voice was a happy boom of sound. *That gives me hope for Astaad, Michaela, and Favashi.*

Alexander had no room in his thoughts for the other three, Zanaya his sole priority. Flying with archangelic fury, his body a scythe through the intense beauty of her sky, he soon landed atop a dune in a small desert region just beyond what had been the north/south border when Titus ruled only half the continent.

His wings ached from the strain he'd put them under, his heart a drum. Trust Zanaya to wake in just the right place, he thought on a wave of raw hope, but though the sky remained a velvety black evocative with scents exquisite, he saw no sign of her.

It made him wonder if he'd got it wrong after all.

Had she woken elsewhere? That didn't matter to him. The only thing he cared about was if she'd woken.

Titus, is there word from any other part of the world of her waking?

No. Her night covers the planet, but no one has yet reported a sighting.

It was taking far too long. Given how distant he'd been, she should've emerged long before his arrival. Worry gnawed at him . . . as the dune melted from under him without warning.

Startled, he flew up into a hover before coming down on what was now a flat area of sand that glittered with diamond fire in the center. He took another few steps back, giving her the space she'd need.

The sand swirled as it rose, spinning faster and faster the higher it got, until the silver glitter of it was a small tornado that blew back his hair and made him stagger on his feet. Arm braced over his eyes to protect them from the grit in the air, he tried to see her through the whirlwind, but that proved impossible, the wind a maelstrom.

The tornado dropped with unexpected suddenness, revealing the back of a woman with hair of purple-washed-silver, her stature small but her curves dangerous. She had a sword strapped to her spine, its hilt studded with opals as well as a single piece of scarlet amber. He'd made sure his Zani had Firelight with her in Sleep.

Now, as he watched with hope and disbelief warring within, she stretched luxuriantly, a cat waking from a nap.

He searched the parts of her body visible to him, found not a single scar or other indication of Lijuan's evil. His Zani had healed.

Then she turned to face him.

He sucked in a breath. "Zani, your eyes."

Smile wiped away, she pulled out Firelight to examine herself in the gleaming metal. The curses that erupted from her mouth were in a language long extinct but that Alexander knew very well—because its repertoire of curses had always been the most interesting.

"That creature born of a dung beetle and a half-dead ass marked me!" She poked at the skin just below the startling pearl gray of her eyes.

Those eyes should've been midnight dark speckled with silvery light, a beautiful and luscious richness that had seduced him throughout time. *"Zani."*

Striding forward, he took his life into his hands and wrapped her up in his arms. Instead of prodding him with the blade for his temerity, she actually dropped her favorite sword to hug him back as tight. "Is she dead?" A rough whisper against his chest.

"Yes. We ended Lijuan that day."

"Good." Short, sharp, satisfied. "I hope my lifeforce gave her indigestion."

Laughing, shaky, Alexander kissed the top of her hair, the side of her face, and then their lips were meeting and it was as if they hadn't been separated by a cold, hard decade. They fit as perfectly as if they'd been designed to interlock. Her lips so soft and plush, his firmer. Her hold fierce, his wings a protective embrace.

The taste of her threatened to bring him to his knees.

Winds encircled them, the swirling sand threaded by glittering midnight as Zanaya cocooned them in a wild privacy that made this moment about nothing but the two of them.

33

The kiss, it was everything, feeding his parched soul and healing broken things inside him. But they couldn't stay thus forever, and soon the sands dropped and they stepped apart. "I'm different," Zanaya said, her expression troubled. "Not the eyes. I could live with that. There's something not quite right with me."

Alexander cupped her cheek, needing to touch her, reassure himself she was truly here. "You're the only one of those who fell to Lijuan's powers who has woken. I thought you were gone forever."

"I know." Rich brown began to bleed back into the pearl of her irises, the effect eerily lovely. "I spoke to Cassandra before I rose. She said that they're still 'caught in-between.'" Flaring out her wings, she then snapped them back in with martial precision.

"There's a reason I'm awake when they're not," Zanaya continued before he could tell her that her eyes were once again as they should be, "and I'm not sure it's a good reason. Especially with these." She pointed two fingers, angled in a sharp vee, toward her eyes. "That insane monster did something to me. Maybe insurance in case she died."

Alexander was horrified at the idea that Lijuan could've somehow infected Zanaya. "Do you have her voice in your head?" He tightened his hold. "Any urge to do things that you'd never do?"

Hands on her hips, Zanaya stared down at the ground. When she lifted her head at last, it was to shake it. "No, my thoughts are my own."

"So are your eyes," he said, finally breaking contact—but only so he could stroke his fingers over the arch of her wings. "The gray has vanished."

She shivered at the intimate caress before saying, "At least I won't see her when I look in the mirror." Biting words, but her expression was taut. "How will I know, Alexander?" A rough question. "What if I *am* infected with her menace, but in a way I can't discern?"

"I will be your lieutenant in this watch," Alexander vowed. "I know you. I'll tell you at once if you begin to act in ways that are outside your personality or your morals."

Zanaya had always had a mischievous streak that led her to stir up trouble—but it was never trouble deadly or dangerous or ugly. No, it was the wicked kind that had almost made him burst out laughing at more than one tense meeting of the Cadre.

Zanaya loved to tweak "the general's" nose.

Now, she pressed her lips together. "I would not have you watch over me, lover," she muttered. "But let us consider this a battle exigency. It stops the instant we know that I'm myself again."

Alexander agreed with a nod. "It appears you'll be ruling the northern half of Africa. Your Nile will welcome back its queen."

Raising both eyebrows, she said, "The Cadre moves faster than it did in my time." She shifted to place one hand over his heart before he could reply.

As if she, too, couldn't bear to be apart.

He closed his hand over hers, spoke through a throat gone rough. "No. Titus has simply made it clear he has no quarrel with another archangel taking over this half. He's caring for it because there was no other option—but he feels spread thin, believes it shortchanges his people."

"I knew I liked Titus." A pause, a tap of her lower lip. "So, how much have I missed this time? Another grandson?"

"It has been but ten years," Alexander said, his voice ragged. "And how could I father another child when I have touched no woman since?"

Her expression softened into piercing tenderness. "Ah, I'm sorry you had to see me fall, lover." Fingers touching his jaw. "I didn't wish to rise until I knew you'd survived the war."

Chest aching, he wrapped her up in his arms and his wings again. She slid her own arms around his waist, laid her head against his chest. And they just stood there for a long time, in an embrace that healed fractures in both of them.

When cool night winds blew through Alexander's hair, he looked up and saw that the stars of early evening had begun to appear. Zanaya's darkness was fading, to be replaced by the natural state of the world.

Zanaya sighed and stepped back.

Fighting his need to hold on, he released her. And picked up the mantle of the Cadre. "There'll need to be a meeting."

"Yes. When can it be arranged?"

"A day or two. We're at peace, so not everyone will be at their strongholds."

Expression pensive, Zanaya nodded but lines creased her forehead.

"Will you spend the night with me, Zani?" he asked, reaching over to smooth away those lines. "Before the world re-enters our lives?"

They were archangels; it was inevitable.

A soft half-smile that held as much sorrow as joy. "Will we begin our dance again?" For an instant, she appeared tired, looking downward again before she lifted her hand and thrust her fingers through her hair. "Do you never wonder if we aren't meant to be?"

"No."

Her lips tugged up. "The general is back, I see." She went to step forward, then frowned, glanced down one more time. "Look."

Following her gaze, he saw the bleached bones of a bird, the black hollow of its empty eye socket staring up at them. "Your winds must've exposed it."

"Yes, I suppose so." Zanaya sounded distracted as she glanced around, as if expecting to see more bones.

"It's only a single bird," he reassured her, and when she scowled, added, "Zani, we were all seeing nightmares around every corner for years after Lijuan. To this day, I flinch every time I pass a small child." He couldn't forget, couldn't erase those memories of a scourge so piteous and horrible.

Features stark, Zanaya said, "Oh, Alexander . . ." and came into his arms. "The answer is yes, I'll lie with you. I need you. I need *us*."

Wanting every moment they could steal for themselves, they flew a short distance to a forest verdant with life and devoid of any mortal or immortal inhabitants. The starry night was their ceiling, her bed his wings. A single magical night before reality crashed into them with the sunrise.

He stroked every curve, kissed every inch of skin, loved her until his scent was on her and hers on him. But it wasn't carnal. There was too much tenderness. Too much trust.

"I lost a quarter of my forces in the aftermath," he told her as he leaned over her while she lay on her back on his wing. "My warriors were broken, wanted to retreat from the world. How could I blame them when I feel the same heart-sorrow?"

Her eyes shone, his Zani who'd always had a far gentler heart than most people realized.

"I wish the memories didn't haunt me," he confessed, "but it's a fitting memorial that they do—because there are no graves for those children, no memorial but this."

Wiping away a tear, Zanaya spoke in a husky voice. "You've grown wise in ten years." She kissed his fingertips, then lifted his hand to trace the lines on it as she'd done when they'd first become lovers. "A mortal I once knew told me that our lives are written in these lines."

"Did he read your palm?"

"Yes. He told me I'd have one great love in my lifetime." A kiss pressed to his palm. "There are no splits at all in my love line." Narrowing her eyes, she stared intently at his palm. "Just as well I spy no splits in yours either, General."

When he shifted to kiss the rounded curves of her cheeks, she smiled, stroked his bare shoulders, and said, "You're the most handsome man I've ever known."

He felt his face go hot. He, Archangel Alexander, was blushing. It made her laugh and kiss his face all over, her hands so loving and tender on him that he let her. As he let her love him in turn, her hands exploring all the ridges and valleys of him, her lips a delicate benediction.

They fell asleep with her head on his shoulder, one of her hands on his heart, and one of her legs thrown over his. He closed his wing over her, holding her close, his Zani who'd returned to him and who he'd never again let go.

Lovers fall and lovers rise. The river stops flowing. This time will be the end.

"Did you hear that?" Zanaya murmured, her voice drugged with rest.

Stroking his hand over her hair, Alexander said, "It's nothing. A dream." That was all he'd allow it to be, he thought as sleep sucked him under.

Our river will never stop flowing. Our love will never end. They were his final thoughts before he fell into the deep.

Above them, the tree branches rustled, the air a sigh.

Had Alexander been awake, he might've seen a ghostly white owl take to the air, its flight as silent as the heart of midnight.

34

Cassandra should've been at rest.

She'd done her duty by one of her charges. Zanaya was safe.

But the slipstreams screamed at her to *look*, to *see*!

Breath shallow and her owls restless, she battled not to hear the screams, battled not to see the spread of rot. Because that putrid death continued to dominate the slipstreams, the single other thread yet thin, fragile.

A breath. A stir.

She frowned, but her owls reassured her that her other Sleepers rested yet.

Astaad, Archangel of the Pacific Isles.

Favashi, Archangel of Persia for a heartbeat in eternity.

Michaela, Archangel of Budapest and Queen of Constantinople.

All lay silent and motionless, their lives caught in a knot in the slipstream that wouldn't unravel, not while the rot spread its putrefaction. But the breath came again, small and stealthy and almost impossible to hear.

Another Sleeper was waking. A Sleeper Cassandra couldn't quite see.

A Sleeper who wanted no one to see them, know them.

35

Alexander woke to Zanaya's jerk.

Immediately vigilant, he found her staring across the span of his chest at what, to him, appeared to be a small wounded animal. His instinct was to assist the creature, but from the state of its fur—patches fallen off to reveal mottled green skin—and the smell that came off it, the poor being had a wound that had gone septic.

"It's sick," he said, stroking his hand down the rigid line of Zanaya's spine. "I'll give it mercy—there's nothing else that can be done for it now." He did so in a way that was both quick and painless.

Expression grim in the aftermath, Zanaya helped him bury the tormented creature, and they cleaned themselves in the icy waters of a nearby stream. It was only afterward, while they were seated on large rocks in a dawn-gray clearing some distance away that she said, "If I hadn't seen that animal move, I'd have thought it dead. It had dirt and leaf debris clinging to it as if it crawled from where it had been buried by nature."

Alexander knew where she was going with this, shook his head. "The animal bled red. Its blood was thick and clearly affected by infection, but it bled red. Lijuan's creatures do not."

A long stare before Zanaya exhaled. "I'm very glad to hear that, lover. The hurt creature must've been disoriented and in pain." A fist rubbing her heart. "I see what you mean now, about seeing nightmares wherever I turn."

"It'll pass," he promised her, and gave her a handful of berries he'd scavenged while she'd been considering the events of that morning.

A sudden smile. "You've picked me berries countless times over the eons, and I love it as much today as I did the first time." Tilting up her head in a silent request for a kiss, she was a lovely whimsical creature with a core of molten steel.

He loved every part of her.

Their first kiss was soft, sweeter than anyone might imagine. Their second kiss tasted of the berries she'd eaten while he'd scavenged for more in the nearby bush. And for a treasured beat, they could just be Alexander and Zani, two lovers who had nowhere to be and nothing much to do.

Then the sun emerged to caress the world in warmth and there were no more berries.

"So," Zanaya said, "let's go see Titus so I can discuss territorial matters with him, face-to-face."

Alexander had little time alone with Zanaya over the next twenty-four hours—at which point they prepared to walk into a meeting of the Cadre.

A *physical* meeting.

The Cadre hadn't met in person for years; there'd been no need, no urgency, and every archangel in the world was content to stay in and stabilize territories badly impacted by the war. Even those who'd paid less of a physical price had a traumatized populace that had witnessed nightmare after nightmare in Lijuan's war.

This modern world with all its devices capable of communication . . . no, there wasn't one corner of the planet that hadn't stood witness to what Lijuan had done. Beginning with the careless mountain of flesh where her people had dumped their wounded fighters, and ending with thousands of decaying bodies strewn across Manhattan.

So no, none of them had seen any need to waste time on meeting in person.

Zanaya's resurrection, however, had set the Cadre abuzz. Everyone wanted to lay their eyes on her.

"Our compatriots," Zanaya had said with acerbic humor, "want to see with their own eyes that I haven't returned a shriveled-up mummy—nor an insane reborn frothing at the mouth."

Alexander had been forced to admit the truth. "I'd be the same," he'd said with a groan. "We are base creatures at heart."

But then Zanaya had laughed, one of those deeply infectious laughs that came straight from her core. "So would I, lover. I was *turned into a mummy*! Had I witnessed that, I wouldn't believe in my resurrection, either."

So it was that they were to meet, the location a sprawling fort in Northern Africa. In the courtyard of which Alexander now stood with Titus, the space expansive and planted with multiple trees heavy with fruit or vibrant with blooms.

"It used to belong to that donkey's excrement, Charisemnon." Titus, the deep mahogany hue of his skin aglow under the sunshine, spit on the ground after uttering the dead archangel's name. "But Euphenia dislikes waste and remembered this place as a haven of beauty and art before Charisemnon stunk it up, so she took charge of having it cleaned and otherwise cleansed. Sharine tells me ancient angelic fire rituals were involved. Phenie also asked a respected mortal healer of places to do his chants and ceremonies."

"Sometimes, the old ways are the best." Alexander couldn't argue with Euphenia's methods when the result was this bright and vital space that carried no echo of Charisemnon's foul mores.

"Well." Titus looked around. "It does have a good air to it, I must admit. I was skeptical when Phenie said she could wipe out that pus boil's stink, but I do believe she has succeeded. There's a freshness to it now, as if it's waiting for its new master."

Titus grinned as they walked inside the main building. "Perhaps it's because—along with her other measures—my sister sent an open invitation to mortal children in the local city. She gave her small visitors paints and sticks of color, and set them free within the fort. Their task was to color the walls with their art. For which activity they were rewarded with much cake and chocolates and the like."

Intrigued, Alexander looked at the stunning wall hangings all around, the walls otherwise pristine. "Where are their creations? Surely Euphenia wouldn't permit her ingenious method of banishing bad energy to be erased?" Alexander knew Titus's eldest sister too well to believe that.

Grin even brighter, Titus lifted the lower part of one heavy wall hanging . . . to reveal an image of flowers drawn in a child's careful hand. "Hidden all over the fort—Phenie says they are a gift of joy for the residents to discover."

Alexander crouched down to trace his fingers over the painstakingly created petals. "Zanaya will love this."

A pause before Titus said, "My friend, I hope you'll excuse some plain speaking." Dropping the edge he'd lifted, the big angel shifted on his feet, uncharacteristically hesitant.

"Speak, Titus." Alexander rose from his crouched position, he and Titus of a height so that when their eyes met, it was contact direct and unflinching. "We've never been formal." Not even when Titus had been a boy.

Alexander had lived long enough to know that some people simply resonated with one another. Age mattered naught beyond a certain point. A friend was a friend.

"I don't know Zanaya beyond our fleeting meeting during the war. But I know *of* her—though but for the odd comment you let slip, you've always been close-lipped on the topic, some of the old ones in my court were around when you two were together."

Alexander nodded, aware that a larger-than-usual number of older angels had woken over the last decade. Per Jessamy's research, it was likely to be a lingering effect of the Cascade, ripples of disturbance spreading in time. "And what you heard worries you?"

"Frankly yes." Titus folded his muscled arms over the shining gold of his breastplate—into which was embedded a hummingbird formed of amber. Titus wearing his devotion to Sharine, the Hummingbird, in a way that couldn't be missed.

Alexander had stopped wearing amber a millennium or two into his relationship with Zanaya. It hadn't been a conscious decision. His ring had shattered during a battle with another archangel, and when Zanaya replaced it, he'd taken to not wearing it where it might become damaged . . . until he hadn't worn it at all.

I have loved you more than I have ever loved anyone or anything in my entire existence . . . But you still love power more.

The echo of Zanaya's accusation stung. He hadn't worried about wearing the amber *because* he loved her so damn much. The entire world knew that Alexander belonged to Zanaya, would never be truly available to any other. What need was there to announce it?

She'd asked about it once and never brought it up again after he explained his reasoning . . . but she'd also never stopped transferring his amber from one sword hilt to the next. And she only used those swords, carried that amber, when they were together. The original Firelight had long since fallen to battle and time, but whensoever she transferred his amber to a sword hilt, that sword became the new Firelight.

Eons of time, and she had the first piece of amber he'd given her—along with the memory of how he'd done it. In a sword designed for her by Alexander and crafted by a master, then held precious and safe by Alexander until he could give it to her . . . while they stood kissed by sunlight, he and his Zani so startled and overwhelmed by the gift of amber.

I never expected amber in my life.

The symbol mattered to her. How could he have been so blind? So certain he was right? How could he have forgotten the tenderness and vulnerability of that moment where both their hands had trembled? Or the wonder of the instant she'd given him his most extraordinary ring? He knew he was arrogant, but to have it go so far? Have it hurt his Zani? It would've been one thing if he was ignorant of her history and what wearing amber meant to her, but he *wasn't*.

"Forgive my words, my friend," Titus said even as Alexander staggered under the weight of his realization, "but it appears you two fought as much as you loved!" He threw up his hands. "Where is the joy in that?"

Struggling to find his feet again as his head spun, Alexander looked at his young friend. "When we loved, my friend," he said, his voice rough with the emotions that roared through him, "it was for thousands of years. And when we fought, it was for hundreds. It is a thing of magnitudes."

Titus was silent for a long time before giving a slow nod. "I see your point. I can't quite comprehend it, but then, by your measure, I've only just this second fallen in love. Still . . . I can't imagine being apart from Sharine." He stared at Alexander. "How did you spend all that time apart from Zanaya?"

"We're both as stubborn as the other, and our anger can fuel wars." It was no boast, just fact; the two of them had the same faults. It was why they loved each other—and why they'd broken so many times over the eons.

Having managed to contain his emotions so they wouldn't leak out among the Cadre, he clapped Titus on the back. "I wouldn't worry that the same will happen to you and Lady Sharine, Titus."

"Oh? Why do you sound so certain?"

"You, my friend, are incapable of holding a grudge against anyone except for the malevolently evil, such as Charisemnon; and Lady Sharine has more wisdom in her smallest finger than either I or Zanaya have ever managed to accumulate." Dry words that were unfortunately true, he and his Zani were both far too hotheaded.

"You are hard on yourself," Titus said, then grinned. "One day I promise to hold a grudge against you. For at least the span of a moon. First, you must insult me. Then I will stew in righteous anger."

Alexander felt his shoulders shake. "The problem is that you find most insults spoken against you hilarious, you malodorous sore on the foot of a dung beetle."

Throwing back his head, Titus laughed that big booming laugh that had always made Alexander laugh with him. It did so, today, as well, and he walked into the meeting chamber with a smile on his face.

What's so funny, lover? Zanaya stood on the other side of the old and starkly unmodernized stone chamber deep in the core of the fort. For once, Alexander agreed with a choice of Charisemnon's. This place was timeless and should remain that way. Built to stay cool in the hottest months of the year, it had no natural light, but Zanaya glowed in the firelight thrown by the torches against the walls.

His Zani, tough and battle hardened . . . but with a softness she permitted him alone to see. And he'd hurt her. Unknowingly so, but that was no excuse. He was an intelligent man, and she'd never hidden her own amber. He'd just been too self-righteous about his decision to accept the evidence of his eyes.

At least he could redeem himself somewhat. He had her amber, too. Not the first piece, for that had turned to ash in a strike of angelfire that had been deadly lightning under his skin as it traveled up his fingers and along his forearm before he halted its progress by literally chopping off his own arm.

Arms grew back.

But there was no coming back from angelfire that managed to reach the heart or brain.

So that piece was forever gone, and he knew Zanaya had never blamed him for it. He had the second piece, the one she'd given him to replace his lost ring. He might be an ass but he *loved* her. To have discarded that most precious gift?

No. Never. He'd gone to Sleep with it, and it lay safe in the chamber from which he'd been so rudely awakened.

He'd retrieve it the instant he was back in his territory.

For now, he answered Zanaya's question about his laughter: *I attempted to insult Titus by comparing him to a sore on a dung beetle's foot. He found it most amusing.*

A slight tilt of her head, Zanaya's gaze flicking to Titus's face as her lips curved. *He will be a good neighbor, I think.* The deep violet of her one-shouldered shift sparkled and glittered in the torchlight.

You, my Zani, are far more likely to be the neighbor who picks fights.

I'll remind you I never had problems at my border except when my neighbors lost their damned minds. I am perfectly *rational when it comes to ruling my territory.*

It's only with you that I'm irrational.

The unspoken words lingered in the air, true enough for both of them.

36

Neha swept into the room at that moment, her skin a dusky brown and her wings a crisp white but for threads of cobalt in the primaries. She'd lined her brown eyes with kohl, but was elsewise in her warrior avatar today. No sari with threads of gold and silver but old and beaten leathers of darkest green that hugged her form. A kukri blade, its curve a wicked sharpness, hung at her hip.

She wore her black hair swept off her face in a sleek bun at her nape and for a startling moment of time, she looked both painfully young—and terribly old, her shoulders bowed by age and grief. But the moment passed as fast as it had appeared, and she was simply the Queen of India, a woman of grace and power.

Caliane was already in the room, chatting to Elijah. The Archangel of South America had recovered fully from the injuries he'd sustained at Lijuan's hands, his wings a flawless white and his hair a richer gold than Alexander's more sunbaked strands.

I hear that Elijah has the longest-lasting relationship in the Cadre. Zanaya's voice in his head, followed by a mental sniff. *We beat that paltry record eons ago.*

She'd always been competitive. *Does it count if we were then apart for tens of thousands of years, Zani?*

Their eyes met again, eons between them. Eons of shouts and fights. Eons of laughter and delight. Eons of history. So much history that it had threatened to shatter them under the weight of it.

Alexander could've kicked himself for reminding her of their failure when he'd just gotten her back. *Titus says his sister cleansed this fort with old angelic fire rituals, the chants of a mortal who heals places, and the art of small children,* he found himself saying. *Now it's fresh and new again. Perhaps we should ask for the instructions for the ritual.*

Zanaya's lips twitched, the heaviness retreating. *Lover, I'm not sure we should be adding fire to our arsenal. Remember that time I decided to be romantic and fill your room with pretty glass lamps? I do hope your housekeeper from that time Sleeps forevermore. I still owe him a hundred yards of curtains, several carpets, hours of manual labor, and of course, my unending apologies. If I never have to face his gravely disappointed face again, it will be far too soon.*

His stomach muscles hurt from containing his laughter.

Another stir at the door and Qin, tall and slender, his wings all the colors of an aurora, and his shoulder-length hair obsidian water, flowed into the room. No one knew his age, but since he'd had a relationship with Cassandra, he had to be the oldest of the current Cadre. Yet it was Caliane who was officially given that honor—because Qin was . . . faded. One foot in this world, one foot in the world where his beloved lay Sleeping.

I've heard he's been moping since he woke, Zanaya said.

Alexander gave her a speaking look. *Truly, Zani. Have you no heart? The man mourns the lover who can never be with him.* Cassandra, with her visions that drove her to claw out her own eyes, couldn't exist in the living world. *I lost you but for a mere moment in time in comparison and I felt as if*

I would break forever. His breath caught even now. *I understand why he is the way he is.*

Zanaya's dark eyes held his, passionate and intent. *But you did your job, Alexander. You never allowed your people to feel a lack. He's an archangel, too. He needs to do his duty and not be a depressed wraith who floats around like a maiden in a moldering castle.*

Alexander fought off an outward wince. Truth be told, and despite his new understanding, he'd had the odd uncharitable thought toward Qin, too. The archangel did his duty, but only just. The territory he'd taken over was doing fine. But fine wasn't good enough for either Alexander or Zanaya. Their territories had always sung, always beaten with a fierce heart, their peoples proud to shout their fidelity to their archangel.

The same could be said of the territory of Raphael, youngest of the archangels.

The Archangel of New York walked in just then with Suyin, the newest of the archangels. Alexander caught Zanaya's mental inhale, understood it. She might've seen Suyin on the screen, and Alexander had told her that Suyin was Lijuan's niece, but to see the new archangel in person had an entirely different impact. For with her hair of ice-white and skin the same, Suyin bore an eerie similarity to her dead aunt—except for the warm darkness of her eyes, and the beauty mark under one eye. Though her wings were mainly white, her bronze primaries and the vibrant energy in her eyes saved her from appearing a being without color.

Today, she wore bronze leathers that echoed the shade of her primary feathers.

Raphael, by contrast, wore black pants of a tough fabric Alexander often utilized, and a sleeveless tunic in the same color—the tunic was strapped to his body by multiple panels of fabric that ended in dull metal buckles. The hilt of a sword thrust over his shoulder . . . and on the fourth finger of his left hand was a ring of amber dark.

Alexander had never seen Raphael without that ring.

His heart twisted all over again as Suyin smiled at something Raphael had said. The newest of the Cadre and the youngest of the Cadre had become close after Raphael permitted one of his Seven to move to China for an entire year to help Suyin set up a court in her devastated territory.

That friendship had continued on over the years, and Alexander knew that it was to Raphael and Caliane that Suyin still looked when she needed to talk something over with a fellow member of the Cadre.

Was Caliane's lover worthy of her? Zanaya asked, her voice soft. *It's strange to be in this world with those I know, and yet their lives have shifted in ways remarkable and unpredictable.*

Alexander thought of his own sudden awakening, the heart-smashing news that Rohan was dead. Murdered. Yet his kind so rarely talked about the disorientation of waking in a world known but unknown.

He realized then that he'd never told Zanaya about Rohan and what had happened to his boy. He'd spoken only about Xander because speaking about Rohan broke his heart. She'd have assumed his son Slept or was in another territory. And he'd thought they had time enough to talk about everything. So much time.

He didn't want to put it off again, but this wasn't the place to share his memories of his precious boy, so he answered the question she'd asked. *Nadiel was smart and good with his hands and he made her laugh, and he loved his son with wild fury.* The other archangel's descent into madness didn't wipe out all that had gone before. *She has never been sorry that she loved him.*

Alexander had spoken but rarely to Callie on the subject of Nadiel, aware the loss and how it had come about had marked her for all eternity, but he had checked in on her in the aftermath. Before her own fall, her own descent into madness.

A good epitaph to a lost love. Zanaya's eyes were soft with sorrow.

She made a hissing sound inside his head the next instant,

and he knew without turning that Aegaeon, with his hair of blue-green, his wings of a darker green streaked by blue, and his insufferably bloated sense of self had entered the room.

"The Cadre is in session." Caliane's voice had them stopping their conversations and turning their entire attention to the meeting.

37

"It is good to see you again, Zanaya," Caliane said on the heels of her pronouncement, her long black hair in a simple braid today and her gown a color-drenched blue that echoed her eyes, her wings a span of white but her skin kissed by the sun. Look at her thus and you'd take her for a maiden who'd never made acquaintance with a blade, far less won many a battle.

Of course, to do that, you'd have to ignore the low hum of her immense power.

"To have you here, whole and healed," Callie continued, "it's not a gift we dared hope for, much less so soon."

Zanaya appreciated Caliane's welcome. She and the other woman had never been friends, but they'd been distant allies of a sort. And they'd never had any hint of jealousy between them. Zanaya had taken one look at Alexander and Caliane together and seen what she had with Aureline. A rare and treasured friendship.

Never would she think to in any way fracture that.

"Healed except for these." She pointed two fingers at her

eyes. "They were gray when I woke. That bitch left a piece of herself in me, and I don't like it in the least."

Suyin stirred, her hand flexing as if she wished to go for the knife strapped to her thigh. "Did she leave any other traces? My aunt might have been a twisted power, but she was a power nonetheless."

Zanaya had to fight from reaching for her sword. She had the feeling Suyin wasn't quite in control of her reaction, shocked into it by the ghost of her murderous aunt. Zanaya couldn't blame her—Zanaya's own reaction to the new Archangel of China was less than controlled. She knew Suyin wasn't her aunt, but the resemblance was uncanny.

Zanaya wondered if that made it easier or more difficult for Suyin to rule the territory that had once been Lijuan's. "I don't know," she said aloud. "I hope to all hells that this is it, nothing but a superficial scar." Even as she spoke, she felt an odd sensation in the back of her brain, a sense of stretching that she'd never before experienced.

As if she was reaching for something just beyond her sight.

Frowning inwardly, she shook it off. Had to be a remnant of her recent—and strange—Sleep.

"I think we all hope that," Aegaeon muttered, the muscles of his arms bulging as he crossed them over the silver breastplate he wore over pants of a tight black. "If I never see any hint of Lijuan again, it'll be far too soon."

Too bad the same couldn't be his fate, Zanaya thought with narrowed eyes. Alexander didn't know that Aegaeon had tried to woo her at a time when the entire Cadre knew full well that she'd never be with any archangel but Alexander. She'd never told Alexander because, quite frankly, it'd have started a war and wasted a hell of a lot of lives.

Her lover was many things. But easily forgiving of such trespasses he wasn't.

Zanaya, however, wasn't going to be responsible for a war. She wasn't some idiot beauty with an empty head who thought violence on her behalf the highest form of flattery. She didn't need or want wars to be fought over her. She fought her own wars—and Aegaeon had learned very well that he should never *ever* put his hands on Zanaya. Or she'd literally cut one off.

She enjoyed recalling the look on his face as he bled all over himself.

The full disrespect of Aegaeon's transgression was the only thing she'd ever kept from Alexander, and she intended to do so forever. She'd mentioned that Aegaeon had propositioned her so that the big blue ass couldn't catch Alexander unawares, but she'd made it a joke—and she'd been careful not to say *when* the proposition had occurred or how *insistent* Aegaeon had been.

"I swatted him like a fly," she'd said with deadly honesty when Alexander's expression began to darken. "He'll dream of me only in his nightmares." Then she'd begun to sharpen her favorite blade.

At which point, Alexander's shoulders had begun to shake. He'd ended up laughing his head off, anger diffused and war no longer a possibility. Because Alexander knew that Zanaya wouldn't thank him for doing violence on her behalf—but he was also an imperfect being, as were they all. Which was why Zanaya had dealt with it as she had.

Today, she smirked at Aegaeon across the circle, willing him to remember the day she'd separated his wrist from his body. It had been worth the loss of one of her favorite tunics— the spray of his blood wouldn't wash out.

Zani, why are you antagonizing Aegaeon?

It's a hobby.

A snort of mental laughter. *My apologies. Carry on.*

Aegaeon, meanwhile, was avoiding catching her gaze. She didn't think he was afraid of her—the ass was too arrogant for that. No, what had stung him the most had been the blow to his ego, the realization that—*gasp*—not every woman in the world would fall to her knees at the merest hint of his attention. Imbecile.

"We're here for one main reason," Titus boomed at that

moment, and though he, too, wore a breastplate and was big and muscled, he had exactly zero other similarities to Aegaeon. "Let's get that out of the way first. Lady Zanaya, as discussed, I have no problem with reinitiating the border in Africa that would give you reign over the northern half, while I take the southern."

"Call me Zan," Zanaya reminded him, grinning at this young archangel who'd somehow become such good friends with Alexander that he made her lover laugh. "No one's ever accused me of being a lady."

A responding grin from Titus. "I think we will get along well, Zan. In all honesty, I would've settled for a merely sane neighbor after putting up with that fetid scum Charisemnon for so many centuries—but you are so much more than that. I would be most pleased to call you my neighbor."

Charmed, Zanaya said, "And I you, Titus." She glanced around the circle. "Does anyone have an argument with our territorial agreement?"

"No—it makes perfect sense," Neha murmured, her tone a touch distracted.

Zanaya didn't know too much about the Archangel of India except that she was fearless in battle. She'd held nothing back in the fight against Lijuan. And from what Alexander had told her of the post-war period, Neha had fought side by side with her squadrons and ground forces to dispatch the reborn children that remained in her territory.

"She was never a general," Alexander had murmured, "but, when it was needed, she behaved like one of the best. Her people would do anything for her."

Today, the rest of the Cadre echoed Neha's statement, and the conversation moved on to matters that had been shelved until an in-person meeting. Zanaya kept her peace throughout, listening and learning the status of the world. It appeared that rebuilding their devastated territories had taken center stage over the past decade until, at last, they lived in a time of peace and prosperity.

"Will such a time bore you, Zanaya?" Caliane asked after

the meeting was over and they'd all stepped outside into the sunlit courtyard to drink and eat and talk. The food had been provided by the staff Titus's sister had handpicked for this reclaimed stronghold, and they'd done themselves proud.

They were all Zanaya's people now, and, as she and Caliane strolled into the low-height maze garden that was the left border of the courtyard, she made a note to praise them for their work. "You know I've battled in many a war," she said, "but despite what some might think, I far prefer peace. I like to rule, to build my territory to be strong. War shatters things."

Caliane's expression was thoughtful. "Yes, I see that now I look back. Your territory was a jewel in the world's crown. I'm only sorry that Charisemnon did so much damage to the part of it he ruled during his reign."

The pull came again at the back of Zanaya's brain, and she could've almost sworn she heard a whisper. The tiny hairs on her arms rising, she flicked her eyes this way and that, but the maze garden and courtyard beyond were empty but for her fellow archangels. The staff and others had been dismissed for the duration of the meeting.

Gut tense, she nonetheless kept her expression calm and continued on in her conversation with Caliane. Afterward, she spoke to others in the Cadre, including with Raphael. The young archangel with his sun-kissed skin, vivid blue eyes, black hair, and wings of white with a metallic glitter to them—a true white-gold—was much the same as during the war, but for the extraordinary mark on his right temple.

Then as now, it reminded her of a mythical dragon, but though the lines were as defined, it appeared . . . flatter to her gaze. As if it had lost its vibrancy. A sign of the end of the Cascade? But that wasn't what she wanted to ask him. "How is your consort?" she said, still fascinated by the fact he'd fallen in love with a mortal—and turned her into an angel.

Raphael's lips curved a touch. "She says that when you last woke, you looked at her like a new and interesting bug."

Zanaya was not often rendered speechless, but her jaw

dropped at that statement. Then she laughed, delighted with both this archangel who'd dared say that to her face—and with his consort. "Alas, I must plead guilty to that. She is the first being of her kind I've seen in all my existence."

Mortals had never registered on her consciousness as anything but fleeting sparks in the darkness. She'd appreciated the art they created, the work they did to maintain the world, but she had trouble bonding with them—she couldn't get past the fact that they'd be gone just as she was settling into a friendship.

"I'll attempt not to examine her with such rude intensity the next time we meet," she promised, ignoring the increased stretching at the back of her mind. It was disturbing but not uncomfortable. "Your territory has recovered from the war?"

"In most senses," Raphael said. "One strip of Manhattan remains scorched and dark, with no sign of new life." A grimness to his jawline. "Suyin is right—her aunt was a *power*. She left her mark on the world in more ways than one." Those eyes so intense in shade as to be impossible pinned Zanaya to the spot. "You shouldn't be awake and whole, Lady Zanaya. We all know that."

So, it appeared Caliane's handsome son was far more forthright than his diplomatic mother. "Do you believe me one of her reborn?" The idea of being one of those monstrous *things* that shouldn't exist made her stomach churn.

"No. A reborn couldn't hold this conversation with me. But, given the nature of your injury, you've healed too fast. We must know the answer as to why."

Never one to shy away from harsh reality, Zanaya said, "Your immunity to her ability. Did you retain anything of it in the aftermath?" Cascade gifts were oft violent, but what they left behind tended to be a gentler kiss of power.

He looked at her with unflinching intensity, his hair blue-black in the sunshine. "Why do you ask?"

Well aware he had no reason to trust her with what abilities he did or did not have, she held out her hand. "Touch me if you will, Raphael. I would like to know if you sense her in me."

A pause as if she'd startled him, but then he gave a curt nod and closed his hand over hers. They both flinched at the discomfort of their archangel-to-archangel contact. She released a breath through clenched teeth. "It's never been this painful."

In most cases, it was a niggling unease that, if left to grow, could turn into violence and anger, pitch predator against predator. Wars had been started by archangels driven to violence by this most primal urge, an urge so vicious and brutal that it took teeth-gritted will paired with millennia of experience to fight it.

With her and Alexander, however, the effect had been dull from the start, and it'd worn down even further over time. They only really got into trouble if they spent too much time together—more than a month of constant contact would do it, but it had to be *constant*. Spending every night in each other's arms and being in close proximity throughout the day. Given their duties as archangels, that was a scenario that rarely came into play.

When it did hit, it took as long—or *longer*—a period apart for the effect to wear off. Which was why they'd learned to ride the edge, go so far and never too far. Far better to take a week apart every two weeks than be forced to keep their distance for a month or longer.

The repulsion effect was worse with others in the Cadre, but never akin to this sharp blade of actual pain.

"No." Raphael frowned. "Usually—and especially at the start—it's a minor irritation at most." Despite that, he didn't release her hand for a full minute. "I taste nothing of Lijuan's evil," he said as they separated at last, Raphael shaking out his hand and Zanaya rubbing hers on her thigh. "But . . . the force of the repulsion between us may be an answer in itself. I react this way to no one else in the Cadre."

38

The young archangel's words whispered in her mind long after he'd moved on to discuss a more local matter with his neighbor, Elijah. Truth be told, Raphael had only vocalized what Zanaya already believed: something was wrong with her. And that something had to do with Lijuan.

Looking up at the sound of Alexander's laugh, she saw him once more in conversation with Titus. Her golden warrior of a lover so handsome and honorable with his openhearted young friend. They'd fallen back into the best times of their relationship after her waking . . . but now fear nipped at her.

What did she carry inside her?

Was she infectious?

Could she hurt Alexander?

Her throat dry, she swallowed. And the stretching in her mind grew stronger, more powerful . . . and aimed itself in a certain direction.

Alone in this corner of the garden shadowed by the spreading branches of a tree familiar to her from her reign as Queen

of the Nile, she shifted on her heel until the stretching settled. As if she'd pointed an internal compass to true north. It
took her a moment to orient herself, to realize the direction
in which she was gazing.

She'd half expected it to be China. That would've made
sense.

This, however . . .

A hand on her lower back, a familiar wing sliding over
her own.

She jerked away, feeling slimy and dirty. *Infected*.

Alexander looked at her with a frown. "Zani?"

"Has anyone checked Antonicus's grave since we buried
him?" she blurted out.

Alexander's forehead furrowed. "Yes," he said. "We've
maintained the regular patrols from Elijah's and Titus's territories, and each one of us does at least one personal flyover
a year." He searched her face. "We've seen no change in the
ice island where he rests, felt no indication that he stirs."

The stretching inside Zanaya persisted. *Insisted*. "I want
to see for myself." Wouldn't sleep easy until she did.

"Zani?"

"I'm different, Alexander. In a way subtle and insidious."
No point hiding from that. "I can sense Antonicus as if I have
within me a thread that ties us together."

Expression grim, he said, "The others? Michaela, Astaad,
Favashi?"

"No, I sense only Antonicus." She had no doubts that he was
the one calling to her. "Maybe because the others are inside
Cassandra's fire, shielded from the world." It was the only
thing that made sense—though none of this made sense. "I
must see where he lies. I won't rest until I'm certain he doesn't
walk." Because he *couldn't* have recovered, not given what
had happened to him.

Then again, neither should she. So perhaps they'd both
come back monstrous.

"I'll go with you."

Burning lines on her cheekbones, she glanced over at the

others. "I don't want anyone else to know." Not yet, not until she knew what she'd become.

"No," Alexander agreed, his skin pulled taut over the bones of his face. "You can't leave straight after taking over your territory either. It'll be noticed."

Zanaya flexed and tightened her hand. "I'll make it seem as if I'm doing a high-level flight over my new lands, taking in all that is now mine. That'll give us enough time to fly there and back."

Alexander's skin felt as cold as the place where they'd laid Antonicus to rest. The idea of Lijuan having left an echo in strong, honorable Zani was an abhorrent one. "Wherever you go, I'll be at your side."

To his surprise, his fiercely independent lover didn't voice a protest. Rather, she said, "I think you should. Just in case there's something *seriously* wrong with me and I try to dig Antonicus up and bring him back to life or commit another act equally repugnant."

Alexander's jaw worked. "Lijuan left pieces of herself everywhere. I was speaking to Neha—she says she just discovered a small cave full of nesting reborn who somehow managed to survive by taking only one person at a time from different villages. A deadly level of cunning."

"Insurance," Zanaya muttered. "Lijuan really believed that, no matter what, she'd survive to come back, even if she lost the war. She believed herself a god, a being far beyond anyone's touch."

"Archangels who lose themselves to power madness often do." His eyes went to where Raphael spoke with Elijah. "I became many things while you were gone, Zani. A father, the most Ancient member of the Cadre for a time, and an angel who almost lost himself to power."

He nodded over at Raphael. "I all but went to war with Caliane's beloved son for no reason except that he was young and had ideas of his own and I was somehow insulted by it all."

"You?" Zanaya's eyes flared. "You were the wildest of the

archangels, the one who thumbed his nose at all the settled members of the Cadre."

"Yes." Such an age ago that had been. "It was another young one, our current historian, who made me confront the path I walked." Echoes of that long-ago conversation in his mind. "Had you not been in Sleep, you would've stood against the man I was becoming. You would've fought at Raphael's side."

Zanaya was yet staring at him. "Did you really come so close to the edge that you would've forced me to raise my sword against you, thus breaking my heart forever?"

Alexander's chest ached at the blunt words. But never had he been a liar. So he said, "Yes. I see it now, looking back. Then, I was in the grip of a conceit that skimmed the edge of the egotistical madness that consumed Lijuan—that she *allowed* to consume her."

That was what Alexander could never forgive, and why he felt no sorrow for Lijuan's death. "She could've chosen to Sleep. You will know exactly how viciously hard it was for me to let go of my territories, to leave the world, but I had a moment where I stood on my fort and I thought . . . Zani would be ashamed of me if I do this. And so I Slept."

Zanaya's throat moved. "I know little of Lijuan's history, but I think she didn't have a friend or lover akin to what you are to me and what I am to you—a being whose opinion matters deeply enough to make us change our course and confront our less-than-humble archangelic natures."

She touched her fingers to Alexander's heart. "You are my touchstone, too, my Xander." A tug of her lips. "Sorry, I keep forgetting that name is taken now. Will you introduce me to young Xander?" The words were followed by a hard shake of her head. "No, not until I know what is happening to me. What *has* happened to me. I would not inadvertently harm this most vulnerable piece of your heart."

Closing his hand over hers, he squeezed. "We'll find the truth, and then we'll find the solution. I *refuse* to lose you again."

39

The lone Sleeper could sense others that were kin to him.

Small pockets.

Hidden.

Secret.

Distant.

But the biggest draw was a pulse that beat hard and strong and *called* to him. As if he were a dog to come to heel.

Anger boiled his blood.

He was no one's pet.

And he was far smarter than the one who would humble him, who would turn him into prey.

Lying as motionless as the dead, no air in his lungs, he smiled and his face cracked, a small frozen piece falling away.

40

Zanaya's mouth was dry and her heart a drum as they hit the edge of the "no-fly zone" around Antonicus's grave. It had been one of the younger angels she'd met in Titus's lands who'd first used that term, explaining to her that it had been created once mortals began taking to the air in their metal machines.

Zanaya liked it. It was direct and to the point.

Today, tired but with her nerves afire, she and Alexander skimmed icy waters choppy from the wind, their caps white, and shards of ice floating on the surface. In acknowledgement of the fact it would get colder and colder from this point on, she'd pulled on a pair of leathers in black.

Her entire current wardrobe was a gift from Alexander. He'd had multiple sets of clothing created for her in preparation for the day she woke—though he'd had no comprehension of when that might be.

He could be so tender, her general sinewy and harsh.

Her top had no sleeves and closed up the front using an invention called a "zipper" that was a sharp strike of silver against the midnight of the leather, but she'd decided to wear a garment called a "thermal" underneath the leather. Long sleeved, it was decidedly warm and covered her arms.

She treasured the clothing, for it was a symbol of Alexander's care for her, but she did miss her favorite worn-in leathers. However, there was a limit to how long anyone stored a Sleeper's belongings. To the credit of those who'd come into her territory after her, they *had* left her stored items in place—and then an earthquake had collapsed the site, along with her long-turned-to-dust clothing.

No one ever talks about having to get a whole new wardrobe when you wake from Sleep, she said to Alexander. *We literally wake up in the clothing in which we went to Sleep, and that's all we have.*

The silver-winged flyer beside her shot her an amused glance. "I was only asleep for a few hundred years—and I had a son as well as my Wing Brotherhood. They stood as guardians over what was mine and were active in preserving my belongings. Most of my personal property came through unscathed."

She made a rude gesture at him.

His responding laughter melted the ice in her lungs. There he was—her Xander. The one with whom she'd fallen in love and stayed in love through forever. "At least I don't have to deal with a crisis of conscience over Charisemnon's belongings."

Her breath puffed the air as she spoke aloud, and she was almost sure she saw the air turn to ice crystals. "Though, having caught up a little on what he did, I'm very certain it would've been no crisis at all. I'd have happily scorched all that he touched with his diseased filth."

"That's why the territory needs you," Alexander said. "Titus has done an excellent job of regaining the trust of the people, so you won't be starting from scratch. But they are wounded and need a leader who can focus wholly on them."

"Nursing the wounded is not one of my winning traits." An unfortunate truth.

"Your second or another can take that role. You'll be the honorable warrior who they'll soon learn will rule them with fairness and compassion."

Zanaya snorted. "Don't make me sound better than I am, lover." She had her flaws—she could be short-tempered for one, liked to stir up small troubles for no reason, and found it greatly amusing when others of her kind acted with idiocy.

"You've never started a war, Zani," was Alexander's riposte. "Not many archangels can say that. Not even I."

She parted her lips to argue, closed them on the realization that he was right. She might like to stir up small troubles, but that was about as far as it went. Oh, she'd fight like a lioness to defend her territory and her people, but leave her alone and she'd go about her business without releasing the hornets of war.

Chewing on that, she flew on in silence with Alexander. They'd never needed to fill their silences, as they'd never needed to ask permission from each other to speak. It was accepted between them that there would be long periods of quiet, and that interruptions were welcome when something had to be said.

She watched him when he gave in to the youth within and dove down in a steep drop, before spiraling back up. He was silver and gold against the white sprawl below, the ocean hidden by a sheet of ice that was getting thicker with each wingbeat.

The Cadre had chosen this as Antonicus's place of rest because it was far from all settled places in the world. No one had said it, but she thought they'd also chosen it because it was so cold. To stop any further rot, to perhaps allow him to heal faster . . . if he was going to heal at all.

Her chest ached from the coldness of the air, but she dove down after Alexander, then raced with him to the sky. And for a moment, they were youths again, playing with each other, rather than two sensible and mature Ancients who should surely know better.

But the laughter and the delight faded in the next half

hour, as they hit the halfway point in the no-fly zone, then moved beyond it. Until at last, they hovered over the cairn they'd built to mark the resting place of Antonicus, Archangel of the lost city of Elysium.

Buried in snow and ice, it had become a small and unremarkable hill in the midst of an ice-coated ocean. Her breath frost in the air, Zanaya landed in an area she remembered as being rocky. Her boots sunk in at once, the snow coming up to her thighs. "Ugh!"

Alexander did a terrible job of hiding his chuckle. Hovering above the snow, he said, "Not been in snow for a while, Zani?"

"I will deal with you later, General Alexander," she muttered, and used archangelic power to melt away the snow so that she stood in a dry hollow.

When Alexander landed beside her, he didn't bother. But he wasn't playing anymore and neither was she, both of their gazes on the snowy hill that held an archangel caught between life and death.

She saw no signs of any disturbance, but still her tendons remained tense, her stomach clenched. Light flecks of snow began to fall, the scene peaceful and lovely, it was so silent and white.

"Do you still feel it?" Alexander asked. "The thread that pulls you here?"

Zanaya breathed in air that was sharp knives in her lungs. "Yes. It almost hurts now. I'm in the right place." Taking a long breath of the frigid air, she held it for a full ten seconds before exhaling. "I need to know for sure."

A short nod before Alexander lifted a hand and began to melt the snow off the cairn with delicate precision. She didn't attempt to assist. He'd always been better than her when it came to such subtle use of power. In the same way that she could generate balls of angelfire at double his considerable speed.

Their differing strengths and weaknesses were one thing about which they'd never fought. Rather they'd seen it as a gift that meant they made a far stronger team. "Why aren't we like this with everything?" she found herself saying in this cold and desolate place that was the grave of an archangel.

He didn't glance away from his exacting work. "What are you talking about?"

"Cooperative, willing to be supple. Why do we always break?" Alexander had been her last thought before she went into her Sleep, and her final thought when she believed she was dying.

He was *so* important to her—so why couldn't she make it work with him?

Why had they never achieved the grace that Raphael and his consort had already managed after but a blip of time? She'd *felt* that comfort between them, that acceptance that they were each other's forever and that nothing could come between them.

Zanaya and Alexander had never come close to such a bond.

"Raphael's consort might believe I looked at her like an interesting bug," Zanaya added, "and perhaps I was rude at first, I can admit it." As the entire Cadre had turned out in person to ensure she wasn't a reanimated mummy, it wasn't every day that an Ancient archangel woke up and saw a mortal who'd been turned into an angel and was now consort to an archangel.

"But," she said, "the reason I watched her and Raphael so intently after my first shock was because they . . . fit. Like two pieces of a wooden puzzle played with and loved so long that its edges are smooth with love and time. They flow and bend and stay."

As the snow fell, she felt her heart break. "Why could we never stay, Xander?" Again, her pet name for him slipped out.

"Zani, they're infants," was the answer of the general who was Alexander. "Barely together for a heartbeat. We were together for millennia." Impatient, annoyed with what he thought was foolishness.

"Never that way, lover," she said, too old not to be blunt in return. "We were never that close and faultless a fit. Too many jagged edges in both of us."

Alexander shot her a look, this one full of aggravation, but kept on with his task. And when he spoke, it wasn't about their splintered history, but the reason they'd flown to this bleak place on the edge of nowhere. "I see a sigil."

The symbol glowed at that instant, recognizing the power that touched it.

"Yours," she said. "Mine was on the other side." It seemed a fitting metaphor for their entire relationship: never quite together, always separated—not by continents or distance, but pride, willfulness, the inability to be vulnerable.

"And there's Raphael's." Even here, Caliane's son wore his love openly, having altered his original sigil to include his consort.

His name in the angelic tongue—twined around the dagger of her.

Archangel and Guild Hunter.

Cadre and Consort.

Raphael and Elena.

Zani and her Xander had never become so entwined, a unit against the world.

"I can see Caliane's," Alexander muttered, his forehead furrowed as he fought to contain his power to a fine beam.

Not disturbing him any further, Zanaya just waited, though the "push" inside her strained at the seams, telling her to go and—

That was the thing. She didn't know what the compulsion wanted her to do.

Her face was ice by the time Alexander unearthed the entire cairn. The lightly falling snow wasn't enough to snow it in again quickly, so Zanaya had plenty of time to walk around, check for any sign of stirring from within—or any indication that someone had tried to dig their way in from the outside.

Archangels usually emerged without any real effort, but

Antonicus had been wounded beyond anything she'd ever seen or could imagine. However there was nothing. Not a whisper. Not a sigh. Not even a rock out of place.

Still not satisfied, she placed her palm against the cairn, ready to sense a weak pulse, a warmth. "It's cold," she said. "Ice." As Antonicus's body must've become, his organs frozen in stasis.

Lifting away her hand with a wince, she shook off the bite of cold, then checked the entire cairn once more. The snow had begun to create little drifts at the edges of the structure, no heat to melt it. "No sign of life." She stepped back. "Antonicus Sleeps."

"I agree." Alexander, his expression grim, had checked with as much care as Zanaya. "But I'm glad we came to confirm. Lijuan was a strange and unknown power."

Unsettled yet, Zanaya stared at the grave the snow was once more on the road to claiming. "I'll fly back here at regular intervals." She wouldn't rest easy otherwise. "Until I'm satisfied that whatever I'm feeling is nothing but a resonance to fading hints of Lijuan's power."

Until she knew she hadn't returned a monster.

41

"Will you stay then?" Alexander asked on the heels of her thoughts. "Is your Sleep complete?"

When she glanced at him, she saw nothing. It didn't shock her. He'd become very good at donning his "Archangel in charge of the universe" face over the years of his rule. So had she. It was a useful face to possess.

Especially when hiding powerful emotions.

"You're angry," she said, for anger was often the thing that came between them.

Hands on his hips, he shrugged. "I was when you first went into Sleep, but it's been eons. I got over it a long time ago." He folded his arms. "I just want to know as a member of the Cadre."

Harsh words—except he was never that fidgety when he was truly being cold. "Ah," she said, a softness in her heart that was for him and him alone. Always had been, always would be; it was a truth as immutable as the sky and the earth. "I was already on the verge of waking when I was pulled out by the Cascade. A few more years, and I would've risen."

"Is that a yes?" A harsh demand.

Irritation surged. "Yes," she said, legs set hip-width apart and her own arms crossed over her chest. "What? You expected me to sit mooning for you while you consorted with concubines and maidens?"

Snorting, he said, "I don't recall you going into seclusion from pleasures of the flesh."

A cold wind whispering past that suddenly made her feel ridiculous. "As if you cared," she muttered, throwing up her hands. "We were always loyal when we were together. *Always.* Not only for the start or the end, but throughout—and for *decades* afterward."

Alexander seemed to struggle with her words. At last, he exhaled and thrust his hand through his hair. "You make me forget that I'm an Ancient, am considered a leader of men and angels."

"Lover, we were never such things to each other." Because Zanaya, too, had glories to her name. Not as many as Alexander—he was simply inclined to heroic and huge quests—but no one who knew the history of the Queen of the Nile could say that she hadn't made her mark on the world.

She glanced over at the cairn, her gut yet chilled and uncertain. "Let us leave this place. It's not where I want to be having this conversation."

Alexander rose into the air . . . after her. He'd always done that. Always waited to make sure she was safely aloft before he took off himself. She'd been infuriated at him so many times over the centuries for what she saw as paternalistic hovering—but he wouldn't budge. The clash had led to more than one break in the timeline of their love.

Now, she shook her head, sad for all the time they'd wasted. "We were foolish young angels, were we not?" What did it matter if he liked to make sure she was safe before he took off? Alexander had long stopped trying to get in her way when it came to dangerous tasks. This? It was a small vagary of his, and she had vagaries of her own.

"Speak for yourself," he muttered over the winds, clearly still in the grip of some mood.

Rolling her eyes, she left him be. And they flew on in a silence taut with the tangled lines of their history . . . their broken love story.

Alexander knew he was acting as young as his grandson. He could look on from the outside and shake his head at his own behavior. But inside . . . inside he was as knotted up as the first time he and Zanaya had fought. Because his emotions for her had never faded. No matter how many years he'd loved her, or how many times they'd shattered.

It had taken him centuries after she went into Sleep to take another lover. Mortals—and even young angels—wouldn't understand such devotion, but when you lived so very long, time ceased to have meaning. He'd waited all those years for her to wake up so they could finish their fight.

But she never had.

"You left me," he said when they landed on an uninhabited island hours from the location of the cairn; its yellow-green grasses brushed his calves, the water that crashed to shore cold but holding no flecks of ice. "How could you leave me, Zani?" The wound inside him had never healed right; it had scarred and twisted and become stiff.

"Because I was old and tired, you stubborn fool!" Throwing up her hands, the passion of her a glory, she said, "You were old and tired, too, but you refused to come with me. I asked you over and over and you always had a reason to remain in the world!"

Alexander clenched his jaw. "I *did* have a reason. I stopped wars while you were Sleeping. I created an empire that stands to this day."

"And how many wars did you start?" was the acerbic response. "Well?" She tapped her booted foot against the sandy soil beneath the grass.

Alexander glared at her, memories of a war he'd *almost* started at the forefront of his mind. "That's not the point," he said. "We had an agreement, you and I. We'd never leave the other to Sleep!"

Zanaya's eyes flashed, then she shook her head. "No, Alexander. You made that pronouncement and expected me to fall in line." She twisted up her lips. "You had a habit of doing that. Just because you had a few years on me."

"A few—" His ability to speak devolving into wordless rage, he turned and strode to the other end of the windswept island, while the seabirds stared curiously with their bright black eyes.

Zanaya didn't follow him.

When he returned, it was to find her seated on the beach of crushed shells, her wings spread in a glorious show behind her. "Look at us," she muttered as he took a seat beside her.

Their wings overlapped.

An intimacy so taken for granted between them that even the worst anger had never torn it in two.

"What?" he said as he dug out a packet of dried fruits, nuts, and chocolate from a pocket in his pants, and passed it to her.

"I've been in the world less than a moon and we're already fighting." Opening the packet, she ate a small handful . . . and made a sound deep in her throat. "This is delicious! This world has many new wonders for me to explore, I see."

He felt his lips curve; she'd always enjoyed trying different foods. "Zani, I love you." A thing so true that it just was. "I've always loved you. I've never loved anyone else the way I love you. You're part of my very breath."

"You always did have a tongue as silver as your wings, lover," Zanaya said, her eyes on the ocean. "Tell me about the woman who bore you a child."

A stab in his heart, his eyes burning from a loss he wasn't sure he'd ever accept.

Putting aside the snack he'd handed her, Zanaya touched her fingers to his cheek. "Alexander, you're hurting." Shock in her flared pupils. "I'm so sorry, lover. I didn't know she had passed beyond the veil."

He shook his head and took her hand in his, weaving their fingers together. "Jhansi is alive, though she Sleeps at this moment in time. She's a gentle creature who has no familiarity with anger. She's . . . like the summer air. Pleasant and tranquil." He forced a smile. "We met one harvest festival, spent the night together. That was the extent of our relationship.

"She had heart wounds of her own that festival, and . . . I was . . . lost, tired." His hand clenched on hers on the admission that his decision to stay awake while Zanaya Slept had begun to haunt him. "Jhansi and I, ours was a joining of circumstance and comfort. Neither one of us had any plans to meet again—until she came to me with news that she carried my child."

He'd never doubted that the babe was his, even before Rohan came out looking like a carbon copy of Alexander but for his coloring, the majority of which he'd inherited from Jhansi. "She's an honest and generous person. You'd like her, but her overall nature is on the far end of the spectrum from either of ours." Jhansi was about as nonconfrontational as an angel could be.

"We never attempted to further our private relationship, but over the years, we became friends, for we were both very present in Rohan's life. Jhansi was a good mother to our son, and I made sure she'll never lack anything in her immortal life." Jhansi had floated through immortality, not accumulating much. "But Rohan was more my boy than he was hers— we were alike in many ways and I loved nothing better than to spend time with him."

Swallowing the knot in his throat, he said, "He was so smart and fearless, my son. Followed me all around the Refuge, and when he was old enough that I could take him to my territory, he couldn't wait for night to fall so I would take him on flights." Safe from the eyes of those who would see in Alexander's child a vulnerability.

"He called me Papa as a child, Father as an adult, and we were friends once he was of an age where he no longer needed me to guide him—though he continued to come to me for advice on various matters. I'm proud of that. That my son respected me as a man as well as a father."

His chest felt as if it was collapsing inward. "My Rohan is gone, Zani." It came out rough, his throat raw. "Murdered by Lijuan because he refused to reveal my place of Sleep." Because his son had *known* that place. Of course he had; Alexander would've never vanished without telling his cherished boy. "His beloved, Citrine, was also killed in the attack on their palace and all I know of her, I know from Xander."

"Alexander, I'm so very sorry." When Zanaya tugged his head down to her shoulder, he went, allowing her to stroke her fingers through his hair, comfort him as the crisp wind bit at their faces and the seabirds padded nearby. "Did Sharine ever paint a portrait of Rohan?"

"Yes." Those paintings were his most prized possessions. "I have them in my fort, and I'll be proud to show you." He wanted her to know his son, all Rohan had been. "Sharine's portraits of Citrine were lost when General Xi sacked the palace, but Sharine quietly repainted her from memory—one just of her, and one of her with Rohan and an infant Xander. Those paintings hang in Xander's rooms."

"I feel no surprise that your son was brave." Zanaya kissed his hair in a caress he'd permit no one else. "Courage runs in your blood."

He shifted to lie with his head in her lap, her beautiful face backlit by the cool blue sky and her fingers gentle as she continued to stroke his hair. "Titus tells me that Rohan became Favashi's most feared and respected general. I see this in how those who served under him speak of him, how much of their loyalty he holds to this day, and my pride, it knows no bounds."

"That is as it should be, lover." She ran her hand over the wing pressed up against her; he'd folded them in neatly, but an angel's wings weren't exactly small. Yet they'd taken this position with each other more than once over eternity and it was no discomfort to either.

"Was he a mischievous child?" Zanaya asked.

Echoes of a boy's impish laughter in his mind, a tiny body "attacking" his as Rohan tried to ambush him, a small hand holding his as big dark eyes looked up at him in a trust innocent and absolute. "The stories I could tell . . ." And because they had time on this isolated piece of rock and shell and grass, he did, pouring out his heart, which would forever bear the imprint of the son he'd loved more than life itself.

He also told her more of Jhansi, a gentle and loving mother whose very being would crumble when she woke.

The one thing he didn't say was that he wished Rohan had broken faith and revealed Alexander's place of rest. Because that would be to dishonor both his son's courage and Rohan's sacrifice. *Never* would Alexander do that. His boy had died protecting him, and that act of love was burned into Alexander's memories, never to fade or be forgotten.

42

"Citrine was a clerk," he said after he could no longer speak of Rohan. "But not just any clerk—she was the clerk who ran Favashi's entire court, the person who juggled myriad tiny and important details to ensure the entire system ran without a hitch." Alexander wished he could've known this woman, intelligent and driven. "Xander says she was a general in her own right—only that her field of battle was the court and politics."

Zanaya's smile was delighted. "A vivid image. It's the role Mivoniel played for me when he decided to come out of retirement and join my court."

Needing a hint of softness, he played with her hair, so luxuriant and thick. "Xander tells me she adored him, and had a streak of mischief in her despite her outwardly quiet manner. The way he colors her with his memories, I can see why my son loved her." Could glimpse the dancing eyes and playful smile.

"My grandson has the same love in his voice when he speaks of his father." Rohan had been the firmer hand of the two when it came to parenting, but not in a way that had hurt Xander. Quite the opposite. "Xander is far more thoughtful than Rohan, and says that he was a quiet child—but his father never made him feel as if that was a wrong way to be; Xander grew up knowing he was his father's pride."

A single tear rolled down Zanaya's cheek. "You raised a son with love and respect, Alexander, and he and his chosen mate in life carried that love through the generations."

Wiping away her tear as his own dried on his cheeks, he said, "It all began with my parents. I dread the day they'll wake, Zani."

She didn't try to tell him it wouldn't hurt, that their lives wouldn't shatter at the news that Osiris was dead. Rather, she leaned down to kiss him with infinite tenderness, her hair a perfumed curtain around their faces, the scent that clung to her only of her. It was the same haunting scent with which she'd ascended—and risen.

Cupping the side of her face, he let himself be so sweetly loved, the taste of salt and sorrow in their kiss.

Her breath was warm against his when she drew back, her features soft, and though this was a cold place far from ideal for intimacy, she didn't rebuke him when he put his fingers on the zipper of her jerkin. Pulling it down, he watched her shrug it off, then remove her sword and associated leather sheath—strapped to her body over the shoulders, and with straps that criss-crossed her upper torso.

She shivered when he stroked his hands under the black of her thermal top, her skin a smooth warmth that he ached to caress, to kiss. Then he felt it, a pulse of her power . . . that created hundreds of *tiny* windstorms around them, heating up the air. Of all the people in his existence since childhood's end, Zanaya alone had looked after him.

Feeling broken open, he just held on to her.

She kissed him again, cupping his face with both hands, while he gripped her waist with his. "Alexander, my Alexander." A murmur against his jaw, along it, down his throat.

Unable to wait to feel her touch on his skin, he stripped

his own upper body. She sighed, removed her top to reveal the round firmness of her breasts . . . then pressed herself against him, the contact a kiss of affection, of love, of two people who'd always been meant to be together.

Running his hand up her spine, he kissed her throat as she touched the hypersensitive arch of his wings. It made his cock ache, his heart thump, such deep pleasure that it was edged with pain. And his heart, it beat only with her name. His Zani.

They sat that way, kissing and touching, for a long time, Alexander healing under the raw wave of her affection so fierce and tender. When she rose to strip herself bare, he simply undid his pants to reveal his rampant cock. And then she took him, coming down to straddle him with an ease that had been eons in the making.

Eye to eye, lips to lips, his Zani rocked them into a release that tore up his spine and made his wings glow as he buried his face in the crook of her neck. He felt her quiver on him, around him, her body going taut before she went limp in his arms.

They lay entwined on the sand, Alexander having used his power to move away the shells. Even so, he made Zani lie on his wing rather than directly on the sand, then curled that wing over her naked body. He still wore his pants and boots, and her whirlwinds yet created a warmth that made comfort possible on this remote and chill island.

"I love you, too," she said when he thought she'd fallen asleep tucked against his side. "Until you're a madness I can't shake."

He was glad she'd stepped away from the grief; Alexander felt raw, could bear no more for today. "Charming," he muttered. "You make me sound a cursed affliction."

Zanaya shrugged, her hand on his heart. "It is what it is; I've driven you a little mad over the millennia, too."

Forced to admit she was right, he grimaced and shifted so that he could look down on her while she yet remained on his wing. "What are you saying? That we're not meant to be?" His gut became as hard as steel. Because that? He'd never, not once considered it. Theirs might not have been a smooth road, but so long as Zanaya existed, she'd one day be his and he'd be hers. That was their destiny.

"No, my love." Zanaya's lips curved in a smile that ached with sadness. "I'm saying that you were the last thought in my head when I went into Sleep, and the final flicker in my mind as that evil bitch of an archangel—" She bared her teeth. "As Lijuan sucked the life out of me, all I could think of was apologizing to you."

He scowled. "Apologizing? For what?" He knew damn well it wouldn't be for her decision to Sleep.

Fingers brushing his lips. "'I'm so sorry, Xander,' I wanted to say, 'but I can't come back this time. There's no more time to fix us'."

His anger, his fear, his frustration, it all vanished under a crashing wave of love and need. *"Zani."* But she held him back when he went to lean down, kiss her with a passion that erased the darkness.

"No, this is what we always do." Blazing eyes. "We fall into the emotion, into the passion, without ever fixing the fractures. Our foundation is rotten, has always been rotten. We never bothered to fix it because it was holding well enough . . . but I don't want that life now, Alexander."

His entire world threatened to burn to ash.

When she pushed at him, he shifted away, releasing her to get up and pull on her clothing and boots. He put himself to rights, too, taking the time to find his footing, ready himself for the battle to come.

Because he *was not* ready to just let her walk away.

The whirlwinds vanished as she took a seat beside him, their wings overlapping once more as they stared out at the ocean of darkest blue-gray. "I see that ridiculously young pup, Raphael," she said, "and I see what he has with his consort, and I'm a bitter and jealous old woman." A scowl. "If you ever repeat that, I'll scalp you."

She spoke on before he could respond. "I don't begrudge them their joy. Rather, I wonder why we could never have that when we had so much *love*."

Alexander took a breath again because at least she was willing to talk about it. The air was blades stabbing into him. "Too proud, both of us. Callie said that to me. Neither one willing to bow to the other."

"Pride mattered naught when I was dying." Zanaya's voice was a strain, her arms wrapped around her knees and the opals in Firelight dull.

"No," Alexander said, his chest so tight he could barely breathe. "I carried you to your place of Sleep and all I could think was that it was over, that I didn't have any more chances. The terror and pain with which I've lived since . . . I would've gone into Sleep forever if I didn't have a grandson to guide on in his path in life."

Zanaya took his hand, twining their fingers together in the way they'd done forever. "I'm glad for your grandson." Her voice was husky. "To have woken without you in the world—" She squeezed his hand. "I'll never apologize for going to Sleep. I needed to Sleep to recover from my eons of life, to ensure I didn't go mad like so many of our brethren . . . but I'm sorry I left you alone, Alexander."

Neither one of you ready to bow to the other.

Alexander fought past thousands of years of being, of personality, to say, "And I'm sorry I put you in that position. I should've listened to you." If he had, she might've agreed that the two of them could, together, go into a shorter Sleep. But he'd refused to even listen, and he'd lost her for endless millennia.

A jerky laugh. "Look at us, being so mature." Sighing, she put her head on his shoulder, as around them, the seabirds went about their business without a care, having clearly decided that Zanaya and Alexander were simply two extra-large birds.

"I can't do it again, Zani," Alexander confessed, slicing right to the agonizing core. "I can't lose you. Not for a few weeks, much less any longer. I've lost too much, am too old and scarred. I want an absolute and unassailable *us*."

Zanaya felt no shock at his words. She'd known exactly what he was about to say—because she'd been about to say the same. "It's always been you, Alexander. Never anyone else."

"Consorts then."

That did make her jolt, stare at him. "We're archangels," she said, her voice lined with grit. "If we become consorts, we'll no longer have a choice as to what we do when the war drums roll. We'll have to pick the same side." Because the enemy would treat one the same as the other.

Eyes of liquid silver locked with hers. "Yes," he said. "We can argue as much as we want behind closed doors—but to the world, we present a united front."

Zanaya had spent her entire lifetime fighting to be her own person. She was too old now not to see why—Rzia's efforts to mold her had turned into a kind of emotional prison that Zanaya had been running from her whole life. Even now, her heart stuttered at the idea of being bound so inextricably to this man who'd battle her tooth and nail when they disagreed.

Yet . . . hadn't she held her own with him since before her ascension? "I refuse to be frozen in amber," she murmured, mostly to herself. "Rzia lies long in my past. I'm no longer the child she attempted to shape with bitter vengefulness."

Alexander understood as only a rare few people in her life would. "As I'm no longer the powerless boy who can be crushed under the boots of others." Even the memory was faded now, hidden by the weight of a reign that had spanned thousands upon thousands of years. "I don't need to cling to power with every ounce of my being."

Zanaya shifted so that they were face-to-face, her expression fierce. "Consorts don't break, come what may. It's a bond to the death."

"I died when you fell, Zani. I have a promise to keep to my son, but it's the only thread holding me to this world should you not be in it. And that thread will break as Xander settles into adulthood." He clasped the back of her neck, beneath the softness of her hair. "I won't be in the world once it does unless you walk beside me. It hurt me to even breathe these past ten years. I'm yours."

Her eyes flared, then she gripped his jaw. "My ability to Sleep is currently compromised—but it'll heal. I've been wounded too many times not to sense that it's not a permanent injury." The certainty of an archangel. "But even if it doesn't, I don't intend to live until madness eats my mind, swallows all I am. I intend for my rule to end."

That was the natural order of life, of immortality. "I won't do this, lover, until you promise that you *will* Sleep. Should I not be able to Sleep, well . . . that will be the end of Archangel Zanaya, and you'll be free."

Zanaya pressed a hand over Alexander's mouth when he would've spoken, her heart thudding as if she stood once more in the ice of the Refuge, Alexander in front of her. A moment that had altered the trajectory of her destiny. "Not soon. You have your grandson, and I'm only just awake. In ten thousand years *at the most.*"

A scowl. "Why ten?" he said when she dropped her hand.

"Because that's a sprawling span of life," she pointed out. "Long enough for us to love . . . but not so long that we'll squander it as we've squandered most of eternity. Wasting time because we believed there'd always be more, an infinite hourglass. We need to shatter the hourglass for it is a seductive cage that keeps us stuck in time."

Harsh words. Brutal in their truth.

"And this Cadre?" she added. "It's too full of Ancients. It's lopsided and wrong. We should always have a balance of young to old, or we'll remain static. From there, it's not too long a journey to stagnant."

Alexander looked out at the ocean for a long time. She wasn't affronted. She'd rather he contemplate the point, be sure where he stood. Because once they declared themselves consorts, there'd be no coming back. Becoming a consort was a choice and a risk so precious that to turn their backs on it would be to spit upon the very structure of angelic society.

And they, neither one of them, was an oath breaker.

Alexander turned to her. "Ten thousand years or less." It was a promise. "And Zani, if you can't Sleep, if you move beyond the veil, have no doubt but that I'll follow."

Zanaya felt her entire world tremble, break, reshape into a new form. Because a promise from the Archangel of Persia was a thing bound in stone. "Alexander, Consort of Archangel Zanaya," she said, the words husky, "I pledge my being and my life to you."

His wings glowed, his eyes fierce. "Zanaya, Consort of Archangel Alexander, I pledge all I am and all I will be to you. To the end, my Zani. Till we are the merest echo of existence in the cosmos."

Hands shaking, she curled her fingers around his nape as she pressed her forehead to his. "To the end, my general. Until time itself stops."

43

Alexander hovered face-to-face with Zanaya at the point at which they had to go their separate ways. He didn't want to leave her with the bond between them newborn and fragile, but he was an archangel—as was she; they had duties to the people who looked to them for stability and protection.

Things had calmed in the years since the war, but the scars lingered. Especially after the post-war vampiric uprising, where thousands of vampires across the world had given in to bloodlust and ravaged the mortal populations.

Alexander had come down hard on the vampires in his territory, his capacity for patience murdered when Lijuan forced him to kill children. "The ones who helped contain the uprising," he told Zanaya after catching her up on that piece of history, "and the ones I know have their bloodlust under vicious control, they of course continue to have my trust."

Alexander had never been one to quickly give—or retract—his faith. "But the others must now earn back the trust of not only the Cadre, but the rest of society. Far too many vampires thought to take advantage of the aftermath of war and some in your lands might consider stirring during the transition of power."

"I thank you for the warning," Zanaya said, her hands on her hips and her features grim. "You're still content to lend me a few of your people?"

"For as long as you need them. All are eager to help set up a territory and I know full well I risk defections." A grin. "How can I blame them when you own my heart, too? So if you wish to make offers in time, I won't consider it a mortal betrayal." He clutched at his heart.

Her laughter was startled and bright. "I plan to steal vast numbers of your people, General. Be warned."

"I will then be honor bound to lure some back."

Smile yet a brightness in her gaze, she said, "Titus advised me that he'd lend me a few of his trusted people, too." She raised an eyebrow. "I'm not wont to trust strangers bearing gifts, but I feel nothing but goodwill from him."

"You can believe him without question," Alexander confirmed. "Titus is as open as the sky. He doesn't do cunning—and he truly does wish for a rational archangel as his neighbor."

"That was my feeling as well." Zanaya shook her head. "I continue to be astonished at this friendship, lover. You, with all your political wiles, and this blunt hammer of a man."

"He keeps me honest. Back when I was itching to start a war with Raphael, Titus wrote to me to tell me he'd heard rumors of the same—and he respectfully called me an idiot." His lips kicked up. "I should've listened to my friend."

"You have much to tell me of your life while I Slept."

"I'll tell you all, anything you ask. For now, I can confirm that if Titus trusts the people he has offered to send you, they won't betray you. Of course, they shall be cheerful spies for him, but that's to be expected."

Zanaya's shoulders shook. "There's another thing—he looked suspiciously gleeful when I mentioned that you'd offered to second squadron leaders Zuri and Nala. Is there something I need to know about the two?"

Alexander chuckled. "The twins are his older sisters—

two of four—and forever ready to tell their younger brother his business. So he is likely delighted at the idea that you'll keep them busy with the innumerable tasks that come with setting up a new court. And there you could have no better help—Zuri and Nala are powerful and experienced warriors who can stand in for your second for the time being."

Zanaya's eyes widened. "An archangel with four older sisters? Titus begins to make more and more sense to me." Lifting her hand, she touched her fingers to his cheek. "I must go now, my consort. But I'll see you again soon."

Taking her hand, he pressed it to his cheek. "Will you come to my territory? Now that we've confirmed that Antonicus Sleeps, I shall like to introduce you to Xander, this bright young piece of my heart."

Open joy in his Zani's expression. "I'll come as soon as I've stabilized the situation in my new land." A kiss passionate before she turned to the right, her wings homeward bound. But she looked back several times to where he hovered, watching after her.

His heart tore in two at seeing her move away from him, his mind bombarding him with memories of how he'd lost her the last time.

Move, lover. A martial order . . . that held a caress. *The sooner we can both complete our duties, the sooner we can meet again.*

Giving a curt nod even though she was now too far away to see it, he turned and headed to his own territory. It wasn't a long flight in the grand scheme of things, and he arrived before nightfall . . . to find Xander flying toward him from the very edge of his lands.

"Grandfather!" His grandson waved, his grin huge and his face so reminiscent of Rohan's that Alexander's scarred heart threatened to spasm with the agony of it.

"Xander." Alexander swept down so he flew wing to wing with his grandson, and he wondered if he'd ever been this young. "What are you doing here? Are you on patrol with your squadron?"

"No, Grandfather. I came to meet you." His gaze was open, his heart on his sleeve.

The child had been hesitant and quiet when he first met Alexander, but Alexander couldn't blame him for that. He'd been nothing but a memory of Rohan's to Xander—and the boy had been grieving for the loss of his parents.

Alexander wasn't a gentle man, but he'd made an effort to be so for this boy. Until one day, Xander had broken down during a private sparring session. Alexander had taken his sobbing grandson in his arms and when Xander tried to apologize, Alexander had said, "Never apologize for loving, Xander. That capacity is what keeps us from becoming monsters."

The boy had splintered that day, and then he'd rebuilt himself.

"Oh?" Alexander said now. "How did you know exactly where I'd be coming from? Surely my spymaster isn't leaking my whereabouts?"

Laughter from his grandson at the mere idea of Alexander's tight-lipped spymaster breathing so much as a word. "I've been learning how to use the mortal device that tracks their flying craft. Angels can't be tracked the same way because—"

"Just as well," Alexander interrupted, his tone granite. "We are not playthings for mortals." On this he would never budge—there was a hierarchy in the world for a reason.

"But," Xander continued, "every time I was on the device, I watched for any hint of a 'shadow'—that's what the mortals call angels glimpsed on the system. And I particularly watched for a shadow with your speed. It was difficult in the extreme—you were invisible but for a split second."

Alexander wanted to be infuriated that the mortal devices could track angels at all, even in so fleeting a way, but he couldn't bear to rain on Xander's joy. "Come then, Grandson," he said, awash in love for the son of his son. "Since you've found me, let us race home. I'll go at half speed." Otherwise, it'd be no race at all, the boy a stripling yet.

Giving a loud "Woop!" Xander took off, a dark streak in

the falling darkness. Look only at the top of his wings and you'd never realize the metallic underside.

Alexander laughed and took off after him. And he thought that an awakening of only ten thousand years was worth it to have such life in his veins, such energy. Zanaya was right, had always been right. He'd just been a stubborn fool to deny her.

It won't be easy, lover. If it was, we'd have gotten it right a hundred times over. We didn't. If we want forever, we need to work harder than we've ever before done. This is our final and most important war.

She'd said that to him on the flight home, an unknowing echo of Cassandra's prediction: *This time will be the end.*

44

Antonicus knew he was damaged. Knew he was not the archangel who'd woken—

His thoughts fragmented.

He couldn't recall why or when he'd last woken, the memories flash-fire flickers in his mind. Images of a devouring black fog. Of screams so piercing they were tiny insects in his brain. Of agony unending.

He turned away from them.

That was the past.

This was his future.

Flexing his hand, he heard the fracture of ice. He'd been encased in ice, left locked in cold. They would pay. All of them.

He'd already started to win, hadn't he?

No breath at all. No warmth. No sign of life.

She hadn't sensed him.

A small part of him that had once been an archangel, once understood life, knew that he should be worried. Angels needed to breathe. They wouldn't die without breath, but it was agonizing after a long enough period. But Antonicus literally didn't need to breathe . . . wasn't sure those organs even worked.

He glanced away from that, too.

The state of his body was . . . less than optimal.

But he could fix that. He knew how. He'd been told how inside the black fog, an insidious whisper worming its way into his mind as the dying mortals screamed and screamed and screamed.

45

Zuri and Nala proved to be as skilled and as trustworthy as Alexander had promised. They were also familiar with Zanaya's territory, having watched over it for their brother when Titus was in the southern half of the continent—and they were generous in sharing their knowledge with Zanaya.

"Are you open to a permanent transfer?" she said a month into her new reign, "Alexander will take no insult if you wish to do so and I'll take no insult if you don't. The choice is wholly yours." She had another thought. "Or perhaps you don't wish to remain this close to Titus?"

Wild laughter from the two beautiful warriors with their long black tails of hair and sharply slanted hazel eyes over dramatic cheekbones, their skin a richness of brown and their wings an amber-hued cream dusted with green that ended up in primaries of dazzling jade. "We adore being able to visit more. Our brother, in contrast, would be *delighted* to get rid of us," Zuri said. "We are a plague upon him."

Nala, the quieter of the twins, nodded. "Our poor brother. He is besieged by sisters who love him and also think they know better." A grin. "We can't help it. To us, he'll always be our little brother who we carried around as a babe."

Zanaya couldn't imagine what it must be like to have so many siblings who so openly loved you. And for all of Titus's muttering about his siblings, he'd glowed with pride when he'd visited of late and she'd told him how much she valued his sisters. She hadn't missed the fact that he'd then spent several hours with the twins of his own free will.

In their bond, she saw what Alexander had once had with Osiris, and she mourned for her lover. "Will you consider it then?" she said to Zuri and Nala.

The twins looked at one another, nodded. "We don't need to; we'd be honored to stay on." Both angels went down on one knee in a single smooth motion, their identical wings overlapping. "We've never been part of building a court and to do so at your side, Lady Zanaya, it's a dream. We need only to speak to the sire and gain his official assent."

Zanaya didn't ask for ornate displays of respect from her people, but she appreciated their formal bow all the more for being made out of choice. "I couldn't have better squadron commanders by my side," she said, then held out both hands, one to each twin.

Accepting the offer, they rose to their feet, and the rest of their conversation was taken up by the necessities of the court. That court was a skeleton yet. Almost none of Zanaya's old court was awake—or alive.

Only three had made their way back to her thus far.

An infinitesimal number, she thought as she stood on a high balcony looking up at the sky where a sleek young angel arrowed toward Alexander's territory. She'd just handed the courier a letter for her consort in which she requested the transfer of the twins' contract. Of course, it hadn't been the least bit formal. In truth, she hoped her glee at winning their loyalty would make him laugh. She loved it when her general laughed.

Her smile faded as she thought on about the damaged land that was now hers. "Auri," she murmured. "I'd very much appreciate it if you woke, my friend." She'd already used a screen device to speak to the slender brunette who was the angelic Librarian and Historian; Jessamy had gone through all available records and told her that there was no record of either an Aureline or a Meher waking in the time that Zanaya Slept.

"I'm sorry, Archangel Zanaya," Jessamy had murmured, the kindness in her eyes so innate that it was impossible to distrust her on any level, "but the records are patchy at best. To go so far back, I had to rely on the memories of the old ones who were awake during the relevant segments."

"I expected as much." Zanaya knew she'd Slept a long, long time.

"What I can say," Jessamy had added, "is that because Aureline and Meher were so powerful, being your second and third, their waking would've been noticed. The Cadre doesn't like to leave such powerful angels to do as they will."

Zanaya well understood that; she remembered how the archangels of old had watched Alexander like a hawk before his ascension. She might've been young at the time, but she'd had eyes and ears. And he'd been her fascination and her obsession.

"So," Jessamy had concluded, "it's highly unlikely that either has woken since they went into Sleep."

Zanaya had turned off the screen with a jolt of hope. She wasn't used to this new way of communicating, and her mind had trouble with the concept, but she couldn't argue about its usefulness.

So much so that she'd asked Nala to teach her how to use it. It had taken effort, but she could now make direct calls without assistance. She input her favorite person's name, and soon enough, his face—harsh and handsome and beloved— filled the screen.

"I hate this device," Alexander muttered with a scowl.

"That's because you're an old man, General."

Narrowed eyes. "I see the twins are being their usual good influence."

Laughter dancing inside her, she pressed her palm to the screen.

He pressed his hand to the screen on his side, his expression softer. "You have something on your mind, Zani."

Oh, he knew her so well. Dropping her hand after their silent and familiar communion, she said, "Do you know if an archangel can wake a person with whom they have a bond?"

"You're thinking of Aureline and Meher."

"It'd be good to have my second and third with me as I rebuild my court. The twins have told me that they don't feel suited to the responsibility of those positions, and I have to agree with them—they're brilliant squadron commanders and that's their strength."

Alexander sighed. "You've stolen them, haven't you?"

"I'm sure I have no idea what you mean. Oh, you'll be getting a visit from a courier soon."

Arms folded but lips curved, he said, "I can't answer your question about archangels, but I can tell you that I was rudely awakened by one of Raphael's Seven and his mate."

Zanaya's mouth dropped open. "Surely, you jest?" To disturb an archangel in their Sleep was a death sentence.

"No, it was needed. Lijuan."

Zanaya echoed his scowl. "Oh."

"But," Alexander said, "in my case, they managed to locate my place of Sleep, then yelled insults at me until I woke up. Turns out a Sleeper can hear such abuses when they take place right on top of him." Amused laughter that belied his stern tone. "You must meet Naasir—he's one of a kind." His smile faded. "The only chimera in all the world."

"He survived?"

"More than that. He *thrived*. Osiris would've been exultant." Head dropping, Alexander shoved a hand through his hair. "But Naasir wouldn't be who he is had he grown up under my brother's dark care. The Naasir we know today was raised with love and in freedom, not tortured and starved in a cage; he's a cherished part of Raphael's court, and Raphael's second may as well be his father."

Hating the old grief in his eyes, and hating his brother for causing it, Zanaya didn't ask any more on the subject. "I should be able to visit soon. The twins can hold the fort in my absence. And . . . I ache for you."

His jaw worked. "I dream of you. Every time I close my eyes."

Her eyes burned, her throat raw.

The two of them closed the connection without saying good-bye. They'd never again say good-bye. For the first time in their existence, they'd decided to put their stubbornness to work in pursuit of their love.

Stepping away from the screen with the urge to hold him close a tightness inside her, she thought of what he'd said. Because the thing was, she *did* know her second's and third's place of Sleep. She'd helped them create it.

"Will you help us find a place no one can disturb even should the earth tremble and split open?" Auri's eyes—that familiar and beloved translucent brown—dull and bruised by the loss of her babe, a loss made all the more agonizing for how late into the pregnancy it had come. Auri had felt her babe move in her womb before her child went forever silent.

Zanaya had been there when Auri gave birth, for her babe was too big to be released in any other way. She'd held that small, *so-small* body in her arms, tears rolling down her face as she pressed a kiss to his forehead, the child's skin blue yet warm from being inside his mother. And she'd held both Auri and Meher as they cried until they could cry no more.

Auri's desire to Sleep had come as no surprise. And Meher would always go where Auri went; she was the sun around which he revolved.

Zanaya had found the couple a safe location. Their babe didn't lie near them. They'd chosen to scatter his ashes in a forest inside Zanaya's territory, so that he'd become a part of the trees, grow as he'd never had a chance to grow in life.

Zanaya had watched over that forest for her entire lifetime prior to her first Sleep, and to her great joy, it had survived all the archangels who'd come after her, its trees tall and strong. Auri would be happy to see that, too. Zanaya had also promised her best friend that she wouldn't disturb her rest unless there was no other choice—and the world was a place Aureline would like to see.

She looked at the screen in front of her, considered the machines that flew in the sky and rolled on the roads, the buildings that speared the clouds, and thought Auri would be fascinated indeed. And Zanaya needed her on the deepest level.

Titus had done much to heal this land, but it remained wounded from the battles against not only the reborn, but Charisemnon's reign of misuse. The population had been decimated, and crops had failed in turn. All these years later, and the populace was yet fighting to get back to where they'd once been.

"They're a strong people," Titus had said to her when they met at the border two days earlier, to discuss what appeared to be a new incursion of reborn at the far end of Titus's territory. "But you can't squeeze blood from a stone, and they were drained to the bone by the time their ass of an archangel got his just deserts."

He'd glared, as if he'd like to kill Charisemnon all over again. "The wounds linger—and, I fear, fester. The current news won't help; I was confident we'd cleared the territory of Lijuan's poison."

"You're certain about it being the reborn?"

"All signs point to it—but it appears to be a single stealthy creature. My people should be able to hunt it down soon enough."

Zanaya hoped that was true, and that no reborn lurked in her own territory. Her people had suffered enough. "Auri suffered, too," she murmured to herself. "Do I have the right to ask her to wake?"

Sleep healed the physical. Perhaps it also healed the heart. And . . . Auri would never begrudge her for asking, not when it had been an eternity since she and Meher left the world.

46

Titus crouched down to examine the body at his feet. It bore all the hallmarks of a reborn—the rotten green tinge to the flesh, the reddened whites of the eyes, even the nails turned into claws that showed up in many but not all of them.

"Only problem," his second Tzadiq said, "is that it's dead. Without being decapitated or burned up." He shrugged. "Not a bad problem."

"But troubling because it raises questions." Titus used the hilt of a blade to prod the poor creature onto its back so he could examine it. He used no extra force—this person had been someone's daughter or wife or mother before she fell victim to the scourge and bore no fault for what had happened to her. "Only mark on her is the single bite to her neck." Clean, neat, a perfect impression of teeth.

"Shows a little too much control for my liking." The sun beat down on the pale skin of Tzadiq's skull. "Reborn tend to gnaw at their prey like feral dogs."

Titus nodded; he was of the same mind. Predators who could controlled their impulses and regulated their kills were far more dangerous than mindless beasts driven by nothing but the craving to feed.

"Should we take the body to the healers?" Tzadiq asked.

"No. Have the healers fly here to examine it." Titus wasn't about to spread any kind of infection.

Staring at the body, he felt a faint hint of familiarity, but this mortal wasn't anyone he could've known. Regardless, it wasn't her face that was familiar. It was . . . He blew out a breath, unable to quantify his response. "Ask the healers to check the creature's brain for differences to the other reborn." Titus had no idea what was occurring, but he knew it was aberrant. "Make sure to station a full guard over the body. The creature might be in some unknown form of stasis. The last thing we need is for it to rise up and attack."

Tzadiq nodded, the mist green of his eyes meeting Titus's over the body. "Did you notice the progression?"

Titus nodded. "No way to miss it." This was the oddest find to date, but their troops had eliminated a number of weak and sickly reborn over the past weeks; the first had been close to the southern tip of his territory. After that, each new reborn had appeared progressively farther north.

As if the reborn who was making the other reborn was heading to a specific location.

"Could be linked to Charisemnon," Titus muttered. "Any sign it's a reborn angel?" An abomination no one had ever expected to exist. "It could be trying to get to what was once home."

Tzadiq shook his head. "But there's no evidence it isn't, either. We have nothing."

Thoughts grim, Titus rose to his feet, Tzadiq echoing him, both of them big men with wide shoulders and muscled thighs—but that strength was useless against this invader cunning and stealthy. "I'll warn Zanaya." Whatever the creature was, it remained far from her at this point—but it would have gained strength with each kill.

It was possible that the Queen of the Nile would yet have to battle this scourge in her new territory.

47

Zanaya had intended to act on her decision to wake Aureline and Meher within the two days following, but—after receiving his message about the unusual reborn activity—she ended up flying to Titus instead. The two of them did a combined flight over a huge span of territory, searching for any indications of the creature's path.

Neither one of them found anything . . . but Zanaya felt eerie beats of sensation that weren't hers. Grass rustling over her skin when she was high up in the air, the bright metallic rush of blood *inside* a body, the feel of dirt under her fingernails. And then, without warning, a wrench on the same thread that had led her to Antonicus's grave.

She landed, her heart thudding as she readied herself to face the half-rotted archangel resurrected . . . but nothing existed around her but waving grasses and trees with a pretty filigree of leaves. The thread, too, had broken. Or had it unraveled when it didn't find what it sought?

When Titus came down beside her, she made the decision

to trust him with the knowledge of her flight to check if Antonicus stirred—and why. "Lijuan left a piece of herself behind in me," she gritted out at the end.

Titus grimaced. "I can see that, Zan." A subtle-for-Titus nod toward her eyes.

Clenching her jaw against the curses that wanted to escape, she hissed out a breath through her teeth. "We need to go over this area with a fine-tooth comb, and then I need to fly to check the cairn again."

"I can do the latter." Titus held up a hand when she would've objected. "You're in the midst of setting up a territory, while mine is stable. And if Antonicus has risen as not what he was, it'll affect us both."

To trust another archangel but for Alexander so deeply, it didn't come easy to Zanaya. But there was an integrity about Titus that shone like the sun. So she nodded. "I hope you find that he Sleeps, Titus, and that what I'm feeling is nothing but the awareness of a smarter-than-usual reborn."

Her discussion with Titus was yet uppermost in her mind when she was finally able to head out toward Aureline and Meher. She'd timed her journey so that she'd arrive in the darkest part of night, be cloaked from any watchers. She was one of the Cadre who had no glamour, but her coloring made up for that in the night hours. She was a ghost, the flecks of white on her wings easily mistaken for stars if she flew high.

She remained in the thin air above the clouds until she reached the point along the rich waters of her Nile where she'd helped Auri and Meher go to Sleep. At the time, the area had been uninhabited due to its dangerous geography. She was pleased to see that, despite the march of civilization, that remained true to this day.

Coming to a hover above the river, she used the power of her tempests to push aside the water and create a tunnel all the way to its chill heart. Dropping into that tunnel while the water swirled around her in a perfectly controlled spiral of liquid, she went down in a measured descent until her boots touched the riverbed.

Aureline and Meher Slept deep below the bed of stone and sand. Once they'd initiated Sleep, Zanaya had closed up the stone chamber she'd built for them using her power as an archangel—however, they were each strong enough to blast through the stone and emerge without her help. They'd get wet without her assistance, but they were of an age not to need to breathe for the duration.

Not wishing to crack the riverbed if they had no desire to rise, she put her hand to the gritty surface of the bed and spoke to her second with the power of her mind. *Auri, will you wake? The world is an interesting place, I promise. There's been a war, a Cascade, and Cassandra even woke up. Now, I need your help to assist in the rebuild.*

Silence without end.

Zanaya ramped up her mental voice to maximum and repeated her words as well as adding a few more—throwing in as much startling and intriguing information as she could in an effort to lure her friend out of Sleep.

Ouch, Zan. A voice so familiar it made time rush backward in a roar. *Why are you shouting?*

Zanaya tempered her tone. *You've been Sleeping a long while. Wasn't sure you hadn't gone deaf.*

You're not funny, my friend, was the grumbling response, Sleep yet heavy in Aureline's voice. *Did you say an archangel made the dead walk?*

And that isn't even the strangest thing to happen. She turned me into a mummy. I wish I could wring her neck but the others already obliterated her.

A mummy? Aureline sounded wide-awake. *You've kept the promise of waking me to an interesting world.*

Auri? I ask for you to stand by my side—but only if your heart wound does not cause you to bleed.

It exists still. Will always exist. But . . . the edges are no longer serrated. Pain in her friend's voice, but not the broken agony that Zanaya had heard before she lay down to Sleep. *Let me see if Meher wishes to wake. If he doesn't, I'll stay with him. Will you be very angry, Zan?*

No, Auri. Never with you. But I'll curse Meher with every breath.

Ah, so no change then.

Smile hot with emotion, Zanaya waited for her second to speak to her love.

The answer, when it came, was in Meher's deeper tone. *Zan, you were turned into a mummy?*

Of course he'd fixate on that fact. *Perhaps it was my destiny as Queen of the Nile.* Her people had, after all, invented the mummification process.

Snorting laughter from both of them, a sound beloved that made her grin.

We're waking, Zan, Auri said after they'd caught their breath. *It'll take time. I feel . . . heavy. Like I'm waking from an afternoon nap gone too long and deep. We've Slept eons, haven't we?*

Yes. She'd let Auri discover exactly how long once she was up and functional. *Take all the time you need, my friend. Alexander will alert me if there's trouble of a kind that needs my attention. Elsewise, I'll remain here.*

Of course you and Alexander remain a unit. Auri's words held no surprise whatsoever. *But did you say something about Cassandra waking up?*

Well . . .

Wait, wait. Auri laughed. *Tell me when I'm fully awake.*

Happiness a blaze in her blood, Zanaya took her place on the bank of the Nile, her gaze on the nourishing waters of the river that might as well be her blood flowing outside her body, it was so much a part of her. Everywhere the Nile traveled, it left behind life rich green and lands fertile—without its generosity, this part of her territory would be an arid and lifeless place.

Zanaya drew in a long breath, taking in the earthy scent of the river.

Alexander had often teased that she loved her Nile more than she loved him. Never could that be; she loved him more than existence itself—and this time around, they'd get it right.

A nagging voice that was a ghostly ricochet of her mother's whispered doubts and passive asides. They hadn't managed to make it work over so many thousands of years. What had changed now?

"An acceptance that we can die," she said aloud, because it needed to be spoken.

She and others of her kind were used to having no real concept of time. To them, mortal lifetimes were of no moment. And yet . . . She'd seen mortals fight with courage and passionate conviction not just in this last war, but in wars before. She'd witnessed their bravery and she'd witnessed their grief.

All of it so potent, so raw.

When, prior to this waking and the stripping of her walls, was the last time she'd been so open to emotion, to the world . . . to Alexander? Sadness washed over her when she realized she couldn't remember.

We need to shatter the hourglass for it is a seductive cage that keeps us stuck in time.

She'd been more right in saying that than even she'd understood at the time.

Movement in her peripheral vision, Aureline and Meher rising from the tunnel of water. They wore only the simple tunics in which they'd lain down to rest, their feet bare and their only jewelry the amber each had given the other: Aureline's was embedded into a metal cuff that fit snugly around her wrist, Meher's a single earring that he'd never once taken out.

Zanaya's pulse speeded up, her throat locking. "Auri." A rasp.

They embraced with fierce affection as Zanaya allowed the churning waters of her river to fall back into place. And when they drew apart, she did the same with Meher. Their relationship would never be the same as the one she had with

Auri, but she did deeply respect and value him—even more so for the eons through which he'd shared his mate's heart with Zanaya.

Many found it difficult to accept such a cherished friendship in their beloved's life.

Alexander never had.

A reminder from the part of her that was oddly young and hopeful after her long Sleep. She loved Alexander for so many reasons, one of which was that he accepted that a person could have many loves in their life. He'd loved his parents, his brother, and his son, now loved his grandson. She loved Auri and perhaps she even loved Meher a little.

It wasn't the same love as she felt for Alexander, for no other love would ever be that, but it was love nonetheless. And it made her greater. "I can't describe how happy I am to see you."

"Even me?" A lopsided grin from Meher.

"Even you." She couldn't help but smile in return. "Well, Auri," she said, looking to her best friend, "will you be my second again?"

"I just woke up from a rather long nap, Zan," Aureline said in the old angelic tongue. "Give me a moment." But her eyes sparkled, a sight Zanaya had thought never to see again. "Though I suppose if you're recovering from being a mummy, I shouldn't tease you so."

"I must know the mummy story," Meher put in, his red hair already tumbled. "Who was able to turn an archangel into a mummy?"

So it was that Zanaya told her friends the story of the Cascade, the Archangel of Death, and the war that had almost devastated the world. Dawn was spreading its golden fingers across the savanna and they were halfway home by the time her friends got over their slack-jawed shock.

Wanting them to know the beauty as well as the darkness of the present world, she landed on a mountain plateau. Her lands fell away in a sprawl of wild beauty below them, while a small city of shining metal and glass rose in the distance.

Charisemnon had stifled his people, so that his territory had no cities as glittering as some of Titus's, but Zanaya had already put plans in motion to undo some of that damage.

It wasn't about cities, however, but about stewardship. She was putting equal effort into rehabilitating wild landscapes that had suffered considerable damage from uncontrolled hunting by Charisemnon's angelic friends. Soon, those abused regions, too, would flourish with life and energy.

"Home," she murmured. "We're home."

A pulse inside her, faint and distant. *Not her own.*

Aureline sucked in a breath at the same instant. "Zan, your eyes have altered color."

Curses upon Lijuan!

"I'll explain later," she said, then turned in a slow circle . . . but she always ended up looking directly toward Titus's lands.

Whatever it was she was sensing, it continued to move up Africa.

48

Titus didn't like the cold. He said as much to Sharine.

She, lover of snow after her long residence in the Refuge, leaned up to press a kiss to his cheek. The caress melted him from the inside out. "We'll be back home soon enough." Her wings were a glory of indigo and shimmering gold against the interminable span of white.

"Yes, I can't wait to be away from here." With that goal in mind, he began to knock the snow off the cairn that marked Antonicus's place of Sleep . . . and perhaps death.

Sharine joined in, neither one of them wishing to use their abilities and inadvertently cause damage. Thanks to Sharine's forethought, they both wore gloves at least. Still, it took time enough that he grumbled his toes were going numb.

His lover, his heart, said, "I'll run you a bath after we get home." A wicked smile that the world would never believe came from the revered Hummingbird.

Titus knew better. "To think I once believed you sedate and beyond carnal matters. I am shocked to my frozen toes," he muttered in faux outrage—for he adored her wickedness as much as he adored every other part of her. And he knew she'd made that comment because she could sense his very real disquiet: this place *felt* bad.

Holding the warmth of her care close, he got back to the task of cleaning up the cairn, grateful at least that no flakes of icy white fell from the sky. What was already here was plenty enough.

"I see no sign of a disturbance," Sharine said after they were done, her eyes sharp and clear. "What see you, my love?"

"Nothing obvious." Frowning, Titus did a full circle of the cairn, as Sharine did the same. "No damage to our sigils, no sign that anyone broke out."

"Archangels aren't known for subtlety when they wake."

"Hmm." Not sure why the scene disturbed him when all was exactly as it always was when he did his routine flights to the cairn, he said, "Let's check the entire island."

But when Sharine would've separated from him, he took her slender hand in his. "Together, Shari. There's something not right here."

She exhaled, the air a puff of white. "I admit it does make the hairs on the back of my neck rise."

But though they searched every inch of the island, they found no debris at all, no sign of an archangel shattering his cairn and rising triumphant.

"Look here, Titus."

When he followed the line of her pointing hand, he saw the small patch of greenish-black liquid that had frozen in place. His gut churned. "Reborn colors. As if one of the creatures threw up."

"From the size, it could as easily be seabird scat," Sharine pointed out. "We could attempt to take a sample for a test, but reborn samples tend to come back as decaying matter, with no other specificity. Illium has explained the concept of DNA, and he says that the reborn process appears to irreparably alter the fabric of what makes us who we are."

"I've also heard this. We should take a sample regardless,

just in case—Antonicus was an archangel, after all. He might not react the same way to Lijuan's evil."

Nodding, Sharine retrieved one of the sample containers she'd brought along in the pocket of the flying jacket Illium had gifted her. "Since you're an adventurer now, Mother," the blue-winged angel had said with a grin.

Of sleek brown leather that was lined within, it suited Sharine's slim form. But he knew she would've worn it with equal joy had it not suited her at all. Because Sharine knew how to love, and she loved her son.

So did Titus. Illium was a difficult angel not to love.

"I suppose," Sharine said after she'd taken the sample, "the only way to be certain is to topple the cairn, look beneath."

Titus grimaced. "To disturb the rest of an archangel without cause is an act of dishonor, even war." Especially when that archangel had been so badly wounded. "This, I can't do on my own—I must have the backing of the entire Cadre. Elsewise, if I find him lying cold in the ground exactly where he should be, it'll cause a wave of distrust and aggression."

"Because if Titus, Archangel of Southern Africa, can so rudely disturb one archangel in Sleep, what's to stop him from doing the same to another?" Sharine murmured.

"You see it, Shari." Titus wasn't a man who liked to walk away from a possible problem, but in simply acting, he'd create a far bigger one. Their world had barely recovered from one war. It didn't need another. "We fly home and I gather the Cadre."

The ensuing meeting, done via screens, went as expected. There was no consensus. Especially after Titus revealed that his scientists' tests on the sample had come back as inconclusive. The material had been contaminated before it froze, and could as easily be a bit of decaying flotsam that had washed ashore as it could be evidence of a reborn.

Aegaeon—and surprisingly—Qin would not have a wounded Ancient disturbed without further proof.

Neha joined them. "I must agree," she said, her face drawn and no sign once again of the saris she'd once always worn for meetings of the Cadre; she did, however, sport a thin snake of bright orange as a necklace.

The creature flicked out its tongue as she said, "If we react to any small disturbance by digging up Antonicus, he'll never have any rest."

She's right, Titus said in a mental aside to Zanaya and Alexander both. *Much as it pains me to admit.*

Yes. Zanaya's voice. *To disturb him when his cairn lies solemn and still, I wouldn't consider it either did I not have the sense of a terrible darkness creeping closer.*

Will you be content to watch and wait then?

Zanaya gave a small nod, while the conversation went on around them. *And hunt,* she added. *Something is in your territory and it's making its way up into mine. Neither one of us can lower our guard.*

If you need more squadrons or for me to join you in the hunt, Alexander said, *you have but to ask.*

We may well do that, my friend. But for now, there's no outbreak. What we hunt is a creature of cunning.

The meeting ended soon afterward. Titus saw Neha's lips part before it did, was certain the Archangel of India was about to speak, but then she closed her mouth and logged off.

The Cadre was no longer in session.

49

Antonicus dropped the body of his latest piece of food and felt it, the stretching awake of his true power. The power of an archangel. At *last*.

He'd been pathetically weak when he'd crawled out of the cold grave in which his so-called brethren had entombed him. But he'd been clever still, hadn't he? He hadn't made a show of it, had used what pitiful flickers of power remained to tunnel all the way out into the ocean before he swam back to shore to regather his strength.

No trace of disturbance. No sign of an awakening to alert the enemy.

He could still feel the ice-cold water shoving into his mouth and nose, wrapping its frigid hand around his throat, burning his eyes. The cold had been immense. He'd known that . . . but he hadn't much felt it. He hadn't drowned either. Hadn't died.

Because you are already dead, Antonicus. A whisper from deep within his psyche.

Shoving both hands through his hair, he roared out a

"No!" to the silent forest around him, while his victim lay twitching below. Removing his sword, he sliced off the food's head. Antonicus had been careful to hoard his energy, only make a *certain* kind of reborn.

It had . . . disturbed him at first when he felt the craving to share the noxious darkness within, create others like him. He'd had flashes of shambling, mindless creatures, images of an archangel whose power was death. And that was when he'd understood: this was *power*. And he wasn't one of Li-juan's shambling creatures; no, Antonicus was an archangel. That bitch hadn't made him a reborn. He'd stolen her power, made himself a master of the reborn.

But Antonicus's reborn were *better*. Stronger, more intelligent, faster. The weakling he'd just fed on wasn't one of his chosen, wasn't worthy of being reborn. His only purpose had been to push Antonicus over the edge of energy.

He wouldn't lie. It had concerned him when the elements hadn't reflected his awakening—though the silence had been to his advantage. The waters hadn't boiled, the sky hadn't altered to the shade of the dark blooms of violet that his people had sown all across his lands in homage to their archangel.

It had made him question himself, question what he was . . . but now he knew that he'd simply roused himself too early. His power had needed a little more time to recover back to the levels appropriate to an archangel.

He wiped his sword on the dead man, then slid it into the sheath at his back. At least he hadn't had to acquire that; the others had entombed him in what he was wearing on the day of his—

His mind buzzed, cutting off the images.

He didn't pursue it, some part of him aware that he didn't want to see the things he'd seen that night, much less hear the nightmare screams.

Once, his heart might've thudded at the thought, but today, his chest was silent.

Ignoring that oddity, he flexed his hand and smiled at seeing the crawl of power beneath the green-tinged delicacy of his skin. *This* was his true waking. His archangelic powers hadn't disappeared after all, as the others would soon see.

Antonicus, Archangel of a fabled city named Elysium, had risen.

50

Strange how slowly time moved when he was far from his Zani.

Now, at last, the time had come that Alexander would see her again. His grandson had, in the interim, taken up a post at one of Titus's forts in order to learn a specific set of skills from a warrior stationed there.

So it was that Alexander and Zanaya had decided that they'd meet at her fortress. That gave Xander enough time to get to them, stay, then return before his leave ran out. But Alexander intended to precede him by a day.

He needed that time to be with his consort.

The skies were a cerulean blue when he took off—the hue so pure and so deep that it reminded him of Callie's eyes. Reminded him too of the son she'd had with Nadiel.

Two archangels in love.

It could be done.

His friends' love story had spanned countless mortal generations, only ending because of Nadiel's descent into madness.

What Alexander had never told Caliane was that—and he was well aware that Zanaya would have raised an ironic eyebrow had she been awake—he'd tried to talk Nadiel into Sleep. But in his defense, he'd only done so because he'd glimpsed signs of Nadiel's subtle decline. "Sleep exists for a reason," he'd said in an effort to make his friend and fellow archangel interrogate his own behavior. "You'll lose nothing by going into it."

But Nadiel had been intractable. Not a man prone to anger, he'd laughed at Alexander's worries, slapped him on the shoulder, and told him not to be "such a grim Ancient." So young and vibrant he'd been, with his hair of mahogany gold and eyes of a vital green mingled with the barest hint of blue, his heart brimming with courage. Raphael might've inherited his coloring from Callie, but his features were an imprint of his father.

So much so that, at times, he wondered how Callie could bear it.

But then . . . Xander carried so many echoes of Rohan in his face and his manner. Alexander loved him all the more for it, for being a living piece of his son. It must be the same for Callie.

He was thinking that perhaps he and Zanaya should discuss hosting a small gathering for their friends in the future when the sky began to darken above him. Alexander grimaced. He could handle the cold and the wet like any other angel—but that didn't mean he *liked* it. Especially since he was wearing his favorite set of leathers, black with accents of silver in the fastenings and buckles.

His third had taken one look at him and said, "Going courting, sire?" a glint in the greenish hazel of his eyes.

Alexander had been ready with his riposte. "Lemei mentioned that General Keemat's favorite flowers are daffodils. In case you had an interest in that knowledge."

Valerius, stocky and contained and not prone to displays of emotion except with his closest intimates, had actually begun to turn red under the naturally pale hue of his skin.

"You should lift off now," he'd muttered as he tugged at the collar of his tunic. "Go impress Lady Zanaya with your sartorial splendor and leave me in peace."

Alexander would much rather do exactly that than turn up at Zanaya's home bedraggled by rain.

But the sky didn't turn the bruised hue of clouds heavy with rain. It went a sickly green, ugly and putrid . . . and reminiscent of how Antonicus's skin had appeared when they buried him.

Life in the process of rotting.

Halting, he hovered in the sky, looked first to the east, then to the west, then north followed by south.

The entire sky was sick.

Gut tight, he turned and resumed his journey at the highest possible speed. Zanaya was waiting for him on the rooftop of her fortress and as soon as he landed, she said, "It's worldwide." Lips pressed tight, she added, "Titus saw it first, asked to initiate a meeting. I sent a message that you were en route, so he's holding off."

His hairline damp with sweat and his wings aching, Alexander nodded. "Let's go."

But when the faces began appearing onscreen, two of the Cadre remained missing. They had, however, been replaced by two people who weren't archangels but who *did* have the right to speak in the place of the two missing archangels.

"Elijah has flown to the cairn," said Hannah, consort to the Archangel of South America, he who'd also become known as King of the Pride in the aftermath of the Cascade. "In absolute terms, he's located the closest to the cairn, can make the journey the fastest."

Hannah, an artist of great renown, had a streak of green-and-white paint in the tight black curls of her hair, and a smaller streak of sky-blue against the ebony skin of her neck. She wore what appeared to be a white painting smock over which rose wing arches of deep cream. The smock was flecked with pigment, silent witness to the speed at which things had taken place this dark day. "He believed it was important he do that at once."

Elena Deveraux's silvery-gray eyes were unflinching in the face of so much power as she said, "Raphael's done the same—he was heading to a meeting with Archangel Elijah when the sky changed, so he won't be far behind him."

That near-white hair pulled back into a tight braid and her upper body clad in a black leather jacket, her expression grim, she could've been an experienced warrior angel of many centuries of age. "Raphael didn't want Archangel Elijah to be alone if there was a possibility that Archangel Antonicus might be rising."

No one had any disagreement with the actions of either archangel.

"That leaves us with no reason for this meeting," Neha said, her voice curt. "Let us reconvene when Elijah has returned."

Alexander considered the other archangel. His spymaster had passed on rumors of Neha's increasing disengagement from her court, and Alexander wondered if the Queen of India was so short with them because Antonicus's resurrection would put a halt to her plans to Sleep.

If, as the signs indicated, the Ancient had risen, he couldn't be in any way healthy. The ugly shade of the sky was in no way akin to the deep purple that had previously announced his presence. The best-case scenario was that he was fully mentally present, just physically damaged. That, they could work with; but if he bore wounds on the mental level . . . that could be deadly.

Archangels had too much power to wield it with anything but iron control.

As for Neha, it wasn't hard to see her exhaustion. Her pain.

He might not have understood her anguish before he lost Rohan, but the man he was today knew what it did to a person when they lost a child. Neha's daughter was never coming back, as Rohan was never coming back. But where

Alexander had a grandson, a living memory of his beloved boy, Neha had been given no such grace.

No. He frowned. Neha had a niece, did she not? One she'd raised? Yes, he recalled her now. Princess Mahiya. An angel lovely and with wings as stunning as a peacock's fan.

Clearly, there were things he didn't know about Neha and Mahiya's relationship if Neha was as alone in her grief as Alexander's spymaster had reported.

Aloud, he said, "Is there any risk it could be one of the other Sleepers?"

Caliane shook her head. "I've consulted with Jessamy in the time since the skies altered. She says the Library has no record of such a perturbing waking for any other archangel in our history."

She clenched her hand around the hilt of the sword she wore at her hip, her sleeveless tunic a faded cream and her pants leathers of the same shade. "Archangels wake in myriad ways, but the signs are *always* a thing of wonder and beauty. This is . . . foul in a way that makes mortals whimper and hide and immortals do much the same."

"It's also not apt to be one of those who went into Sleep with Cassandra," Suyin said in her quiet voice, while Elena Deveraux ducked to the side as if listening to someone else. "Antonicus alone was wounded in a way that relates to these colors."

"None of the others were even close to waking when I rose," Zanaya added.

Elena Deveraux returned her full attention to the meeting. "Our lead squadron just overflew the area where Cassandra's fire opened in the territory—they report no disturbances," she said. "We get that her past behavior is no predictor as to her location, but it seemed a good idea to confirm."

Alexander nodded, well appreciating the caution of Raphael's consort and Tower.

"Then Neha's right." This from Aegaeon. "We meet again after Elijah's return."

Alexander didn't miss the fact that Aegaeon hadn't mentioned Raphael. Not exactly a surprise; Aegaeon continued to be humiliated that his son chose to serve the Archangel of New York rather than join his own father's court. Alexander was in full sympathy with young Illium. Because where Aegaeon had squandered his child's love, Raphael had earned the powerful young angel's loyalty.

Now, the Ancient was one of the first to vanish after they agreed to the interval.

Titus remained onscreen after the others all followed suit. "Alexander, Zan," he said. "We've had no signs of the reborn threat over the past two weeks. It might be that the original creature has either gone back into hiding, or died in the same sickly way as some of the reborn it made."

Next to Alexander, Zanaya frowned. "You don't think it's Antonicus anymore." A statement.

"With the sky altering color now . . ." Titus shrugged. "Should the signs not have been present earlier if this was him?"

It was a good question. "Do you sense him as you did before we flew to the cairn?" Alexander asked Zanaya, aware she'd shared her discomfiting ability with Titus.

She made a face. "No, not as then . . . but I do continue to get random snatches of sensation. Always pointing in the same direction." Glancing up at Titus, she said, "I would ask, my friend, that you not lower your vigilance."

"Never," Titus promised. "Not until you confirm you no longer sense anything. Because even if it isn't Antonicus, it does appear to be a dangerously intelligent reborn." He glanced to the left. "I can see the skies through my window. They look to be clearing of the accursed color. I might fly out and shake the edginess off my wings."

"We'll talk again, Titus," Zanaya said.

Alexander nodded a good-bye to his friend, said, "Let us hope Elijah and young Rafe have good news for us."

After they ended the conversation, Zanaya turned to him. "Young Rafe?"

Wincing, he pressed the bridge of his nose between thumb and forefinger. "I try not to do that, and it usually only comes out in conversation with friends. I can't stop thinking of him as Callie's mischievous boy—he once flew to my Refuge stronghold and infiltrated it. He was a babe at the time."

Laughter from Zanaya. "Oh, you must tell me this story. Why did he do so?"

"Because he'd decided to set himself a challenge." Hands on his hips, Alexander shook his head, then, as the two of them walked side by side to Zanaya's chambers, he told her the full story of Raphael's quest. "He was a smart, fearless boy. I always liked him." Which was partially why he was so mortified by what he'd almost done prior to his Sleep.

"Nadiel and Caliane," he continued, "raised him with love, but also taught him to be clever and self-reliant. With the two of them unable to live together always, the boy was well used to switching strongholds and courts, and I think it gave him a flexibility of thought that many of our kind lack. He was also intrepid—he began to fly between the two courts on his own at around seventy years of age."

Zanaya gasped. "So young? Were Nadiel and Caliane neighbors like you and I?"

"No. They were separated by two other territories." Alexander's lips tugged up. "One of those was mine, and the other was under the reign of another ally. Let's just say the boy had a discreet escort for the first few years, until it became clear to all four of us that he could be trusted to follow the rules— *and* that he was capable of thinking on his feet if he hit an unexpected storm or the like."

"That makes me realize something," Zanaya said with a frown. "I haven't known any archangels as children before their ascension. I can see how you would've had trouble with the transition." She pushed open the door of her suite on that.

As always, it was a place of plush fabrics and art, the air sweetly scented. But there was nothing heavy about it. The fabrics she preferred were soft and lovely to the skin, the art bringing the outside in: pieces of Africa captured in canvas, carved in wood polished to a shine, or woven into fabrics made with utmost care.

A candle burned in a glass holder, a thriving green plant sat in another, while a small white cat jumped off a window ledge to come over for pets from her mistress. The slinky creature deigned to rub her body against Alexander's leg before she padded out of the room. "The Queen of the Nile and her familiars," he murmured with a smile, well used to the way she'd always had a cat or a hound—and once or thrice, a falcon.

A smile as she shut the door behind the cat. "I have no idea from whence she came—but she has decided I am acceptable. Her name is Duchess. Now, General, strip."

Well ready to get out of his sweaty clothing, Alexander began to do as ordered. He was reaching up to unbuckle his sword sheath when Zanaya froze, then took his left hand, raised it up. "What's this?" A soft question, the pad of her thumb brushing over the ring of melded onyx and amber that he wore on his finger.

"A ring I should've been wearing for eons." Taking a deep breath that trembled, he said, "Will you forgive me, Zani? I never meant to hurt you, but I did, and for that, I will never be sorry enough."

It had taken him far too long to understand that his way of thinking wasn't the only way. "But know this—it was the only item aside from my weapons and my clothing that I took with me into Sleep. So it would be safe, protected as the seasons and the centuries passed. Even this bullheaded warrior wasn't a total idiot."

Zanaya didn't speak for so long that he felt his heart drop. Then she lifted her head, her eyes bright in that way they got when she was holding back strong emotions. Though she didn't speak, she lifted his hand to her lips and pressed a tender kiss to his ring.

Her next words were pragmatic . . . but she touched her fingers to his jaw in a caress sweet. "I'll order food from the kitchen so you can refuel after your flight, and the clothing you sent ahead sits beside my own in the wardrobe."

Alexander wanted only to tangle himself with her, but he

knew she was right. He had to be at full readiness in case of
the worst news from the two archangels who'd flown to check
the cairn.

The war drums might yet sound again.

Still . . . "Elijah and Raphael have hours to fly, and neither
Titus's nor your people have reported any worrying disturbances," he murmured, and reached for her. "Can we not
steal but a moment of that time?"

51

"Alexander." A purr of sound against his lips as she allowed him to tug her close, allowed him to unhook the two clasps on her short wrap of icy green, allowed him to run one hand over the smooth dark of her skin while holding her with his other arm.

"You're wearing lace," he said when his fingers brushed the soft black fabric that hid her sex from him.

Husky laughter. "I was quite prepared to be bare, but I find I like this modern bit of froth. Each is equally pretty and useless and I have gathered a collection of them."

Smiling because he adored her in every way, he shifted so he could roll the underclothing down her hips and over her legs. "Since they are so dear to you, I won't tear them off like a ravenous wolf." It was no big thing to go down on his knee in front of her so he could complete the disrobing.

They were beyond such petty power plays, he and his Zani. She'd been on her knees in front of him, too, doing things to him with that lush mouth that destroyed all sense of reason and turned him into nothing but a mindless being who craved the pleasure she could give him.

Today, she lifted one foot then the other to help him remove the scrap of lace. Crushing it in his hand, he lifted it to his nose and drew a long breath. She gasped out his name even as the scent of her musk engorged him near to pain. "Always," he said, leaning in to press a kiss to the juncture of her thighs, "always you have been my addiction."

Her fingers in his hair, her wings fluttering restlessly.

It was a simple thing to nudge her thighs apart as he dropped the lace. It was even simpler to spread her with his tongue, taste the liquid core of her. She shuddered, gripped harder at his hair. Grasping the back of one curvy thigh with his hand, he held her in place for his exploration, his thirst for her a thing that had been building eon after eon after eon.

"Alexander."

The tremor in her voice as she said his name erased all extraneous thought, his only aim her pleasure. He had so much knowledge of her body, as she had of his, and he used all that knowledge to drive her to a quivering release, then gathered her up in his arms to carry her to the bed.

She smiled up at him, her hand rising to run through his hair.

The softness of the moment, the tenderness he allowed no other in his life, it stopped his heart.

When he laid her down on the bed draped in sheets of sunset, the colors fading from orange to cream, it was with equal tenderness. He didn't hide himself from her in any way as he finished undressing—and it was nothing to do with the physical. Of all the people in this universe, it was Zanaya who knew him below the skin and above.

All his flaws.

All his gifts.

All his mistakes.

And still she opened her arms and embraced him when he came over her, his wings spread above them. Eyes soft, she ran her fingertips over the sensitive underside of one upper arch, making him hiss at the pulse that shot directly to his cock.

"I always somehow forget how very beautiful your wings are, lover, and then I see you again."

Alexander wasn't a vain man. Strength had always been more important to him than looks, but he found he was vain when it was Zanaya. "I shall do sky tricks for you, like I did as an infant archangel." Playing with her in a way they hadn't done for millennia before her Sleep. "You may act the maiden and admire me."

Her laughter was sunshine over his skin. "I shall expect far better flight tricks now, for you've had centuries upon centuries to practice." Round curves to her cheeks, her smile a light in her eyes.

"For you, Zani, I'll learn such aerial tricks that they'll put me in the history books and call me Alexander, Archangel of Aerial Acrobatics."

She was still laughing when he kissed her, the contact intimate beyond bearing. It reached his heart, made it expand and expand, so big that he didn't know how it could be contained within his chest.

Then she was stroking his back, wrapping her legs around his waist, and all he knew was her, all he felt was her. "Zani, my Zani."

Zanaya had been in bed with Alexander plenty of times through their long history. Her favorite wakings had always been by his side . . . but she'd never told him that, she realized. She hadn't wanted to give him that power, hadn't wanted him to know just how important he was to her.

Foolishness.

"I hope to wake beside you again and again, lover," she said, turning to look at him as they lay side by side. "Those dawns are always the most beautiful."

"Yes," he said simply and with the potent power of the general he'd always be, no matter how many other titles he wore.

"We need to work out exactly how long we can be together before our powers begin to push us apart."

Frowning, Zanaya said, "We know that already. More than a turn of the moon of constant contact puts us over the edge."

"Caliane and Nadiel managed it longer," he told her. "They also switched territories halfway through each 'safe' period, so that neither was without its archangel for long. And, unlike them, we're neighbors, can meet for shorter visits more regularly. We should run trials, find the rhythm best for us."

Hope bloomed inside her. Everyone knew that two archangels couldn't live together always. It was a natural law. To hear that they might be able to see each other more often . . . "Will you tell me about Nadiel? I feel lost not knowing such an important element of Caliane's history."

"Come," he said, an echo of old sorrow in his voice. "We'll talk as we bathe."

As one of her staff had filled up the tub after Alexander flew in and they just had to top it up with hot water, they were soon sinking into the heat. She joined him, then picked up a pitcher and poured water over his head so he could scrub his hair and face. After that was done, he began to methodically clean the rest of his body and tell her the story of two archangels who'd fallen in love.

"He was young in the grand scheme of things," Alexander said, "but he was powerful—and he was a warrior I respected, for all that we often competed for Callie's attention."

Zanaya raised an eyebrow where she knelt in the water in front of him. "Did something change while I Slept?"

"No. Caliane has only ever been a friend and compatriot. I suppose I did it out of a different kind of jealousy—that of a friend who sees his friend paying more attention to another." He looked up. "More so because my own lover Slept."

Zanaya caught the edge there. "No, General, I will never countenance your anger on that point. I gave you a choice. You made yours and I made mine." She softened her rebuke with a kiss. "We'll never go forward if we look only to the past."

Her consort, the man who'd led countless armies into battle, held her gaze with an implacable one . . . that softened until he gave a harsh sigh. "I'm making the same mistakes, aren't I, Zani? Being obdurate and unbending."

Unused to such a lack of confidence from him, Zanaya might've struggled to find an answer—except that he'd already given it to her when he spoke. She took the hand on which he wore her ring, ran her thumb over the smoothness of the onyx and amber. "The Alexander I knew before I went into Sleep would've never once admitted that he might be fallible."

Cupping his cheek, she pressed her forehead to his. "Neither would I. Both of us were willing to break us to get our own way. This time, I'm not willing to break us." It was a weapon she gave him, that knowledge.

But he crushed her close and took her mouth in a kiss so deep and boundless that it shattered her heart. "Never again, Zani." His big, muscled body trembled, his skin slick with water and his wings aglow. "We've earned our right to get it right this time—but now Antonicus might be rising, and bringing back the same evil that nearly took you."

"My love." She kissed the side of his face, his jaw, his lips, trying to make up for the pain she'd inadvertently caused him. "I'm so sorry you had to watch me fall." She knew exactly how being made helpless to assist her would've affected him.

"You were so broken, Zani." The words came out ragged, his breath catching. "So small and so—" He bit off the rest of what he'd been about to say, but she heard the tears he refused to allow to fall.

Her own eyes turned wet, the tears mingling with the water in the bath. And it was she who held him now, she who comforted this archangel of war and courage. "We'll make it this time, lover," she whispered. "Lijuan's evil won't part us again." It was a vow.

* * *

Alexander felt naked to his core by the time he exited the bath and dressed in a simple sleeveless tunic in a cream shade, paired with the pants from a set of brown leathers. The sensation of innermost vulnerability left him wanting to strike out, wanting to put up walls, shields to protect himself. Create a front guard to defend his flank.

Fighting that urge took everything he had.

She was his consort, had every right to be *inside* his protective walls. Never would he shove her outside.

Zanaya smiled at him, already dressed in a wrap of glimmering blue-black held together by a jeweled clasp at her shoulder and one at her hip. The violet silver of her hair was a tumble down her back that she'd scraped away from her face with diamond-studded combs, her skin aglow with health.

"You are lovely," he murmured. "A piece of starlit night given form."

"You've always been a charmer," she said, padding over to rise on tiptoe and kiss him.

No one else had ever thought him charming, not in this way. But perhaps it was because she was the only person he'd ever thought to charm. "Make sure to tell my grandson that when he arrives. I often think he believes me a creaky old Ancient with no skills with women at all."

Husky laughter. "Ah, he's young. He knows not the value of a rare and aged vintage." A little bite of his throat before her face turned solemn. "We should make a plan in the event that Antonicus has risen and is not who he once was. We must both be on the same page."

"Yes," Alexander said without hesitation, and then he set aside his arrogance and took the most logical action. "You must be the lead, Zani. You have a connection to him that is an advantage."

Zanaya looked out through the large windows to their right. "I hope that it is, lover. More, I hope that we're all wrong, that Antonicus Sleeps and what we saw was nothing but a strange natural phenomenon, a final remnant of a terrible Cascade."

Yet he could tell from her tone that she didn't believe it any more than he did. Shifting to stand by her side, their wings overlapping, they looked out at the rich golden light of late afternoon . . . but saw only a fast-approaching horror.

52

Raphael caught up with Elijah not long after the Archangel of South America had landed by Antonicus's cairn. Hardly a surprise when Elijah had been flying toward the border for their meeting at the same time as Raphael; they couldn't have been that far apart, and—thanks to a lingering Cascade gift—Raphael was now a faster flyer than any other archangel in the world.

The latter didn't make him any more powerful than Eli, however. Each of them had talents or skills of their own that kept the Cadre in balance. Eli, for example, had always had a mind capable of such razor-sharp strategy that even Raphael's equally gifted second had been known to tell him never to go to war with their closest neighbor.

"I can't promise we'll win," Dmitri had said, his dark eyes glinting. "Eli thinks seventeen moves ahead. He must've been a hell of a general in his time."

Since it was Caliane who Elijah had called his liege before his ascension, Raphael had an excellent idea of just how good a general the other man had been. He also knew the depth of Elijah's capacity for loyalty—it had taken him a little while to get it, to understand that Eli would never stab him in the back, literally or metaphorically, but perhaps that was a lesson of age.

Now that he'd learned it, he would never squander the gift.

"Eli," he said, his heart thumping from the effort of his flight as he came down beside his friend. "Any signs?" He'd spotted nothing from the air.

"I knew you'd be just behind me." Elijah thrust his hand through golden hair gone dark from sweat. "I've done a full walkaround and multiple flights over and around." His jaw worked, the pure white of his wings blending in against the snowy background. "No signs of an ordinary archangelic awakening."

Shards of stone, rocks thrown about, melted metals, the entire island obliterated to sink into the ocean, any of those things would've been a clear signal that an archangel had risen here. "We can't ignore the skies." The sweat that had dripped down Raphael's back began to turn to ice—he was glad now that he'd listened to Elena and worn an item of clothing that she'd gifted him.

"It'll wick away sweat, dry quickly, and keep you warm in the aftermath," she'd told him. "Hunters use it when we go into cold areas."

Long sleeved and black, with built-in wing slits, it fit snug to his frame. He wore a lined leather jerkin over it—an item of clothing he'd almost ripped off and thrown aside on the flight here, but now appreciated. He always forgot the brutal cold of this piece of the world.

"We'll have to unearth Antonicus." Elijah's voice was grim. "I don't suggest this easily—"

"—but it must be done," Raphael completed, for he wouldn't have his friend and ally believe he walked alone into this decision. "No one can argue with us. Not after the bilious stain on skies across the world."

"We'll be careful," Elijah murmured. "It'll take longer

than if we blast it open, but if he *is* in there, we go too hard and we risk causing him further injury."

Raphael nodded. "Agreed." Antonicus might have been an insufferable ass, but he had done his duty as an archangel and deserved their consideration.

The two of them got to work, not speaking except when necessary. This wasn't the time for idle chatter or even friendly conversation. The work went faster than they'd anticipated and they soon found themselves looking at the mix of shattered rock and frozen soil below which they'd laid Antonicus to rest.

"I should do this, Rafe. I'm older, less apt to be made a target by certain others in the Cadre."

Even though Eli had known Raphael as an infant then a boy, he'd *never* slipped up and called him his childhood nickname after Raphael became an archangel. That he'd done so now gave Raphael an insight into the strain behind his fellow archangel's cool expression. "No, Eli, we do it together. United."

A glance at him out of eyes of golden brown before Elijah nodded.

And they turned their power into lifting the cold and stony earth below which should lie an archangel.

53

Alexander tracked Zanaya to her library after he'd finished speaking to Xander; she had the doors open to the balmy night, was looking over a detailed map of her new territory. Her hair was violet rain under the overhead lights, her wings velvet dark and held tight to her back with warrior control.

"My grandson remains intent on flying to us tomorrow," he told her. "Says his leave hasn't been revoked since there's no uncontrollable outbreak or any real sign of trouble." He rubbed his forehead. "I couldn't argue with him—he might be a child to me, but to the outside world, he's a junior squadron commander who's often out on solo flights."

"That doesn't mean you won't worry about him." Gaze soft, Zanaya took his hand, squeezed. "Even if Antonicus does walk, he's doing so in stealth and cunning. He has no discernible reason to target your grandson—if he even knows that Xander exists."

Alexander frowned, exhaled on a wave of shattering relief. "No, he can't know. He wasn't awake long enough for us to converse much—and he'd have no reason to dig into my family on his own. As for the past, while we were cordial when our reigns collided across time, we were never either intimates or enemies."

The realization was welcome but did nothing to ease the tension that had him as taut as a wire. "Do you think you'll be able to sleep before we hear back from Elijah and Raphael?"

Zanaya shook her head. "And we've done as much forward planning as we can." Her gaze shifted to the huge balcony doors open to the falling night; the carvings in the wood glimmered with flecks of gold paint that had faded and been left to their weathered state. It suited all the old books against the walls as well as the well-worn carpet made by gifted mortals in his own lands.

"Much as I despise Charisemnon," Alexander murmured, "this room is both warm and rich in texture and history."

"Immortals are complicated beings," Zanaya muttered, then scowled. "But in this case, he erased all he did in the past with the actions he chose to take prior to his death. As far as I'm concerned, this room belonged to a man who died long before Titus ended Charisemnon in battle."

"I find myself thinking the same with Lijuan." Alexander could still remember how bright of heart Lijuan had been before she became addicted to the drug of power. "She looked at me with stars in her eyes once." A memory old and fragile, a shimmering thing he'd almost forgotten until this very moment. "So young she was, so earnest in her devotion."

"Did you—"

Alexander shook his head before Zanaya could complete her question. "I felt nothing the same for her, Zani. But I didn't want to hurt her. I told her she was too young, that to ignore the difference in our ages would be an act dishonorable on my part."

Soft laughter. "A predictable response if one knew your history."

Alexander treated her to a mock glare. "Will you hold that grudge for eternity?"

"Yes, to the very last second of our existence."

Laughing, he looked out at the night again. "I wonder sometimes," he said, laughter fading, "if she held a far deeper grudge that I didn't welcome her into my arms, if that's why she murdered my son and his mate."

His entire chest ached from the pain of it. "But that is foolish and arrogant, is it not, Zani? She was young, would've forgotten me soon enough."

"Yes," Zanaya said. "At the end, all she cared about was being bloated with power. The identities and histories of her victims didn't matter."

Alexander had to believe the same—else he'd go mad. "What a waste of what could've been an extraordinary life." He could still see Zhou Lijuan as she'd been then, smart and driven and beautiful in her courage. "The young angel I knew was a different person. I can mourn that long-ago angel with her hopes and dreams without feeling any pity for the person she became."

Fingers touching his in silent agreement, Zanaya said, "I think you need the embrace of the sky, lover." In her tone was a deep knowledge of the grief that would never leave him, Rohan's name tattooed on his very heart. "Shall we fly?"

His chest expanded at the idea of being in the air. This land might not be his own, but it sang with Zanaya's fierce spirit even after so short a time under her reign. "Yes."

They took off together, flew wingtip to wingtip in silence for a long time, a portentous sense of an oncoming future bearing down on both of them. While her fortress wasn't located near any major cities, they did overfly multiple smaller settlements, all lit up golden bright as the residents conversed, ate dinner, did business, or had central gatherings.

As with his own lands, the heat of the day was an uncomfortable pressure at present, the early part of night far preferred. He'd ended up overheated and enervated when he'd raced to Zanaya's home after the skies sickened—and he'd been in the cold air of the clouds, high above the scorching glow of the earth.

"We should walk the night marketplaces when all is calm," he said to his consort. "Act as we did when we loved in the streets of what is now old Marrakech."

A startled huskiness of laughter. "Will you buy me trinkets for my wrists and ears again, lover?"

"I already have, Zani. But I intend to hold them hostage until you're next in my territory." Glancing down, he wasn't the least surprised when those who spotted Zanaya against the night sky jumped up to wave, their grins obvious even from such a distance. The bows that followed were deep, and reverent, her people already in love with the Queen of the Nile.

More settlements than not already flew her flag, the colors of her reign violet and black. From the homemade nature of those flags, Zanaya hadn't sent out a mandate. No, this came from the hearts of those she ruled. "You are beloved."

"No, lover, I am new." A quiet power to her. "Your young friend did much to lay the groundwork, but he's right in saying the people believed he continued to feel more loyalty to the south. Now, those same people pin their fragile hopes on me, look to me to heal what Charisemnon broke."

Always, she'd seen with a painful clarity.

"The people of neither your lands nor mine are ready for another war," he said at last, thinking of all those he'd lost to Sleep or to tortured nightmares. "I can say the same for the rest of the world without fearing I speak a falsehood. Some of the structural damage has only recently been fully repaired—and a number of young immortals who were wounded yet struggle through their healing."

Ofttimes mortals didn't realize how long it could take a young immortal to recover from the worst injuries. Yes, an angel could grow back an arm or a leg, but it wasn't a thing done without pain and suffering. Yet he could see it from the mortal side, too—after all, the mortal fighters who'd lost limbs in the war would never regrow them, would live their lives in a body forever altered.

"War is never good for anyone." Potent emotion in each and every one of Zanaya's words. "All it leaves behind is carnage of the body and fractures of the mind."

"Yes," he said, awash in memories of the rows of immortal and mortal dead, of the angels who'd fallen to Lijuan's black fog, of the vampires who'd lost their lives on the cusp of freedom after their mandated century of service, of the children Lijuan had turned into a piteous plague . . . and of the piercing cries of the survivors.

Parents. Lovers. Children. Friends. Comrades.

War spared no one.

"I don't believe it." Zanaya came to a hover in the air, above a tree under whose wide canopy slept a family of cheetahs, their bodies curled and tails flicking as they dreamed. "The general is agreeing with me when it comes to war?"

Halting across from her, hands on his hips, he dipped his head a fraction. "I've witnessed too much suffering to see battle as a thing glorious anymore." Always before, he'd focused on strategy, on the mechanics of war. This time around . . . "This war wasn't 'clean' in any sense. Lijuan crossed lines that should *never* be crossed, and she made us all her accomplices."

So long as he lived, he'd never forget having to cut down child after reborn child. Their blood had stained him, would forever haunt him. "And so long as war exists, there will be those who fight in a way that is without honor. Better then, to have a world without war."

Softness in her expression, she said, "If only it could be so, lover," before they both swept down and over lands bathed in the light of a fertile moon, round and heavy.

His consort, his Zani, led him eventually to a landing spot on a grassland that appeared to go on for miles, interrupted only by the majestic form of a single baobab tree in the distance. Its smooth trunk was a heavy weight of thickness, the thin branches high above crowned with leaves.

When he folded back his wings and turned, however, he

saw another stand of trees in the shadows of the opposite direction. More akin to a small wood or nascent forest. He guessed it had grown up around a source of water.

It was toward those trees that Zanaya walked. He strolled with her, content to be in this time and place with her while a nocturnal bird rode the drafts above. Not an owl from the form and size. Likely a nightjar.

It was Zanaya who spoke first. "You were right on one thing during our previous debates on the topic of war—such violence will always occur in a race as powerful as our own." Whispers of melancholy. "It's as inevitable as the rains of a monsoon or the chaos of a Cascade, a law of nature that we can't alter."

Alexander had seen too many archangelic alliances falter over the centuries to argue with her on the point. He took her hand, their fingers weaving together in a familiar pattern. "At times, I've wondered if we are prey to more subtle Cascades. Ones we never notice, but that light a flame of slow rage under the cauldron of archangelic power."

Not answering in words, Zanaya shifted so that her wing brushed his own. And they walked through the tall grasses while the moon shone overhead and other nightjars joined the solo flyer. Small insects and creatures become comfortable with their presence soon added their noises, busy and active, to the rustle of the grass.

"I've had many names through time," Zanaya murmured at one point, the fingers of her free hand trailing over the long grass. "Perhaps one day, I'll be Queen of the Savanna. I would like that, I think."

Alexander would love her under any name, in any of her guises. Walking with her, neither one of them in any hurry, this night was restful in a way he hadn't experienced in a long, long time . . . until Zanaya came to a sudden halt.

"I feel it again," she said, rubbing a fisted hand over her chest. "A strange mirrored heartbeat. As if I'm hearing my pulse and another's at the same time."

Alexander's hand clenched on hers. "Which direction?"

Halting, Zanaya moved—her consort moving with her—until they looked in the direction of the frozen wasteland where they'd buried an archangel . . . but that direction also included Titus's entire territory. "Any sense of distance?" he asked her. "Is the heartbeat close?"

Zanaya "listened" harder, but the beat was difficult to pin down, the "sound" of it oddly fuzzy. "I can't tell," she said at last. "It's so strange, but it's almost as if the pulse I hear is an *echo* of a pulse, a beat made in an empty sp—"

A stirring in the grass that wasn't a harmless creature going about its business.

It was too . . . cold. Cold as the grave.

And she could *feel* it.

Hairs rising on her nape, she released Alexander's hand to draw Firelight from its sheath. Alexander shifted into warrior readiness beside her, a subtle change but one that was as obvious to her as if he'd yelled out a battle cry. They'd always been in sync when it came to the physical, whether that was a thing of pleasure—or of war.

But what came at them wasn't an enemy or a threat. Neither was it one of the wild beasts that prowled this landscape and that Zanaya cherished with all her heart. The wild should be left to be wild; she'd kill no animal if all it was doing was protecting its young or its territory.

"Alexander." Her voice came out a ragged whisper, horror a saw rubbing on her every nerve ending to produce a jangling and manic melody. "Do you see this?"

"Lift off," he said, his voice clipped. "Rise above so they can't touch you."

Zanaya wasn't one to take orders, but this one she'd needed. Her shock and refusal to countenance that this could be had threatened to freeze her in place.

Snapping out her wings, she made a rapid vertical takeoff.

Alexander, his own sword in hand, waited until she was aloft before rising himself.

Now that she was in the air, she could see the full horror of it. A gleaming white skull on which clung dusty tufts of hair, arms and legs that had all but skeletonized, the skin gone a strange inhuman shade of greenish dark from decay or another process she didn't understand.

Dirt covered the whiteness of bone where the moonlight glinted on it.

The *creature* had stopped crawling when she lifted off, now twitched its head up to stare at her through a blank eye socket . . . and that was just the one who'd been the closest to her. Others crawled through the grasslands, all of them in a similar—or worse—shape. Some were missing limbs, as if the bones had fallen away, but each and every one had a head that was yet attached to their neck.

Mouth dry and stomach a churn of nausea, Zanaya said, "Reborn? They look nothing akin to the ones I've seen previously, not even the most recent reborn in Titus's lands."

"I've never seen the like," Alexander said, the silver of his eyes unearthly in the moonlight and his wings a blaze of metallic light that was the moon's reflection. "But I think they *are* reborn. They were either missed in Titus's sweep of this territory, or . . ."

"Or?" Even as she waited for his answer, the creatures below attempted to rise up and reach for her, but they were too weak, kept collapsing in a rattle of bones.

"There was a time when the reborn in this land hauled the dead from their graves and fed on them," Alexander told her. "Those dead then rose as reborn. It may be that some dead who were so mauled didn't rise at the time."

Zanaya's gorge threatened to erupt. "Are you saying—" She halted, unable to think of the right words. That these wretched beings might be the buried dead whose slumber had been broken just made the entire thing even more obscene. "These creatures," she finally managed to say, "are they risen from their graves?"

54

"Titus ordered his people to dig up and cremate their freshly dead." Grim words. "But the reborn wiped out entire settlements—easy for the squadrons to miss a desecrated graveyard or two, especially with the chaos of what was taking place at the time."

Zanaya heard a faraway and wretched scream in the back of her head as the creature she'd first seen, the one who seemed the strongest of all those below, tried to rise toward her once again, its face bearing just enough skin to reveal a paroxysm of pain.

Unable to bear it, she used her power to scrape the area in a pinpoint strike. There were no more skeletal reborn after she was done, nothing but dust where they'd once crawled. The grasslands fell silent. Suffocated by the weight of that silence, she and Alexander flew a meticulous and sprawling grid to ensure no more hid within the grasses.

I've found the graveyard, Zani. Alexander's voice in her mind. *Tucked into a corner of the forest we saw as we walked—it lies adjacent to the remains of an abandoned*

*hamlet, and is difficult to see from an aerial scan. I only did
so because of a token left behind in a grave—it glinted in the
moonlight.*

I'll come.

*There's no need. I can tell you that every grave is empty,
and that trails of dirt lead away from each. This is from
whence the reborn appeared. The dead must've been partially dug up, then abandoned—after the living who looked
after them were all already dead or reborn themselves.* A
pause. *Let me protect you this once, my heart.*

Bile scalding her throat, Zanaya swallowed. And allowed
herself the respite—and Alexander the need to protect. *I see
no signs of any other reborn. Let us meet again on the plain.*

When she landed, she did so in a patch of grass untouched
by the risen dead. "They were coming toward me," she said
to Alexander when he landed beside her. "It was obvious
from an aerial perspective."

Turning before he could answer, she strode through the
grass, then came back, the grass prickles against her wings
where before the blades had been caressing fingers. Her entire body felt as if it had been beset by tiny insects. "That
fucking blackhearted bitch." She spat out the words. "She
infected me."

Alexander grabbed her hand when she would've swiveled
away again. "Zani, no. *Think.*" He squeezed her wrist. "The
infected were slave to her will—you are slave to no one. Do
you feel any compulsion to serve a master?"

Unable to shake off the sense of violation, she tore away
her hand and strode through the grass. This time, she walked
until she was far from the memory of the crawling reborn,
her mind cooling with each step that passed.

When Alexander flew over to land beside her, she exhaled.
"No," she said. "I feel no compulsion to serve anyone." It was
a relief to say that aloud. "But—" She cut herself off because
she didn't want to say it, but Alexander had to know. "I *felt*
them, those creatures. Like a hum inside me. And . . . I heard
a screaming faint but pitiful."

Trembling not with shock but blackest rage, she looked at Alexander. "How could she live with those screams? They would've been so loud for her, the trapped begging her for release."

"Because she was evil." Flat words, the silver of his gaze as hard as a sheet of metal.

"I might not be reborn," Zanaya said, "and my eyes might have settled into their ordinary shade—"

"They changed to gray when the reborn were coming toward you, are only fading back into dark brown now."

Uttering a small scream, Zanaya kicked at the dirt, hard enough to send a clump flying. "Bitch. Vicious, murderous *bitch*!"

Whatever Alexander said in response to her tirade was drowned out by Aureline's voice in her head: *Zan! We've received an alert on a modern device that bears Raphael's sigil and that of Elijah. I can't access it. It's sealed for archangelic eyes only.*

Blood cold, Zanaya shared what Auri had told her with Alexander.

They took off in grim silence.

That the Cadre had buried Antonicus in the ice was a secret between archangels and their consorts—no one else could ever know that their most powerful could get sick, could become *infected* with disease. It was too catastrophic a piece of knowledge, would shatter the belief in the invincibility of the Cadre that kept the world relatively stable.

An archangel being killed in battle against another of their kind was one thing, but to be maimed in the way Antonicus had been? No, that information couldn't be permitted to spread. Theirs was a world of vampires prone to bloodlust and mortals so vulnerable to angelic power that they simply *couldn't* fight back.

No weapon created by a mortal mind would ever kill an archangel.

Zanaya had caught up on a large chunk of more recent history in the past months, and so she knew that a mortal had once built a thing called a bomb and used it to blow up an angelic home. The saboteur had managed to kill the angel's entire household, vampires included, and he'd blown the angel to pieces.

But not enough pieces.

The angel's head had been found still attached to his spinal cord. His skull was cracked up, his brain badly damaged— but not obliterated. That was all it'd taken. Because that angel had been one of the *old* ones full to the brim with power.

Five years and he was whole again.

By then, the archangel who was his liege had destroyed every hint of the mortal and his bloodline, no matter how far-flung. Mortal after mortal and even a number of kind-hearted angels had pleaded that the members of his family were innocents—with many so distantly related to him that they didn't even know the bomber.

The archangel had refused to show mercy to even the smallest babe.

Zanaya's stomach had churned as she listened to that history. She didn't believe in a scorched-earth policy of punishment, but she understood how the other archangel's mind had worked: to show even a drop of mercy might be to encourage others to act out.

The annihilation of the bomber's bloodline followed by the resurrection of the angel who'd been blown apart—an *angel*, not even an archangel—had made the futility of such attacks crystalline.

Bombs still existed.

As did flamethrowers and missiles.

Those weapons and more had been used in angelic wars and battles. But every human on the planet knew that to attempt to use them against angelkind as a whole would end only in a carpet of red across the world. Because even if they blew up every single archangel in the world, those archangels would come back.

Over and over and over again.

For only an archangel could kill another archangel.

Even the black fog that had devastated Antonicus had been spawned by an archangel.

There was no way for mortals to win against the Cadre, destruction of humanity the only end result . . . except of course, angelkind would never kill *all* the humans. Their need for humanity was her kind's greatest secret, one that had been kept with ruthless ferocity across time. Without humans into whom to eject the toxin that built up in their bodies, angelkind would be a madness of wings and blood.

"Rather make the creatures cattle—breed them and use them." She'd heard it said in her time, and she was sure there were those who yet believed the same.

Angels could be cruel and heartless and without pity.

Zanaya had no illusions about her people. But any further thoughts on the subject would have to wait. They'd arrived at her fortress, and she soon spotted a familiar form spotlit by the moon. *There's Auri on the roof.*

They landed as one in front of her second.

The other woman handed over a sleek black device. Larger than the machine called a "phone," it had many of the same functions. Zanaya thought of it as a knowledge bank, for it held all the information of the world.

Attached to it was another small, square object.

"It's set to open to a scan of your iris," Alexander said before Zanaya could ask for the procedure to access the message.

She remembered now, how the Cadre had requested that she put her eye to a machine so that the image of her eye could be recorded and used as a key, along with her voice. She'd been newly awake then, hadn't processed much of what that meant.

As she nodded, she heard Alexander say, "Aureline, I'm glad to see you awake. A pity we couldn't meet again in less fraught times, but let us hope for peace in the future to come."

Auri, who'd always been ambivalent about Alexander due to her loyalty to Zanaya, gave a polite nod before retreating from the roof.

Having worked out that the smaller device was the lock, she touched it to activate it as she'd been taught worked with many such devices, then allowed it to scan her eye. After which, it asked her to speak.

"This is an astonishing device." Zanaya's eyes were pinned on the black screen that showed a turning hourglass, the skin of her face tight over her cheekbones. "Is it not, Alexander?"

"I'm still on the fence about all these advances," he muttered even as he spread his wing behind her own, the contact as much for him as it was for her.

A coldness spread through his limbs, a premonition of news terrible.

An image appeared on the main screen at the same instant: the insignia of the Cadre—a simple circle with all their emblems arranged inside it. It changed with every change in the Cadre, emblems being added or removed.

Zanaya's emblem, an ankh below which ran two curving lines representing her Nile, sat opposite Alexander's: an outline of a raven in flight. Titus's updated emblem sat next to his—the familiar outline of a baobab tree remained unchanged . . . but now, there soared above it a hummingbird.

It was Sharine, the Hummingbird, Alexander remembered all at once, who'd drawn the original outline of *his* iconic emblem. It had taken place soon after his ascension. He'd been talking to Caliane about what he wanted his emblem to be, while her quiet best friend sat sketching nearby, the gold-tipped black of her hair glossy in the sunshine, and the next thing he knew, she'd shown him her sketchpad and said, "Akin to this, Alexander?"

Because the thing with Sharine was that she'd never been intimidated by archangelic strength; she'd always had a power of her own that no one could explain. It wasn't of the Cadre, wasn't martial. Yet it clung to her, a tranquil yet potent cloak.

Dragan, rough-edged but insightful, had once looked at her and said, "Perhaps she is evolution, Alex. A better, kinder, more intelligent us."

How odd that, until this instant, he'd forgotten such a critical memory and all the others connected to it. Another example of the tangle of age. He wondered if *Sharine* remembered the genesis of his emblem? He'd ask her, perhaps delight her with a remembrance long lost.

A flash on the screen in Zanaya's hands as the insignia split into ten unique emblems before vanishing to reveal a crisp visual of Elijah. Standing beside him was Caliane's blue-eyed son, both of them situated against a backdrop of snow and stone. What Elijah had to say was the worst news of all: "Antonicus has risen. There is no body in the grave."

55

Antonicus had fed again. The more he fed, the more of himself returned to him . . . and the more disgust he felt at—

The thought fragmented, his eyes narrowing as he kicked the half-shriveled body whose lifeforce he'd acquired. At first, he'd thought he needed their blood, but blood, rich red and metallic, was a mere transfer mechanism for the energy that fueled him. Soon he'd have so much that he wouldn't need to bother with the distas—

Another fragmentation.

Frustrated, he roared and kicked the body again. Again. Again.

Until when he stopped, the once-whole form was in bloody pieces, bones shattered to punch through skin, and Antonicus's reborn crouched nearby, waiting to scavenge what flesh remained. Dark green plants grew at their back, the leaves plump and wet in comparison to their emaciated state.

His upper lip curling, he waved a hand and they swarmed to feed.

Repulsed by their slurping and lack of control, he was

about to turn away when he caught a movement in the sky in his peripheral vision. He looked up into the late afternoon light with the instinctive caution of a man who'd won more wars than he'd lost; it was highly unlikely even a flyer skimming the canopy would see Antonicus and his reborn, for he'd chosen his feeding ground with care—deep in the heart of a rainforest verdant with life and thick with shadow.

Still, there was no point in becoming careless now.

The angel *was* skimming the treetops, but that wasn't what caught Antonicus's eye. It was the underside of his wings. Pure silver. The kind of silver he'd seen in the wings of no other angel in the world but Alexander.

Alexander wasn't his enemy.

But Alexander had oft lain down to sleep with the one who *was* the enemy.

All at once, Antonicus knew what he had to do. And he wasn't going to use his resurrected power to do it—no, he had to hoard that for the fight to the death to come.

Instead, he grabbed the crossbow he'd acquired from a pile of weapons beside the barracks of a remote squadron. That had been his first taste of returning power—he'd fed, and had soon after been able to don his glamour.

No one could or had seen him.

Crossbow in hand, he rose up through the waterlogged air of the forest . . . and fired.

56

The sun's rays flowed to red-orange with the oncoming sunset as Alexander stood with Zanaya on a wide balcony that faced the direction from which his grandson would fly toward them. Alexander's chest stretched in prideful anticipation of seeing Xander's powerful wings in flight—and in painful joy at the thought of introducing this most precious piece of his heart to Zani.

Below them spread a rolling span of land golden and rich through which meandered a herd of elephants while birds caught rides on their backs in return for taking care of troublesome insects. One intrepid flyer, black as soot, its beak a familiar curve, came to sit on the railing of the balcony alongside his leaning arm.

Alexander chuckled. "We have an honored guest, Zani."

"A raven." Zanaya smiled. "I've never seen one this far north—but then, you're here. Obviously, it's come to greet you."

As if hearing her, the raven turned and gave her the gimlet eye, then walked over to peck at Alexander's arm hard enough that he frowned. "My ravens rarely act in such a fashion." His wasn't a true gift; he couldn't control or call ravens as Elijah could the pumas and other big cats that prowled his territory.

Regardless, he *did* have a bond with them—they'd often acted as both harbingers and messengers for him, and once, when he was in great peril, they'd appeared en masse to peck out the eyes of his enemy.

Now, he nudged the bird's beak away. It opened that beak and croaked at him in that way that was distinctive to ravens, impatient and demanding and far deeper than a crow's caw. The marks on his arm were inconsequential, the *kraa* call of the raven familiar . . . except that his grandson should've been here by now.

Heart encased in ice, he said, "Zanaya, ask your squadrons if they've spotted Xander."

Well aware what ravens meant to him, Zanaya hissed out a breath and went silent as she communicated with her people. The guards had already been informed that Xander had free reign to come and go from this territory, so Zanaya'd had no reason to tell them to keep watch for him today.

Hands clenched to bone whiteness on the balcony railing, he stared at the raven. "Where is the child of my child?"

The bird croaked again, loud and angry.

And in the distance lifted an entire conspiracy of ravens, a massive black wing that arrowed south with the same loud *kraa-kraa*.

As if yelling at him to follow.

At the same instant, Zanaya said, "He hasn't been spotted." Words edged in steel. "Not by the fortress guard nor by the border guard."

Alexander was already shoving back from the railing to spread his wings. "Follow the ravens."

Then they were aloft and racing through a sky afire in all the hues of flame—toward the border that Xander had never passed. *Zani?* It came out curt, hard, for Alexander had to be a general now and not a grandfather.

All squadrons alerted, Zanaya replied in a tone as curt

and martial. *Message is being forwarded to the border, and from there, will be passed to Titus. He knows how to use the phone device, is apt to have searchers in the air within minutes.*

Alexander couldn't speak, not even with the mind. His entire focus was on finding his grandson. Even now, the raven who'd landed on the balcony flew to his left, keeping up with an archangel going at relentless speed. Impossible. Perhaps it was no real raven but the ghost of the one who'd burned up during his ascension.

So it was written in myth: that Alexander's raven would rise with Alexander's need.

Zanaya flew with equal speed next to him, and her voice when it entered his mind was fierce. *We'll find him, my love. He's strong and he's smart.*

Alexander swallowed hard. *He's not an archangel, Zani.* Because they both knew the biggest threat out there: an archangel touched by a murderous black fog, an archangel whose rising had caused the sky to sicken.

None of them knew what had returned wearing Antonicus's skin.

The two of them flew on into the rapidly encroaching night, then farther still, halting only when hailed by a squadron commander near the border. "Sire," he said to Zanaya, "Archangel Titus has activated all his squadrons and they search along Xander's most likely flight paths. So far, there's no news."

Gut a creation of ice by now, Alexander looked forward.

His ravens, black against the moonless night, invisible except when they moved, had landed on the buildings of the border but croaked in harsh impatience now.

Black wings filled the air.

Zanaya swept out with him in the ravens' wake, any orders or comments she had for her border commander given on the mental level. "They're tiring," she said at one point, and he realized she was right. Members of the conspiracy had begun to drop away, their tiny chests heaving and wings drooping as they searched for a place on which to land.

Alexander went through his arsenal of power, but he had nothing with which to help the birds that were so loyal to him in their own independent way. Intelligent and capable of far more than most knew, ravens were ever their own masters— but they never forgot a favor or a friend. And for reasons of their own, they'd chosen Alexander generation after generation.

That was when he felt it, a subtle wind that kept the birds aloft without forcing their flight path. He always forgot that Zanaya had not only tempests at her fingertips, but this far-more-subtle control over the air. It was why she was the best endurance flyer among archangels living, dead, or in Sleep.

Thank you, he managed to get out past the fear clogging his throat. It was an emotion he despised, but had come to accept came bundled with the fury of love and protectiveness he felt toward his grandson.

I'm here, Alexander—anything you need, was the fierce reply from the consort who didn't expect grace from him in this endless beat of time where his heart threatened to shatter inside his chest.

Zani, I survived losing Rohan only because Xander existed. The words were torn out of him. *I can't*—He shoved the thought aside, unable to even countenance it.

I've been thinking of why Antonicus—if it was Antonicus— would target Xander. Coolly strategic, the voice of the commander she'd once been. *He's not your enemy.*

Finding his footing in the familiar chessboard of war and politics, Alexander's brain kicked out of fear mode and into gear. *No. How would he know Xander was mine, in any case?*

The underside of his wings, Zanaya suddenly said. *Did you not say they are identical to your own? And that's what a person on the ground would see when they looked up.*

That he'd missed the obvious was a testament to his current state of mind—and it was a cold slap across the face. He couldn't help his grandson if he wasn't thinking clearly. Wiping away all emotion using the brutal control he'd learned over millennia of disciplined rule, he considered Zanaya's words. *Is it possible he thought he was taking me?*

Perhaps. Or he took the chance that it might draw you to him. He may well hold the Cadre responsible for his predicament and want to take vengeance against each of us in turn.

Alexander fisted his hand as the raven beside him—tireless, seen only at the periphery of his vision—shouted its croak, then dived. He went with the bird, the wind rushing past his face at vicious speed and his wings sleeked until he was a falling arrow.

He landed in a hard crouch on the ground, one hand pressed to the earth. The metals far beneath sang to his touch, but his attention was on the single feather beside which stood the raven: the filaments a pure silver that glittered in the glow thrown off by Alexander's wings, it was splotched with a substance he didn't want to see, didn't want to touch.

Zanaya landed opposite, immediately saw what held his gaze. "It's my turn to protect you, Alexander," she said and picked up the feather. "Silver on one side, earth tones on the other."

Then she ran her finger over the splotch, lifted that finger to her nose. "Blood." A single word that made veins of rare metals ooze from the earth in a metallic spiderweb as Alexander fought to control his rage and panic. "But there's not enough of it here, not even enough feathers."

Zanaya's own wings glowed, too, her eyes pearl gray shot with light as she scanned the area. "Xander was wounded, but he didn't die here."

Zanaya was right, he realized—he could see more than one feather, but the number was far smaller than it should be for a major injury to an angel of Xander's age and size.

He went to look to his raven . . . but the bird was gone, though Alexander hadn't seen it take off. When he searched in the trees and in the sky, there were no more birds with hooked beaks riding the winds or perched in the branches.

"I believe my ravens have said all they wish or need to say." Alexander was never sure quite which; the birds had their own minds and ways. "He must be close by." Looking into his consort's eyes, he said, "Gray."

From the harsh curse that escaped her parted lips, she knew exactly what he meant. "No mirror pulse, but I feel . . . an absence. So strange that I should feel what is missing, but that's all I can describe it as. A numbness where a pulse should be." Her head jerked to the left. "That way."

Alexander never went into battle without being fully informed, but he'd follow Zani anywhere—and he knew the child of his heart was now of her heart, too. Because Xander mattered to Alexander.

They took off into the cold chill of a grayness that told him dawn was approaching. He and Zanaya and his ravens had flown through the night. He looked below, scanning in every direction.

But when the answer came, it hovered in the sky directly ahead of them.

"Antonicus."

57

Zanaya snapped into a hover while using every skill in her arsenal to keep her face expressionless. She couldn't, however, do anything about the shock and revulsion that curled creeping tendrils throughout her blood.

Because while Antonicus could fly, his wings were not . . . right. His tendons and fine wing bones had healed enough to keep him aloft, but a greenish film so transparent that she could see the entire understructure was all that connected the myriad pieces.

He had no feathers.

The only thing to which she could compare his current state were the wings of a newborn angelic babe. Yet even that wasn't right. An infant's wings might be frail and transparent, beyond easy to tear and break, but they were also hauntingly lovely in their delicate translucence.

A skeletal smile from a face out of nightmare, Antonicus's eyes wet orbs in a shrunken face. Those orbs flicked to the archangel at her side. "Would you like to see my prize, Alexander? Your son, I would guess."

The tiny hairs on Zanaya's arms quivered. Antonicus's voice was . . . broken. There was no other way she could describe it. Perhaps she might say he had shattered rocks clogging up his throat.

"Where is he?" Alexander's question was quiet—and all the more deadly for it.

Smirk on his face, Antonicus dropped through the mists above the trees without warning.

Zanaya followed, Alexander beside her. Yes, Antonicus was drawing them into a trap, but they were two against one. *Xander is your priority, Alexander. Antonicus is mine. I can feel him.* Like slime in her head, a putrid malevolence that whispered things just beyond her ability to hear.

Zani, he's no ordinary archangel, said her consort, who would die inside should his grandson perish.

Zanaya was not about to allow that to happen. *I'm an archangel and a general, lover. Your grandson is but a youth. Our duty is clear.*

A wrenching moment of eye contact before they landed.

Antonicus stood a number of meters from them, his wings folded back to reveal the barest arches over his shoulders. What arches he had were mismatched and mutilated. To her, it looked as if his bones remained unbelievably soft and malleable, Antonicus a melted doll.

"You're yet in the process of healing," she said, not able to believe how he'd even reached the sky when his frame was so emaciated, patches of green rot on his face, his neck, his arms . . .

"Thank you for not mentioning the smell." At that moment, he sounded like a cultured Ancient.

"It is of no moment. You have but risen." But no Sleeper ever came out of Sleep so damaged. On the other hand, Antonicus had been a rotted corpse when he was buried, so perhaps it was to be expected. "Where is the angel you brought down?" She had to be the one to speak, because Alexander was vibrating with the need to kill—and it was clear Antonicus was baiting him.

Antonicus bared his teeth, the loose skin of his face quivering in a way that made it seem as if he had things crawling beneath. "I gave him to my creatures." A small, mean laugh. "They will fill their bellies with him while we converse."

She snapped out a hand to press it against Alexander's chest when he would've stalked forward. *He wants you close.* A cold realization. *He wants to make us like him.* It was there in the greed of his gaze, in the breathless quiver of him.

I must find Xander.

Antonicus hissed. "Why is he beside you . . . mistress?" The last word seemed torn out of him, his face twisting through a hundred emotions before it settled into one of utmost devotion.

Queasy unease in every part of her. Archangels served no one, were laws unto themselves. But she wasn't about to walk away from this opportunity. "Antonicus, where is the angel you took down?"

A sly smile. "I left him by the river with my reborn." His features twisted, his next words gritted out through clenched teeth. "By the river, mistress. You can hear the waterfall."

Alexander, go! Save the boy!

Alexander lifted off, Zanaya's hair blowing back in the wind of his passage. Did he possess that intangible thing the mortals called a soul, it was now torn into two ragged pieces that fluttered in the cold morning gray of the rainforest.

In the power games of archangels, Xander was the innocent, had to come first.

Zanaya knew that, too. She would have asked him to make the same choice had she been faced not with one reborn archangel but an entire Cadre of them. *I'll return as fast as possible,* he promised her. *Keep him talking.*

I can't get anything beyond the river out of him. Can you spot the ribbon of it from above?

No. The entire forest was concealed by heavy morning

fog as soft and welcoming as Lijuan's had been an ugliness of black death. But its ethereal beauty made it no less an impediment to his need.

His grandson hadn't yet developed mind speech, was too young for it, so Alexander couldn't contact him that way.

That was when he saw it—a familiar black form in the distance, circling and swooping. *My raven shows me the way. Zani, stay safe! I'll be back soon!*

She said nothing in reply, might even now be in battle. Teeth gritted as even more of his soul tore away, he flew so hard and fast that he wrenched something in his shoulder. The hurt was a welcome bite as he dove through the cloud of fog where his raven had circled . . . and heard the thunder of a waterfall.

He thought he knew where he was now, Titus's lands as familiar to him as his own after his many visits to his friend. He lit up the sky with his power as he landed, and in the glow of gold, he spotted Xander. One of his grandson's wings was torn and bloody, while the other had been sliced off at the back and not cauterized.

The blood loss must've been catastrophic, but Xander was somehow conscious—and he had a knife in his hand with which he was swiping at the reborn that scuttled around him, attempting to sink their teeth or claws into him. He was faster, more skilled, but he was tired, and Alexander saw a number of scratches and bites on him.

He didn't roar out his rage.

He simply encased Xander in a bubble of his power, then killed everything else. He was certain he hit no targets but those he sought; the wild creatures who called this forest home would have long abandoned an area ripe with the stench of the unnatural dead.

Reborn erased out of existence, Alexander dropped his bubble of power to see his grandson shoot him a fierce grin. "I knew you'd come, Grandfather," he said.

Then Xander collapsed, as if giving himself permission

to let go now that Alexander was here. The knife that fell from his hand was one Alexander had given him, a blade that he wore in a hidden sheath in his boot.

Already running to him, he reached out to his love. *Zani, he's alive! Xander is alive!* Broken and battered but alive.

Her voice in his mind, a breathlessness to it. *Burn out every scratch and cut he has on him. I don't know if Antonicus's creatures carry the same poison as him, but we can't risk it. Deeply excising the wounds may stop it from reaching Xander's bloodstream.*

The idea of harming his grandson was a knife to his heart, but Alexander didn't hesitate. Zanaya would die to protect that which Alexander loved, as he'd do for her. Her counsel held only care. So he lay his wounded grandson flat on the ground, then began to use the brutal power of an archangel to excise literal chunks of flesh from Xander's body.

His grandson flinched and moaned but remained unconscious.

A small mercy.

But the boy was silent and cold as death by the time Alexander was done. At least there'd been little to no further blood loss, as Alexander had cauterized the wounds as he went—though the scent of Xander's flesh burning was a hard thing to bear.

Wrapping him up in his power, Alexander gathered him in his arms. He knew why Antonicus had taken Xander now. Son or grandson, he had to have realized the child was of Alexander's bloodline—and Alexander was known for his loyalty.

He was also known for his love for Zanaya, she for her love for him.

Find a way to draw one . . . and the other would come, too.

Xander had been both bait . . . and a distraction for Alexander. *Zani, the goal was to get to you!*

I know! Take Xander to safety! Get him out of here now!

It was the only choice. Xander was badly wounded, needed

a healer as fast as possible. Yet to leave his Zani? But he must. Because his consort was an archangel, too, honorable and good and with courage infinite.

Hold on, Zani, he thought as he took flight with Xander in his arms. *Hold on.*

58

Shoving back the strands of hair that had blown across her face during Alexander's ascent, Zanaya breathed through her mouth in an effort to filter out the stench that came off Antonicus. He smelled . . . rotten. Not the rot of the earth, musty and rich. But the putrid rot of meat left out too long, until maggots began to wriggle in it, their plump bodies gleaming and wet.

Even as her gorge threatened to rise at the image, she tried to keep Antonicus talking. "Why did you take the stripling?"

"Because you are *mine*." Bared teeth. "I knew he'd be with you. Zanaya and Alexander. Alexander and Zanaya." He said that in a mocking singsong way, then spat at the earth. "I heard it throughout history, but it's wrong!"

It was difficult to maintain this conversation while also speaking with Alexander, and she had to fight not to betray her relief when her consort told her that his raven showed him the way to Xander.

Please be alive, Xander, she said inside her own head. *He has a warrior's fierce heart but it will break beyond repair if he loses you.*

Aloud, she said, "Tell me about your reborn."

A twisting wrench of his head, his face distorting in ways that should've been impossible.

Molten bones.

Melted bones.

She almost took a step back on the rich green of the dew-laden grass, stopped herself just in time. Around them, the forest was as silent as the grave from which Antonicus had come . . . but a white owl with eyes golden sat motionless on a branch of the young kapok tree behind Antonicus.

"I must rise," he grated out. "I must . . . serve." Hate in his eyes, but he answered her question as if compelled. "I must be your instrument."

A cold tendril of understanding wormed its way through Zanaya's brain. This was why the dead had risen from their graves to come to her. Lijuan, that blackhearted bitch, had made Zanaya just a little like her.

But even Lijuan hadn't been able to control *living* archangels.

Her chest heaved, her breath slicing razors in her lungs as she remembered the pulse that was an absence, an echo of what once was . . . and no longer existed. And the smell that clung to him, so noxious and *unalive.*

Yet surely Antonicus was too rational to be dead, to be reborn. "Are they like you?" she asked. "Your reborn?"

He snorted, his face a ripple of distortion. "In a minor way. Basic speech. Basic thought. They are vectors to spread the glory of *you.*"

Alexander's voice blasted into her mind at the same instant, with the joyful news that Xander lived. But along with her happiness came a creeping fear. *Burn out every scratch and cut he has on him. I don't know if Antonicus's creatures carry the same poison as him, but we can't risk it. Deeply excising the wounds may stop it from reaching Xander's bloodstream.*

Antonicus leapt at her without warning, his claws bared and eyes red.

Blasting out with angelfire, she blinked as he moved with reptilian speed to avoid the blow. That hadn't been normal, hadn't been natural, not for their kind. Now, he crouched opposite her and screamed, "I serve no one! I am an archangel! I am Antonicus!" Curling bolts of power of putrescent green at the tips of his clawed fingers before he shot them her way with a speed that was vicious.

Then Antonicus smiled . . . and vanished.

Shit! Fuck!

The bastard knew Zanaya had no glamour. And those without glamour also couldn't see through it. Her consort's voice in her head, a warning about Antonicus's plans. *I know! Take Xander to safety! Get him out of here now!* Antonicus would go after Alexander if Zanaya fell, with Xander collateral damage.

A whisper of cold at her nape.

Falling back on the instincts Mivoniel had drilled into her, she dropped, rolled, and came up on her feet some distance away. Then she went airborne at brutal speed, at the same time calling her tempests to pummel the earth and the air.

A flicker of mud-green power as her winds smashed Antonicus hard enough into a tree that it disrupted his glamour. Dropping her tempests, she targeted him with angelfire, but he was invisible to her gaze once more, and in that moment, she saw Lijuan, *felt* Lijuan. How the Archangel of Death had gained the ability to go noncorporeal, until even the archangels with glamour could no longer see her. How she'd appeared behind Zanaya.

This time however, Zanaya was ready.

She'd reactivated her tempests as fast as he'd vanished, and she hoped to hell her winds were shredding the gelatinous webbing of his wings.

Then it came. A crossbow bolt shot hard and with power enough that it ripped through her left wing—with another bolt hitting her in the neck seconds later. Gurgling at the blood that threatened to drown her, she gripped the bolt in her throat and tore it out as she spiraled to the ground.

Even her winds couldn't keep her aloft with her wing so badly damaged.

She landed, but didn't crumple. Her throat was already healing, but she remained at a disadvantage with her lack of glamour. But she had other assets, including her mind. "Fight like an archangel, not a sneak thief!" she challenged when she felt claws swipe by so close they almost sank into her.

A hiss of anger and then there he was, his face a rictus so tight it was animalistic, his eyes no longer holding much sentient thought. Teeth gritted, he said, "Kill you. End you. No mistress! I am Antonicus!"

Too wounded to move fast enough to avoid his power, she took a blow directly in the gut. But though it burned and seared and made her grimace at the pain of it, it didn't dig into her bones like angelfire . . . and she knew. "You're not Antonicus," she whispered, drawing Firelight. "Antonicus is dead."

Screaming, he came at her with claws bared, all sense and reason gone. She thrust Firelight deep into his heart, then used her winds to shove him back until he was pinned to the nearest tree by her sword. This close, the scent of him clogged up her airways and made her gut want to eject itself through her mouth.

Red eyes locked with hers, hatred in their depths. But when he attempted to hit her with his power, nothing came out but the merest trickle. "Food," he growled. "Food. Fuel."

Zanaya thought of Lijuan's mound of the dead, the bodies of her loyal fighters hollow and empty of all life. Silence where so many voices had rung. Hands stretched out in death, as if they pleaded with their beloved goddess for mercy.

Cruelty beyond cruelty.

"No archangel needs to prey on others to gain power," she said to this creature that had once been a man of integrity and honor. "Even Lijuan only used others to bloat herself—she always had an innate level of archangelic power. You are no longer an archangel."

He screamed . . . but the words he spit out in the aftermath were unexpected in the extreme. *"Kill me."*

She hesitated, the tone of the demand so much of the Cadre that she questioned her conclusion that he was become reborn. "Antonicus? Do you exist?" Never would she end him without being dead certain. "If all you need is a much longer Sleep, then that may be the best choice."

A single tear rolled down his face, the eyes that held hers no longer feral but so sad as to be despair in its purest form. "I will do as my mistress wishes."

It was her blood through which rage burned now. "I am not your mistress," she said. "You are an archangel!" Forcing herself to touch his putrefying body, she clenched her hand over his shoulder in the manner of comrades.

He was a shiver of bones beneath skin that felt as if it would fall off him at any moment. But his face was tranquil now, a faint smile on his lips. "What do you wish of me, mistress?"

Inside the faint screams within her head, however, she heard one that was loud and clear and of an archangel. *End this! End me! I beg of you, Zanaya!*

She staggered, her eyes burning. "Antonicus." A whisper. "You are an Ancient." To kill so much life, so much history when there might be hope of a recovery, it was an abomination.

But the scream inside her head was suddenly echoed by words forced out of a throat that didn't want to cooperate. "I dream only of her," Antonicus rasped, the strange half-smile yet on his face as the man who'd once been an archangel battled the evil in him that compelled him to submit. "My Sleep is nightmare. Now she has made me a slave."

Rivulets of blood dripped down his face as his skin tore open from the force with which he was clenching his jaw. And that blood . . . it was green and dark, fetid and rotten.

In front of her, he struggled to find his voice again, while inside her mind, his screams became guttural. He was losing the last pieces of himself, she realized. Soon, he'd be nothing but a mindless beast beholden to her will.

"No," she said, and locked gazes with him for the final time. "I will not allow her to do this to you, Antonicus, Archangel of Elysium." Wrenching Firelight from his body, she took a step back, rage and pain locking her throat.

Zani! Alexander landed beside her, so hard that she felt an earth tremor. *Xander is safe with Sharine. She flew this way to search with a squadron.*

Sharine, the Hummingbird, was one of the very few people, she knew, with whom Alexander would trust his grandson. She should've known the general would find a way to look after both pieces of his heart.

"You're hurt," he said, his hands fisting as he stared at the bloody hole in her throat.

It's all right, lover, she said mind-to-mind. *I will heal. Today, we are charged with a task terrible and necessary.*

Aloud she said, "Antonicus is ready to go," as the archangel who'd died in front of their eyes only to be forced awake as a monster managed to hold his feet, though his chest was a bleeding maw, his face cracked rivulets of death.

Antonicus had been arrogant and oft an ass, but he'd done his duty as an archangel. He didn't deserve to be humiliated at the end, his entire history reduced to this creature that was no longer Antonicus even if some part of his mind yet existed within. But she would give peace to that final flicker of the being who'd once been an archangel.

"Alexander, you and I must vow to never reveal this Antonicus to the others," she said. "His history will end the day he flew into the black fog. With courage and heart. We will say we have no other knowledge of his whereabouts. Soon enough, he will become legend, the Sleeper lost."

Alexander gave a curt nod even as Antonicus's mien turned grateful—and proud. His shoulders squared as much as possible, his expression resolved.

"We were never friends, you and I," Alexander said to the dying archangel, "but you were a great archangel. Good journey beyond the veil."

Antonicus didn't reply, his face twisting again as he fought to retain the last pieces of himself as inside her, the screams grew ever louder. *Lover, this must be a private act. He is too proud to accept you as witness.*

Alexander took to the sky without argument.

And a pale gray beam of dawnlight hit the decaying flesh of Antonicus's face.

"You are no one's slave, Antonicus, no one's servant." She made her words hard, absolute. "You are an archangel. And you have chosen your ending." Then she unleashed her power.

He didn't fight back. Couldn't fight back.

Her midnight fire, a thing not of heat but of the cold heart of night, engulfed him. His face was a torment of pain as he died, but inside her head, she heard the clarity of words spoken in the voice of an archangel respected and honorable—and at peace: *Thank you.*

It was over quickly.

That told her more than anything how little of Antonicus had remained inside that rotted shell. Archangels didn't die easy. What had turned to ash in front of her had been as much an automaton as the reborn who'd crawled to her through the grass.

Tears still rolled down her face at such an end to a life glorious.

Unwilling to just leave his ashes there, she created a small whirlwind that sucked up the remains. Then she rose into the sky with the whirlwind beside her. Alexander, who—as she'd expected—had waited close enough to assist should the situation turn, joined her, and they flew together until they were deep over the sunlit waters of the ocean.

There they halted, the whirlwind in front of them.

There was no need for more words, but she felt she must say them. "Archangel Antonicus died a decade ago. But what remains here, we give to the water, in the hope that this being, too, will find the same freedom."

Alexander took her hand in his as she released the whirlwind, and the ashes dropped gently onto glittering blue. "We made a mistake that night on Neha's border fort, didn't we, Zani?"

Throat yet thick, she shook her head. "No, we couldn't consign him to death when he might have a chance at life. This way . . . he made the choice. He asked for death."

Alexander's fingers clenched on hers. "Do you think the others who Sleep will rise as he did?"

"I would say no for Astaad and Michaela—they were injured in battle against Lijuan, and while that comes with dangers of its own, Antonicus flew into the death fog. You told me Favashi sickened after being in China?"

"Yes, Lijuan left an unknown trap for her."

"So, she is the one most at risk. But she has also spent the longest in Cassandra's embrace thus far—and she looked nothing akin to Antonicus when she woke before the war. Chances are high she's safe, but we won't know until she does awaken." Zanaya could no longer see any hint of ash, the last echoes of an Ancient life gone without a trace. "I have a piece of Lijuan's gift with the dead."

Alexander cupped her face, his skin golden in the sun's rays. "You are a woman of heart, consort-mine. You give mercy. You don't use."

Simple words that had a profound effect on her understanding of who she was now—an archangel who could draw the lingering dead to her, give them true peace. "Yes. I accept this charge and this honor." Never again would she fear the infected dead or the reborn that remained in the world—for they were creatures trapped and screaming.

With each one that she gave mercy, she brought a little more light into this yet-healing world.

"Hold me, General," she said and, wrapping her arms around his waist, laid her heart on his chest. "And I will hold you. Both of us were wounded this morn."

Alexander's indrawn breath was a painful thing as he wrapped his arms tight around her where they hovered above the water, two archangels who trusted each other enough to lay down all their weapons, lower all their shields, reveal all their wounds.

High above them, a solitary white owl soared until it vanished into the clouds.

59

Xander was very much of his grandfather's bloodline, Zanaya thought not for the first time as she ducked her head in to check on Alexander's grandson. While Sharine and the squadron with her had taken him first to Titus's nearest stronghold, the healers had authorized a transfer to Zanaya's fortress once Xander had stabilized.

So now it was that Zanaya had a most amusing and clever houseguest—who also possessed a delightful tendency to blush despite his best efforts to squelch the trait. A junior squadron commander of two hundred, he wasn't a boy except to her and Alexander. And as a commander, he was well loved by his wing and wider comrades.

So many young angels had requested permission to visit the fortress that Aureline had assigned a separate aide to the task. "I'd forgotten the impatience of youth," her second had said at the time. "An hour after the request and they contact us to ask why the delay in our response." Laughter. "I had to put on an exceedingly severe 'dusty old Ancient' tone to get the entire lot of them to calm down and leave my aide in peace."

Today, however, Zanaya found Xander on his own. With sleep-tumbled hair as dark as the cocoa bean, and skin of deepest gold, Alexander's grandson sat upright in bed; his lithely muscled upper body was bare but for the salve that coated his healing wounds, his forehead furrowed as he focused on a "laptop."

The word made no sense to Zanaya. Yes, it sat on his lap. But it was hardly a spinning top, was it?

He looked up at her entrance, sniffed the air . . . and put his laptop aside, his healthy wing rustling against the bedding with the movement. Not to say the wing was undamaged; he had taken wounds there, but they'd proven minor in the grand scheme of things and would heal without any major intervention. Xander, however, had wanted the wing excised, to balance out his body while it healed—a common choice among warriors. But to his dismay, the healers had vetoed that option: with Xander's other injuries being what they were, they didn't wish for his body to waste energy regrowing a wing that bore no significant damage.

"I am *not* in the habit of amputating perfectly healthy wings, young man," the most senior healer on the entire continent had huffed. *"Warriors."*

Unlike the irritable healer, Zanaya felt for Xander. She'd lost a wing in her time, and had gotten rid of the other as a matter of course. Else she'd have been useless as a ground fighter, her balance shot and muscle strains a certainty—angelic wings weren't exactly small or weightless, after all.

But her houseguest wasn't one to sulk; he'd groaned at the decision, then got on with learning how to be as stable as possible with one wing. Today, he whispered, "Tell me my nose doesn't lie, Lady Zanaya, and that you've brought me angel-mead."

"Drink fast," she said, putting the amber brew in his eager hand. "We must get rid of all evidence before Healer Apanaia catches us."

A playful glint in eyes of palest brown shot through with

shards of gray, he said, "I never knew archangels were scared of healers before."

"All smart angels are scared of healers," she drawled, and took a seat in the comfortable armchair beside his bed. It was one of two. Alexander had returned to his territory for a short period to handle a most unexpected matter, but elsewise, they often visited Xander together.

Who, after taking a healthy drink, leaned toward her. "Will you tell me?" Though his butchered wing had barely begun to heal, the area against his spine where it had been so viciously hacked away was covered in salves and the like, and his other injuries made it appear as if a giant insect had taken bites out of him, there was no dimming the light in his gaze.

The healers had been concerned about lingering trauma, but he was more a general's grandson than even Alexander had realized, pragmatic and hardheaded. Xander saw his attack by the pack of reborn as nothing more than an unpleasant encounter with an enemy they'd been fighting for years.

And while he hadn't recognized Antonicus at the time, he'd vowed to honor the promise Zanaya and Alexander had made to the Archangel of Elysium. "Never will I speak of him as I saw him," he'd said. "As far as the world is concerned, I will say I was assaulted by aggressive reborn after I landed to eat a meal. With my wing gone, there's no evidence of the crossbow bolt, no question to answer."

Yes, this child of Rohan's was a young man Zanaya was proud to call family.

"Tell you what?" she said, amused an inordinate amount by her secret knowledge.

"Why Grandfather got a stunned look on his face while he was sitting right there next to you, and flew off the balcony all but two minutes later," was the dry response. "As if he hasn't been watching me like a hawk over its chick."

"Not a hawk," Zanaya murmured. "A raven. Like the one sitting on the balcony railing right now, keeping an eye on you in your grandfather's absence."

A pause, a slight tilt of his head as he glanced out through the wide-open doors. The bird spread its wings and croaked a greeting before settling back down to its unblinking watch.

Xander looked slowly back at her. "I thought I'd imagined the raven that watched me from the branches as I fought the reborn."

Zanaya gave him an enigmatic smile; let the child discover the mysteries of his grandfather in his own time. "If I share what enticed Alexander to leave your side, you must keep it to yourself until the knowledge becomes widespread."

"I promise," Xander said at once.

Still amused, she said, "First General Avelina has just woken up."

Xander's mouth dropped open. "You mean Archangel Titus's *mother*?"

Zanaya's shoulders began to shake with mirth. "Four sisters—and now his mother is awake!" She slapped her thighs. "And she wishes to surprise her children." Keeping her mouth shut and expression composed around Zuri and Nala was taking all of Zanaya's considerable willpower.

As for Phenie and their other sister, Charo, no doubt they'd been bemused to receive a formal invitation to visit Zanaya's lands in a week for a special dinner, but they could hardly say no to an archangel who "wished to make the acquaintance of the family of two squadron commanders" who she held in the highest esteem.

Alexander was in charge of getting Titus to the table.

"I must admit I can't wait to see her children's faces," she confessed.

A wicked grin that reminded Zanaya of a younger Alexander. "Grandfather always talks about her. Says she should've been his permanent second, but that she didn't feel ready for the position then. Do you think she might consider it now?"

Before she could answer, Xander added, "Tarek and others from the Wing Brotherhood handle a lot of court business, but Tarek's been at Grandfather to appoint a true second—

Tarek's a sentinel, a warrior, wants to go back to focusing on that."

"Avelina's position is in discussion." Though, per Alexander's last message, the first general *had* declared herself "old and moldy enough" that she might be willing to take up the mantle of second.

"Did you know her?" Xander asked with youthful curiosity. "Will you tell me more about her? She's a legend among warriors."

Zanaya granted him his wish, but his eyelids began to droop mere minutes later. She could, however, see him struggling against the need to sleep. "Rest, Xander, child of my heart. It's a critical part of your healing."

"Warrior," he muttered, "not child." But he smiled when she ran her fingers through his hair.

She sat with him until he fell into a deep sleep.

Her heart felt tight, full of too much love. "I am honored to know you, Xander, Son of Rohan and Citrine, Grandson of Alexander and Jhansi," she said quietly. "I can't wait to see who you become." Leaning down to press a kiss to his temple, she then tugged a blanket over his healing body, and whisked away the mug that had held the mead.

She got caught as she was leaving his room.

"Sneaking in contraband I see." Aureline raised an eyebrow above lashes decorated with tiny feathers she'd gathered from her own wings.

Zanaya's best friend had fallen in love with the current fashions in cosmetics and body decoration, and was experimenting with the clothing to see which she liked best. Today's was a short and fitted dress in autumn orange with elongated triangular cutouts on one shoulder and at the waist. She wore the dress with the torture devices called "high heels." Today's were a dramatic pink.

"I like the dress," Zanaya said. "How did you get into it is my question." She twisted to look for the wing slits.

"Don't change the subject," Aureline said, mock stern.

"How is our resident invalid who can't seem to sit still? You know I had to chase him to bed yesterday after he decided to do laps of the inner garden?"

"I am shocked."

As Aureline burst out laughing at Zanaya's utterly transparent lie, Zanaya handed the mug to a passing member of the staff while putting a finger to her lips. The vampire of four hundred years grinned. "What mead?"

"Exactly so." Tucking her arm through her best friend's afterward, she said, "Xander will heal. It'll take time, but he's young yet."

Wings companionably overlapping, the two of them walked out into the same garden heavy with scent and color that Xander had chosen for his illicit exercise. "And you, Auri?" she asked. "Are you happy to be awake?"

"Every day, Zan," was the immediate answer. "This new world is most strange and lovely—though I do miss our old fortress on the Nile."

"As do I. I intend to rebuild it." She paused. "Speaking of our residence, Xander has suggested we add faux mummies to the entranceway of our current home. 'For authenticity, Lady Zanaya.' He also recommends I add one to my sigil."

Aureline's snorted laughter was a thing wonderful and familiar.

But no one was laughing two hours later, when word came through from General Rhys that his liege, Neha, Archangel of India, Queen of Poisons, of Snakes, and Mother of Anoushka had gone into Sleep.

"She was tired and heartsick," Caliane said after the general's resolute but grief-stricken visage disappeared from the screen. "We all saw it, but I was hoping she would be able to stay awhile longer."

Titus was more blunt in his summation. "We needed her to stay longer," he said, his hand fisted tight around the ceremonial spear he'd planted on the ground. "The world has just stabilized. None of us can afford to leave our territories and take on more."

Zanaya half expected her lover to volunteer to absorb India into his lands. Alexander had always been hungry for more, still more. But today, his gaze went to another. "Callie, the times are exigent. You can no longer rule only the city of Amanat and the land on which it stands."

Caliane sighed. "Yes, and Neha's people know me as an ally. It will be as gentle a transition as such things can be."

No one had any objection to that. If Zanaya had to guess, she'd say it was relief that rippled through the Cadre. It certainly appeared so from the cheerful conversation that broke out among the group. *Are we, do you think,* she asked Alexander, *in a time of peace?*

Eyes of pure silver met hers. *A precarious one. I would venture Qin is kicking himself for not vanishing the instant you appeared on the scene. We may yet drop from nine to eight.*

Zanaya flicked a glance at the archangel who'd remained silent throughout the meeting. *Perish the thought. Ruling with eight is exhausting—the vampires keep talking themselves into uprisings and stupid angels start to believe they can steal and hoard territory. Never fear, I will risk life and limb and the condemnation of your Sleeping housekeeper to attempt the fire ritual in order to cleanse the cosmos of your wayward thought.*

He ducked his head slightly to hide his smile, while the others of the Cadre finished up their happy discussion. Well, but for Qin. He was never happy. And in truth, she wasn't so hard of heart that she didn't pity him his separation from Cassandra. *I hope Qin finds his happy ending one day, lover. What anguish it must be, to be alive in a world in which your beloved can't exist without going quite, quite mad.*

A white owl landed on Qin's shoulder at that moment, fluffing its feathers before it settled. The creature's eyes were a vivid gold.

60

Alexander flew back to Zanaya five days after the meeting about Neha. Arriving in the gray light of dawn, he looked through the open balcony doors of his grandson's room to ensure himself Xander was in no distress—a worry without need, but he couldn't help it.

"Grandfather." Not only was Xander not in distress, he was walking around the room dressed only in the silken pants he'd taken to wearing in bed so he wouldn't blush when Zanaya came to visit him.

His joy at seeing Alexander was unfettered and open.

"I thought the healers told you no exercise."

Wincing, Xander took another step. "Don't tell me you agree with them?"

Since Alexander was no hypocrite, he gave his grandson his arm . . . and gently tugged the boy's tousled head close to press a kiss to his hair. "You are a beating piece of my heart, Xander. Never forget that."

"I love you, too, Grandfather," Xander said with the ease of a stripling who'd never had to question the love of his family.

Deciding to assist his grandson with his small rebellion, Alexander helped him into a jacket to protect his ravaged body from the cold morning air, then the two of them walked out to the balcony and down the small set of steps that led to a garden that thrived in the sandy soil of the region, the earth in which the plants buried their roots a blend of brown and orange.

Around them, leaves shimmered with dew, the flowers already open to the morning light, and the mist that curled up off the ground a delicate accent. The local peafowls, squat of form and with iridescent feathers of blue and green and black, tiny crests on their equally tiny heads, wandered the neat pathways, while in the distance came the trumpet of an elephant.

He imagined he could scent Zanaya in this space—though perhaps it wasn't his imagination. This was her home, after all. His home, too. Theirs.

A place they made wherever they chose to be together.

"She's amazing, Lady Zanaya," Xander said when they paused so Alexander's injured grandson could catch his breath.

Ah, the boy was half in love with her already. "You'll get no argument from me, Grandson. I've loved only one woman in all my existence, and her name is Zanaya."

Xander shot him a look, the gray-brown of his eyes kissed by dawn light. "I've never seen you this way, Grandfather."

"Sweaty from a long flight?"

"Young." The word was soft. "When you laugh with her, smile with her—if I didn't know you for an Ancient, I'd never guess it. Papa was like that with Mama."

It stopped Alexander's heart each time his grandson used those affectionate terms to refer to Rohan and Citrine. To know that his son and Rohan's mate had loved their son so well that this boy would forever carry them in his heart? It meant an amount indefinable.

"We've not often spoken of your mother," he said, sorrow in his heart for the absence of his own memories of Citrine.

Xander lit up as he talked of his mother. "She was clever, but gentle and calm with it, while Papa was a fighter to the bone—he wasn't hotheaded, but he was . . . *big*. In his emotions, in how he spoke, in what he wanted out of life."

"Yes, Rohan was always a child bold."

"It wasn't until I was well past a hundred that I saw that Mama had her own power—and it came from being at peace. True peace, Grandfather, I've come to realize, is a rare commodity. Not many, mortal or immortal, ever achieve it. But my mother had it all my life. As if . . . as if she could hear the breath of the universe and was attuned to it."

"I think," Alexander said roughly when he could speak again, "you have more than a little of your mother in you, Xander. I see Citrine clearly now."

A deepening of Xander's smile. "She liked you, did you know that?" When Alexander shook his head, Xander said, "She used to tell me stories about my legendary grandfather, and she taught me that my father was such a good papa because you'd been a good papa to him."

Alexander swallowed the lump in his throat. "You've given me much joy today, Xander."

The two of them walked a touch farther before Xander spoke again. "May I ask how you met Lady Zanaya?" Adoration in his tone. "I've never known anyone like her."

"Will you challenge me for her then?"

Streaks of color on Xander's cheekbones. "Grandfather, I would never—"

Alexander laughed and hugged an arm around the boy's shoulders. "I'm sorry, child. I couldn't help myself."

A sharp look. "See? You're younger with her, because of her. Not so . . . weighed down by power and life."

Alexander found himself mulling over his grandson's words long after Xander was back in bed, fast asleep due to his exertions. Alexander had since washed before joining his Zani in bed. Warm and bare to the skin, she welcomed him with her kiss and her heart and he, a man who had always wanted more, still more, was happy to just *be*.

When he stroked the curve of her hip, his lips on the back of her neck, she smiled a smile soft and lazy, and reached up to curl her hand around his nape. They kissed again, her skin so warm, his yet cool. But it heated up with each kiss, each caress, each question asked and answered as they danced the slow dance of lovers who didn't need to rush.

"Do you think we stopped living at some point?" he said to Zanaya as they lay tangled in the aftermath, all liquid limbs and honeyed pleasure. "We did more than exist. We did our duties. We took care of our people. But . . . did we stop living as we once did?"

Zanaya's answer was simple. "Yes."

Staggered by the blow of it, he fought to find his voice again. "You say that with such ease, Zani."

She drew a delicate pattern on the skin of his chest as she lay on his shoulder, his wing below her body and one of hers arching over him. Her hair was a softness of silk against his arm, the weight of her too slight for the power in her frame.

"It wasn't easy at all when I first realized it," she said. "I struggled against the truth of it for years—but I had to face it. Where once my life was fire and color akin to a sunset over my Nile, it had become a muted palette. You remained the brightest spark in my existence, and even you had begun to fade. I couldn't bear it, lover."

Alexander took a painful breath, asked, "Is your world sunsets and fire again, Zani?"

Rising on her elbow beside him, she ran her fingers through his hair. "It's wild and beautiful and *bright*." Her gaze searched his. "Is it the same for you?"

"Yes. Because of you." She was the fire in his blood.

A long silence full of memories spoken and unspoken.

"I wanted to ask a gift of you," he said at last.

Lips tugging up in a curious half-smile, she waited.

"I would like to alter my sigil to include your Nile. So that my raven flies over your river."

She sucked in a breath, her pupils expanding to overwhelm her irises. *"Alexander."*

Fisting his hand gently in her hair, he said, "I love you, my Zani. I will love you till the end of time, whether that is tomorrow or eons from now."

Eyes shimmering, she ran trembling fingers over his cheek. "I'll give you my Nile," she said, her tone husky, "if your raven perches in my ankh."

An expansion inside his chest, a sense of endless possibility. "It is done then." No doubt the Cadre had noticed his amber ring, perhaps even the amber in the hilt of her sword, but no one had said anything on the point. This mingling of sigils, however, was a statement that couldn't be ignored—or undone.

"Till the end of time, lover." Zanaya's kiss was starlight and ebony rain.

Alexander, Archangel of Persia, opened out his arms and surrendered to it, to her, to *them*. Till the end of time.

Above the fortress, a conspiracy of ravens buoyed by a wind of perfect strength and direction flew a pattern intricate. Had anyone below been able to track their movements, put it on paper, they'd have seen a gift between consorts.

Not so far distant, in a land of sand and life, people pointed and cried out in wonder as the Nile rippled with fallen stars in a shape no earthbound mortal could hope to divine, but a rare few lucky angels high in the sky managed to see: an ankh in which sat a raven.

And far below the earth, a seer mad with her visions smiled . . . and allowed herself to rest.